# THE NOBLE ASSASSIN

...ristie Dickason started writing at the age of three, ...fore she could spell. She went on to read English ...Harvard, then won an MFA in Directing at Yale ...ama School. After spending fourteen years as a ...eatre director and choreographer, with the Royal ...akespeare Company and at Ronnie Scott's, among ...hers, she returned to her secret passion for writing ...hile convalescing from illness. In addition to her ...ovels, she also writes poetry, music lyrics and for ...e theatre. As a child, she lived in Thailand, Mexico ...d Switzerland and has now lived longer in ...ndon than anywhere else. For more information ...d to contact her, please visit her web site, ...ww.christiedickason.com

By the same author

*The Lady Tree*
*Quicksilver*
*The Memory Palace*
*The Firemaster's Mistress*
*The Principessa*
*The King's Daughter*

# CHRISTIE DICKASON

## *The Noble Assassin*

HARPER

*Harper*
An imprint of HarperCollins*Publishers*
77–85 Fulham Palace Road,
Hammersmith, London W6 8JB

www.harpercollins.co.uk

A Paperback Original 2011
3

A catalogue record for this book
is available from the British Library

ISBN: 978 0 00 728913 4

Set in Meridien Roman by Palimpsest Book Production Limited,
Falkirk, Stirlingshire

Printed and bound in Great Britain by
Clays Ltd, St Ives plc

**MIX**
Paper from
responsible sources
FSC™ C007454

Find out more about HarperCollins and the environment at
**www.harpercollins.co.uk/green**

*For John*

Thank you to:
John Faulkner, my personal Google
Stephen Wyatt, my creative SOS, as always
Olena Kostovska
Lindsay Smith
Stephen Siddall
Tom French for IT support and rescue
Emma Faulkner, for the title
Orly, for listening, among much else
Leonardo, Giuseppe and Rosa Giannini for
my office away from home
Sarah Ritherdon and Victoria Hughes-Williams at
HarperCollins
My agents, Robert Kirby and Charlotte Knee
Jon M. Moore, Chief Executive, Moor Park Golf Club
The Museum of Richmond, Richmond Surrey
The Richmond Reference Library
Jeremy Preston and the staff of East Sheen Library
for invaluable support in research, readings, and
readership involvement

(And, welcome to Matilda, who arrived in this world
just before I hit 'SEND'.)

Francis II [1]  m.  MARY, QUEEN  m.  [2] Henry Stuart
King of France       OF SCOTS         Lord Darnley
                r. 1542–67           d. 1567

JAMES VI and I  m.  Anne of Denmark
r. 1567–1625 (Scotland)      d. 1619
r. 1603–25 (England)

Henry         Elizabeth  m.  Frederick V       Margaret
1594–1612    1596–1662     Elector Palatine     b. 1598
                                            d. in infancy

Sophia  m.  Ernest Augustus
1630–1714      1630–98
           Elector of Hanover

# Elizabeth's Family Tree

CHARLES I    m.   Henrietta      Robert     Mary     Sophia
King of England     Maria       b. 1601    1605–7   b. & d. 1607
and Scotland            d. in infancy
r. 1625–49

George I    m.   Sophia Dorothea
Elector of Hanover      of Celle
King of England      1666–1726
and Scotland
1714–27

           (*via Victoria*) - - - - - - - Elizabeth II
                                         1952–

# PART ONE

# 1

## LUCY – MOOR PARK, HERTFORDSHIRE, NOVEMBER 1620

The air is so cold that I fear my eyelashes will snap off like the frozen grass. Only my two youngest, most eager hounds have left the fireside to bound at my side.

I do not want to die. But I cannot go on as I am, neither.

I ride my horse closer to the edge of the snow cliff. I imagine turning his head out to the void and kicking him on. I imagine the screams behind me.

We would fly, my horse and I, falling in a great arc towards the icy River Chess far below. My hair would loosen and tumble free. His tail and my darned red gown would flutter like flags.

Then we would begin to tumble, slowly, end over end, like a boy's toy soldier on horseback, my bent knee clamped around the saddle horn, his legs frozen in mid-gallop. The winter sun reflecting off his black polished hoofs. My last unsold jewels scattering through the air like bright rain. For those frozen dreamlike moments, my life would again be glorious.

I feel the alarmed looks being exchanged behind me on the high, snowy ridge, among the moth-eaten furs and puffs of frozen breath. I quiver like a leashed dog, braced for the first voice to cry, 'Take care!'

I walk my horse still closer to the edge.

It would be so easy.

I look down again at the river. Why not? What is left to lose now?

The in-drawn breath of that vast space pulls at me. The serrated edges of the snow cliff glisten, sharp enough to slice off Time.

Welcome, the space whispers. Below me, I see the smiling faces of my two dead babes. Welcome. I see the face of my poet, my only love, now dead to me.

One kick, then no more fighting. No more debts. No more loss. No more of the scorn and silence already denying that I am alive.

Even my Princess is gone from England.

I listen to the uneasy stirring behind me. Who would break first and call me back?

You can die from lack of a purpose to live.

'Your Grace . . .' The waiting gentleman speaks quietly lest he startle me, or my horse, and send us over the edge. Speaking carefully, as if I were poor, maimed, self-indulgent Edward, who suffers so nobly before witnesses then beats his fist against his chair when he thinks himself alone.

The cold air is a knife in my chest. The sun on the snow blinds me. I am made of ice.

I let my small band of attendants hold their breaths by the edge of the snow cliff. They should be grateful to me for this small gift of fear, I think. Salting the bland soup of their day.

I look down at the river again. Edward is wrong to say

4

that I lie to myself. I face the reality in front of me. Listen to its melody. Then I rewrite it, sometimes on paper, sometimes only in my head. I give it more beauty, or terror or meaning. I tell the story better. But I never deceive myself as to which is which.

For instance, I can see that the scene I am now writing in my head is impossible. The fall would be messy, not glorious. Almost certainly, the horse would have to be shot. I would land at the bottom broken but still breathing. And then I would become a captive with my husband in his fretful rage.

I see the pair of us, invalids side-by-side in our fur rugs, dropping malice as the stars drop the dew until we die.

I still brim with unwritten words, unsung music, unplanted gardens. I still keep most of the looks and all of the wit that had made me the darling of the Whitehall poets. I feel like a piece of verse begun but not finished. There is one poet who could have written me but never will.

In the void below me, I see him striding up and down the gravel path of my lost garden in Twickenham, stirring the air, reciting a poem born from the passionate union of our thoughts. I hear words I had offered him, whole lines, even. An easy rhythm where my ear had pointed out a stumbling line for him to revise. All now made his own. He recites the completed poem for the first time, to me alone, too intent to notice that spray from the fountain spangles his dark hair and coat with sparkling diamond chips.

He glares up at the sky and down at the gravel path. I watch his clenched hands spring open to mark each stress of his metre. Watch his long fingers and feel them on my skin. His words sail out of his body on the fierce current of his breath into the wide air of the universe.

5

I imagine them sailing on past the moon, past the sun, until they reach the farthest heavens to lodge as new stars. He comes to the end of the poem, listens for a moment to its last echo in his head, then turns to look at me, almost with fear. Was it good?

I have lost him along with all the rest.

When I had been the Queen's favourite, she bathed me in her generosity. Passing it on with an open hand, I became that bountiful goddess known as a patron, a source of prizes, favours and preferment.

But my fortunes had declined with the Queen's health and the vigour of her court. My husband and I never recovered from his fine for treason. I often spent what I did not have. Our growing debts had forced me to sell the lease of my Twickenham garden to that reptile Lord Bacon. When the Queen died, almost two years past, I was finished. Her court was dissolved. I lost my place and the wealth that went with it. I could no longer afford to be patron, to my poet or anyone else. Now I am branded a 'court cormorant', a beggar, wife of a debtor, a woman of no use to anyone, burying her shame in the country. Like the pox, my fall from grace threatens to infect others.

What remains for me? Why not open my wings and fly? If not here, somewhere higher and more certain.

My gelding suddenly shies away from the shining ice edge.

I lean forward and pat his neck. 'Don't fear,' I murmur. 'When I jump, I won't take you with me. I swear it. Nor anyone else.'

Not today.

But I have never yet given up on anything I set my mind to.

I will do it, I promise myself. Soon.

My poor hounds have begun to shiver, up to their shoulders in the drifts.

I turn my horse's head to let him begin to pick his way back down along the icy track towards Moor Park, with the dogs racing ahead and my attendants behind, no doubt relieved. I press my old beaver muff to my cold face then bite savagely into the fur like a hound on a hare's nape.

I have little patience with wilful misery, least of all my own, but I see no way out for me now. I clench my teeth on the side of my hand, deep inside the muff. I want to throw back my head and howl. To crack open the steady deadly progress of time and set loose demons and angels with flaming swords. I would welcome the novelty of a second Great Flood, cheer on the Four Horsemen of the Apocalypse. Anything to change what my life has become.

When I drag my frozen skirts back to the fire in the hall at Moor Park, I learn that those demons and angels have already escaped. As my skirts steam and drip and my shivering grey hounds curl close to the flames beside their fellows, I listen with horror to Edward's urgent report.

The dark, gaunt Horseman of War had heard my desperate plea.

'There is war in Bohemia.' My husband can scarcely conceal the pleasure he takes in telling me.

I didn't mean it! I think. Not like this! Not Elizabeth!

'They lasted scarcely a year on the Bohemian throne, your English princess and her little Palatine husband.' He shakes his head and waits for me to ask if she is dead.

Queen Anne's daughter Elizabeth. My father's former charge, raised in our home at Combe Abbey. Elizabeth Stuart, the only woman I love who is still left alive. In spite of her younger years, she could always match me thought for thought. At times, she had left me, the older girl, laughing in her wake.

7

When I remain silent, he can't contain himself any longer. 'All reports say the Hapsburg armies have invaded Prague, routed the new young King's Protestant forces and arrested the rebel leaders.'

'How certain is this news?'

'A courier arrived from my cousin today.'

'What of the King and Queen?' I ask when my voice is again under control. My Elizabeth and her Frederick, who had been pressed into accepting the crown of Bohemia.

'Fled, I'm told . . . and still in flight. Declared outlaws by the Hapsburgs, under Ban of the Empire.'

I want to hit him for the pleasure in his voice. 'Will England go to war to save her?'

'That's for her father to decide.' I have asked a foolish question. Then he smiles and shrugs. 'King James is England's self-styled *"rex pacificus"*. Draw your own conclusions.'

'There'd be no honour in his "peace" now.' I wish I could say that my feelings at that moment are pure, generous and patriotic, but honesty insists otherwise. A sudden jolt of excitement runs through my horror.

'The Bohemians might prefer to call their leaders "heroes" not "rebels",' I say mildly while my racing thoughts drown both Edward's voice and his quiet malice.

I survived my first seven years of marriage chiefly by pretending to ignore my husband. He had soon proved to be a master of the puzzled tone, the helpless shrug, the meaningful glances over my head. He let my words fall to the floor as if they had no meaning. Or he would seize on one and examine it with puzzled incomprehension before tossing it away. Or he shook his head sadly and told me what I had meant to say. In the company of other men, he ignored me altogether. When he managed to provoke me past endurance, he would smile with satisfaction. Look at her! See what a harridan I have married!

Having once again failed to goad me into an unseemly outburst, my husband now purses his lips. I scarcely notice.

If what Edward tells me is true, I know that the future of England has just changed. My future could change with it. I see escape from Edward and from Moor Park. I see the return of warmth and true companionship. I see purpose for my life again. I confess that I begin to listen to his news of unfolding disaster in Bohemia with a heart turned suddenly light with renewed possibility.

# 2

## ELIZABETH STUART – PRAGUE, BOHEMIA, NOVEMBER 1620

In the royal palace in Prague, the King, Queen and guests pretended to eat. The young, Scottish-born Queen of Bohemia, Elizabeth Stuart, jumped at a sudden boom and spilled the sauce from her silver spoon. She set the spoon down on her plate and picked up her French fork. She looked at the fork, unable to remember what she should do with it. With its two long sharp tines, it resembled a weapon. She found herself gripping the gold mermaid of its handle in her fist.

They no longer pretended to converse, in any of the several languages spoken around the table. All words had now deserted them. Up and down the long polished table, people stared at their food as if puzzled by it or chewed on morsels that they forgot to swallow. All their senses seemed to have deserted them except that of hearing. Sir Edward Conway, one of the two ambassadors sent by James from England to parlay for peace with the Hapsburg enemy, sat with one hand at his hip, resting on an absent sword hilt. Even the servers standing behind each chair forgot to offer the food they held, frozen in listening.

Cannons had begun to boom far too close, from the west.

The child in her womb jumped.

Elizabeth could almost have persuaded herself that the guns were summer thunder bouncing off the mountains.

'It's noisy for a Sunday that was meant to be a day of truce,' said the other English ambassador, Sir Richard Weston.

'We're high here,' said Elizabeth. Her unspoken meaning – the Hradcany Palace, home to the King and Queen of Bohemia, sat on a rocky summit high above the Vltava river. Sounds from far away reached them with unnatural clarity. Therefore, the fighting was not as close as it sounded. She was reassuring her white-faced husband as much as the rest of them.

Her husband shook his head. Frederick, elected King of Bohemia for a little more than a year, had been weighed down beyond his strength from the age of sixteen by his leadership of the German Union of Protestant Princes. 'They're fighting on the White Mountain. I should be there, not at table.' He stood abruptly. Fabric rustled and stool feet squeaked on the stone floor as everyone else rose with him. Then he paused uncertainly, head lifted, listening to the sounds of the battle.

The forces of the mighty Catholic Hapsburg Empire had engaged Frederick's twenty-five thousand German mercenaries and Protestant Bohemians less than half an hour's ride from the city.

'But we have them outnumbered,' said Frederick. 'They're only seventeen and a half thousand men.'

'Go tell the stables to prepare His Majesty's horse,' Elizabeth ordered a serving groom.

The fear and relief on the boy's face as he ran from

11

the hall made her question whether he would take her order to the stables or flee from the castle entirely.

'You must go arm yourself, my love,' she told her husband quietly.

'Oh, Lizzie!' He looked at her with terror in his large dark eyes. 'I fear that we can't . . .'

'I shall come serve as your armourer, myself.' Elizabeth, First Daughter of England and child of its King, married to Frederick at fifteen, now the twenty-four-year-old Serene and Puissant Queen of Bohemia, took her King firmly by the arm and led him towards the door of the great hall.

'You must leave Prague at once,' said Frederick. 'Go early to Bresslau.' She was to spend her confinement in Bresslau. He had already ordered some of her furniture sent there.

She shook her head. 'I stay here in Prague as long as you do.'

The doors had no sooner closed behind him than they opened again on bad news. The arriving messenger smelled of gunpowder, blood and horse. Elizabeth could scarcely hear his words through the thunder of cannons inside her head.

The messenger finished speaking.

Behind her, Elizabeth heard screams and the crash of falling stools. Courtiers ran past her out of the hall, pushing and jostling in the door.

'Where are the other German princes?' she demanded. 'Our allies? Where's Thyssen? Bethlem Gabor and his Hungarians? Are they on their way to relieve us?'

'I don't know, Your Majesty. But our army is on the run with the Imperial army on their heels.' The messenger looked back at the door.

'Go run with the rest of them, then!' she said with contempt.

She stood in a small still centre of the maelstrom unleashed by his message. She saw a man run by her carrying two jewelled goblets from the royal table.

'Your Highness, do you wish me to take your knives and forks?' A voice at her elbow, her chief lady-in-waiting, balanced on her toes, wanting to run, but still at her English mistress's side.

She looked back and saw a waiting woman rolling up one of the Russian carpets on the royal dais.

Reality hit her. A hostile army was about to invade this very space in which she was standing.

Feeling unnaturally calm, she nodded at her lady-in-waiting. 'And all my jewels.' She turned to the two English ambassadors, still present, heads together. 'You must return to England and tell my father to send soldiers and money at once!'

Weston nodded, but looked away.

Into the maelstrom, a white-faced, trembling Frederick returned. 'It's too late, Lizzie. My army has deserted. Even Anhalt and Hohenlohe were clamouring at the city gate in the midst of their own soldiers, begging to be let back inside the walls. We must all leave Prague now!'

'Then you can ride with me and the children,' Elizabeth said. 'We will need you and the castle militia to protect us.'

Scarcely a year after she had arrived in Prague as the new queen of Bohemia, Elizabeth packed to leave again.

First, the children. The boys must not become Imperial captives! Thank God the Crown Prince had already been sent to safety in Berlin! Get the others away from here! Look to their needs. Clouts for the coming babe, petticoats, toy soldiers, cups and spoons, coverlets, shoes and boots, bread and wine. Gloves.

Oh God! She could not think with that thunder in her head.

Cradle . . . a welcoming gift from her new people less than a year ago, for Rupert her first Bohemian child . . . Too heavy to carry?

She looked out of a high window as if expecting to see Hapsburg soldiers climbing towards the castle.

Snow, falling. Great pillows of snow fell onto the thick coverlet that already hid steps and cart tracks. The staircase down to the river looked like a smooth white slope. They would have to take the wagons and carriages the long way round, to the north where the land rose more gradually, towards the advancing enemy, before curving south again.

Money chest, she thought. Petticoats, riding boots. Fill brass warming pans with charcoal. Likewise the iron heaters for the carriages. Feather mattresses . . . Leave all farthingales behind to save room in the carriages.

All the time, her ears listened to the gunfire, growing closer.

'Madam . . .! Madam!' cried frightened voices. 'Do you want me to take . . .?'

No time. They must leave now!

The First Daughter of England, child of the would-be Peacemaker English King, could not become a prisoner-of-war.

Apart from all else, she thought, my father would never forgive me for forcing him to take a stand. Not after he had advised Frederick to stay at home in Heidelberg and refuse the Bohemian crown.

'Into the second and third carriages,' she ordered the children's nurses with their bundles. Where was the castle steward who should be overseeing this rout?

14

Food! she thought. And ale. Who was supervising the packing of food and drink for them all?

How many were they?

She sat on a packed chest, pulled up her skirts and hauled on her riding boot unassisted. Her ladies were all running with loaded arms. Or had vanished.

And who can blame them? she thought. She hauled on her other boot.

How far away was her intended refuge in Bresslau?

Too far. The mountains would be impassable in this weather.

Our departure from Prague is merely a series of problems to be solved, she told herself. But they all needed solving at once. There was no time . . .

Think!

Food, she thought again. Don't let yourself become distracted from the most important things.

She found the steward in the kitchen courtyard, making a tally of flitches of bacon and smoked hams as they were thrown into carts.

'Where are your clerks?' she asked.

He gestured at the mêlée around them and shrugged. 'I want to be certain, myself . . . Bread already in that cart, madam.' He pointed, then ran across the courtyard to chivvy along two men who were loading barrels of ale onto another cart. She saw a guardsman carrying a pike.

The armoury! She ran back to the steward. 'Weapons,' she said. 'We must not leave weapons for the enemy to take.' He nodded and pointed at bundled pikes and stacked shields waiting to be loaded.

We must go to Berlin, she decided. A long ride in this weather. But once there, they would find warmth and food and safety, for a time at least. Time to think about their suddenly unthinkable situation. She didn't entirely believe it, even now.

Snow was already blanketing the contents of the carts. Churned-up slush washed past the ankles of her boots as she ran back into the castle to oversee her own chests, which were being loaded onto carts in the main courtyard. And her money chest and jewel case, stowed in her carriage at the front of the forming line. And the chest holding state papers.

Letters!

She turned to go back to her apartments, but a militiaman blocked her way.

'No time, madam,' he said. 'You must leave now!' The militiaman disappeared again.

She lifted her head. The cannons had stopped. For a moment, she felt an intense silence, as if the world had stopped turning. Then shouts and gunfire, and the screaming of wounded horses arrived on the wind, far too close.

Children already in their carriage. Shadowy heads and the heads of their nurses . . .

Cloak. Gloves. Money pouch tied under her soft riding skirts, over her seven-month bulge of belly. Dagger.

She clambered up into her carriage. Two women in it already. Her chief lady-in-waiting sat huddled under a bearskin rug with Elizabeth's jewel case in her arms.

She helped to wrap Elizabeth in another rug. 'Put your feet here, my lady.' Elizabeth lifted her soaked boots onto the iron warming pan of burning charcoal. Melted snow was already making a puddle on the floor of the coach. She lifted back the curtain over the window to watch their departure. In both directions along the line, indistinct figures took shape in the snow then disappeared again, both mounted and on foot. Though the light felt unnaturally bright, she could scarcely see the walls of her adopted home.

Frederick appeared on his horse, armed for war. 'I'm giving the order to go forward.'

She nodded at him through the open square of the window. 'To Berlin.'

He leaned close and said quietly, 'I'm sorry, Lizzie.'

'Don't be a fool,' she said. 'We're having another adventure.'

'Do you think we'll survive?'

'I shall. And I don't like the prospect of widowhood, however you imagine you might arrange it.'

He nodded, then swallowed. 'If I could face your father to win you, why should I fear the army of the Hapsburg emperor?'

She smiled more brightly than his sally warranted, to reward him for attempting it at all. They clasped gloved hands through the carriage window. The ends of his dark curly hair were tipped with snow. Flakes were already settling on her skirts.

'I'll see you safely to Berlin,' he said. 'Then I must ride north to try to raise more men. I've learned that it was only the mercenaries who deserted, not our local troops. The people of Bohemia will defend us yet.'

'And I will give you all my jewels to pawn to pay them.' She held up the curtain and watched him dematerialise again as he rode away to the head of the long line.

Her carriage jolted forward, throwing her back against the seat. Behind her the shouts of the drivers travelled like a wave back along the line of carts and carriages. The carriage dropped suddenly as its wheels slid into buried ruts in the frozen mud. The seat banged the ends of their spines.

'Dear Lord!' exclaimed her lady-in-waiting. Elizabeth

heard the horses groaning and blowing. Behind them, oxen protested. The carriage swayed and creaked like a ship in a storm. She dropped the curtain across the window. She needed both hands to clutch the front of the seat. The interior of the coach was now dark and no warmer, but the curtain at least kept out the snow.

'Stop!' A scream rose behind her. She leaned from the window again, into the icy needles of snow. A voice fought its way to her against the wind, through the shouts of the carters and coachmen and the protests of the horses. 'Wait, Your Majesty . . .!'

Then the wind blew the voice into ragged tatters.

'Stop!' she cried. Cold air filled her open mouth. Her teeth ached from the cold. 'Who is that?'

It's too late, she thought. We've been overtaken.

'Your Majesty!' The voice shouted again.

Then she saw the man staggering and sliding through the snow alongside the track. Not a Hapsburg soldier: one of Frederick's gentlemen. Clutching a bundle of cloth in his arms, he fought his way forward towards her carriage.

'Your Majesty,' he shouted again. He overtook the carriage behind hers. 'Dohna, the King's Chamberlain went back . . .' He slipped and almost fell into a drift. '. . . into the castle to check that everyone was gone . . . That nothing valuable had been left . . . Look!' He stumbled alongside, panting, beneath the carriage window, holding up the bundle of cloth. 'I was in the last carriage. Dohna threw him in . . . left behind in the nursery!'

The bundle gave an angry wail.

The carriage slid sideways. Elizabeth nearly fell from the window as she reached out. The man shoved the bundle up into her hands just before he fell. Elizabeth fumbled, re-gripped and fell back into her seat. It was her youngest son.

18

'Rupert!'

One of her ladies whimpered.

Alive. Very much alive. She could now hear his steady screams and feel the pumping of his breath. The scrap of his face that showed amongst the wrappings was brick red. His body arched with rage.

Frightened faces stared back at her across the carriage.

'Where's the prince's nurse?'

But she already knew. She remembered now. She had not seen Rupert's nurse waiting with the others. The woman had fled.

Behind her she heard the coachmen and carters cursing and shouting as their beasts piled into the ones in front of them, trying not to run into her carriage.

'Onwards,' she shouted through the window and heard the order reverse itself back down the line. As the carriage lurched forward again, she braced herself against the motion, with her son pressed against her guilty heart. For the first time, she truly felt the enormity of what had happened to them all, of what was happening, and would go on happening. However calm she had pretended to be, what had happened was so terrible that it had almost made her leave behind her youngest child.

# 3

## LUCY – MOOR PARK, 1620

I lie in my cold bed, breathing out warm clouds, my feet close to the iron brazier filled with coals at the end of the mattress. My maid Annie snores gently from her pallet on the floor. A nodding house groom tends the fire.

I think about the news Edward has given me. The daughter of the King of England – my Elizabeth – is in flight, pursued by the armies of a Catholic empire that rules most of northern Europe from Russia to Flanders, only a short sail away across the North Sea. The long rumbling of war on the Continent between Catholic and Protestant powers has suddenly turned to the thunder of guns that can be heard in England.

She will be frightened and confused, though, as always, she will seem to command. She will fear for the children. They are all in danger.

I know I should not feel happy. How dare I rejoice?

I duck down under the covers to warm my hands on the brazier, curling like a cat in the small warm cave.

I am being given another chance. If I can think how to take it.

The next morning I rise as if the world were not changing. I dress, eat my frugal breakfast of bread and small beer. Wearing old fur-lined gloves with the fingers cut off, I sign orders to buy sugar and salt that we can't afford. I approve the slaughter of eight precious hens. I count linens as they come back from the washhouse, and the remaining silver returned from being washed and polished in the scullery. While Lady Agnes frowns at a peony she is working in tiny knots to hide a patch on a sleeve, I try to do my own needlework. But I prick myself so often that I throw the torn pillow cover across the room.

Agnes tightens her mouth and ignores me. After a time, I pick up the pillow cover myself.

After the midday meal, I write to my old friend from court, Sir Henry Goodyear, begging for news. I would have written to Elizabeth, but do not know where to send a letter. I take out her many letters to me and re-read her joy at her babies, her excitement at moving to Prague, her confession how she had offended her new subjects by misunderstanding their early gifts.

> . . . *So I made certain to display the gift of a cradle for the coming babe on the dais in the great hall, as if it were a holy icon. I believe that the people were puzzled by this strange English custom, but pleased . . .*

She had always trusted me with her indiscretions as well as her joys. I press the letter to my forehead.

If she were dead or captive, Edward would have told me. Therefore, she must still be alive and free.

As the early winter darkness closes in, to get through

the time, I try to write verse as I had once done so easily at court.

Remembering the good-natured, bibulous, literary competitions, I attempt to write an ode in the style of Horace – a challenge we had often set ourselves after dinner, made arrogant by wine and youth. But my metres now trudge heavy-footed where the Roman poet's had danced and skimmed like swallows.

No thoughts or words seem important enough to distract me. All my being waits trembling on the surface of life. It should be anguish, but I confess that, even while tearing up my attempt at Latin verse, I feel alive once again.

Above all, I need more news. Even without the distortion of malice, accounts of past or distant events are always slippery. The truth often proves to be, insofar as one can determine it, a little less vibrant than the tale as told. The tale is almost always simpler. The true narrative most often proceeds by bumps and hiccoughs, not in great sweeps.

I need a letter from Elizabeth. She has clung to England by writing letters, first from her husband's German Palatine, more recently from Bohemia. I know she will write to me as soon as she can.

Goodyear writes back by return of messenger. He has heard that Elizabeth and her children struggled down the mountain to spend the first night in Prague, in the house of a Czech merchant near the Old Town Square across the Vltava river from the palace. There, she waited while Frederick and his generals argued whether to try to defend Prague. With Hapsburg soldiers already looting the Hradcany Palace, the cavalcade of carriages and carts left the city by the West Gate just after nine o'clock the following morning.

*There seems to have been wide-spread panic,* he writes. *The royal family were deserting Prague! Frederick was forced to make a speech to reassure the terrified mob that the Bohemian officials, who were in truth escaping with them, would escort the royal family only a short distance then return to defend the city. The heaviest snow caught them on the Silesian border.*

The world has changed. And I see a part for myself in this new world. Not at Moor Park.

Her first letter reaches me at last, from Nimberge.

*My Dear Bedford* (Elizabeth writes), *I have no doubt that you have heard of the misfortune that has come upon us and that you will have been very sorry. But I console myself with one thing. The war is not yet over. Frederick has gone into Moravia in search of reinforcements. I will await him in Nimberge. I have also written to my father, the King, begging that he send immediate assistance to the embattled King, my husband . . .*

By the time I receive this letter, she has almost certainly moved on. I must track her flight. Find her. Go to her. Elizabeth's need and mine will meet. Her need will rescue me, just as her mother's need had rescued me once before. I can do it again.

But the first time I changed my life had been half my lifetime ago. I had been just twenty-two years old and known that I could do anything as well as any man, if I set my mind to it.

# 4

## LUCY – EAST ENGLISH COAST, JUNE 1603

My right knee had cramped around the saddle horn. My thoughts jolted with the thud of the horse's hoofs. The pain in my arse and right thigh was unbearable.

For tuppence, I'd have broken the law, worn a man's breeches and ridden astride. Then I could at least have stood in the stirrups from time to time to ease the endless pounding on my raw skin.

But I could not break the law. I was the Countess of Bedford. Even if I had not been riding at this mad, mud-flinging pace, strewing gold hairpins and silver coins behind me, my progress would have been noted and reported. Therefore, I had to ride side-saddle like a lady and wear a woman's stiffened, laced bodies and heavy, bulky skirts.

*. . . worth the pain . . . worth the pain . . . worth the pain . . .*

Two days in the saddle so far, one more to go. A man rode ahead of me to confirm food, lodging and the next hired horse. I had never before ridden so far, so fast, nor for so long. Our speed and the effort of keeping my seat at this constant killing pace prevented coherent thought. A woman's side-saddle is designed for stately progresses and the occasional hunting dash, not for this hard riding.

But a gentlewoman riding full tilt, scantly accompanied, leaping from one post horse to the next, was not invisible. I dared not risk man's dress lest word of my crime reach the wrong ears and ruin my chance for advancement forever. Meanwhile, my body screamed that I was murdering it.

*. . . worth the pain . . . worth the pain . . .*

I pointed my thoughts ahead along the green tunnel of the forest track, to Berwick, on the eastern coast just south of the Scottish border, where the new queen of England would arrive the next day on her progress from Edinburgh to London.

Elizabeth, the sour Virgin Queen, was dead. Good riddance to Gloriana! England now had a new king, James Stuart, who was already King of Scotland. This new king brought with him a new queen, Anne of Denmark.

*Berwick on Tweed . . . upon Tweed . . . upon Tweed . . .* The hired post horse wheezed and panted, throwing his head up and down in effort as his hoofs drummed out the rhythm of my destination.

Sun flashed through the trees. We splashed through pools of white light on the wide dirt track, where I rode at the side to avoid the ruts ploughed by wagon wheels.

*. . . a new queen . . . a new queen . . .*

Days and miles behind me, other would-be ladies-in-waiting advanced on the royal prey at a more sedate and comfortable pace. Even my mother, as ambitious as I but with an ageing woman's need for bodily comfort, had fallen behind me. I would be the first to greet our new queen. My best pair of steel-boned bodies, finest green tuft taffeta gown and ropes of pearls jolted behind me in

25

my saddlebags, with my collapsed-drum farthingale lashed across the top like a child's hoop.

When the new Danish-born Queen Anne had been married to the King of Scotland, Scotland became her country. Now she was moving again willy-nilly with her husband-King to yet another of his strange kingdoms and another strange tongue. Queen or not, she was a mortal woman with mortal fears and must surely be wondering what, and whom, this new foreign country would bring her.

If I had my way, it would bring me. Before any other English woman, I would be the first to make her feel welcome in her new country. I would be the first in her thoughts and in her royal gratitude. The first to receive her favour.

My thoughts drummed in my head with the beat of the horse's hoofs.

Edward pretended not to know what I did. If he had seen me at this moment, he would have paled like a slab of dead fish and railed yet again against the day he let his aunt Warwick persuade him to marry me, my modest bloodline redeemed only by the size of my dowry. But now that he had spent my money, the Third Earl needed me to succeed in this venture as much as I did myself.

When I had been married at thirteen and become Countess of Bedford, I was not fool enough to hope to love a man so much older, with a noble title, no self-control and an empty purse. But secure in my innocence, youthful confidence and the protecting glow of my dowry, I had never imagined that our chief bond would grow to be rage, at circumstances and each other.

Though I had fought him at the beginning of our marriage, when we still lived at Bedford House in London and were still received at court, my husband's scorn had burrowed into my head and replaced my childhood nimbleness of mind with a sluggish anger. In the pit of my stomach, I soon began to carry a heavy worm of resentment and guilt.

I could write verse well enough to be admitted, as an equal, to the company of poets, wits and literary men at court, known as the 'wits, lords and sermoneers'. Among our other games, we competed to write 'news' in set rhythms and poetic forms. But my paper and ink were too costly, Edward said, even before his own stupidity had cost us everything. Why did I imagine that I could write like a man?

From the first days of our short time at court, he ridiculed my early gestures of patronage. 'Why waste money that we don't have on playing patron to cormorant poets and playwrights?' he asked. Surely, I must know that they wrote their flattering lies only to earn a free meal at my expense!

And of what use were my languages? We couldn't afford to entertain anyone, English or otherwise. My closest friend at that time, and fellow poet, Cecilia Bulstrode was no better than a whore. Our former acquaintances of good repute would sneer at our growing poverty. I should concern myself with beds and linens, not the houses that contained them. What other wife created uproar and muddy disorder by building pools and fountains, or wasted money on infant trees when she had not yet produced an infant heir?

Then his actions put a stop to our life at court, to my literary life and to all my hopes of becoming a patron. After his folly, we could no longer afford even to buy my books, nor strings for my lute and my virginal, nor trees for my gardens. No matter how distant and faint, my singing gave him megrims.

Because of his treason against the Old Queen, which might have cost him his stupid head, I was trapped with him in exile from court and all that I loved best. Exiled from the place where I was valued, where my skills and education had purpose and employ. The worm of resentment gnawed. The rich life in my head was going quiet. I was losing myself, spoiling from the core like a pear.

I was already twenty-two years old. The new queen just arrived in Berwick was my chance for escape.

'Why would she favour you when she has all the nobility of England to choose from?' my husband had asked when I told him what I meant to do.

I dared not tell him. The avid rumours circulating in London, which had reached me in letters, even in exile from court at our country seat at Chenies in Buckinghamshire, where we then lived. I had heard the same from my dear, faithful friend Henry Goodyear, from the incorrigible gossip Master Chamberlain, and from my friend Cecilia Bulstrode, who collected a terrifying amount of pillow-talk. All three wrote the same vital news. The new queen was said above all else to love drinking, music and dance.

I kissed their letters in a passion of intent. Tenderly, I refolded them, to trap in the folds their promise of escape from Chenies. All my skills that my husband disregarded would serve me at last.

My father had educated me like a boy in the Ancient philosophies and languages, including Greek, Latin and a little Hebrew. I spoke French and could write passable verse in both Latin and English. But I also had been taught the female skills. I sang, danced, played the lute and plucked out not-bad original tunes. I could stitch well enough. Like either sex, I could tipple with the best, having learned young (and to the outrage of my mother) how to drink from court poets, musicians, artists and playwrights.

Even my lowly birth, so disparaged by my husband, would soon be put right. My father, a mere knight, a sweet, gentle man, had just been appointed guardian to the King's young daughter, the Princess Elizabeth Stuart. A baronetcy was sure to follow soon.

In short, I would make the perfect companion for a lively young foreign queen who loved to drink, dance and sing – if I could get to her before she chose another.

In truth, my husband could not lose in permitting me to ride for Berwick. If I succeeded in my aim, I might restore both our fortunes. If I broke my neck in the attempt, I would set him free to seek a wealthier wife. And if I failed, I would give him the pleasure of punishing me with his disappointment for the rest of my life.

*. . . worth the pain . . . worth the pain . . .*

A new time had begun for England with the death of the sour Old Queen and the naming of King James VI of Scotland as her heir. A new time had begun for me, Lucy Russell, the young Countess of Bedford. The new king would not hate my husband, like the Old Queen, for having been fool enough to entangle himself in the Essex rebellion against her. If I succeeded, I would entreat the Queen to ask the new king to end our exile from court. He might even forgive my husband the Old Queen's punishing fine.

But I knew that good fortune is not a reliable gift for the deserving. You have to see where it lies and ride towards it. The future will find you, no matter what you do. Why not take a hand in shaping it?

*. . . upon Tweed, upon Tweed . . .*

We crested a hill, broke briefly out of the tunnel of

trees, plunged down again, taking the downward slope at a reckless speed.

Two sets of hoofs drummed and flung up divots of mud. A single armed groom, Kit Hawkins, rode with me. Like me, he was still young enough to delight in the brutal challenge of our shared journey north.

My knee had set solidly around the saddle horn in a constant blaze of pain. I would scream if I could not straighten it.

Just a little longer . . .

You promised the same an hour ago! shrieked my muscles and bones.

Just another mile, I coaxed, as I had been coaxing myself for most of the day. Then you and the horse can rest . . . for a short time. Less than half a mile now to the next inn . . . a quarter of a mile . . . then a little water for the horse – but not too much. A short rest, no eating for either of us yet or the galloping pace would cramp our bellies as hard as rocks. Then just one more hour of riding, to our arranged stop for the night and the next day's change of horse.

And then . . . My thoughts escaped from my grip . . . I would dismount, straighten my leg if it would obey . . . lie down . . . sleep for the night on a soft, soft bed. Sleep . . . lying still, flat on my back . . . on tender down pillows . . . quite, quite still. Not moving a single sinew. Heaven could never offer such pure bliss as that.

I felt a jolt, something amiss, too quick for me to grasp. The horse buckled under me. Still flying forward, I detached from the saddle and felt the horse's neck under my cheek and breast. Sliding.

His poor ears! I thought wildly. I somersaulted over his head.

Don't step on me!

The world rushed past me, upside down.

Stones!

A crashing thud.

As I emerged from darkness, I found that I could not breathe. I sucked at air that would not come. Searing pain burned under my ribs. Dark mist in my head blurred my sight. My several different parts felt disconnected from each other, like the limbs of a traitor butchered on the scaffold. An ankle somewhere in the dark mist began to throb. Then an arm.

'Madam!' said a tiny, distant voice.

The mist cleared a little more. I blinked and moved my eyeballs in their sockets, still trying to breathe in.

A wild accusing eye met mine, only a few inches away. It did not blink.

With a painful whoop, I breathed in at last.

My groom, Kit, stooped beside me. 'Madam! Are you badly hurt?'

Whoop! I gulped at the air. Then took another wonderful breath. I swivelled my head. My neck, though jarred, was intact. I tested the throbbing leg. Also not broken, so far as I could judge. My left hand felt like a bag of cold water, but my fingers moved. 'Not fatally . . .' I sucked at the air again. '. . . it seems.'

'Thanks be to God!' He offered his hand to help me rise.

In truth, he had to haul me up. I stood unsteadily. My left ankle refused to take my weight. 'Did you see what happened?'

'No . . .' He inhaled. '. . . madam.' He was having as much trouble breathing as I. 'No hole in the road . . . just stumbled and fell without reason . . . that I saw.'

'How does he?' Carefully, I turned my head.

We blew out long shaky breaths.

31

The hired gelding lay with forelegs crumpled awkwardly under him. Flecks of foam marked the sweaty, walnut-coloured neck. Wind stirred his near-black mane. White bone showed through the skin on his knees. The wild, staring eye still did not blink. The arch of ribs hung motionless. The stirring mane was only the illusion of life. He had not stepped on me, not fallen on me, had saved me but not himself.

We stared down at the long, yellow, chisel teeth in the gaping mouth.

The absolute stillness, where a few moments before had been heat and pounding motion, pricked the back of my neck with incomprehension. I had seen the sudden death of a vital creature before in hunting, more than once. But I could never grasp the sudden nothingness – one moment alive, the next moment a carcass that could never change back.

One of the horse's ears had been turned inside out in the fall. I pulled off my right riding glove with my teeth, knelt painfully with Kit's help and straightened the ear with my good hand, as if this act might somehow help undo what had happened. I brushed away a fly already crawling on the horse's eyelash and looked again at the long, yellow teeth. An old horse. Too old for our pounding pace. I had killed him with my ambitious urgency.

I felt the skin between my shoulder blades quiver, touched by a Divine reproving finger. I laid my hand on the smooth, hard neck, still warm, still damp with sweat. This death was surely a sign. A warning of failure. The skin of my back quivered again.

'He was too old to keep up such a pace,' Kit said. 'Forgive me, I should have seen . . .'

'Merely old,' I said to the sky. 'An old horse, dead from wicked carelessness perhaps, but by natural cause.'

God sent no sign of rage that I was ignoring His sign. Lightning did not split a nearby oak. A hail of toads did not fall.

'Help me up.' I stood and tested my ankle again. Still watery, as if the bones had dissolved.

'I should have . . .' Kit's voice shook.

I felt his hand trembling. My thoughts had now cleared enough for me to remember that he would have been blamed had I been killed in the fall. I looked at his white face.

'Not your fault,' I said. 'Mine. And the ostler who hired the horse to me . . . knew that we meant to ride hard. I should have paid more mind to . . .' I meant to touch his arm in reassurance, but found myself clutching it in a wave of giddiness.

After a moment I patted the arm and let go. I was on my feet. Alive. A clergyman would no doubt call me innocent of wrongdoing, in the case of the horse, at least. But, insofar as I could define a sin, failing a creature in my care was one of them.

However, sin was not the same as a warning. To my knowledge, sin seldom seemed to prevent worldly success.

'Please take my saddle and bags from the body,' I said. 'I'll ride behind you until we can find me another horse.'

His eyes widened but he obeyed. He also had the grace to pretend not to notice my gasps of pain when he lifted me up behind his saddle.

We made a curious sight, when we rode just before sundown into a modest farmyard, scattering pigs and hens. Faces appeared in windows and doors to stare at a liveried groom with a dirty, dishevelled lady behind him, their horse's hindquarters lumpy with too many saddlebags, a spare side-saddle and a flattened farthingale.

I paid the farmer far too much to sell me an ancient

mare that fitted my saddle. He could not believe his luck. I was overjoyed to find any mount at all.

I did not try to gallop her. I was grateful that she managed to move me forward. In truth, I could not have survived a gallop, even though I had bound my ankle to steady it.

By the time we stopped at our scheduled inn to sup and sleep, much later than intended and long after dark, my left wrist had swollen so that I could not hold the reins in that hand. My head thumped. Preparing for sleep, I found blood smeared on the back of my linen shift, from my raw thighs. Because I could not remove it, I had to sleep in my boot.

The next morning, I could not move. Slowly, cursing, I forced each limb into action. Inch by inch, I pushed myself upright. I had to call for a kitchen maid from the inn to help me dress.

I blinked water from my eyes as Kit carried me into the stable yard and lifted me up into my saddle, now buckled onto the new hired mount. As we set off again at a gallop towards Scotland, when he was behind me and could no longer hear me nor see my face, I wept openly with pain and cursed my rebelling sinews.

The reward had best be worth what it was costing.

I arrived in Berwick at midday the following day.

# 5

## BERWICK CASTLE, NORTHUMBERLAND, 1603

Queen Anne, my intended prey, stood by a window in the little presence chamber in Berwick Castle, gazing out towards the foggy, darkening sea. I fastened my will onto her like a hound setting at a partridge.

She ignored me and continued to look out into the dusk.

I tottered towards her, past curious courtiers, inhaling sharply with each step and hobbling like a one-legged sailor. At a respectful distance I sank into the deepest curtsy that I could manage.

'The Countess of Bedford, Your Highness,' said the gentleman usher, in French.

Let me rise! I begged her silently. This was no time to faint from pain.

She gazed out of the window, still ignoring me.

If she ever let me speak, I could show her that I spoke French. But then, I must have seemed an unlikely companion, with my limp, misshapen hand and pain curdling my wits.

There's nothing to see out there but fog! Please, let me rise!

Five grooms began to light candles against the sudden fall of darkness. A sconce on the wall threw a sudden wash of unsteady yellow light across the Queen's face.

I did not like what I saw.

Her tall, lean figure stood half turned away from me, dressed in grey satin, one hand clenched on the pleated lip of her farthingale. The nearest corner of her tight lips was turned down under a long, large nose made larger by the shadow it cast across her mouth.

I could not imagine that shadowed, unsmiling mouth open in song, nor that clenched fist raising a wine glass in a tipsy toast. This new queen was not the lively, deep-drinking, dance-loving, frivolous creature of my friends' letters. Not for the first time, rumour had been wrong. She might as well have been holding a prayer book and wearing black.

From under my lashes, I tried to read her. My mother had taught me that, to survive, you must learn to read the people who hold power over your life. What you learn will give you power. They think they hide themselves, but the set of shoulder, or twitch of a hand, an uneasy sideways look or overloud voice always gives them away, if you know how to look and listen. Learn what they truly want and give it to them, my mother had said. Then you will not only survive, you will succeed.

More sconces bloomed around the walls. I saw the new queen clearly now.

Another sour queen like the old one, I thought unhappily. To advance in her court, I did not have to like her, but she had to like me.

I had to make her like me. If not, it was back to Chenies with my tail between my legs. Back to Edward and silence.

To my lute without strings. To living with my husband's infinite reasons for saying 'no'.

I glanced at the three Scots ladies attending her, all soberly dressed, their hair covered. They eyed me coldly. The story of my undignified arrival had quickly spread.

If they were what pleased her, I was finished.

I had nothing to offer this woman except the usual obsequious court flattery that drove me mad with impatience and fuelled a dangerous urge to blurt out the truth. While many of my friends at court before our exile had celebrated my reckless candour as wit, this dour queen would not. Experience had taught me that sour women tended not to like me, however modestly I tried to behave myself. For the first time, it occurred to me that I might fail.

I knew that I made a sorry picture. Both my thighs now trembled violently. I could see the fabric of my gown shake. Though I had paid a castle woman to dress my hair and lace my bodies, my gown was still wrinkled from the saddlebag in spite of all her shaking and brushing. I had managed to cram my injured foot into a shoe, but only after cutting away my riding boot.

My bad ankle trembled on the brink of giving way. My good leg wobbled from having to support my entire weight. Pain brought tears to my eyes.

The Queen turned suddenly, as if she had just noticed me. An unexpected brightness of diamonds and amethysts flashed when she waved a bony hand for me to rise.

'I thank you, Your Majesty.' I straightened with care. It was still possible that I might fall at her feet. Then I looked at her face. Our eyes met in shared assessment.

I tried not to stare.

Unlike Old Gloriana, Anne wore no rouge or other artifice. Her naked face looked drained by weariness and older than her twenty-nine years. In the candlelight, her skin was grey against the creamy pearls hanging from her ears. On the jewelled hand she had waved, the nails were bitten short and the skin around the nails nibbled raw.

Forgive me, I thought. I read you wrong.

We studied each other with equal intensity.

Do you not yet understand the need for masks? I ached to ask. Old Gloriana understood that need, most of all for queens.

The weary pain in her eyes tightened my throat. The last emotion I had expected to feel with the new queen was kinship.

I had prepared an amusing, pretty speech of welcome, but could not begin it. Those words were meant to charm a different woman.

I saw now that she had not been ignoring me from spite, nor to assert her position. I recognised the heaviness that had held her unmoving at the window. I knew that long stare into nothing. She had been searching for strength to begin conversation with yet another stranger, who, like all the others, undoubtedly wanted something from her and would require her to make a decision.

I dropped my eyes to her childlike bitten nails again.

Not sour, after all, I thought. Queen or not, she was melancholy and past hiding it. Her youth was being worn away by misery. Like me, she was spoiling from the core.

I felt a rush of gentle ferocity, like the tenderness when I cupped a new chick or saw a fragile green shoot pushed up through clods of dirt and stones.

The Whitehall wolves would tear this poor woman apart. I had felt their teeth and knew how sharp they could be. She must be protected. She must be told. Somehow, without giving offence. But to tell her would give offence, no matter how carefully worded. One does not pity royalty.

'You made good speed here, Lady Bedford,' she said. 'Though perhaps at a dear cost.' She gestured at my bad hand. So, she had heard the tale too. But between her native Danish accent and her acquired Scottish one, I could not tell what she thought of my journey.

Trying to decide whether to risk speaking my true thoughts or to hazard a jest in return, I stepped onto my bad ankle. A flash of searing pain together with exhaustion betrayed my training.

'Oww! God's Balls!'

I staggered, hopped sideways, caught myself and clapped my good hand over my mouth. I heard outraged gasps from the attending ladies, then unbreathing silence. Even the six men-at-arms standing behind the Queen had frozen.

Raw arse and dead horse were for nothing, after all. The touch between my shoulder blades had been a Divine warning. I had ignored it. I would have to slink back to Chenies, confess to Edward . . . for rumour would soon tell him if I did not . . . that I had managed to marry obscenity to blasphemy in two short words. And been thrown out of Berwick for offending the new queen.

The silence grew.

I began to rehearse my long, painful, slow hobbling retreat to the door . . . desperately slow, stretching out my torment . . . the averted eyes of the men-at-arms, the suppressed smiles of the ladies-in-waiting . . . their hungry gossip when out of the Queen's hearing. I imagined their tutting and lip-smacking disapproval and raising of eyes to Heaven.

I waited to be dismissed.

The Queen was studying me with . . . I tried to resist

39

hope . . . what looked like the first real interest. 'Lady Bedford,' she said at last. 'I think that I must engage you to improve my English. I'm certain my other ladies don't know so many useful words.'

I imagined a glint of mischief in the swift look she gave her three tight-lipped Scots.

I wagered my future.

I became an angel balanced on a pinhead, precarious yet suddenly sure of my footing at the same time. I must abandon protocol, I was certain. She had had too much protocol. Her carelessness with her person told me that she had put herself beyond the reach of a courtier's empty flattery. I wagered my future on what I felt she needed most from me.

The words sprang raw and unexamined from my mouth. 'It will be my greatest pleasure to give you pleasure, madam,' I said. 'Pleasure.' I repeated the word. I let it hang in the air. '. . . in English lessons and all else.'

Play, I thought.

'I will shake my sack of words,' I said, 'until every last "zounds" and "zwagger" has tumbled out for your instruction – and enjoyment, if you so choose.'

She gave a minute nod at my return of her serve.

I advanced carefully towards my leap. 'If my honesty ever oversteps, or I play the fool too far, I beg your forgiveness in advance.'

Her intent stillness gave me courage to go on.

'Because even my errors will have only one purpose – to give you joy.' I heard another intake of breath behind me at this presumption.

Joy. The word flew out of my mouth and circled in the air above our heads. A dove. A butterfly. A scarlet autumn leaf.

Joy. My offering to her. Not service, not loyalty, not

reverence, nor adoration, nor awe, nor blind obedience, which royalty can always command. Joy. A precious commodity that cannot be commanded of another person, nor bought, nor wrestled into being. It was delicate and fleeting, as I knew very well. You must stalk it, surprise it. It's a seed that may or may not grow. You can't force it, but you can dig out the stones, till the ground and stand by with expectant heart and watering cans. Among other things, I was also a gardener. I knew how to make the desert bloom.

The Queen had tilted her head, not looking at me now, listening.

'Madam, at my birth I was christened Lucy . . . *lux*, *lucis* . . . light. In your service, I swear I will earn the right to my name.' I held her now in my thoughts as gently but firmly as I would trap a moth. 'If the light and laughter ever fail, you may banish me.'

I heard her draw a deep breath.

Quickly, to lighten my earnest words, I threw open my arms, imitating a player-warrior accepting the fatal sword thrust. 'And I must beg your forgiveness already, madam. I dare not risk another curtsy or I will sprawl at your feet.'

To my horror, she did not smile at this extravagance. Instead, tears welled in her eyes. I had misjudged and cut too near the quick.

I had made the new queen cry in front of everyone. Now she would hate me. I had dared to pity her and let her know it. Shamed her in public, before those tight-lipped, but almost certainly loose-tongued, women. I had made a second fatal error. Back to Chenies after all.

Then she swallowed. 'Thank you, Lady Bedford.'

The gowns of the waiting women rustled. There was a tiny pause.

I tried to think what to say, unable to hope that I might somehow, perhaps, survive my own mistakes for a second time.

Then she pointed at my swollen hand. 'You must have that hand bandaged. I shall ask my doctor to see to it.' She waved away my renewed attempt to curtsy. She was mistress of herself again.

And she had offered me her own royal doctor.

'Thank you, madam.' I dropped my arms. 'I am honoured . . .' I caught her eye and noted the slightly raised royal brows and the waiting chilly half-smile. I bit down on the formulaic gratitude.

Lightly, Lucy, lightly now.

She saw me catch myself. Her brows stayed up. But she knew that I had understood her.

I glanced at the row of cold eyes and tight mouths behind her.

She needed a playmate in the pursuit of joy.

'I will limp gratefully from the field for treatment,' I said. 'But before this herald retires injured, she must first deliver urgent news. Two thousand richly jewelled royal gowns await Your Highness in the royal Wardrobe in London.'

'That's good news for any woman, royal or not!'

Her Scottish women laughed politely.

Now the Queen was reading me as closely as I had read her. 'And tell me, Lady Bedford, who brings such good tidings, can you give me more good news? Does it truly rain less in London than in Edinburgh, as I have been told?' Even through her double-layered accent, I heard a testing playfulness.

'I could never speak ill of Scotland, Your Highness. Even when the truth demands it.'

She smiled at last. The air around us loosened. We

42

exchanged another assessing look. Together, we had averted danger. We exchanged the most minute of nods. Miraculously, we seemed to stand at the first fragile beginning of friendship. The way ahead felt as tentative as a garden path marked out in sand, but it held the same implied promise that it might be laid, rod by rod, in brick and stone.

In the next days before setting off for London, I tested what gave our new queen pleasure. I soon learned that she did not share my taste for debate and philosophy but did like music and dancing, just as rumour had said. Above all, she needed to laugh.

Therefore, I brought these pleasures together. I taught her – and several of her women – to sing two English songs whilst I played the fool with a borrowed lute and one good hand and made her press her fingers in place of mine onto the strings so that together she and I made a single musician and all of us almost fell off our stools with laughing.

She liked to gossip and would be living among strangers.

Therefore, I improvised scurrilous rhyming couplets to help her, and her Scots ladies, to remember the different English courtiers waiting in London.

'"Her flattering portrait is like Lady C . . . Only in this – that they both painted be",' I recited.

'Does she still whiten her face with lead?' Her Majesty clapped a hand to her mouth in mock horror. Her women clucked 'tut-tut' and shook their heads. One or two touched their own hair or mouths thoughtfully.

She fancied herself a poet. Therefore, we began together to devise her first masque to celebrate her arrival at the court of Whitehall.

When she grew weary, I made herbal tisanes to help her sleep. I quickly learned not to mention children or the King.

I watched her shoulders loosen. Her eyes began to sparkle. Once, at some trivial jest of mine, she laughed so immoderately that I feared she would veer into uncontrolled tears. Then she patted her breastbone, wiped her eyes and stood up to foot-fumble her way into a half-remembered Danish country-dance, which she promised to teach me when I had two good feet again.

I had ridden north driven by cold ambition and need, in search of advancement. I had won royal favour just as I had intended. I did not expect to have my ambition disarmed by my heart. The more I saw that I was able to please Queen Anne, the more she captured my love. She needed me when no one else did. She needed Lucy in all her brightness. I loved her for her need and shone ever more brightly in the effort to give her joy. It was more than I deserved.

I had ridden into my rightful life where I was needed and where my skills had value. Chenies did not need me as the new queen did. My husband's other estates at Woburn and Moor Park did not need me. He too would profit from my renewed royal favour. I was saving us both.

I heard the mutters among the disappointed English women who arrived three days after I did. No lady would have done what I did, they said.

But the truth proved them wrong. Three evenings after I had ridden into Berwick, hatless, hair flying, limping and with a wrist like a ham, I was made first lady of the bedchamber to Queen Anne, wife of the new Scottish King, James VI of Scotland who was now also James the First of England. I was elevated to be chief among all the court ladies-in-waiting. If that was not lady enough for anyone, I cannot say what would be.

My new position even silenced my mother when she

arrived in Berwick with the other women. This was a woman who, when she later died, was widely said to have gone to see that God remembered to wash behind His ears.

I was twenty-two years old when I rode to Berwick. Power and privilege were in my grasp again. I was happy. I thought I had tamed the future.

This time I don't know where to point myself. Time is now the enemy. Elizabeth is on the run and may be taken prisoner at any time. She is expecting another babe.

She has not written to me since that first letter.

I must go where powerful men gather intelligence, where news and rumour are born. Someone will know where Elizabeth is. I will ask until I learn. Then I will go to her, on the run or not, however it can be done, and persuade her to come home so that I can help her find joy again as I once helped her mother. She will keep me by her, and I will have a purpose again.

# 6

## ELIZABETH STUART – BERLIN, DECEMBER 1620

Elizabeth understands the message she holds in her gloved hand. The letter's language is formal. It twists and turns, slithering around the brutal meaning without ever quite arriving. But the message is clear.

No.

She is being turned away yet again with flattering words that fail to hide the writer's fear.

No friends here, neither. No room at the inn for the queen and children of a defeated king. They are enemies of the imperial House of Austria who are not known to forgive an affront. The rebellion of the Bohemian Protestants has been an affront. Daring to elect their own Protestant king in place of the Hapsburg Ferdinand has been an affront. Helping the fugitive king and queen will be an affront. The Hapsburgs would not forgive.

With the back of her fur-lined glove, she wipes a clump of falling snow from her left eyelash. Snow is already blotting out the words on the paper she holds.

*. . . Madame, in spite of the great . . . in which I hold your esteemed husband . . . and your . . . circumstances alas . . . regret . . . unfit to entertain you in a way suitable to your elevated . . .*

Not possible, she thinks. I am the wife of a king, and daughter of the King of England. If these cowards don't fear my poor Frederick, they must feel some respect for my father and for England! Surely, England would not tolerate such treatment of its First Daughter, even if she were not also Queen of Bohemia.

The letter is from Frederick's brother-in-law, who regrets his unavoidable absence. Even family lacks the courage to help them.

She should have been prepared for refusal. The Imperial armies are close and marching closer. England is very far away. And, so far, resolutely refusing to take sides.

The messenger stands respectfully, head bowed, awaiting her response. Behind him, at the far end of the snow-covered causeway, stand the closed gates of the city. Behind the gates lie the castle and lighted fires, heated wine, warmed beds. Roasted meats that have not frozen solid. Dry shoes.

Her fingers, even gloved, are almost too cold to hold the Elector of Brandenburg's message.

With disdain, Elizabeth drops the letter into the snow. She tightens her grip on the belt of the man riding in front of her and re-balances her shivering, pregnant bulk on the back of the saddle. 'Ride on.'

Captain Ralph Hopton understands the spirit of her order as well as the words. He kicks their horse, turning it so that he forces the messenger to leap back out of their way. One large rear hoof drives the letter deep into the snow.

They have lost carts and carriages to the drifts and to desertion. Looters had not waited until she was out of sight of Prague before beginning to strip the contents of the caravan.

A wave of disbelief rolls back along the line behind her when the remaining drivers and horsemen see that they are turning away from the city. She hears shouts as men heave carts onwards out of ruts in the frozen mud. One by one, the straggling remains of the procession lurches into movement again.

She looks back to see that the light carriages now holding the children and their nurses still follow Hopton's horse. The first carriage slips on a frozen rut and lurches violently like a ship hit broadside by a wave. Then it rights itself and tilts to the other side. Behind it, straining horses and oxen are lashed by violent English, German and Bohemian curses aimed at the circumstances.

She straightens her aching back and cradles her belly with her free hand. If their eight-month-pregnant queen can carry on, so could the rest of them. Those who remain.

The child in her belly gives a violent kick. Her womb is riding very low, a sign that the birth is not far off.

Not yet, she begs. Please, not until I find refuge! Or else, I may give birth to an icicle. You know you don't want to be an ice baby.

From here at the front of the line, she cannot see the end of the caravan, but she knows that farther back men and women are still slipping away into a familiar countryside. Back to their mountains, back to their villages. Like Rupert's nurse.

She imagines the nurse's husband or lover, perhaps a soldier, pulling her by the arm away from her charge. Saying, 'This fight is nothing to do with us. Leave the royal brat. Come home!'

The army would not fight for us, she thought. If soldiers desert, why expect more of maids and grooms and ladies of the bedchamber?

She ducks her head under her hood against sudden needles of sleet. If all her new subjects left her, she would manage perfectly well without them.

Without a palace, what need did she have for so many people?

Once past the approach to the city gates, the road divides. Before word of the onward advance has had time to reach the rearmost carts, Hopton asks, 'Where do we ride, madam?'

'Custrin,' she says at once, with authority. Another of Brandenburg's castles, just as unsuitable, he said. But she is running out of choices. 'A few days more. Perhaps only two. At Custrin, we'll have fires and real beds. Tonight we will find a sheltered place to stop and sleep in the carriages.' Her ears catch the sound of a child crying behind her. 'We shall curl up together as warmly as a litter of pups.' She lays a calming hand on the agitation in her belly.

There is still enough charcoal left to keep their braziers alight for another night. The two remaining cooks might even manage hot soup. They will lose a few more animals to exhaustion and the cold, but that can't be helped. A few more men will slip away to warmer beds.

'We won't be able to wash,' she says cheerfully. 'But there are worse things than beginning to smell like a dog as well as sleeping like one.'

# 7

## LUCY – MOOR PARK, DECEMBER 1620

'I must go to London,' I say. We are at dinner in the damp, draughty hall at Moor Park, eating vegetable soup from pewter bowls, the silver plate having long been sold. The long table is half-empty. Though we still keep our personal retinues, they have shrunk. Only three servers stand behind our chairs, where once there would have been one for every diner. Once, musicians would have played while we ate. Once, when we had finished eating, we would have pushed back the table to dance.

The Third Earl sets down his spoon, hugs his injured arm to his chest and looks at me over his barricade. 'Why?'

At the bottom of the table, our steward holds up a finger to signal the coming point of his story to the four heads leaning towards him, including that of my chief lady, Lady Agnes Hooper, the widow of a local knight. I have no patience with the strict Protestant protocol in which I had been raised, and keep an informal house.

'To mend our fortunes,' I say quietly.

The steward's listeners laugh, settle back on their stools and resume eating.

I am tempted to add, 'as I did before'. But my husband's agreement would make my project easier and a great deal more pleasant.

I chase a cube of turnip around my bowl, braced for the frown and pursed lips that always precede refusal.

Even before his accident, Edward had preferred to say 'no'. 'Yes' pained him. It suggested action, feeling, thought.

'I believe that the muscles of your cheeks and lips will creak if you say "yes",' I had once observed.

'No' lets him purse his lips. 'Yes' hints at a smile. Whenever he is forced into agreement, his mouth stiffens with reluctance, as if it hurts him to stretch it wide enough to let 'yes' escape.

The dislike I see in his eyes still startles me. Eyes that are too close together, huddled near his nose.

'London?' he echoes, puzzled and querulous like the old man he is rushing to become.

I would have preferred him to shout.

My tongue speaks of its own will. 'You remember London, do you not? A city to the south of us, on the Thames? Less than a day's ride . . .'

He flinches. I have used a wrong word again. 'Ride.' He had been thrown from his horse, against a tree, while hunting. He could no longer tolerate the word 'ride'. Even 'horse' makes him uneasy.

Why could I play the courtier with everyone but my husband? Close your ears. Keep your eye on your destination, I tell myself.

'I forbid you to go,' he says. 'This is another of your fancies. And certain to cost us dear, like all the rest.' He bends to his bowl again.

Eyes around the table suddenly grow intent on soup and the roasted duck from our ponds.

That was not a request, I think. I was telling you what I mean to do.

I have had many such silent conversations with him.

The smell of the soup sickens me. I set down my spoon. I fold my napkin exactly on its creases and lay it on the table – once we could have afforded a waiting groom to take it from me. I stand up. 'I pray you all, excuse me.'

Stool and bench legs scrape on the stone floor as the others rise with me. Everyone but my husband.

'Sit down!' He speaks as if to one of his dogs. Even whores are granted the courtesy of 'mistress', and I am a countess.

'Sir, I need air.'

'Sit!' he snaps again.

I hear breaths drawn around the table and see glances exchanged. My thoughts cloud as if I had drunk too much wine, though we were making do with over-watered ale. My heart grows white hot and swells against the inside of my ribs, pounding as if I were at court, in costume, waiting to fling myself onto the table of a thousand eyes. I have the sensation that my bones shift subtly inside my skin.

I catch the eye of my lady and the steward. I widen my own eyes.

'If you will treat me as one of your dogs, sir, you must allow me out for a run.'

Someone snorts. Agnes Hooper hides a smile. Followed by my husband's astonished gaze, I leave the room. Calmly. I walk through the cold passages to a side door. Unhurried. I open the door and step outside.

I run. My heeled shoes slip on patches of mud in the

vegetable gardens. The long icy orchard grass turns to glass under my feet.

I look back. No one follows me. I plunge deeper into the orchard, colliding with trees like a drunken dancer, cursing and wiping my nose on my lace cuff.

A sow nosing for frozen windfall apples squeals and flees from my path, baggy teats swaying, followed by panicked, flap-eared scraps of piglet.

No farther, or else my heart will explode. I fling myself back against a tree. My throat opens. A scream rises from my feet, swells, pours out and quivers the leaves above my head, a dark animal scream like the demon shriek of copulating foxes.

I am drowning in 'No!'

I scream again, pounding my fists into the tree behind me.

Everything gone! Fallen from chief lady-in-waiting at court to this! Tied down by my husband's constant 'No'. By poverty. The Queen, dead, and her court dispersed. My dear friend, Prince Henry, dead. My Elizabeth, married, gone, and now a fugitive . . . another exile.

Stop! The voice in my head is firm, the necessary voice that had always before pulled me back from folly, just in time.

I scream again.

Stop! the reasonable voice repeats. Someone will hear you and come.

The thought of anyone coming to force me back to the dining table is even more intolerable than the sudden storm inside me.

My thick brocade skirt and winter petticoat, together with the padded sausage of my bum-roll tied around my waist, have rucked up in a lump behind my waist and hips.

The rough grey, lichen-covered apple bark snags at my hair.

I clamp down on the next scream and press my hands to my face to close out the world.

Into the darkness float the faces of loss. My parents. My queen. Elizabeth. And my infant daughter, who had lived inside me, kicking at the inside of my belly, dancing at music, stirring when I laughed. At the sight of her, complete and perfect, a miraculous new person who met my eyes with puzzled astonishment, the milk had leapt into my breasts and flowed from my nipples.

I had never suckled her. Even the sow could suckle her young. My daughter stayed with me for only two hours. I lost her. Like my son, my first babe, Edward's precious heir who had lived one whole month. Long enough to be christened, at least. Losing my babes had cut out one of my vital organs and left me diminished, like a fatal illness from which I would never recover.

I drop my hands and try to narrow my thoughts to the fan of brown grass near my left foot. But another lost face arrives there.

John would have seen a metaphor in that dead grass, would have resurrected it with the miracle of his words, given it new, eternal life in verse and human comprehension. He would have made its little patch of mud here under an old apple tree as huge as the world of the soul.

The rough grey tree bark tugs at my hair when I shake my head. Don't think of him.

Though still in this world, he is now dead to me, but his words are still alive and insinuating in my head. I have them trapped in ink shaped by the movement of his hand, locked into my chest of papers like hostages.

I stare down, puzzled, at the blood on the sides of my fists.

I am meant to be the wild, merry Countess of Bedford, who can be relied on to lead each new diversion, who lightens the heavy spirits of others. Who soars in witty debate. Her spirits are never seen to weigh her down. In my thirty-nine years of conscious life, I had met Melancholy more than once, but always in secret. I had refused to entertain it.

Now, I feel too heavy to move. I could not even have kicked my horse over the edge of the snow bank. I bow my head, pulling my hair free. I lick the blood and flecks of bark from the side of my right hand, absently noting the tiny points of roughened skin that scrape against my tongue.

From the age of thirteen, I have tried to be a dutiful wife. I knew what was required of me.

After Edward had spent the modest fortune for which he had married me, losing his own money along with mine through his folly and bad judgement, I made over to him my own portion, which should have been mine alone, my protection, my safeguard. He had insisted. I was still, then, a dutiful wife. My portion was long gone.

There is nothing he could do to me now to make me any unhappier than I am already. Except to lock me away like a madwoman or chain me to my bed.

I imagine rising from the table again, but this time, I walk to the stables. I mount my horse, standing already saddled with a gold-embroidered, red velvet saddle-cloth. I turn his head south to London and kick him gently. It is spring. I wear a fine silk satin gown, deep blue, not frayed and not mended. The African ostrich plume on my hat curves down to tickle the lobe of my ear. I again wear my wedding diamonds, and the pearl eardrops I had worn when I first danced for the Queen.

I hear the sow grunt in the distance. A woman's shadow

moves among the trees. I slide around the tree to buy a few more moments of freedom.

'Madam?' calls a tentative voice. Agnes Hooper, my chief lady.

At least, my husband has not sent the watchman, or a man-at-arms to restrain me like a madwoman.

Take care, warns the voice in my head. You've just behaved like a madwoman. Don't risk being thought possessed. Don't hand a naked blade to your enemy. Even Edward might be tempted to use it.

I sigh and step from behind the tree.

Back in the big house, I smile at my husband, nod pleasantly to the others at the table and sit down again as if nothing at all had happened. Reassured by my smiles, the diners unfreeze and begin to murmur and chew again. The surface of the afternoon closes over us though it remains a little uneasy. Only Agnes glances at me from time to time with a small frown of concern. With grim satisfaction, I note that I still have the power to bend the spirits of others and to shape the mood.

Except that of my husband.

Edward Russell, Third Earl of Bedford, is watching me over his dinner with an air of puzzled reproach. In public, as always, he endures with heroic patience the harridan that his wife has become.

Look at her! his eyes beg the other diners. What man has ever been so tormented by his spouse?

Let it pass! I warn him with my eyes. Can't you see the danger you're in? Can't you feel how your dutiful wife has just changed?

# 8

My husband continues to eat slowly and calmly, to show everyone who rules in this house. But he eats without appetite. He still watches me, with the progress of his thoughts clear in his eyes.

He had seen. He had noticed. He feels the change in me and doesn't know what to do. I almost pity him in his confusion.

Everyone waits for his response while they pretend to eat. By rights, he should assert his male authority. Perhaps even try to beat me later.

But he does not know what to do and hates himself for not knowing. He hates me for making him not know.

His eyes shift away. I have long suspected and am now certain. He is afraid of me. Just as he had once feared his formidable father.

Poor, poor Edward, I think.

Whatever manhood he ever had seems to have leaked away through his cracked arm bone, along with his youth and any vitality, as if the crack had let in a sense of death. The tree trunk that met his head had not cracked his skull, but it seemed, nevertheless, to have shaken his wits.

After the horse threw him, he had surrendered himself to becoming clumsy and lop-sided. He seemed to aim at the world askew, anticipating dislocation and, therefore, finding it.

At first, I had tried to coax him into healing. 'It's only an arm,' I said. 'Not your neck, or back. It will soon mend.'

'What do you know of twisted sinews and constant aches that gnaw at your spirits?'

I had bitten back my impatient reply and offered him the cup of pain-killing draught.

Now he gives up on eating, shoves away his plate and stands up from the dinner table. Everyone else stands. He lifts a foot, then hesitates.

I recognise that hesitation. He lurches forward. Looks around. Everyone pretends not to see.

His secretary, his steward, his three attending gentlemen, and all the rest, stand politely, waiting to see what he will do, or wish them to do.

A show of respect for his position, I think. Not for the man.

Every year since his accident, the Earl shrinks a little more. Everything grows less. His movement, his appetites, his will. His fortune. His dignity. The space he occupies in this world.

He looks at me accusingly, as if I had caused the floor to shift beneath his feet.

I have to look away. I cannot bear his wilful determination to suffer.

On the last time that we truly spoke to each other, he had pointed at me with his good hand. 'I stumble towards the grave,' he had said. 'I'm dying, and no one on this earth cares that I am afraid of death yet wish for it at the same time – least of all you, who should care most of all. My wife.'

'You're not dying,' I said. 'You can walk. And you could ride again, if only you would.'

'What do you know of suffering?'

I could only look at him, wordless.

'Get out of my sight,' he had said. 'Stop taunting me with your lithe moves and your sudden little dance steps.' His gaze had fallen on the ridged mud plot outside the window, a frozen maze of ditches and string, which would one day become my new garden. 'Go look for joy out there in the mud you love so much.'

Unless I shared in his misery, I insulted him with any pleasure I took in life.

'And in case you hope to make a life without me here in this godforsaken place,' he said, 'I will tell you that no one of any consequence will ever come see your blasted garden!' He steadied himself against the tabletop, waving away my offered hand. 'What good do you imagine that making a garden has ever done anyone?'

He turned his face away from the window, squinting his eyes as if hurt by the light.

'I know that you hide from me out there, amongst all those costly infant trees we can't afford. I've seen you wrapping them tenderly against the cold. And when it's too cold to coo over trees or seedlings in some gardener's hands, you bury yourself away from me making sketches and diagrams. You make your garden only to torment me, to punish me for what I have become, even though it was not my fault.'

I had stood wordless, unlike my usual self, my breath taken away by this mistaking of the truth, and from fear of what I felt coming.

'How dare you imply reproach, as if I were a useless husband?' His knuckles whitened on the edge of the tabletop. 'I lifted you from country into court. And to no purpose! You have killed my family's line. You can't even produce me a living heir!'

I keep my eyes averted now until I hear him move away from the table. I watch him leave the hall. He walks uncertainly, as if unsure where to go. His two gentlemen of the bedchamber, the sons of neighbouring knights, exchange glances then follow him. I see his old nurse hobble to meet him in the passage outside the hall, take his good hand and lead him away to the safety of her care.

# 9

Falling asleep that night, the heaviness of the orchard ambushes me again. To fight it, I repeat to myself all the reasons that life has changed and will continue to change.

Elizabeth, in flight and without a home, needs me. The newly married princess, in love with her young husband, headed for his beloved Palatine, had not needed me. Then she had lost her one close English friend, Lady Anne Dudley Sutton, gone with her to Germany after her marriage. She will need to see a well-known face. She will need a trustworthy friend. She needs me now as much as her mother ever did.

I turn over in my bed and yank at a wrinkle in the sheet that feels like a mountain ridge under my shoulder. I listen to Annie's gentle snores from her pallet on the floor.

If she is to come home, Elizabeth must believe that the English still love her. I must reassure her. And that I too still love her. That I will protect, inform and amuse her. Then, when she returns, she will make me her first lady of the bedchamber as her mother did. I will again be the older almost-sister, trusted once more with private access to both her person and her secret thoughts. I will be back where I belong and have purpose again.

My restless foot meets the solid weight of one of my small hounds, which has managed to slip into my chamber and jump onto the bed. I feel the animal go very still, pretending to sleep, waiting for the command to get down. But I welcome the heavy warmth. After a moment, the dog sighs and softens in sleep.

I cannot sleep. She might already be a captive. Or even dead, executed by the Hapsburgs, or from loss of blood in childbirth. Her confinement must be soon.

I close my eyes and feel for her in the darkness of my bed. Surely, I would feel an emptiness if she had died?

Elizabella, please write to tell me that you are well!

I am still awake to hear the first birds warming up after the night.


I do not tell my husband that I mean to defy him. I make an inventory of my remaining jewels not yet sold to try to pay our debts or to buy winter feed for the horses, or salt and sugar for our table. Or Edward's claret. I rifle through my secret, shrinking store of plate, silver pomander cases, embroidered gloves, silver-gilt boxes and other baubles for the gifts and bribes needed to navigate Whitehall.

At Whitehall, appearances matter. The surface is held to reveal the inner man. Or woman.

And I am going back to Whitehall.

With my lady Agnes Hooper and my maid Annie, I lay out my old court gowns, pairs of bodies, embroidered petticoats, cloaks, gloves, hats and shoes to choose what to take with me. I examine worn cuffs and finger torn lace ruffs. One pair of heeled shoes, in which I had once danced before the whole court, had been mended twice and the leather of the toes rubbed nearly through.

I imagine the aghast astonishment of my former protégés, the poets, artists and musicians who had once received my generous patronage.

Or worse: no longer being of use to them, I might have turned invisible.

The thought of being pitied makes me hot. My skin burns as if I have a rising ague.

'Poor thing!' I could hear a woman whisper it, the Rutland girl, or one of the acid-tongued Howards. 'She may have risen to become a countess, but look where it got her.'

'An invalid husband, mended shoes . . .' says another voice.

And the constant search for someone to loan us more money.

My skin has grown thinner, I think as I stitch a loose strip of gold sequins back onto the front panel of a petticoat.

'If I brush this carefully, it will serve, don't you think?' says Agnes, holding up a hat of Muscovite beaver fur.

I nod as I bite off the thread.

Once, I would not have cared. But now, unprotected by the love of my queen or my poet, I feel an urgent need for at least one new gown to face both my enemies and my friends who remain at Whitehall.

'You too must have a new gown,' I tell Agnes.

'Madam.' She curtsies and tries not to look too pleased, but the severe planes of her face rearrange themselves into something like a smile. Though her husband had been a knight, his estate was sold to pay old debts and she now depends on me for survival.

I glance at the patched soles of her shoes where she kneels by a chest. I need a pair of new shoes, I think. We both need new shoes.

So much for my 'learned and masculine soul', once praised by Master Jonson. But, as I have said, we are impure creatures. Only saints and demons can be entirely consistent.

Then Agnes shakes her head. She knows most of my secrets, good and bad. 'Where will you find the money, madam?'

'Watch me,' I say.

I fetch one of Edward's old doublets that I had filched from his chambers. He has not worn it since his exile from court by the Old Queen for his entanglement in the Essex rebellion, seven years after our marriage – when he was old enough to know better. He would never miss it now.

I pull my little knife from where it hangs on a ribbon under my skirt.

I begin to cut off the jewelled buttons on the front of the doublet.

At least, this is not your foolish head, I think as I slice off the first button with my knife. You had a lucky escape from the scaffold. Though the fine of five thousand pounds imposed by the Queen had begun our ruin. And his exile had made it impossible for him to acquire all the money he'd borrowed to pay back the fine.

I give the button to Agnes, who sets it carefully on the table.

I saved us once before . . . with my ride to Berwick . . .

I slice off another button.

I shall have to do it again . . .

Another button off.

Whether you want me to, or not.

This one jumps from my fingers and rolls away under my bed. Without losing a fraction of her lean, straight-backed dignity, Agnes sinks to the floor in a pool of skirts, presses her head to the side of the bed and extends her arm into the dark space beneath.

I cut off another button.

'I have it!' cries Agnes in triumph. She unfolds upwards, puts the escaped button beside the others on the table, shakes her skirts and begins to pick dust kittens from her sleeve.

'Thirteen,' I count. We look down at the glittering line of small golden baskets, woven from gold wire, each set with a diamond.

'Lucky thirteen,' she says. 'If you believe such things.'

One button buys me rich golden taffeta a little darker than my hair and the making of it into a court gown in the latest style, with a soft farthingale and embroidered sleeves. Two more buttons buy a gown for Agnes, and new saddlebags for me, along with a new side-saddle to replace the old one that is stained with sweat, patched, and has a girth as crumpled and limp as an old stocking. The other ten, I put into a purse against the expenses of London.

Losing your position at court . . . I tighten the cord around the neck of the purse . . . means losing all the means by which money can be made. You no longer receive fees for granting licences, patents, monopolies. You might lose all the rights formerly granted to you – the income from harbour fees and taxes on imported goods. You lose the gifts of gratitude given in exchange for favours, like access to the Queen, or a kind word spoken into a powerful ear, or finding a position for a young female cousin as a lady-in-waiting, or placing a young son as a groom in a noble house. You can no longer grant favours for favours in return.

I tie the purse around my waist and tilt my Italian glass to be certain that my petticoats hide the bulge.

*Voilà!* No purse.

A week later, while my maid Annie, assisted by my chamberer, makes piles of clean linens and matches stockings, I start to pack a few books into my travelling chest. *To Lucy Russell, Countess of Bedford*, begins one of them. *To the Countess of Bedford*, begins another. And, *To My Golden Mistress* . . .

The only verses I truly value have been written but not yet published.

*To the Most Esteemed* . . . I snap the book closed and return it to the cupboard.

A poor woman cannot serve as patron to poets and playwrights. A poor woman is not called 'the Morning Star' or 'Brightest star in the Firmament' in exchange for putting food on a poet's table.

But poverty means more than merely losing the flattery of your protégés. Or even scrimping to buy feed for your horses or the lack of fashionable gowns. It means hopelessness. It blocks the means by which you can hope to prosper and progress. Poverty closes doors. It stitches up your pockets so that no money can enter them. It dulls your senses and your wits with constant grinding need.

I know that I should be grateful. Compared to a beggar, I am rich.

I know that the soul should rise above such worldly concerns. It should console you for lack of material goods by a richness of the mind and hope for the Next Life. But in truth, I have never met an artist or poet who did not tell me that poverty crowds out the imagination and dulls the action of the wits with its endless round of the petty problems of daily survival. I share their conclusion.

On the other hand, I think as I brush the feathers on my beaver hat, if you're poor, no one marries you for your money. I try on the hat and assess my reflection in my glass.

Plausible, though not impressive. If I squint, I can ignore the tracks of Time on my face. Praise God, my hair still keeps its original bright red-gold.

I set the hat on top of my folded winter cloak.

My route is not yet clearly mapped, but I know where I am headed. I can take the first step.

To London.

I will let the whispers and raised eyebrows in Whitehall roll off me like water off wax.

And then . . . when I have found Elizabeth and brought her back, and we are close again . . . The excuses and closed doors that drove me away from court will be retracted and opened again. And I will forgive, or not, as I decide. Lucy Russell, born a Harington, is not finished yet.

When I am ready, I go to Edward's chambers. He looks up from his brooding examination of his fire, startled to see me there. His old nurse pauses in her folding and smoothing of a shirt to glare at me.

'I leave for London tomorrow,' I say. 'All is arranged. I will send back word how the house and gardens have been tended in our absence.'

He does not pretend surprise. If he has failed to notice the dressmaker and the loss of his doublet, he must have seen the cart that is to follow me with my belongings as it stood being repaired in the stable yard. Or the chests standing open in the hall. Or the ale kegs and small stack of hams in the screens passage. He must have heard the noisy chase after a dozen laying hens and their indignant squawks at being crammed into their travelling crate.

'Back to your poets and lovers?'

'You know that I can't afford poets any longer.' I weaken, foolish enough still to hope for a word of approval. 'I have a purpose that will benefit us both.'

'Another of your schemes?' He hugs his shattered arm to his chest, swaddled in its fur muff. 'What will this one cost us?'

'Less than my ride to Berwick.'

He rolls his eyes to Heaven. God spare me her impudence!

But he waves his good hand to dismiss me. 'Do as you will, madam. I'm too weary to fight you. I don't care where you go or whom you see. You're of no use to me.'

I take that as his formal permission. I have already sent word to our London house that I am coming.

# 10

## ELIZABETH STUART – CUSTRIN, GERMANY, DECEMBER 1620

'Are you ordered to turn us away?' Elizabeth demands.

The castle steward shifts uneasily on his horse. 'The Elector of course welcomes you, if you truly wish to stay. In the circumstances.' He had intercepted them at the bridge before they could enter the town.

From behind him on his horse, Elizabeth stares over Hopton's shoulder. Custrin Castle looks very much like the grim fortress described in the Elector of Brandenburg's letter.

> . . . *the walls are without tapestries, the cellars empty of wine, the granaries bare of corn. From my own sense of honour* . . .

Elizabeth had snorted when she read that word 'honour' in Berlin. Now all impulse to laugh has left her. She could have recited the vile letter word by word.

*. . . I cannot allow Your Majesty and your attendants to suffer the inconvenience of lodging in a place devoid of food and fuel, without fodder for your horses.*

'I wish to stay,' she says. 'Just for one night. No civilised man would make a pregnant woman sleep in a snowdrift, even if she were not a queen.' The child in her womb heaves and kicks as if infected by her fury and despair. A belt of muscle tightens around the base of her gut.

The steward shrugs and turns his horse back to the castle. Hopton kicks his mount to follow. Elizabeth grabs clumsily at his belt with numb hands to keep from being jolted off when the horse slips on the ice on the bridge.

We are turned enemy, she thinks, still disbelieving the speed and distance of their fall. One moment at dinner together in Hradcany Palace, monarch and ally. The next moment in wild flight, the guest no one dares to entertain.

The great fireplace in the hall of Custrin Castle stands cold and cave-like. The huge iron firedogs are empty of logs. No waiting fire has been laid. The bare stone walls ooze damp. Although the absence of icy wind makes the interior of the castle warmer than the back of a horse, her teeth still rattle. Her feet are numb, untrustworthy blocks. The tight belt of muscle around the base of her belly has slackened, but she knows it will tighten again at any moment.

'There must be firewood in the village, if you have none here,' says Elizabeth. 'We badly need fires. And food.'

Someone in the village must have food, even if the castle larders do not.

'Your Highness.' The steward looks past her, wild-eyed, at the shivering crowd of attendants and royal children.

The Elector must have believed that the English princess

70

would understand the true message of his letter. He had given no orders what to do if Her Highness ignored it.

'I'm certain we can find enough for one night,' the steward says. He would have to see that the captain of the castle garrison doubled the night watch.

The child shifts in her belly. Elizabeth pulls off her gloves and flexes her icy fingers.

The Elector did not lie in his letter. The place does not suit a queen. Cold air flows down from the small, high windows. Icy currents seep under the door and wash around their ankles. Everywhere she looks, she sees only more grey dampness.

But she is in.

'I assume that you have a suitable chamber for me, with clean sheets on the bed,' she says. 'And chambers for the Prince, the Princess and my ladies. The rest can be laid out on pallets so long as there are fires. The carters and drovers, too.' She gazes around the grey, grim hall. 'I'm quite sure that your master has a few bottles left in his cellars for just such emergencies as this one.'

'Madam.' The man bows and begins to back away. 'I must just . . .'

As he is about to leave the hall, she adds, 'And bring me pen and ink. Tomorrow morning, I will give you a list of my needs for the next month, including a midwife. As soon as we have fires, I will also write to the Elector to tell him that I have decided to stay here at Custrin until my child is born.'

*If he dares to throw me out,* she writes to friends in England, *. . . let him try to explain to the English people – and to their King – why an heir to the English throne was born – and very likely frozen to death – in a German snowdrift.*

## LUCY, DECEMBER 1620

Her letter reaches me just before I leave Moor Park for London. She is not only alive but sounds like her former undaunted self. The tale is almost comical as she relates it, but her anger glints through her words.

She must learn to be more guarded in what she writes, I think. Or at least use a cipher. I put this letter with her other ones in my writing chest that will travel under my eye on my horse's hindquarters.

# 11

## LONDON, JANUARY 1621

I turn my horse left out of St Martin's Lane. The house stands ahead of me on the north side of the Strand, as lanky and narrow-shouldered as I remembered it. I have never liked Bedford House, built in London for my husband by his father in the days of the Old Queen. It strikes me as unfriendly, with its long roof, seven steep sharp gables and the empty posturing of a mock-military turret tower. It looks south across the Strand, past York House, home of the Lord Keeper Francis Bacon, to the Thames. Only being near to the river is in its favour.

I can hear the distant shouts of boatmen from the different water stairs as I let my horse pick his way through the frozen rubbish in the street. After passing under the arch of the gatehouse at the far end of the house front, my small party clops into a large, irregular, open courtyard.

A tall, fair-haired man bursts out of the higgledy-piggledy wing on my left. 'I hear that a new horse has arrived for the stables! And it's not half-dead, neither.'

'Sir Kit!' I cry.

He runs to take my horse as if he were still a groom, but I'd had Christopher Hawkins made up to knight as soon as he was old enough – one of the first favours I asked after arriving in London with the new queen. The young groom who had ridden with me to Berwick is now my London Master of Horse. When he married the year after his advancement, I persuaded Edward to give him the lease of a small house in the tangle of streets that abut the west wall of Bedford House, along with a small annual income. So far as I know, he survives the paltry stipend granted to him by Edward by teaching the aspiring sons of successful London merchants how to ride.

Now I look down at the delight in his face and watch him stroke my horse's nose with a broad callused hand. Here is one of the few men I know I can trust.

In the big entrance hall, steward, clerk, secretary, cook, house grooms, chamber grooms and maids wait to greet me. It is a smaller company than it had once been, even allowing for absent scullery grooms and gardeners. But a London house can supply itself from the city bakers, fishmongers, butchers, brewers, vintners, poulterers and pigmen, and does not need its own. It need not pretend to be a self-feeding country estate.

The steward looks ill, I note. I will ask later if he needs to give up his position.

I hand my fur-lined gloves to my maid. Agnes Hooper unhooks my travel cloak and takes it away to dry. I look about me.

I'm pleasantly surprised. Bedford House feels drier than either Chenies or Moor Park, and far more welcoming than when I had first seen it as a new young wife. When we married, my husband was lodged there with his aunt, the Countess of Warwick, for whom I had been third choice.

Raised from slumber by my arrival, the house smells of the lavender and rosemary used against moths and of hastily applied beeswax polish. But there is not the odour I remember from other visits of mustiness and mice. The entrance hall and chief receiving room, like much of the house, are half-empty, their paintings and furniture having been sold to help pay Edward's fine. But the smoke rises straight in the fireplaces. The wooden floors are warmer underfoot than the stone floors of Chenies and Moor Park, the low-ceilinged rooms easier to heat.

The steward, who bears the unfortunate name of Mudd, escorts me to the chief sleeping chamber. Looking through open doors as we pass, I see that some of the upholstered chairs and stools still wear their protective linen covers. But then, I had given very little warning of my arrival.

At the threshold of the great bedchamber, I stop. For a moment, I think I will not be able to enter. The ornately carved bed, with its newly brushed silk hangings and velvet coverlet embroidered with harsh, slightly tarnished gold threads, wrenches open the door of memory.

My wedding night at Bedford House: duty on both our parts. Impatience on his. Pain. Sticky slime.

I had counted off the month. I bled. I had failed to conceive.

Tried again. Again, not with child.

I felt sick in the mornings, but not in the right way.

Again. Still not with child.

My husband's eyes were cold and resolute when he bedded me.

I must not want to conceive, he said. I wasted my vital force in court frivolities. I unwomaned myself with my pen, by aspiring to have a manly soul. I loved the Queen

75

and played the man with her so that I was no longer a true woman. I murdered my babes with my mind before they could grow.

Again I bled.

I conceived but lost the babe soon after.

My guilt grew plainer in his eyes.

Again we mated.

Again, I failed. I disappointed and disgusted him in every way.

And my money was going fast.

It was because I could not give him an heir that I had signed over to him my own marriage portion, my own money, my protection. Because I was still young and hoped to be valued, even if not loved.

In spite of many offers, I was not tempted to repeat the carnal experience with another man. I hid my distaste with flirtation and outrageous talk. For the next several years, I was that rare case, a woman who was as virtuous in life as she was painted in verse.

'I will sleep in my old parlour,' I say now. 'A smaller bed will do.'

Mudd disappears to arrange it.

I summon Sir Kit to the little parlour and call to a groom to bring us warmed wine and tobacco pipes.

Kit brings with him a faint odour of horse and cold fresh air. His new leather jacket creaks as he shifts in his chair, smiling at me. I feel that he would rather be in motion, but will sit for the moment to please me.

'Now, tell me all the gossip,' I order. 'How has London entertained itself in my long absence?'

'Very ill, without you.'

'Kit! Please don't turn courtier on me or I'll have your knighthood revoked. Tell me the worst.'

'Lord Bacon is on trial for corruption. His old enemy

Coke leads the prosecution.' He grins with glee. His firm chin wears a stubble that it had lacked on our ride to Warwick, but otherwise, he looks no older. 'With Killer Coke sniffing after him, he's done for.' Coke had also prosecuted the Gunpowder Plotters. All of them were executed.

I pass Kit a long-stemmed clay pipe and light my own with a coal from the fire.

'Rumour . . .' He draws on his pipe. '. . . whispers that Buckingham already has his eye on Bacon's house, York Place.'

'My neighbours do not improve,' I murmur.

'Buckingham still climbs in the King's favour.'

'That may not be entirely bad.' I had plans for Buckingham.

We finish our pipes with the special relish of wickedness. Smoking defies authority. The King loathes the 'stinking weed' tobacco. My friend Henry Goodyear had written that courtiers at Whitehall are forced to huddle in furtive groups in the open air if they want to share the fashion for smoking pipes.

Sir Kit drops his voice. 'Buckingham now controls all access to the King . . . and I know this from more than gossip during riding lessons.' He takes my mug and warms my wine again with the poker. 'He drives others from the court.'

'My friends?'

'Southampton.' The poker hisses in his mug. 'Cranborne and Suffolk . . .'

'So many?' All these men were old friends. Henry Wriothesley, Third Earl of Southampton. Lord Cranborne, the son of my old protector and friend, Robert Cecil.

'And what of my dear old letter-writing friend, Sir Henry Goodyear?'

'He's with the King, in all things. Sings the praises of a Spanish marriage for the Prince.'

Perhaps to be trusted, perhaps not.

The number of safe allies at court has dwindled.

'And Arundel?' I ask. 'Does he still chase after antiquities with his old hunger?'

From a prominent Catholic family, Thomas Howard, Earl of Arundel had survived the taint of Catholic treason after the Gunpowder Treason against the King in 1605. Who could blame him if he found art safer than politics?

Kit sets the poker carefully on a trivet. 'He now woos Buckingham.'

'And so must we all, from what you say.' I upturn my mug and drain it with an unladylike gusto that would have made my husband purse his lips and look up to Heaven.

Neither of us asks after the other's family. Kit's wife, like me, has failed to breed, and like me grows near the end of her child-bearing years.

'Now I will inspect the gardens, before it grows too dark.' I call the steward.

His face bleaches when I say what I wish to do. 'Tonight?' He swallows.

'Is there some difficulty?'

'None, madam.'

The house groom kneeling by the fireplace grows intent on placing a new log. I glance at Kit but he is engrossed in buttoning his coat.

The Bedford House gardens run in a long narrow belt along the wall, beyond the outbuildings at the far end of the big courtyard and the stable yard to its right. Beyond them and our wall lies the open space of Covent Garden – forty acres of rough land and patches of wilderness.

Standing below the garden wall, I can hear the voices of people using the diagonal track that cuts across the Long Acre between Drury Lane at Holborn and St Martin's Lane near the Royal Mews.

At first, I see no cause for the steward's ill-concealed distress. The box hedges in the small knot garden just behind the house have been neatly trimmed. No weeds or other disorder explain his unease. I head for the arched gate to my right that leads to our kitchen gardens, orchard and the small wilderness that provides coppiced garden stakes and firewood.

'There's little to see there at this time,' the steward warns. 'And the paths will be muddy.'

'Frozen mud.' I go through the arch and stop. Edward would have called it 'theft', a crime punishable by hanging.

Before me lie row upon row of neatly tended cabbages, late turnips, and the remains of vast onion beds. A long line of old diamond-paned windows leans against the wall, protecting dung-heap hot beds, recently dug over. I see a vast bean patch with dried haulms hanging on some of the tripod supports. A mountain of frosted carrot tops rises from the corner of another cleared and newly manured plot. Far more vegetables are being grown here than could ever be needed by the skeleton-house family left in residence when the owners of Bedford House are elsewhere.

I know that we lease some of the garden to local people who lack growing space in the crowded city. But those gardens lie beyond a farther, locked gate. This is private land, for the use of Bedford House only. The knuckles of Mudd's clenched hands gleam white under his skin.

'Your labour, our land,' I say mildly. 'I see no difficulty with your enterprise, so long as you pay fair rent.'

'Of course, Your Grace! It's just that I . . .' He makes the wise choice and swallows his excuse.

'How long have you been growing vegetables to sell?'

He clasps his hand over his mouth, then mumbles, 'Two years.'

I weaken in the face of his distress. And the thought of how little Edward pays him. 'We shall calculate what you owe . . . and start from now.'

He drops to his knees on the frozen earth. 'Madam, I thank you! God bless you!'

'But when you next undertake commerce using someone else's land, ask permission first. Or you might find yourself hanged after all.' Before he can begin to weep and protest his gratitude any further, I tell him to get up or else he will freeze his knees.

The truth is that I need all the allies I can muster.

'Before the light goes,' says Kit, when we are returned to the warmth of the house, 'you must come with me to admire a wonder.'

# 12

Ice crunches under our boots. The silence is eerie. No slapping of water against the stone steps. No would-be passengers shouting, 'Oars here! Oars here!' No thump of colliding boats, no rattling of rowlocks. Standing on the Strand water stairs, I look out over the Thames. Knives of icy air stab my lungs. I hold my silky beaver-fur muff to my face, inhaling the musty animal smell, warming my nose with my exhaled breath.

Kit points at the sinuous black ribbon at the centre of the river. 'The water grows narrower every day.'

It is the coldest winter in living memory. The Thames is freezing outward from its banks.

A flock of gulls arrives suddenly out of a grey sky and swoops to land on the river. They slither and slide on the ice in a comical flapping of wings. Dignity recovered, they sit, perplexed, on the new, hard lid over the water, waiting to reconnect with what they knew.

I watch two small boys testing the ice, too far out.

The air is luminous and thick in the growing dusk. On the opposite bank of the Thames, Southwark, where I had visited only four years past as the favourite of the Queen, is dissolving into a faint hint of buildings in the beginning of snow. Soon it will disappear altogether and leave me looking across the river at nothing. As insubstantial as the past.

Time behind us might as well never have been. It's gone. Today is what there is.

Suspended there above the freezing river, I feel a cold clarity enter my thoughts.

I was right to have come. Too many women in my position lay meekly down in the narrow coffin of duty. The Lord would have to forgive me. Whilst I am alive, I mean to live. Until Death steps into my path and raises a beckoning finger, I will not accept impossibility.

I'd had a close call on that ice cliff between Moor Park and Chenies. I'd almost given up.

The first icy needles of new snow prick my face as we watch the two boys arguing. Their bodies tell the story as clearly as words. One of them slides a foot a little farther out towards the black ribbon of water, which looks as lithe and alive as the back of a moving snake. The other boy steps back, ready to sprint for the shore.

A dark crack opens in the glinting white surface. With shrill cries, they fall onto their bellies and push furiously with their arms, sliding like young seals towards the bank.

Kit runs down the icy steps towards them. Then they are safe on the thick ice near the shore, brushing snow and ice from the front of their coats, their excited voices as sharp as the cries of the gull. Kit returns to my side. A dog barks from the far side of a nearby wall. The rhythm of horses in the street behind me is jagged as they struggle on the ice. Church bells begin to crack the cold air with metallic hammer blows.

Two weeks ago, I was prepared to kill myself, even at the risk of damnation. I had not imagined how soon

82

I would be here in London again, half fearful, half filled with exhilaration, examining my weapons like an old warrior coming out of retirement to fight once more for his life.

We turn away from the river to return to Bedford House. A passer-by would see only a handsome woman of middle years, in fine but mended clothes, crunching across the ice-filled street attended by a single waiting gentleman, and a maidservant and groom who can scarcely contain their eagerness to get back to the warmth of a fire. He would not have seen a fallen countess who meant to raise ghosts and make them dance again.

Later I lie in my narrow bed on down pillows and feather bed over the base of wool and straw. Agnes has been given a cot in the next room, with her maid on a pallet on her floor while Annie snores on mine. Unable to sleep, I listen to the old familiar night noises of the city. Moor Park already feels distant and a little unreal. The creak of its damp leaning walls and the screams of foxes have been replaced by church bells, dogs, shouts of the night watch, and fainter, more distant voices and music from the tightly packed houses and inns around our walls.

I hear an explosion of shouts in the street. Then abrupt silence.

Perhaps from the Savoy. The derelict hospital stands nearby, across the Strand from Bedford House, its rooms now occupied by vagabonds, criminals, indigent students, and the occasional poet.

I shift my head on the pillows. I will not think about poets tonight.

Tonight, I will not think about loss, only what I hope to regain. I pull the coverlet up to just below my nose, close my eyes and breathe in the resinous smell of pine

from the fire that still burns brightly to warm the room.
I would make it all happen again.

With the scent of burning pine branches in my nostrils,
I again pulled on red silk stockings. Fastened a white
heron feather in my hair. Draped a veil. Little by little,
Lucy Russell, Countess of Bedford, transformed herself
into a magical creature.

It was the masque, *Hymenaei*, celebrating the marriage
of the new young Earl of Essex to the daughter of the
Duke of Suffolk, Frances Howard.

I pinned a jewel at the front of my hair. I turned my
head. My third eye, my Cyclops eye, flashed and winked.
My jewelled shoes turned my steps to bursts of spangled
light. Behind me revolved a huge golden globe. 'Behold the
world, how it is whirled round,' a court poet had written.

We all floated together on the music. The space beneath
my ribs grew as large as the sky. We inhaled starlight.

I smiled as I spun past the silent mouthing and hungry,
anxious eyes of Ben Jonson, the poet and playwright
whose words we sang. Then I spied the straggling locks
and thoughtful frown of the court painter Master Jones,
the God who had created the revolving world that would
soon open like a flower bud. Together we three had made
these 'lies', as my husband called them. I had defined the
terrain, helped to devise the songs. Together, we had waved
the wand that transformed the plumpest lady-in-waiting
into a goddess for the evening. Following our queen, we
floated and spun in a better world than our own until the
candles blurred.

At the end of each performance, in the silence after
the music died, I would drop heavily back onto my feet,
attacked by a vague sadness. But even before my Cyclops
eye could be counted back into the Jewel House and the

smoky threads of extinguished candles could fade from the air, I was in conference with the Queen about the next masque, display of fireworks or other prodigy of illusion.

I understood the code of royal flattery that must underlie every word and action. I knew that we all worked for the glorification of England. Even the new king, who preferred the hunt to dance, and was an awkward gnome crawled from under a Scottish stone – even he understood how the extravagant glories of our masques made him shine brighter in the eyes of visiting envoys and ambassadors.

But we also made a deeper magic than mere politics. Once I caught even the King watching a forest transform into the undersea kingdom of Neptune, with an open mouth and the eyes of an enchanted child.

When not devising masques or other entertainments, my everyday self had chased after other urgent purpose. The Queen gave me the right to sell positions in her household. I could also sell licences to ship wool, cut wood, or drive your beasts to market in London. I sold monopolies on certain trades. I could collect customs duties and was granted the right to mint coins.

Much of my profit went to repay the Russell debts. But I also made my gardens. I bought paintings and antiquities. I wrote. I debated, sometimes even at the King's table of wits. I entertained poets and playwrights and threw gold at their metaphors.

Alone in my own chamber in Twickenham or in the apartments the Queen had given me to keep me near her in her own residence at Denmark House, I filled the silence with the sound of my lute or the scratching of my pen. I left no cracks for sadness to take root.

\*    \*    \*

The fire in my chamber at Bedford House is almost dead. The dream music fades but the smell of burning pine remains and is real. I wrap myself in a coverlet and go to put another log on the greying coals of the fire. A piece of rough bark catches and sends up tongues of blue and orange. I will the log to catch.

Then the little tongues of flame stretch out and embrace the log. My entrails unclench. It feels like a good omen. I warm my ankles for a time. A ragged chorus of church bells announces one o'clock.

'All is well,' cries the watch.

Amen.

I am on my way back to the good times.

I return to my bed.

I get up again, light a candle from the fire, and search until I find where Agnes has put my little writing chest. Then I put on my old fur-lined robe. I sit on the floor in front of the fire, cooking my face while my back chills, and open the chest.

Now I will test your gratitude, I think as I lay out my paper. Remember who lifted you onto the ladder that led you up to your present power and position.

*To the Most Esteemed Lord Buckingham*, I write.

To reach the most powerful man in England, I must go through the second most powerful, the King's favourite, George Villiers, Marquess of Buckingham.

I do not expect trouble. I helped to put George where he is.

Lord Buckingham. My George. How he has risen!

To hold power at court, you must first observe and read those above you to discern their deep desires. Then you fill those desires without seeming to see either weakness or need. And then, you must see off your rivals. When the royal family arrived at last in London, late in the summer of 1603 – King, Queen, and children, with their Scottish courtiers and eager new English ones – the chief enemy of the English courtiers was Robert Carr.

I rise from beside the fire to get my knife. As I sharpen my quill I remember how urgently many of us had wanted to see off this adored favourite of the King, the worst of the loud, greedy, land- and title-grabbing Scots who had trailed down from Scotland behind the new monarch.

Carr was a tall, fair, self-satisfied Scottish lunk, with moustaches like tufted squirrel's ears. He was far less able than he believed himself to be, a handicap that, nevertheless, did not prevent him from beginning almost at once to believe that he ruled England through the King.

The English soon learned to despise and fear him in equal measure. His word to the King could ruin a man. A wistful sigh could win him another man's house and lands. Before he died, Cecil, the Chief Secretary of England, had hated the man as much as the rest of us. But it was I who read the King's desires and found the weapon to bring Carr down – a beautiful, witty, ambitious young Englishman named George Villiers.

Georgie Villiers, a graceful, charming youth whose fragile beauty and well-formed thighs had made more than one lady-in-waiting weep with desire.

Together, I and one of the most powerful lords, with the willing connivance of many others in the English faction at court, had used Villiers as one nail to drive out another.

Anything to see off the wretched, overweening favourite, Carr, we had thought. Dark beauty for fair. Englishman in place of Scot. An amusing wit to leaven the required adoration. Villiers to replace Carr.

I test my newly sharpened nib. There must be no blots or torn places in this letter.

*It would give me great pleasure to see you once again . . .*

We had sung in the flickering light of candles, the jewelled seawater on our costumes sparking. Cool air caressed my bare ankles. The tall young sea god beside me stroked the bare skin of my arm. I had chosen him from all the other men to be my partner.

I balanced the silk seaweed and gilded shells twined into my hair as we made a reverence to the queen of the Sea, my queen. Joy poured out through my throat. I was safe in a magical place where the whine of growing debt could not be heard. Where men and women could live briefly as creatures better and more marvellous than themselves. Disappointed petitioners, unhappy wives, heartbroken suitors, secret cheats who feared discovery. The bored and the tedious, the ambitious and the hopeless. For a short time, in this shared place out of time, they could all forget their true lives and live in earthly Paradise.

And the ambitious could rise.

I let George Villiers lead me into a dance, with the rhythm of beating waves in our heads and in our blood. George Villiers was rising in the King's favour and owed it to me. At my side, beside the chief lady of the court, he had become chief lord. He stood at James's side and I at the Queen's. The two separate courts, insofar as they mingled, had mingled in us.

He had sworn his undying gratitude. I had seen his beauty and his ambition and drawn him into the court circles. I had trusted him to make the most of the preferment to which I helped him. He knew how I ensured that he always appeared to advantage, as he did that night in a pale glittering costume that gave his eyes a dangerous gleam and showed off his legs.

My baron father was the guardian of the King's daughter.

Poets praised me. I was the Queen's favourite lady and ruled the revelry of the court. No wonder he thought that he loved me. No wonder I had loved him with the pure heat of a creator. I was the begetter and breeder of his new being as favourite of the King. He was my creation, and my investment in favours owed.

Once, no one could enter the King's presence without Carr's consent. Now, George holds the keys. Where he was once my supplicant, I am now his. This reversal of roles follows the natural ebb and flow of favours done and returned, and does not trouble me. My request now, small as it is, should flatter him in his new elevation. In my experience, great beauty dooms a man to vanity, a weakness that can make him malleable. And, besides, he owes me a great deal.

Clever, ambitious Georgie, I think as I sign the letter, *Your most grateful and admiring Lucy* . . . I hesitate, then add, . . . *Russell. Cs. of Bedford.*

We would soon see if his sense of gratitude is as finely developed as his thighs.

'If you wish to achieve power here at court . . .' I had once stood on tiptoe to breathe into his ear during a pause in the dance, '. . . learn to read those above you and divine their deep desires . . . give them what they want without seeming to know that you do so. You won't be forgiven for seeing weakness or need.'

'I already know,' he had said, looking at the King.

I should have been warned then.

# 13

## LUCY – THE PALACE OF WHITEHALL, LONDON, 1621

Like a country mouse, I peer into the Great Hall where I once ruled on behalf of my queen. My jewels, which felt so overdone in Hertfordshire, shame me here in Whitehall. I advance from the door, past dense clusters of men, some of them friends, some not.

I nod to the tall, thin, soberly dressed figure of Thomas Howard, Earl of Arundel, said by Kit to be wooing Buckingham. He smiles back. Though he ranks far above me, being old nobility amongst all the bindweed knights and barons created by King James (of which my father had been one), Arundel and I share a passion for beautiful things that we cannot afford. He is talking now to the King's Surveyor, Master Inigo Jones, progressed from designing masques to designing buildings, in what will no doubt prove to be a costly conversation.

Many people think Arundel cold and aloof, but I found him a steady friend when poverty had turned many people against my husband and me. His own experience of childhood poverty may have left him softened by understanding.

I exchange chilly nods with two of the bindweed knights and move on through the packed bodies.

The hall smells worse than a barnyard. I had forgotten the nasal assault of the court. Civet, musk, and herbal waters applied to freshly shaved chins. The reek of anger and aggression seeping out from armpits. Damp wool, leather, foul breath, horse and farting dogs. Woodsmoke overlays the dark heaviness of old ashes and damp stone. Through the open arches and passageways, smells of sewage, rotting weed and fish seep in from the river. The herbs burning on the fire fail to sweeten the air.

On the low dais at the far end of the hall, the King's empty chair confirms his absence hunting at Royston. George Villiers is standing as close as is possible to the royal chair without actually occupying it. Even if he were not at the centre of a gaggle of courtiers, I would have spied him at once by the bright flashing of diamond buttons and the wide, stiff white-lace collar that sets off his handsome face.

Nearest to him in the crowd stands Cranfield, the Lord Treasurer, looking wary, and the Lord Chancellor, Francis Bacon, nodding and smiling at Buckingham's words. Buckingham's brain-sick brother John, now made Viscount Purbeck by the doting King, sits on the edge of the dais, picking at the cuticles of his left hand.

Buckingham's other brother, Kit, amiable enough if little more than that, stands smiling when other men smile, laughing when they laugh. Though still only a groom of the royal bedchamber he has been promised an earldom by the King. Just behind Buckingham hover two secretaries, ready to note down any licences or patents or letters of favour that his lordship might grant.

The beautiful youth has become a striking man. He is still lean, in spite of the indulgences of James's court. Since I last saw him, he has grown a neat, elegant stiletto beard and a moustache that flicks up at the ends. These frame his full, sensuous mouth, which – I would have sworn – he has reddened with carmine. His eyes, edged with long thick lashes any woman would envy, shift thoughtfully from face to face as if choosing from a flock of chickens which neck to break for the pot.

He seems more sharply drawn than the men around him, larger than his true size. A five-strand yoke of pearls, like the diamond buttons and red and white fires sparking on his fingers, make him seem a source of light. Even in a daytime doublet of yellow silk, and leather shoes instead of evening silk, he looks as rare and glamorous as a player in a candlelit masque.

My eye had been as good for a man as for a painting when I chose him.

I watch him speak to an eagerly nodding courtier, whose face I do not know. As he does so, he places a casual hand on the back of the King's chair.

I see no sign of his poor credulous, wealthy new wife, little Katherine Manners, the only daughter and now, on the death of her brother, the sole heir to the Duke of Rutland. However, I spy his monster mother holding court in the far corner of the hall, at the same time she sees me.

I nod coolly to the three-times married Lady Villiers. We loathe each other. She always saw me as an enemy. I despise her for the coarse hunger of her ambition for her entire family as well as her son.

Then Buckingham sees me. He breaks through the circle of courtiers and holds out his hand. 'Madam! My dearest Lucy! Such a long time!'

I smile brightly and put my hand in his. The offering should have been mine and the taking, his. In his civil-sounding words, I hear a subtle reminder of my absence from the heart of the court, and all the reasons why.

I smell the musk and violet scenting his beard as I study George Villiers – once my George. I feel the first sense that things might go wrong. The long legs might be just as fine as they had always been, and the stockings somewhat finer. I'm not certain that I care for the other changes since Pembroke and I had introduced him, a handsome youth, blushing prettily (George, that is) to the King, six years earlier.

'I would wager that you're not here just for love of me,' he says.

'I've never needed any other reason.' An iron nail now seems even more apt an image than it had done six years ago.

We smile into each other's eyes as we once did. I daresay that mine have turned as cold as his.

He has never forgiven me, I think.


He had pulled me behind a statue at the end of the dance and kissed me, which was common enough behaviour at such moments. Then he inserted a hand between the layers of my scanty costume, probing for my cunt.

'Are you mad?' I yanked his hand away and looked around. 'Will you make the King jealous?'

With a flash of anger, he stepped back.

'George, you're too fine now to be spent on trifling with me. Don't risk everything you've won.'

'The King doesn't mind what I do, so long as I swear I love only him.'

Then the King's a fool, I thought but did not say.

'Stop sulking,' I said. 'That's our next music.'

No matter that the English secretly complained of his manners, our Scottish King was not a fool.

Smile at me again, George, I begged as we advanced hand-in-hand down the hall, young god and goddess. Those sharp magpie eyes of your royal master are reading your sudden stormy face like a handbill. You put me at risk even more than yourself.

'I presume, after so long, that you want something from me,' he says now.

'Always.' I hold my smile. And I believe that you owe it to me. 'Georgie! How well you have assumed the tone and posture of a great courtier. I'm most impressed.'

Ice forms on his features. His eyes slide sideways to see who might have heard. The pink lips tighten under the horizontal moustache.

'I'm in earnest,' I say. 'You were always handsome. You've grown magnificent.'

'And you still know how to flatter.' As chilly as his voice has turned, I see his vanity wanting to believe me.

'But you still don't like to be teased. Forgive me. And I do come as a petitioner to you, I admit.'

He waves a gracious hand, showing me his rings. Too many for my taste, gifts from the King, no doubt. 'Your faithful servant – if it lies in my power.'

'A trifle, for a man in your position. I would speak to the King in private.'

'Why?'

'Why "speak", or why "private"?'

'I can't imagine what you have to say to His Majesty.'

Once, I had been able to brush off insult. I know that he saw me inhale. I want to slap the self-satisfied smirk off his handsome, rouged face. To say that, to me, who had once dined at the King's own table and joined in the duels of intellect and learning that the King so relished.

I hold his eye, silently, drilling my thoughts into his head. Remember how much you owe me. I helped you to the position where you can grant such favours. Or have you forgot?

'I will understand,' I say, 'if you are unable to arrange it.'

'I can do it. Don't fear. If I ask, the King will agree.' He turns to leave me again. 'But you must understand, "in private" will include me.'

He asks.

The King, of course, agrees.

# 14

## THE PALACE OF WHITEHALL, FEBRUARY 1621

'Majesty, the Countess of Bedford,' says Buckingham, so smoothly that you would never guess I once had to tutor him in court behaviour.

'I know who she is, Steenie.' The King frowns and sticks out his lower lip. 'I had to sit through too many of her masques and far too much dancing. What's your purpose with me, madam?' He looks down and brushes at some large crumbs on his doublet. Next to Buckingham, who today wears a golden sash, fringed garters and a single diamond earring, the King looks like a house sparrow in his plain grey and black.

'Not to dance, I swear, Majesty,' I say. 'You're quite safe. I left my costume for Terpsichore at home.'

The King looks up and smiles, just a little.

A good beginning. Yes, I tell him silently. In spite of my worn plumage, I'm still the same girl who once made you laugh and could enter your disputes as fiercely and effectively as any of your tame poets and wits.

'A private word, if it please you,' I say.

The King looks uncertain. His wits are too sharp for him not to guess why I might suddenly risk humiliation by presenting myself at court again. He glances at Buckingham.

'If Lord Buckingham does not object,' I add sweetly.

Georgie proves the truth of at least one poets' cliché. His eye beams turn to daggers. I feel them pierce the surface of my assumed composure as surely as real steel.

The King frowns. 'Lord Buckingham has nothing to say in the matter.' He nods dismissal and Buckingham goes, through a small private door near the dais, followed by two other attending gentlemen. The remaining lords and gentlemen retreat to the far end of the hall.

First point to me. It's good to learn the limits of Buckingham's power. But I see the King's eyes follow his favourite from the room like an anxious hound.

The face he turns back to me is guarded.

'My father is not dangerous because he is the King,' Elizabeth had warned me shortly before she left for the Palatine with her new husband. 'He is dangerous because he is easily bored and because he is afraid.'

'So, speak, madam!'

'Majesty, you know that my family have always served you . . .'

'To the matter! Stop blowing wind from your backside. What d'you want?'

I've seen his abrupt humour too often to be shaken. And if he expects me to blush at his coarseness like a child virgin, he's mistaken.

'The honour of England,' I say.

Whatever else, I now have his full attention.

His face darkens. 'Why do you need a private word for

that? D'you mean to say that I don't want England's honour? And you wanted no one to hear your accusation?'

I stare back at him. 'If you were not the King, Majesty, I would tell you not to be a fool. Firstly, for believing that I could think such a thing. Secondly, for thinking me to be enough of a fool to tell you if I did.'

I stay silent whilst he chews on his tongue and re-crosses his legs, studying me.

'Insolent as ever,' he says at last. 'Now that you've called me a fool, how else d'you mean to insult me?'

I hold up crossed fingers like a child in a game. 'King's Peace? No penalty?'

'Nay, madam. Your head's safe. For today. Get on with it.'

I have him entertained now. He leans forward into the fray, just as George had described to me in the early days of his preferment. Scottish James, who fears tedium almost as much as he fears an assassin, eager to dispute philosophy over roast duck with the wits and scholars he invites to dine with him. Who lays out sugared almonds to mark the points in an argument and sulks when he loses a debate (which, not surprisingly, is seldom).

But I know to take care. Some of the English at court still mock his thick Scottish accent and mistake his coarse language and behaviour for a similar coarseness of mind. Beware, I warn. Unless I wish to let them hang themselves.

'The Princess, your daughter . . .' I begin.

'Audience over!' he shouts. 'George! Where've you got to?' He pushes himself to his feet. 'Don't presume to advise me on statesmanship, madam. I know what has befallen my daughter and that silly little German princeling of hers. But I am a king as well as a father!'

I drop my eyes at the oratorical ring of his final words. I wonder what he would do if I were to applaud. There had been times when he would have laughed.

'D'you think I don't know?' He begins to stammer with rage. 'D'you think me ignorant? D'you think no one writes to the King of England, nor reports to him what is happening abroad?'

Applause, a bad idea. I abandon all thought of asking where I might find the Princess. I sink into a deep curtsy and stay there.

'D'you think I don't weigh and consider and make a judgement on what I know? To the best advantage of England and English honour?' He looks towards the re-entering Buckingham. 'Steenie, this mincing little smock has come all the way from the country to advise me on English policy in the Continent! Come here! Tell her that England will send no military aid to the former King of Bohemia!'

The two other gentlemen attending Buckingham linger uncertainly outside the door as if they fear that the King might suddenly pick up his foot stool, as he has been known to do, and throw it at someone's head. The other men, at the far end of the hall, do not risk even curious glances towards the King's raised voice.

From the depth of my curtsy, I murmur, 'With your permission, Majesty, I would slink back to the country, where I will confine my advice to the making of cheese.'

The King stops in mid-flow. 'Get out!' He shoos me away with both arms.

I treat this most informal of monarchs to a formal backwards exit for the full length of the hall, turning only at the door, where I catch the eye of Arundel above the heads of the huddle of gentlemen waiting out of earshot. He widens them ever so slightly. No doubt, given his noble breeding, I merely imagine the roll.

Though I failed to speak more than four words to purpose, my audience with the King has not been entirely wasted. The great, like everyone else, imagine that they tell you nothing when they refuse to speak. The King's anger told me a great deal.

I had prodded a raw spot. I never mentioned sending aid. He flared into rage before Elizabeth's name had fully left my mouth. Without prompting, he told me that he did not intend to send aid to his daughter, nor to his son-in-law Frederick, nor to the Protestant princes in Germany. James was both father and king and was suffering for it. He was angry, in this case, not from tedium but from fear.

He might be surprised to learn that I'm happy enough with his stated intention not to send aid.

Bring your daughter back to England, I think. It would solve all problems: yours, hers, and mine. But I'm only a mincing smock down from the country. Such a suggestion from me would only set the King more stubbornly against it.

# 15

Still quivering from the force of the King's rage, propelled by frustration and, I confess, by curiosity, I walk through the once-familiar palace with Agnes and my maid at my heels. Agnes, who has waited for me outside the King's receiving chamber, at first eyes me expectantly. Then, reading my dark face, she sighs and falls behind.

I note the new faces, the new chips and cracks. Passing from the Great Hall into the open court that separated the King's Side from what had been the Queen's Side, I look through the Court Gate into the public street of Whitehall. I turn back. A newly restored and gilded garland above a door reminds me of my old friend, Master Jones, the painter and artificer who had designed the Queen's masques and is now the King's Surveyor and designer of His Majesty's masques.

'I don't know where the King finds the money,' ventures Agnes, gazing up at the golden garland. 'From what I hear.'

'Spends what he doesn't have, I imagine. Like the rest of us.' I turn and head for Scotland Yard to the east, half-hoping to find Jones in his lodgings there. On the way,

101

the wife of one of the King's gentlemen of the bedchamber looks through me.

I hear Agnes sniff. Neither of my women curtsies.

I'll make you see me again, I promise the woman. When I shed the cloak of invisibility called Poverty and return in triumph to Whitehall.

I can see it so clearly. Elizabeth safe. A new life for me as her most favoured lady-in-waiting, able again to give pleasure. And to sell influence and licences, with the power once again to grant and withhold. Able again to make money and wear shoes without patches on the soles. Straightforward enough, if it weren't for a stubborn, self-willed monarch.

As we walk, I examine my position.

I was not given the chance to ask for Elizabeth's return and now dare not try the King again. I still do not know where she might be. Even if I did know where to find her, I do not have consoling news to take her. You are never loved for bearing ill tidings. Every schoolboy is taught that the Ancient Greeks killed messengers who brought them bad news. Bad news is not the way to Elizabeth's heart and favour. And, even if I had good news for her, I need royal permission to leave England to take it.

See where your goal lies and ride towards it. The voice of my dead mother, Lady Harington, wife of Lord Harington, made Baron of Exton, the guardian to the young Princess Elizabeth, speaks firmly in my head. It does this more often than I would like. When alive, she had been certain that she was right about everything, from the height of her ladies' necklines to the existence of God. When I once rashly dared to challenged her, she retorted, 'Be certain of all, or be certain of nothing. If you begin to question, that's where you'll end – certain of nothing. Climb to the top of the hill, my dear, or stay at the bottom. In between, you'll find only slippery slope.'

Your map leaves out the sloughs of confusion, I tell her. Now that she is dead, I can answer back.

Jones is not in Scotland Yard. My ladies and I return to the main palace and find ourselves back on the King's Side, to the west, outside the gate of the privy garden, gazing through it. Beyond the sinuous iron lace, a flock of weeding women shuffle forward like geese, squatting with skirts gathered around their knees, overseen by the head gardener.

A man I do not know. I feel too fragile to risk another rebuff by trying to enter my old playground and being turned away.

I hear footsteps on the stone paving behind me.

'Madam?' One of Buckingham's men. We follow him back through a private door into the palace. Buckingham is waiting in the ante-room to his lodgings near the King. Through air that is hazy with plaster dust I see Master Jones in a far room, framed by a series of doors, busy with refurbishing Buckingham's apartment.

Buckingham pulls me into a window bay, out of hearing of my women and the six gentlemen who are gambling with cards by the fire. Four dogs lie at their feet, curled near the flames. The fire's warmth does not reach us. A cold draught spills down from the window.

'Are you mad?' he demands, tight-jawed. His breath makes little dragon puffs in the chilly air. 'How dare you ask me to solicit the King on your behalf when you intended to make trouble? You'll ruin us both!'

'Poor George. Have I put him into his Old Dad's bad grace?' He does not frighten me. I've seen him in a temper often enough.

'You don't amuse me.' He purses his pink woman's

mouth and turns the rings on his right hand with his left. 'What do you think you're doing?'

'I seek only permission to visit an old childhood friend.' The jewels on his doublet alone would repair the Moor Park roof.

'You abuse our friendship by involving me in your politicking!'

The once-grateful youth has turned as slippery in my grasp as a trout.

But I will not be rebuked once again and sent scuttling off without an answer. Villiers is not the King. Not yet, whatever he might imagine. Any more than Carr had been.

I wipe pale dust off the window seat, sit down and smooth my cloak over my skirts. '"Politicking", you say? How so? His Majesty was shouting that the audience was ended before the Princess's name had even left my mouth! How is a natural concern for an old childhood friend fiendishly transformed into "politicking"?'

I look up at him. 'Don't glower, George. It spoils your face. You know that I can't damage you with the King. Those legs and shoulders will surely protect you from his wrath.'

'I hope you're not trying to flirt with me, madam . . .'

I raise an eyebrow. 'Madam' is it? No more 'George' from me, then.

'I'm no longer a green boy, easy to impress,' he says. 'And, in truth, madam, you grow a little long in the tooth for my taste.'

Like a blow beneath my ribs, his words make it hard for me to breathe.

'I would never presume to rival a king.' I keep my voice calm but feel a treacherous heat in my cheeks. He has never forgiven me for that rebuff, after all.

We eye each other. He must know that I will never forgive him for this second insult. Then I understand. He does not care whether I forgive him or not. That is his true message. I feel a chill far deeper than the coldness of the room.

War is so quickly declared. A favour so quickly forgotten. I am indeed dulled by country life. Once I knew very well that the best way to make a man dislike you is to do him a good service. If he admits the need for gratitude, he lessens his own achievement. And George Villiers, with all his charms, has never suffered from humility. I never mistook him for a good man. It was my mistake to have imagined human weakness anywhere in him.

One of the dogs pushes its snout under my hand. I stroke its head to try to calm myself. For certain, I can no longer rely on his gratitude. But without Buckingham, I cannot reach the King. Without the King, I cannot reach Elizabeth.

'Hertfordshire has dulled your wits and kept you ignorant,' he says.

'Which of my many points of country ignorance do you mean?'

Without Elizabeth back in England, I might as well kick my horse over the edge.

'Why does the mention of his daughter's name send the King into such a rage?' I watch him consider refusing to answer.

Then his pride in knowing the King's mind triumphs over spite. 'He means to make a Spanish marriage for the Prince. To the Infanta.'

I throw up my hands in mock despair. 'He has forever been arranging a marriage for one or another of his children to France or Spain! Was not poor Prince Henry to marry the Infanta before he died? Is the woman just as satisfied with his baby brother? By now, she must be a good deal older than the Prince of Wales.'

'The parties to the marriage are irrelevant.' He speaks with condescension, as if I, who have suffered one myself, did not understand the politics of dynastic marriage. 'It's the union of allies that matters.'

'A Catholic ally in this case,' I say. 'Who's also an ally of the Hapsburgs.' My face grows hotter. 'An ally who would be displeased if the King of England dared go to the aid of his own daughter and the Protestant cause.' I spring up, unable to remain still a moment longer or to remember why I sat in the first place. The dog shies away and clacks back to the fire. 'I can't believe that the King would sacrifice a princess of England to please an ally of the Hapsburgs!'

'He's not sacrificing her!' Two red spots bloom in his cheeks. 'The King wishes to mediate between the warring causes, not join them. He will make the restoration of Frederick to the throne of Bohemia one of his terms for the Spanish marriage.'

'If it ever happens. Can he not read the humour of his people?' I demand. 'They fear Rome and want their princess safely back in England. Not running from danger abroad or clinging to a shaky throne.'

'Have you forgotten all discretion in Hertfordshire, madam? If I weren't your friend, I could say that those words were dangerously close to treason.'

'Then I thank the Lord that I can still be counted among your friends.' I manage to smile while my thoughts rearrange themselves. I let myself begin to believe that this man, no longer my grateful George, might indeed be capable of naming me a traitor if it suited him or advanced his cause.

'You still call her a princess of England!' A ruby flashes

as he points his finger at me. 'The Princess chose to marry her little German princeling . . . fought to marry him. She's wife of the Palatine now. She belongs to the Palatinate of the Rhine. She's German, not English. She's lucky to have any friends at all left here in England.'

'She's second in line to the throne of England,' I say. 'The English people would welcome her back.'

'Against her King's wishes, she preferred to become queen of Bohemia. You know as well as I that her little husband would never have accepted the crown of Bohemia if she had not urged him to it . . .'

'What nonsense!'

But I can hear Elizabeth reassuring her young husband that he could manage perfectly well to be a king.

Heads lift from the cards.

Buckingham lowers his voice again, his pupils two dark points. 'I assure you, madam, the King was not pleased to have his daughter join the Bohemian rebellion against an anointed king, the Archduke Ferdinand. Now she tries to yoke him to the cause of the German Protestants. The Peacemaker King will not lead his English subjects into an unjust and needless quarrel! He will negotiate peace as he did with Spain. He owes those royal rebels nothing now that they reap the harvest of their own ambitious folly. And so I will write to them in his name.'

My nape prickles, like a hound seeing a ghost. Buckingham would never dare to label the Princess a rebel if the King had not already done so. From rebel to traitor is a short, slippery step. Later, I cannot remember how I escaped from his presence.

I walk all the way back to Bedford House, my skirts swinging like a bell as I try to outrun my rage. I slip on ice, recover, march fiercely, slip again. By the time I reach the Strand, I have begun to think straight.

In spite of Buckingham's talk of rebels, James is a father, after all, as well as a king. Perhaps he raged because he does not know what to do. He prefers hunting to government. '. . . and so I will write to them in his name . . .' Much of Buckingham's power grows from his willingness to deal with the tedious details of governing while appearing not to do so.

I must learn from Georgie how to play midwife to royal decisions. Think of the present situation as the plot for a new masque. Devise a surface of glorification and flattery to hide the secret acting out of private ambitions and desires. I wish I dared ask the advice of my old friend, Master Ben Jonson, who seems able to spin endless new plots, but I do not trust his need to brag, nor can I be certain that I wouldn't see my actions exposed in one of his plays or blasted in an epigram.

Back in my bedchamber at Bedford House, I burn the letters Elizabeth has sent me.

*. . . I beg you to go to the King, my father, and tell him that, on my knees, I beg for his help, as his only daughter, the only true Daughter of England and a queen who would regain her rightful crown, and her husband's crown, and the birthright of her children . . .*

I push every scrap of paper into the flames with the poker and smash the ashes. Her words now seem both innocent and dangerous, an invitation to what hostile eyes might read as treason. I'd not given enough weight to the King's thick padded doublet cross-embroidered with wires to stop an assassin's knife. Nor remembered that he had been used at the age of two years to unseat his own mother from the throne of Scotland. I had under-reckoned his fear of being dethroned in turn by his own son, Henry.

He feared even his daughter, who is as loved by the English people as her brother had been.

Until Buckingham alerted me, I had not considered that King James might see the Bohemian rebellion as bringing down a fellow monarch, Ferdinand of Austria. Frederick, Elector Palatine, had been crowned in Ferdinand's place by popular acclaim. Crowned with him, Elizabeth had become the usurper that James had always feared. His own fear of being unseated made him kin to the displaced Hapsburg Ferdinand, not to his unfortunate daughter and son-in-law.

'Rebel.' I can still hear the echo of the King's voice in the words of Buckingham.

Clearly, Elizabeth does not realise her full danger from her own father. She must be more discreet in her letters. She must curb her voiced anger, which has so inflamed the King. She must not try to raise support among the Protestants of England – or they, and she, will be branded traitors. I must make her see that her only safety lies in giving up Bohemia. She must return to England and reclaim her place as second in line to the English throne. She must come back to me.

I have to make the King let me go to her. Letters are too dangerous. Letters can be intercepted. If this mincing smock from the country could do nothing else, she can take a warning to a friend. All she must do is find the Princess, devise how to reach her, and get royal permission to do so.

# 16

In my bleak humour, I can't sit quietly by the fire. Kit is busy and unavailable to share a pipe. I put on a heavy fur cloak, wool scarf, rabbit-fur gloves and hat. 'I will walk down to the Strand water stairs, to see the progress of the ice.'

Agnes sighs and puts on her own cloak to accompany me.

The ribbon of water at the centre has dwindled to a narrow black thread. A sluggish current toys with rafts of floating ice.

'I'll stay here, if I may, madam.' Agnes huddles against a wall behind me, out of the wind. Alone at the far end of the deserted stairs, I watch a small ice floe bump into another, almost block the thread of black water, then pull away again, turning slowly as it heads for the sea. Below me, people crunch heavily along the shoreline. A man's hat blows from his head and skims away, low and dark above the ice like a cormorant. A sharp-nailed finger of wind prods through my scarf to my breastbone.

The wheel of Fortune has cast me down but now offers to lift me up again. Not many are given a second chance.

There must be a way to seize this chance, if only I can see how.

Footsteps approach on the ice.

'It will be frozen solid by midnight.'

I recognise the man at my elbow. I nod to let Agnes know not to fear.

A silver-haired soldier in his fifties, Sir John Holles was Prince Henry's Comptroller in the golden days at St James's Palace. Though some people thought him quarrelsome, I'd always found his provocative manner entertaining and his architectural interests surprising in such a rough and plain-spoken military man.

'Fools!' He points his beard at three men skating on the frozen shallows near the bank.

'I thought you enjoyed skating on thin ice,' I say. 'Will you deny others the same pleasure?'

'But I never break through. That fat one's sure to.'

I expect him to say more, but he does not.

We watch the three men in silence. I hear the ice crunch under Holles's boots as he shifts his weight. He clears his throat. Rubs his hands together as if to warm them.

'It's not the weather for discussing gardens,' I say at last. Like me, he is fluent in both French and Italian, and together we have fought over the virtues of Palladio and admired the work of de Caus in the Prince's gardens at Richmond.

'Indeed not, madam.' He clears his throat again.

I study him sideways. I recognise the signs of a man minding his pennies. Old-style stacked ruff. Neatly patched boots. Balding fur on his cloak collar. When Prince Henry died, Holles had fallen out of favour at court, even before I did.

We continue to stand in silence, watching the skaters. A boy passes below us pulling a sledge stacked with firewood. We watch him slipping and sliding down the river towards London Bridge. I look back over my shoulder. Two armed attendants wait for Holles in the lane leading to the steps, well out of earshot. One of them has struck up a conversation with Agnes.

'Did you follow me here?' I ask, unable to wait a moment longer for him to get out whatever he had come to say.

'There!' Holles looks at me with satisfaction. 'I told them you were the right choice.'

'Right for what?'

'To take a letter to the Princess.'

I stop smiling. My hair prickles as if I were hot and not freezing. 'I don't know which question to ask first. Who is "them"? Or which princess?' But I already know the answer to the second.

'Quick,' he says, as if to himself. 'Nimble.' The sharpness of his eyes undoes any first impression of a slightly shabby, harmless old man. 'You already hope to visit her.'

'I can't think how you know.'

He waggles his head in disclaimer. 'Rumour spreads.'

But intelligencers are more certain. I had not told the King what I wanted to do. Only Buckingham. 'They' seemed to have someone placed in Buckingham's court.

'We need a true friend of Her Highness.'

We? I feel Fortune's wheel begin to creak and turn again. I see it as a heavy mill wheel in a rising leat, dark and dripping, taller than twenty men, timbers thicker than a horse, carrying life forwards in its buckets, dumping it into the fast-racing current beyond.

'. . . who would not raise suspicion as one of us would,' Holles continues.

'Send an intelligencer. Such men are skilled at being unnoticed.'

'Better someone untainted by either diplomacy or war.'

112

'In that case, it can only be a woman,' I say tartly.

'A woman and a friend would be most fit for the purpose,' he agrees. 'Her Highness is watched constantly by people whose allegiances are not known to us.'

'Is this letter dangerous, then?'

'Not so much the letter, madam, as the mere fact that it's sent at all. One woman can comfort another without raising suspicion. Whereas, comfort from men with military experience, who command soldiers, will never be seen as innocent.'

Nor would any associate of theirs, woman or not.

'Does this mysterious "we" know where I must take the letter?' I ask.

'Cleves or The Hague. Prince Maurits has offered them refuge.'

'At last.'

'We will soon know which city it is. And you can bring us back word of the new prince.'

'She had her babe? Safely?'

'At Custrin, at Christmas. All is well, on that front at least.'

I tell myself to take a moment to reflect. Elizabeth is well and has found a protector. On the other hand, this request is not without danger. 'Comfort' from men who command soldiers can mean only military support. The King refuses his daughter such support. 'They' are not friends of the King.

'Who is "we"?' I ask.

'Men from Prince Henry's court while he lived – most of them – who would have served him at the highest levels if he had survived to become England's king.'

Henry's Protestant knights, I thought. Good men but war-like, as their prince had been.

'You'd find that many are already well known to you,' Holles adds.

'And what is this message from men with military experience?'

I want Elizabeth brought safely home, not fighting to be restored in Bohemia.

Holles wags a finger at me. 'Madam, you already know too much.'

I look at him thoughtfully. I had arrived at the water stairs in despair. Now, of a sudden, I might have powerful allies, men who command soldiers, old friends, even if I do not yet know who they are. But Holles clearly respects them. And I respect Holles.

Their message to Elizabeth does not matter. If only I can reach her and speak to her in person, I will persuade her to return to England. These men and their letter will help me to her. They might not be friends of the King, but I have just thought how to decrease my risk.

Holles stands facing me, gripping the front edges of his cloak in gloved hands, waiting for my answer. I remember the scars and sword nicks on his knuckles, which the gloves hide. He cannot imagine how I see him at that moment, rising, white hair and beard and all, carried upwards with me on Fortune's wheel.

In case we are being watched by other eyes than those of Agnes and his own men, I do not nod. 'I'll do it.'

'You'll need this to buy off someone, I'm sure.' Holles passes me a small hard object wrapped in a handkerchief. 'Ask if you need more.'

The next day, in my little parlour at the back of Bedford House, I grovel twice-over to Buckingham, once in a letter, and once with the gift of a gold pomander case set with pearls, which Holles had given me on the water steps.

Writing the letter to Buckingham makes my back teeth

114

ache from grinding, but I cannot stomach meeting him again face-to-face.

*Having done my duty to the daughter of my late mistress, the Queen,* I write, *I am now free to serve whatever purpose you might command me . . .*

My hand rebels. I sit at my table for a moment. I stare up at a corner cobweb missed in the rush to prepare Bedford House for my arrival. I stand, put on a cloak, and walk out into the kitchen garden at the back of the house. I glare at the frost-glazed cabbages lolling on their stems. I yank at some dried bean haulms still tangled on their tripod support and send ice crumbs flying.

I march back into the house, breathing on my fingers to warm them, and make myself finish, implying . . . I cannot bear to write it outright . . . that I have transferred my loyalties from the dead queen and absent princess to the new masters of Whitehall.

I suggest humbly (hah!) that with my knowledge of French, Italian and German – and my close family ties to the Princess – I would be the ideal emissary from the King to urge the Princess to curb her complaints against him. I could warn her how gravely she and her husband are displeasing His Majesty by their stubborn struggle to regain the throne of Bohemia. I could carry her a letter from the King himself, if His Majesty wished it. All this would, of course, already be clear to Buckingham's states-manlike mind. I wished only to state my willingness . . .

I swear that I hear a growl somewhere in the room as I sign myself, *Your Grace's most Obliged and Faithfull Servant.*

I send for Kit to take both letter and gold pomander.

I see him look at the name on the letter. Not a muscle of his face moves. Then he gives me the quickest of upward glances. If, by any chance, I do get the King's permission to leave England, I will take him with me.

Then I wait.

Vanity does indeed make a man pliable. And the golden bribe may have helped.

Buckingham must have interceded.

The King sends for me.

# 17

'*Beati Pacifici!!*' says the King. 'Blessed are the peacemakers! Beat that into her stubborn head.'

'Sir,' I murmur.

'I'm only letting you go so y'can impress upon Her Grace, my one-time daughter, that she and her warlike husband are rebels! D'ye understand me?'

'Yes, Majesty.'

I'm going! The King himself is sending me.

'Rebels against an anointed king – Catholic or Protestant, it matters not! Ferdinand of Austria is the rightful king of Bohemia, and all who oppose him are rebels. And I told them so. D'ye understand?'

I nod. A child of three would understand. Rebels against a king are traitors.

Treason. King James has not yet used the word outright, but I hear it flapping its great ugly black wings around my head. The leathery snap of its wings bangs against the ceiling.

'I warned them! A year ago! Now the bloody pair of them undo all my good work.' The King glares as if I were the guilty party. He seems to chew his tongue. Then he rubs his mouth angrily. 'My poor emissary, Doncaster. Might as well have saved himself the trouble of banging his chops together over all those negotiating tables. What good does it do me to send an emissary of peace to Paris and Madrid, and Italy, and Austria, if my own blood then makes him a laughing stock? Tell her that she's twice a rebel. As my child and as my subject.'

'Sir.' I feel his eyes watching me for the full distance of my backward retreat to the door, his letter in one hand, my other hand controlling my skirts.

'Watch her closely when she reads my letter,' he shouts down the hall. 'Come tell me at once how she takes it! I want to know every twitch, every word she speaks. Be sure to take note!'

He has not mentioned his new grandson.

# 18

James changes his mind about whatever he has written to his daughter. Sends to have his old letter returned. Dictates a new letter. Changes his mind back again. My passport letter is lost and must be re-copied.

Headed back to Bedford House with Kit after my third fruitless visit to Whitehall, with instructions from one of the King's secretaries to return for the royal letter in two days, I make a detour to the water stairs. The transformation I find surpasses the most God-like imaginings of Master Jones with his heaving mountains, disappearing forests and rising suns.

London and Southwark are no longer cut off from each other by a barrier of water. Order and Lawlessness have joined hands. London Bridge, formerly the sole link between worlds, stands ignored by all but its residents. The customs officers who usually guard it like trolls have thrown up their hands and gone to sit somewhere warm.

The black thread at the centre has disappeared. The Thames has frozen solid into an opaque landscape of ruts, bumps, and occasional shiny grey patches of translucent ice mottled like a skin disease. And noise has returned.

But now the steps ring with the shouts of men on the ice with sleds for hire, of people wanting to be pulled across to Southwark, people selling hot pies, roasted chestnuts, and gloves. Vendors shout from market stalls set up on the ice. Dogs race deliriously back and forth between the banks, no longer barking at each other across the water. A vicious, snarling fight has broken out on the Southwark side. No doubt, other dogs mate and the spring will see litters of cross-Thames pups.

Sniffing the smoke from fires lit in braziers, the succulence of fatty meat and of browned pastry, ground spices, fresh horse droppings still steaming in the street behind me, I realise that these smells ride on a clean white current of icy air. The frozen Thames does not stink. The rotting weed, drowned dogs, unwanted babes, and human ordure have been covered with a lid of ice. Decay has been suspended.

'Madam! I pray you!'

'I don't wish to buy,' I say. The winter has stopped time, I think. It feels like a gift.

'Madam,' he insists. His voice booms all out of proportion to his skinny frame.

He is about eighteen years of age, teetering between youth and manhood. With his hat removed for a bow, his ears stick out through lank greasy hair. Their rims glow pink with cold. On second look, I see that he is far too well dressed for a vendor or beggar. Better dressed than I am, for that matter, in a new fur-lined cape, heavy silk breeches, and fine riding boots.

Then I see his manservant waiting a short distance away.

'A word in private, I beg you.' He bows again.

'You may speak in front of Sir Christopher,' I say. 'And do please replace your hat. You'll freeze your head.'

The young man blushes and bows again to Kit. 'Forgive

120

me, sir . . .' He gives me a wild look, clearly having been instructed to speak to me alone.

I glance at Kit. The young man is an unlikely assassin. 'I believe both honour and life are safe,' I murmur.

Kit delivers a warning glare before stepping back.

The young man follows me out to the end of the water stairs.

'So?' I ask.

He blushes again. 'Your friend will be in Cleves.'

'I beg your pardon?'

'Cleves! Where you mean to go. With her new baby.'

A man and woman on ice skates slide carefully past, below us. I watch them testing this unfamiliar means of advance.

'Did Holles send you?'

He looks appalled at my indiscretion. Nods curtly.

'I must go to Cleves?'

He nods, glancing around for any intelligencers who might be freezing their feet, or anything else, on the water stairs. I watch him try to swagger away without slipping on the ice in the street.

'Hot chestnuts, madam?'

'Too hot for me to handle?' Then I smile at the boy offering me a tray of paper twists filled with his charred, aromatic wares. 'Yes, I'll have some.' I dig in my purse for a few pennies and give them all to him for good luck. On the way home, I share them with Kit.

A week later, the young man waylays me again, this time in the street near Charing Cross. My friend will be in The Hague, after all.

He is well chosen as messenger. His blushing awkwardness would convince the most suspicious watcher that he follows me out of puppy love for an older woman. He may or may not realise that he himself is a hidden message

121

to me. Holles and his friends have intelligencers abroad. They have the money and power to buy information even before it leaks out of Whitehall.

In the last week of March, with my passport letter from the crown in hand at last, I sail for The Hague, in the Netherlands. The two letters that I carry rustle under my bodice. I don't let myself touch them. I'm certain that everyone can hear them.

In our dark, low-ceilinged ship's cabin, while Agnes fusses trying to make us comfortable, I touch both letters – a royal reprimand to the daughter of England's King and a message to her from the King's enemies. With my hands pressed over the letters, I stare into the shadows of the beams a few inches above my head.

Agnes straightens up too fast, hits her head on a beam. 'God's Body!' she curses under her breath. She has never sailed on a ship before and is more agitated than she will admit. 'Don't look at me like that, madam,' she says. 'I've heard you say worse.'

I look at her tall, unlikely presence in this cramped, dark, floating closet that smells of sea, fish, wet wool and tar.

This is not a masque, nor a poem. It is real life.

I try to believe it. When I left Moor Park for London, I never imagined turning double agent in the effort to re-shape my life. Part of me wants to laugh at the absurdity. Another part of me, which has been asleep in its cave for a very long time, comes fully awake. It stretches and sniffs the air, feels a keen, cold thrill of excitement and fear.

I have been followed. The man crossing the North Sea with me has not troubled to pretend otherwise. He rode out in the lighter with me. When I first leaned on the ship's rail, he leaned a little farther away.

Quietly, I open my cabin door. I think I see a figure in the shadows, beyond the steep wooden gangway. I hear the King's voice again. 'Watch her closely. Report back to me . . .' I have permission to visit the refugee princess, but my behaviour as well as hers will be reported.

I close my door carefully. I send Agnes to beg a hot posset from the galley. Then Sir Kit raps on the door. He is temporarily back in livery, travelling as plain Kit Hawkins and sleeping in a hammock slung somewhere amongst the cargo.

'Comfortable enough,' he says now, having inspected his allotted sliver of space. 'If you don't mind snuggling up to bales that smell of wet sheep.' He smiles to show that he does not mind in the least. He spends much of his life in stables amidst warm animal smells.

Because the creaking and banging of the ship disguises footsteps, I set him to guard my door. Alone in the close, dark cabin, with Kit's broad shoulders between me and my watcher, I take out Holles's letter and weigh it in my hand.

I swivel, shift eight inches backwards and sit on the bunk to think.

I know only what Holles told me. I have no proof of his intentions or those of his reported friends.

I would be a fool to act in ignorance.

I turn the letter in my hand and study the seal.

Tampering with a sealed letter is a crime.

But treason is a greater crime and I have already turned traitor by carrying Holles's letter, if its contents are what I believe.

Believe. I can't be certain.

Ignorance would not protect me from the charge of treason.

In for a penny, as my mother would have said.

123

I push up the glass shield of the hanging candle lantern, heat my knife and prise up the brittle red seal on the letter.

The message is not encrypted. The writer trusted to the enclosing folds to hide the contents. And to the honesty of the courier. The lack of cipher implies a first communication, not an established exchange.

I rub my lips with my fingertips. The letter's meaning goes far beyond my happiness or even the personal safety of the Princess. I'm not a fool. I thought I had understood the purpose of Holles and his friends, whoever they might be. Nevertheless, their letter gives me pause.

Friends of the Princess are mustering three hundred horse, Holles writes. Eight companies of armed militia. Eight sappers, two fire-masters. Engineers and pikemen, with more men promised. Flesh and steel bound for the Continent. Holles and his friends want war with the Continental Catholics, just as their dead hero Prince Henry had hungered for war.

As a father, the King is a monster. But this letter makes me see that, as a monarch responsible for his people, he has some reason on his side.

Like the dead Prince, Holles and his friends mean, if they can, to settle the conflict of two religions by the total, bloody defeat of the Catholic enemy. The King believes that he can avoid war for England through compromise and negotiation, even if it means sacrificing his own daughter.

I re-read the letter.

If war, for how long? And how brutal?

In the shadows of the tiny cabin, I see cut flesh and flowing blood, real men and horses, slashing swords. I see bellies opened. Legs sliced off. The blood of dying men

124

turns the dust to red mud. I see my head gardener, dead. Sir Kit, fatally wounded . . . I imagine his wife's grief . . .

These men will not stand up again when the music stops and bow to the applause.

I should not want war for my country.

But War already rode its horse across the Continent. It already threatened an English princess. Men already smirked when the honour of England was mentioned. Refusing to fight meant that England meekly accepted dishonour.

Tear up the letter, I think. Pretend it was lost . . . never existed. I have legitimate purpose for making this voyage in the letter I carry from the King.

The letter I hold from Holles and his friends will encourage Elizabeth and Frederick to continue the fight to regain Bohemia and the Palatine. If I deliver it, I work against my own aim to bring her home.

I refold the letter carefully on its original folds, hiding away the dangerous words. I reheat my knife, soften the base of the seal and press the red wax circle exactly into its former place. My hand is steady. No blurring of outline betrays me. No more than an ear pressed to my cabin door could have known that I carry an offer to commit treason.

What if I don't deliver Holles's letter?

Elizabeth need never know. I would deliver the King's letter, then speak to her about my true purpose.

I lay my hand on the door bolt, to ask Kit what he would do. Then I return to my bunk. He is already too far drawn into my guilt.

You need not decide now, I tell myself. Take a little more time to think.

I can see the paper jumping as it slides back under my dress over my heart.

When younger, I would have flung myself into this thrilling new adventure, hungry for experience, certain of the final applause at the end of this particular play. Now I can also see myself kneeling at the block.

Even I am not fool enough to meddle with the letter from the King.

I look around the damp closet that is my cabin. If the winds are with us, I might have to sleep here only one night. If the winds die mid-channel, it could be my prison for days or even weeks. But even one night gives me time to decide what to do with Holles's letter.

# 19

## LUCY AND ELIZABETH – THE HAGUE, LATE MARCH 1621

Following the Dutch page through the long, black-and-white tiled halls of the Wassenaer Hof, past endless lines of half-open doors, I find myself as short of breath as when I was about to enter in a performance at court, when I imagined eyes fixing upon me, and I wanted to be loved. I feel as excited and raw as if going to meet a lover.

I see her caught in a tall gold-framed mirror before I see her in the flesh. A half-turned back, a head taller than her ladies, standing quite still, arms against her sides.

That's never she, I think in dismay. Then she turns and I shift my eyes from the reflection to the reality.

This is no longer the ebullient girl I had known, bright-haired and radiant among her brother's friends at court.

As an irrepressible seven-year-old, still rough-edged from running wild in Scotland, she had been sent by the King to my parents at Combe Abbey for safe-keeping. My father was appointed her guardian. Whenever I visited Combe from London, the young Elizabeth had followed me like a puppy with her pack of dogs clicking after us. I first took interest in her because she was the Queen's child. Then I found that her ready adoration helped me to endure the coldness of my marriage. And then we became friends. I could feed her eager questing nature where my parents' quiet estate could scarcely contain it.

I was older, already married, midway in age between the Princess and her mother, my queen. Like an older sister, I could describe the wonders of London, reveal adult secrets and whisper the misdeeds of the court. Because no one else would, I showed my bloody monthly clouts to her horrified, awe-struck eyes, and warned her to expect the same. I allowed her to consider me her oracle in all things and tried to tell her only what was true.

With her I could also let my years fall away and shed the tight-lacing of good behaviour. Once, in the dark, silent night kitchens of Combe, I had hugged her smock-clad legs and hoisted her up to feel along a beam for the key hidden by my mother. I myself unlocked the food cupboard and hacked two lumps from the sugar loaf. We grinned at each other in the faint light as we stood sucking our stolen lumps, relishing the shared adventure even more than the sweet taste.

I cobbled together costumes and wrote both words and music for masques that she and I then staged with her pet monkey and dogs playing gods or demons while we reserved the nymphs and goddesses for ourselves.

'Do you make me play the River Thames,' she once asked, 'and Queen Hippolyta of the Amazons, because I am a princess and should play the principal part?'

'Of course, madam.' I dropped a playful curtsy. 'And

also so that you will learn to sing and dance well enough to lead the company when you are a queen yourself.'

In truth, I dared not risk otherwise. From what I saw of her, she gave herself so entirely to whatever part she played that I could never rely on her to remember to step out of her role in order to unhitch a dog from a miniature carriage. Or, without losing her place in the music, to hammer on an old washtub to make thunder at the same time. It was my pleasant role as her experienced courtier to do all that she did not. When the King called her to Whitehall at last, she made me a lady-in-waiting, shared with her mother.

Now, I curtsy formally, considering the marks the last eight years have made on her. Since I saw her last, my princess has, of course, become a queen. And a mother. And then a refugee. But, in spite of all that has happened to her, I had not thought to find her so dimmed.

As I rise, she grabs both of my hands. For the first time, I see her mother's bones beginning to press through the golden roundness of youth. She wears the familiar russet colour that once echoed her hair. But her wild bright red-gold hair has now dulled almost to brown and is pulled back tightly under a lace-edged coif. For the first time, I see that she might age into plainness. I feel the new distance between us.

'I am overjoyed, and I confess, somewhat relieved to see Your Highness so well,' I say.

'"Well"?' She still grips my hands, but frowns a little, as if testing the taste of the word. 'Do you truly find me "well"?'

'Not dead, I mean,' I say tartly, reassured by this flash of the old Elizabeth. 'In London, you're dead many times over. Women everywhere talk only of your tragic end . . . how you died in childbirth. Or died of ague in a German prison as a prisoner-of-war.' I laugh, still startled by my failure, in spite of her letters, to imagine her in her new life. 'One can buy handbills in the streets claiming to show your funeral. I do indeed call it "well" to see you alive and in such comfortable surroundings.'

I had seen the physical and political dangers clearly. I did not imagine that her cheerful gallantry could be dulled. I had come to The Hague to woo a stranger.

I smile around me at the well-born Dutch women attending Her Majesty, but meet only cold stares. My red gown and flower-embroidered petticoat glow over-vivid and gaudy against their rusts, greys and blacks.

So much black! I think. Their hair is as closely veiled and coiffed as their smiles are tight. Elizabeth's closest lady and intimate friend, Lady Anne Dudley Sutton, who had left England with her after her marriage, had died almost at once in childbirth, soon after her own marriage. Like her mother, Elizabeth is alone.

I want to comfort her as if she were still a child. She could almost be my daughter, I think suddenly. I want to embrace her but dare not.

Elizabeth ignores the stares of her ladies. 'I am agog to hear all the news of your family, and the Russells, of course. And the Talbots, the Villiers, the Bacons, and the Cornwallises.' She drops my hands and moves towards the door. 'Bedford, you must come walk with me in the gardens, which I know will interest you. Or have you moved on to another passion since we last met?' She raises her voice. 'The rest of you may stay. I won't have you wearied with our tedious English gossip.'

Taking her lead and chattering lightly, I follow her, leaving Agnes to outstare her Dutch counterparts. 'Your Highness, I am still so much in love with my Moor Park garden that, if I were as fond of any man, I were in a hard case.'

'Don't mind them,' she says under her breath. 'They're jealous of my precedence here, and now yours.'

Three greyhounds trot after her. As soon as we enter the gardens, she scoops up the smallest, a pale grey, half-grown pup, and hugs it to her while it licks her chin. 'Who's the most beautiful greyhound in the Low Countries?' she croons. It wriggles and jumps free. She watches it run ahead with the other two.

'And what of my other friends . . . my dear Camel Face, Doncaster? How is he? Did you know that my father sent him to Antwerp to sue for peace, but did not permit him to visit me here? I would also have liked to see his chaplain, that wicked poet of yours, Master Donne. I hear that he's turned Doctor of Divinity – a fate surely as unlikely as my own!'

In her preoccupation, she does not seem to notice the deep flush that rises from my neckline to my hair. 'I have brought a letter for you from England,' I murmur.

I don't say that I have two.

We walk until out of earshot, along the neat geometric, green-hedged gravel paths, our skirts rustling together with each step. The gardens are very finely kept, if a little stern, square-cornered and old-fashioned for me with my passion for Italian running water, curves and artful wildness.

I trail my fingers along cut-leaf edges of the low, green hedge then sniff my lemon-scented fingertips. 'I would like to take back some cuttings of this small-leafed box. I don't have it at Moor . . .'

'How can you call it "well",' she interrupts, '. . . to live on the charity of my husband's uncle and of the States General, banished from England and from my husband's

131

rightful country? How is it "well" to be a refugee, when I should be a queen?' She throws up her hands in outraged disbelief. 'Is it "well" to cower in a borrowed palace, an outlaw, under the Ban of the Empire if I dare to cross the Dutch border?'

She always had a quick temper, even as a small child, but I had never before heard her bitter. 'However did you persuade the King to let you risk contamination by seeing me?' she asked.

'By offering to act as his messenger.'

She recoils like a touched snail pulling back into its shell. Her eyes harden. 'The letter you bring is from my father? I did not expect that of you.' I am turned enemy.

'Carrying His Majesty's letter was the price of his permission to come here.'

'Give it to me, then. It must weigh unbearably heavy in your purse.' She holds out her hand.

I pretend not to watch her while she reads it.

She inhales sharply, seems to hold her breath, then crushes the letter in her hand.

At the next crossing of gravel paths, she throws the balled letter into the small lily pool at the centre. She does not speak. Together, we watch the water slowly unfurling the paper again.

The water blurs the words into unreadable clouds. '. . . my deep displeasure with your *husba*—' I read, before I look away discreetly. No surprise there.

At last, I say, 'Madam, the King's seal . . .'

Though the King's words are fading, the red sealing wax gleams brightly through the greenish water. Two pale carp dart at it and retreat.

'You're right, of course.' She stoops and fishes out the dripping letter. 'The less anyone here knows of His Majesty's true feelings, the better.' She stands, tight and silent with misery, while the letter makes a wet stain down the front of her gown.

'Allow me, madam.' I reach across the distance she has put between us, take the letter, squeeze it and refold it to hide what is left of the contents. I offer to return it.

She waves it away. 'I'm sure you already know what it says.'

In chilly silence, we round the end of a high yew hedge and walk into the shade between yew and a high brick wall. No strollers, no gardeners in sight.

I look at the misery in her face. Still holding the sodden lump of the King's letter, I give her the letter from Holles, urging her on to war.

She tears it open, too angry with the King to notice my tampering. She reads a line or two and stops walking. 'You took a risk in bringing me this.'

'A delicious risk, which I thoroughly enjoyed! I must seek another at once.'

She smiles a little. Less unfriendly. Then we both lift our heads. Footsteps crunch on the gravel on the far side of the yew hedge. She folds Holles's letter and puts it into her skirts. 'I thank you, Bedford. You are a brave friend.'

'No more than when I sat awake with you in your bedchamber that night at Combe, to outface the ghost of the abbot said to walk there.'

'Alas, he never came.'

'And how disappointed we both were!'

We exchange half-smiles, remembering.

In a silence that is now collusive, we walk on, turning back out into the sunlight at the first opening in the hedge.

I look around for my shadow from the ship. Elizabeth watches the back of a retreating gardener, lopsided with carrying a basket of pulled-up weeds.

'The Dutch are kind, but they abhor secrecy.' She glares

133

back across the garden at the crowded, higgledy-piggledy red-brick gables of the Wassenaer Hof. 'Eyes at every window! If they can't see you, they know that you must be trying to hide something sinful.' She raises her voice. 'Look! Here we are, in plain view!' She trembles on the brink of further excess.

'How fares your husband?' I ask while I try to think how to raise the question of her return to England.

'Ah, poor Frederick.' She turns towards a stone bench set in a yew niche and sinks down onto it. 'He can't forgive himself for leaving the Palatine undefended . . . for losing it and all that our son should have inherited. And Bohemia. He's turned dark and cold with melancholy, can think only of raising an army to fight the Hapsburgs, to try to repair his bruised honour and our fortunes.'

I wait for her to ask me to sit.

'God's Breath, Bedford!' She suddenly slaps the seat beside her. 'We're not at court now. And we should have brought our hats.' She glares out at the unexpected spring sun that is drying out the damp gravel of the paths.

'I'll go fetch them.'

'Are you mad? Will you venture back alone and unarmed among those cheese-faced gorgons?'

'Gorgonzolas,' I murmur. 'If only they were Italian, not English and Dutch.'

She smiles at this feeble attempt to lift her spirits.

'What do you wish Frederick to do?' I ask, using his name as I had once done, testing our renewed amity.

'Whatever will make him happy.' She looks down at her hands on the shelf of her lap. Her nails are bitten short, as her mother's had been when I first saw her in Berwick.

'But fighting on against the odds won't make him happy if he meets only defeat in the end,' Elizabeth continues.

'I fear that he won't give up until forced . . .' She looks up at the sky. 'Or killed.'

To the east, a band of black horizon slices off the bottom of the bleached blue sky.

'No one would dare kill a prince . . . a monarch,' I say. 'Not in cold blood. Not any longer. Not in our days. Not even the Hapsburgs.'

'I'm not so certain. The Hapsburgs have already arrested and sentenced to death most of Frederick's supporters and counsellors, including an eighty-year-old man. And they followed poor old Slik into Saxony to capture him. Many of my train here fear for at least one member of their family.'

'Do you believe a Protestant defeat is inevitable?' I ask. A Protestant defeat would send her home, but at terrible cost. If she survived or were not made a prisoner-of-war.

'Consider the power of our enemy!' she says. 'And our allies here on the Continent blow hot and cold. Volunteers sign on . . . run away. Heroes offer themselves as our champions, then desert to the Catholic cause. Ambassadors shift position more often than . . .' Her voice trails off.

I hear her swallow.

'My father is a monster! He is angry with us . . . with Frederick and me, when we are the ones suffering. Why is he not angry with our enemies? Why must friends who offer us aid be forced to act "against the present will of the King"? Why must I curb my tongue and stop making trouble for England? Why are my rightful complaints and pleas for help as dangerous to my country as treason?'

She brushes fiercely at the wet spot on her skirts made by the King's letter.

'I know that I, myself, count for very little with him, but I am a princess of England. The Hapsburgs have insulted England, not just the Protestant cause in Germany.

135

England's honour fled along with her First Daughter. Why doesn't my father's vanity, at least, prod him into action?'

She pauses for breath. 'He has always railed against usurpers. The Emperor stole Frederick's hereditary Palatinate . . . my husband's throne. Why does my father tolerate this usurpation?'

I lack the cruelty to reply that she and Frederick are the usurpers, and wait for five heartbeats to see if she has exhausted her rage. 'He hopes for a Spanish marriage for the Prince of Wales.'

'To the Infanta?'

I nod.

'Still?' She flings up her hands in her familiar gesture of exasperation. 'Will he never give up on an alliance with Spain? First for Henry, now for Baby Charles. That poor Spanish breeding bitch has been kept dangling on the marriage market longer even than I was!'

'The King may change his mind. Or negotiations for the Spanish marriage may come to naught.'

I hear one of her feet kicking at the gravel. 'Is it true that Buckingham knows the King's mind better than any other man?' she asks.

'I fear so.' I hesitate, then give her a delicate push. 'He told me, one of the King's terms for the Spanish marriage is that you and Frederick are restored to the Bohemian throne.'

She takes my meaning perfectly. 'And that means we never will be! Unless the Spanish stop insisting the English bridegroom turn Catholic.' Her foot kicks at the gravel again. 'Do you see the English people ever agreeing to a Catholic convert for their king?'

I shake my head.

'What should I do, Bedford? Everyone else advises me. Once I trusted only you. What do you think best?'

We are again, almost, as we once had been, but she has a hard edge on her voice that I have never heard before.

A sudden knowledge of ageing strikes me silent. I feel the years behind me as a string of losses, never to be recovered. I don't mind, just then, if we never make a bright new court together in England. I don't mind if I remain penniless.

'Let me join you here,' I say on impulse. I do not care who might be listening. The Hague is far enough from Moor Park and Chenies. The end result would be the same for me, if a little more modest than I had intended. I would escape from Moor Park and I would be with Elizabeth again.

She shakes her head. 'It's a mean, pinched, dangerous life, my dear Bedford. Not for you.'

'I live a mean, pinched life in England.'

'I can't imagine . . .' She leans and peers into my eyes. 'In spite of your gardens at Moor Park?'

I nod, unable to speak. Then I shrug.

She takes both of my hands firmly. We are friends again. 'When I imagine the joy of being able to talk to you every day, it makes me want to weep, but I will not put you into danger. And you're a married woman, with estates to run.' She looks down at our joined hands. 'Forgive me for speaking plain. I've had to learn a brutal truth. I'm a beggar queen who must take care not to offend her allies – who happen at this moment to be the pious Dutch. I can't encourage a married countess to run away from her husband, no matter how dearly I love her. And no matter how much she wants to.'

She looks up at the crowded brick gables of the Wassenaer Hof. 'And please don't tell me to be grateful for the refuge the Dutch have given me! I turn myself inside out every day, behaving well in order to earn it.'

'Behaving well? Is that so hard for you?'

She snorts, as I intended. 'And please don't tell me to be patient.'

We're back on old, familiar ground. I have a little influence with her again, if I can think how to use it.

I raise a hand to ward off her indignant protest. 'Yes, I do tell you to be patient. The King has two choices: restoration, or bringing you back to England. In either case, it's best not to anger him past his endurance.'

'By continuing to fight, do you mean? But I anger him whether we fight or not! You've left out his third choice. To abandon me! Yes!' She cuts off my protest. 'We will continue to fight without his help! Frederick wants to fight. He is my husband. I love him. I will not leave him.' She scrubs at her eyes with the heels of her palms. 'Oh, Bedford! Why do husband and father have to be opposed?'

I know now what she wants. And what she wants is not what I want. But I, too, have loved. Like her, I could not have left my love if he had wanted me to stay.

'How can I serve you?' I ask. 'Just tell me.'

Her reply comes with the quickness of previous thought. 'Speak to my brother. I'm told that he wrote to our father, volunteering to come fight at Frederick's side. If you will risk it . . .'

I glance up at the windows of the Wassenaer Hof where one pair of eyes might belong to whoever had followed me. I see myself kneeling at the block again.

I revise quickly: Elizabeth becomes queen of England. Elizabeth the Second. I am her chief lady-in-waiting in her court.

The scene reverts back against my will. I kneel at the block, accused of aiding a would-be usurper.

Neither scene is yet true, but the block seems more likely.

'He must carry some weight with the King, now that he's heir to the throne,' she says. 'He must be almost a man now. He won't abandon his sister.' She blows a strand of hair out of her eyes and suddenly looks, not like a queen and mother, but a frightened little girl.

I look away. 'I will speak to the Prince.' I try to imagine Baby Charles standing up to either the King or Buckingham. 'Lizabella . . .' My old pet name for her, to console her for what I dare not say. 'You will not be abandoned. We . . . your friends in England, of whom there are many . . . will not abandon you.'

'Are you saying that my brother will?' Her voice sharpens.

'I won't know until I speak with him. But the people of England love you still and will not allow it. You carry a double love – their love for you and the love they once gave to Henry. They would have you safely at home.'

She closes her eyes. 'When I was small, I believed you could do anything. I remember how you once made me a crown of gold wire and leaves. I believed that it transformed me into a real queen.'

The young Elizabeth had trusted me when I once told her to jump and catch a lower branch, and that my horse would not bite her open, outstretched hand.

'This time, I'm not alone,' I say.

'Then send us help.'

Please don't ask that of me, I beg silently. 'We will see you restored in Bohemia and the Palatine,' I say. 'If that is what you want. Or else bring you safely home. I swear it.'

Home! I pray silently. Please, come back to England.

'We must fight,' she says tiredly. 'Until we can't fight any longer. You're not afraid to help us?'

'No, madam. I am not afraid.'

139

She lays her hand over the letter hidden in her skirts. 'Tell my friends in England that they must send us money and soldiers soon.'

I nod, agreeing to what I do not want, feeling like a traitor, but not certain to whom.

'Please, Bedford. Soon! I don't know how long we can survive.' She stands abruptly. 'Now you must come admire the new prince.'

Still carrying the wet letter with King's seal, I follow her.

While we wait on the flat muddy shore to be rowed out to our ship back to England, Kit reports on what he has learned from the gossip in the Wassenaer Hof. While claiming to be a simple man, he has a gift for extracting the meat from every conversational nut.

We stand on the wooden pier above the grey, churning water while the boatmen below us prepare their oars. My cloak snaps in the wind. Kit holds his hat clamped firmly under one arm to keep it from being blown away.

'I spoke to wives and sons of men arrested by the Hapsburgs.' Sea winds beat strands of fair hair against his ruddy face. 'They fear that the Austrians mean to make an example of the so-called "rebels".'

'So Her Majesty said to me.'

'To execute such respected men . . . civilians, not soldiers . . . scholars, even – would be against all honourable practice of war.' He shakes his head firmly. 'Once, perhaps. But, surely, not now.'

'I wish I shared your certainty.'

'Please don't trust my opinion on my fellow men, madam. You know that I like my pupils less than I do their horses.'

140

# 20

I spend most of our voyage back to England hanging over the ship's rail, voiding my stomach while trying not to be blown overboard. Sir Kit clings with both hands to the rail beside me. Blown spume darkens his fair hair and drips from his eyelashes.

'Go below!' I shout at him more than once. 'Get out of the wet!'

He shakes his head and plants his feet against the steep tilting of the deck.

Though I'm certain the sailors would have liked us out of their way as they struggled to hold steady the plunging, rolling ship, the cabin feels like a coffin. If I'm going to die, I want to do so in the open air.

This is a metaphor, I think once, when able to lift my head and look about me at the crashing, broken seas and vibrating ropes. For my confused, risky venture. For the English ship of state . . . A metaphor more to the taste of Master Ben than of John . . . Dear God, what have I undertaken?

I carry back two letters from Elizabeth. One to the King, the other to Holles. I don't dare to open either of them.

When I return, I must first play intelligencer for the King. And then I must seek out Holles.

The ship pitches forward. The rigging drums and clatters. My thoughts skew. The ship twists into a roll. The water rises in a slanting wall towards my head.

My skirts will pull me down, I think. Then, I'm looking up at a dark grey sky.

Bedford House embraces me in welcome. Dry and unmoving, the floor stays in its place. The walls stand more or less upright. The cook tempts me with a vegetable stew made from dried beans and carrots from Mudd's gardens. A fire burns in my little bedchamber. A kitchen groom has found a new-laid egg under a hedge to make me a warm, reviving posset. Edward is still at Moor Park.

Joy.

I have survived.

Kit's wife greets him as if she had thought never to see him again. Lady Agnes vanishes, straight-backed but grey-faced, to her bed.

A little later, in a dry, loose gown, wrapped in a flowered Russian shawl and cradling my posset mug in both hands, I stare into the fire in my bedchamber. In my lap lies a letter, delivered while I was away.

I know the writing that shapes my name on the front. I can see his hand holding the pen. I can hear his voice. Why has he written to me now, after three years of silence? I find it hard to believe that his timing is coincidence. More like the deliberate, unlikely, and sometimes perverse marriage of one of his metaphors. And no easier to read.

He's a Doctor of Divinity now, I think. Royal chaplain. Chaplain to my old friend Doncaster on his peace-making embassy to Germany for the King. Then, quite suddenly, Dean of St Paul's. A miracle of transformation, from

Catholic clerk to Anglican divine. I can't be alone in asking just how he has managed it.

For certain, he no longer needs me as a patron. The Dean of St Paul's cannot be the lover of a married countess. I press my fingertip into the dip of the red wax seal.

I set down my mug and touch the letter as if my fingertips could read his intent through the folded paper. The letter feels as dangerous as the man.

I wonder if Ben Jonson knows what he did.

# 21

## LUCY – LONDON, 1613

I was in my lodgings at Denmark House, called Somerset House before it was given to the new queen. There, I could always be near her and answer her call. To have my own apartments where I could work and entertain took the sting out of the constant tedium of waiting on another's pleasure. I could even look out over the river from my windows, push them open and fill my lungs with space and sky.

I heard the rumble of Jonson's voice.

'Madam, I have an urgent petitioner to you,' he said.

'I already feed too many poets,' I had replied. Including Ben Jonson himself. Some weeks, though I tried to hide it, I was hard pressed to find money to feed myself.

'None like this one.' Bright, burly, his sails always billowing before a private following wind, Jonson was as sharp-eyed as a woodpecker. 'And he's in dire need of a patron. Has a young wife and a child for every year of marriage. Four, at last count.'

'When does he find time to write?'

Jonson grinned. 'I'm not fool enough to try to answer that one. But, to my mind, he's a very good poet.'

'How generous of you to help a competitor. I suspect you. You'd advance only the least gifted of your disciples.'

Jonson shook his great, blunt head that held a formidable, if self-educated mind. 'He's no disciple of mine . . . has no taste for my gods and goddesses. Won't deign to write masques . . . he's with Bacon on that. But, alas, he looks more like the author of my masterpieces than I do.'

'And do you look more like his work than he does?'

'No one looks like his twisted verse, thank the Lord! They'd be very strange-looking creatures, else, with feet that tread where you least expect them.'

'You make him sound like a perverse poet.'

'No, no, no! A confused soul, I should say. He's a double man. I believe you'll like one of him very much.'

'And the other?'

'A fight to the death.' He grinned again.

'Which you will relish watching.'

'Of course not! *Absit invidia* . . .!' Mock-wounded, he clutched his broad chest. 'It would be an act of mercy if you took him on. No one else would tolerate him.'

'I can't afford another poet,' I repeated. Not when Edward's aunt Warwick had just asked again for further repayment of her loan to him.

'He needs you. And, if I'm not mistaken, you need him.'

'I need a poet? If you imagine, sir, that I need flattery . . . even yours . . . you're mistaken.'

'I could not flatter you, madam. It's beyond the power of mortal man.' The lines of his craggy face drooped into a lugubrious mask. 'All words come too far short of the truth.' He unfolded the paper he held in his hand.

The brand on his thumb flashed briefly. 'Listen how I have failed:

> . . . *Lucy, you brightness of our sphere, who are*
> *Life of the muses' day, their morning star!* . . .

He intoned his outrageously flattering epigram as if announcing a death.

I shook my head in laughing disbelief. 'All that to advance another man's cause?'

His brows met above his fight-crooked nose. 'Is it not good?'

Enough mocking. I knew from past experience that his humour would not tolerate critical disdain. I did not fear him in the least, but that brand told the world that he had killed a man in a fit of rage. 'It's very fine, if undeserved. And if I'm truly both morning and evening star at the same time, I suppose I can deal with your double poet.'

I held out my hand for Jonson's epigram and his protégé's offering.

*Satires*. By Master John Donne.

I had heard of him.

'Wild Jack Donne,' I said. 'Gossip's favourite boy. An ambitious lawyer's clerk with a taste for outrage. Who carried off his employer's well-born niece and married her. And still a smock-chaser. Is that true?'

'I never gossip,' said Jonson. 'But, with his little wife always pregnant, what do you think?'

'He'll get no satisfaction from me.'

'He'll tell you what he wants from you fast enough, beyond the money and *entrée*. Ask what he can give you.'

146

# 22

## LUCY – LONDON, 1621

Jonson knew very well what he was doing, I think now.
You are never safe with a writer. Writers have a cruel,
childlike curiosity. They want only to watch and feed.

I look down at the letter in my lap.

Except for this one, who hungered for more than he
could grasp.

I break the wax seal and unfold the letter.

*Madam* . . .

A cold greeting. The letter could have been for anyone.
So much for my secret hope that I was still his Lucy, his
Pole Star, his First Good Angel and God's Masterpiece . . .
once openly called all these in his public readings, his
praise of me repeated aloud over wine, around winter
fires to assembled companies of fellow poets, eager imit-
ators and the noble owners of deep pockets.

*Madam* . . . I blink to clear my eyes. *This letter is brought
to you by one of the German prince's men, an English soldier*

*who once pined for you in execrable verse which he has forced
to my attention . . .*

At least his tone is familiar.

*. . . When he and I last met, while I was in Heidelberg serving
as chaplain to the Vi. Doncaster, he begged me for a letter of
introduction so that he might offer you the fruits of his
admiration in person . . .*

This is nonsense! I think. The man I had known would
never inflict an execrable poet on anyone, even in cruel
jest. Donne might be wicked, ungrateful and confused,
but I could not imagine him exacting a petty revenge of
that sort. To be merely troublesome was beneath him.

*. . . But my chief purpose is not to inconvenience you with
his plodding deities and tarnished love darts.* (Aha!) *I believe
that he may, amongst other gossip bring you news of dear
friends whom I'm certain you wish only good speed.*

He had signed the letter 'JD'. No 'Doctor', no 'Dean'.
No 'John' or 'Donne'.

I look again at that anonymous 'madam'. Perhaps less of
a slap than I first felt. He did not name the execrable poet,
neither. Nor the 'German prince'. But in the context of
Heidelberg and Doncaster's mission for the King, I conclude
that the 'dear friends' must be Frederick and Elizabeth.

Not coldness but discretion.

No date on the letter. No one named. Written in plain
English, not a cipher. An innocent letter of introduction
that does not introduce.

Wits as quick as his never gave birth to words without
intent.

Like the approach of Holles, this letter is not coincidence. It comes too hot on my visit to The Hague as a double courier. My earlier importuning of the King and Buckingham set off rumour that must have reached St Paul's. Or Donne may even have been in Germany while I was in the Netherlands.

I feel the light brush of a strand of spider's web.

I re-read carefully . . . an English soldier met in Germany. Donne mentioning his own service in Germany with Doncaster.

He did not say if, or when, he had returned.

I can read no other story in his letter. He is offering to introduce a soldier who can give me word of Frederick and Elizabeth and, perhaps, might be able to help me fulfil my vow.

I no longer know him, I think. I most certainly do not know the man who now writes sermons and preaches at Paul's and owes his high position to the King. This letter could be a possible invitation to collusion. Or it might be a trap.

When he was still a mere poet, I had known how to read him. Poets always lie, but in predictable ways. I knew better than anyone how unpaid bills and pre-dawn fears invade that deep quiet place where poetry breeds. Therefore, I had paid their bills and thrown gold at their metaphors. From gratitude, they flattered me, but also increased the sum of human joy.

The letter in my hands hums with politics. Written by a man I no longer know. It opens a door I'm not certain I wish to enter. I lean forward to put it on the fire then sit back again, appalled by my own weakness. His ghostly hand lies under mine on the paper. I can't bring myself to destroy even this shadow of him.

I chew at a broken fingernail.

If I met this execrable poet, I might learn more of Donne's purpose.

In seeking Elizabeth, I had imagined only how I might recreate a world of pleasure and joy. Imagined dancing again before I grew too old and stiff to bend my knees. Making music, giving people respite from their daily lives.

I can cope with the petty politics of court. I can cope with running estates. I understand colour, metre, rhythm and how to strike cuttings. I can look at an acre of flat mud and transform it in my head into a garden. I can't see where I am going now.

I send for my steward.

I learn that the man who first delivered this letter during my absence has returned every day and now waits by the porter's lodge.

I have my maid redress my hair and put on a square, starched lace collar. I flutter as if this man's eyes were Donne's.

# 23

I do not like William Turnor. At first glance, he seems the model for the man who will never be remembered nor closely described. A neat tapered beard like that of most other men and of a middling colour disguises the true shape of his chin. A very ordinary brownish moustache blurs the line of his upper lip. The set of his shoulders lies hidden somewhere under the padding and slashed old-fashion shoulder-rolls of his doublet. Under the stiff lines of his soldier's leather jerkin, his waist might be slim or blown up like that of an ale drinker. I see nothing to explain my dislike, except that he is not Donne and is not what I expected Donne to send me.

He offers the usual effusive greetings, flattery, gratitude for my gracious condescension, *et cetera*, then proffers me a paper.

Not a piece of his 'execrable' yearning promised by Donne. Instead it was 'An Elegy to the Lamented Prince Henry'. Dead for nine years.

'This is your work?' I ask.

He inclines his head.

I look at him more closely. 'Are you a poet before you're a soldier? Or the other way round?'

'A soldier by choice, madam, a scribbler by compulsion.'

'If an empty pocket compels you, I can be of no use.'

'I don't want a patron.'

We eye each other.

'I would speak with you alone,' he says.

I lead him to a window niche, out of the hearing of my maid and Agnes Hooper, who stitch by the fire in my receiving chamber. He positions himself with his back to a wall where he can watch both my women and the door. His eyes make a quick circuit of the room.

Not ordinary, after all, I think. Disguised. And far more soldier than writer.

'I swear that there's no one behind the hangings,' I say. I catch a flash of irritation before he lowers his eyes.

He's not a good enough actor. Having come prepared to play the courtier, he lacks a true player's ability to adjust to his audience. When I snatched his script away from him, the killer showed. And he cannot hide his swordsman's hands.

I can't imagine that he was sent by my Donne, Master John Donne the poet. This was a creature of Doctor John Donne who had risen high and fast, against the odds.

'If you don't want a patron, why did you bring me this verse?' I offer to return the paper unread. 'The object of it is long dead. We've all moved on to other griefs.'

His eyes glint under his hat. He shifts his weight while he searches for words. I notice a thin pale scar that runs along his jaw and disappears into his beard like a snake into long grass. 'To save time,' he says.

'To what end?' His lack of grace now infects us both.

'Read the verse, madam. The prince whom I mourn is indeed long gone, but other sorrows remain alive.'

I unfold his paper. He watches me read. My women pretend they aren't watching both of us.

John, I think . . . into what do you draw me?

I frown. 'This verse is workmanlike enough, but it's not the news that Doctor Donne promises in his letter, of dear friends whom, I understand, you've lately seen in The Hague.'

'I'm not alone in still feeling grief,' he says quietly. 'A lingering sorrow reaches up into the highest realms of the court. I'm a mere messenger sent to bid you to come learn more.'

'Are you not allowed to speak plain?'

'A mere messenger, as I said.'

I want to slap him from frustration. I've known other men like him, who take pleasure in balking others.

'I go nowhere unless I know where and why. And whom I will meet.'

'Don't fear. You'll be in good company – at least three knights and an earl.'

As if the rank of my fellow company is what concerns me.

'Is Sir John Holles among them?'

'Yes, madam.'

'Are you allowed to tell me where?' I ask through clenched teeth.

'There's no mystery.' He gives me an amused look that doubles my urge to clip him on the ear. 'The occasion will be a meeting of the Adventurers of the City of London for the First Colony in Virginia. I can't tell you the place, because it's not yet agreed. But I believe that you carried a letter for them to The Hague.'

The Virginia Company, as it is more shortly known. I did

153

not expect that. I remember that Donne once applied to be their secretary.

The Virginia Company had been born as Prince Henry's great venture into the New World, where the Prince set out to build another, better England, a Protestant kingdom that would see off the Catholic Spanish in the Caribbean and send back the riches of the New World to England. Gold, timber, beaver and other furs, fish and all the wonders that were yet to be discovered. Almost all of the Prince's close associates had invested, including me, in my husband's name.

'Will it be a formal meeting of the Court of the Company?'

Turnor shrugs.

The Company is a consortium of venturers of two sorts: Venturers of the Purse, who merely invest money, and Venturers of the Person, who risk themselves bodily in the New World. Their first landfall in the Americas had been at a peninsula later named Cape Henry. They named their first settlement Jamestown and the area in which it lies, Virginia, thus neatly complimenting two monarchs at the same time. So far as I know, no investor has yet made back his stake. I have not. Since the Prince's death, the Company still limps on but has been badly wounded by political feuds, ineptitude and foul weather.

I look back down at Turnor's mediocre verse bewailing the loss of England's honour along with the loss of its warrior prince. Written by a man who looks more suited to a battlefield than to my receiving chamber and whom I do not like but was sent to me by a man I once loved beyond imagining. Whatever they might be, this verse and this bidding are not the usual public invitation to a Virginia Company meeting of the Venturers of Purse and whichever Venturers of Person might happen to be back in England.

I feel suddenly entangled in a thicket of sharp branches, a tangle of court poet turned cleric, a struggling joint stock company, and this soldier of fortune in front of me. Together with the dead Prince who tied those three together. And the Prince's sister, who is a refugee sheltering from the greatest power on the Continent.

'Perhaps they mean to pay dividends to their investors at last.' I fold his 'Elegy' and hold it, uncertain where to put it. 'In that case, I must not be absent.'

Accepting this invitation will, at the very least, save me the trouble of seeking out Holles. I might also learn who had been watching me in The Hague. I might learn why Donne thought I should attend, which might tell me what he still thought of me.

# 24

## LUCY – LONDON, SPRING 1613

The courting dance between poet and patron is stately. The steps are well known. The poet woos ardently, but patrons vie just as hard among themselves for the glory of sponsoring the most successful poets. And painters. And musicians.

The sponsored artist flatters. The sponsor expects to be flattered in exchange for giving the artist living expenses, or lodgings, and all the advantages of intimate contact with the great.

My little pack of poets was well known. When he and I first met, I should have been thinking that Donne would be flattered to join them.

He showed no sign of feeling flattered by being welcomed here in my small receiving chamber in Denmark House where the rich embroidery and inlaid chests were marks of the Queen's love for me. He had thanked me for meeting him. Then he fell silent. He should have been uneasy with the hunger to be accepted. He should have advanced the courting dance with an eager, seeking eye and flattering tongue. Instead he stood back from the surface of the moment and studied me, lost in deep thought, not seeming to notice or care how I stared at him.

He was in every way unlike Jonson. No billowing sails. Donne held everything in reserve. This man did not feel like the wild Jack Donne of whom I had heard, the writer of outrageous, challenging verse and deadly satires, seducer of noble maidens, one of whom had eloped with him, to her guardian's fury.

I could not stop staring. My easy words, so often spoken before with other men in this exact same circumstance, had dried up. I had forgot how to be gracious and how to charm.

Our continuing silence did not seem to worry him. His stillness felt like a necessary rein on an impatient inner force. He did not need to speak to me because he seemed to be in silent conversation with himself.

I'm ill, I thought. Gone mad. A worm has eaten my thoughts. I wanted to smash into that silent inner conversation that excluded me. I did not want him to leave me out.

I clasped my hands behind my back. Then unclasped them and cupped one fist in the other in front of me again. My thoughts grew so addled that I could not think at all. I was appalled.

I was the virtuous Countess of Bedford. The Muses' muse. I was adored. I was worshipped. But I was not loved, as my friend Cecilia Bulstrode had been loved before she died, with heat and sweat and rumpled sheets. I flirted, but I did not dally. My marriage had taught me the disillusions of bed.

I heard my tongue click with dryness as I tried to swallow.

My heart had just turned whore.

I wanted to touch this man who was watching me from the distant centre of his stillness. I wanted to touch his

157

hand, his shoulder, those fingers, his lower lip – it did not matter. I wanted to lean against him, as I sometimes leaned against a horse or a beech tree. I wanted to put my hand on his body the way I would lay my palm against a water-polished stone warmed by the sun.

Don't be a fool, whispered my dead mother's voice. This man will gain you nothing but grief.

I wanted to feel his breath warm on my ear as he spoke to me. I had never before felt this terrible hunger for physical touch.

He's not even so handsome, I told myself. Not like Buckingham, or Arundel.

Even I recognised the lie.

'Sir,' I managed to say. 'Master Jonson has begged your cause very prettily.'

He raised his brows very slightly but inclined his head in acknowledgement.

'. . . for him.' I had not meant to answer that hint of disbelief.

He was almost too pretty for a man, but that 'almost' made all the difference between Buckingham's fragile female beauty joined to a man's body and this sinuous male perfection of a large tomcat or finely bred hound.

Donne was slim, long-faced, and dark as a Spaniard, with high cheekbones, smooth chin and soft dark moustache. A long, strong, elegant male nose balanced his large eyes and full mouth. The dark willow leaves of his brows echoed the arch of his eyelids. He held long, slim fingers linked together in front of him.

I stared at the chiselled curves of his upper lip and the voluptuous fullness of the lower one. His silky moustaches drew my fingertips like the pieces of down you catch floating in the air.

'A child for every year of marriage . . .' Jonson's words

leapt into my mind, along with the naked back and hips of Donne in bed, making love to his wife.

He's still waiting for me to speak, I thought in alarm. I could not remember what he might have said. Why was he looking startled? Had I said something out of keeping? Without knowing I spoke?

His lips parted slightly. Behind his full lower lip, I saw the top edges of white teeth. I saw words forming from the thoughts in his eyes.

I felt the brush of his fingers on my face like a memory. I needed to feel his flesh against mine so intensely that I thought I would weep.

But I did not love. Love was not part of my life, except in friendship. Outside my marriage, I did not give myself into the power of any man – that was one valuable lesson taught to all women by the old virgin queen who had refused even marriage. I held myself apart and intact. This elusiveness was part of my strength.

Why was I even thinking such thoughts?

'What is it, madam?' He frowned a little, leaning forward to read my face.

'Why do you ask?'

'I see it . . .' He stopped.

I shook my head. There was silence while he still studied me. Then he seemed to make a decision and let out a long sigh. 'What are we going to do?'

'What do you mean?' I stammered. I could not breathe.

He opened his arms in a gesture that embraced us both.

I shook my head and raised one hand to ward him off.

'Do you mean that you don't feel it too?' he asked.

'I won't,' I said.

Dear God! Straight into the deepest mire!

I shook my head again, angry at my own awkwardness.

He half-smiled and rubbed his forehead with one hand.

'Please believe me, in spite of what my friend Jonson may have told you in his pretty plea, I'm no happier about it than you are.'

'I cry you mercy . . . I don't . . .'

'Do you want me to trundle out the usual empty phrases? Would that set you at your ease?' He observed me again. 'No, I fear that you and I will survive only by plain speaking.'

Plain speaking about what? I should have asked. 'But I need to dissemble,' I said. 'I can't . . .'

He nodded, then stood silent. We looked at each other.

I had heard the women's talk. I even pretended to join it. A lover, discreetly managed, was almost a requirement at court. But this was not a manageable lover. I felt something intent and unyielding in him. In another man, I might have disliked it.

With another man, I would not be considering the question of lovers, manageable or not.

'Lucy . . . *lux* . . . my light,' he said as if testing the words aloud.

I did not know whether his marriage had been politic or from affection. But, even if I sent him away this instant, my politic marriage would not survive him. I already felt a power in him that had begun to unpick the fabric of my carefully woven life.

John Donne, penniless lawyer and rising coterie poet. Not a manageable lover for the virtuous, untouchable Morning Star of Whitehall. And not, for certain, being already married, a suitable husband . . .

What was I thinking?

'Is this usual?' I asked, echoing his earlier gesture of embracing arms.

'Not in my experience.' He did not laugh.

Neither the cold misery of my marriage bed nor my

experience of light-hearted flirtation had prepared me to deal with such a moment.

He crossed his arms across his chest and gripped his elbows, his hands pale against the black velvet of his coat. 'Please believe me. I did not come here intending to try to seduce you.'

I clutched indignation to keep myself afloat. 'Did you dare presume that you could?' Our gazes collided and held.

'If I am not to offer you lies . . . we both know that I could. But I will not, I swear, not without your agreement. I am seduced already.'

'How dare you?' I sounded feeble to my own ears. We had already moved far beyond such posturing.

'I wish that I did dare.' He gave the flash of a smile. 'Then we wouldn't be edging around each other in this uneasy way. Instead, I'd be turning myself inside out to charm you, quoting my own love-struck lines as if inspired on the spot by your presence. As if I'd never struggled through hours of lonely, painful work by candlelight.' He held up his hands in the swordsman's gesture that concedes defeat. 'I swear to you that I came here intending no more than good, honest flattery and hoping for a patron.' The smile returned to where it had lurked at one corner of his mouth.

I crossed my arms tightly across my breasts.

'Oh, God!' he cried in mock despair. 'Who has warned you against me?'

I stared back.

'Friend Jonson?'

I nodded.

'He exaggerates both my appetites and the number of my conquests . . . please, don't protest that he did not. I can hear his glee now, in the recounting.'

'He did warn me to take care.'

'Did he also add that I love my wife?'

The young wife with a child for every year of marriage.

I blinked. It was an unusual line for a would-be seducer, of whom I had had many. But I liked his admission. She was present in his life. Not dismissed, not disregarded. He did not belittle her, as I had heard so many men do when they pursued another woman.

'I wrecked the smooth advance of my career for her,' he said. 'And do not wish I had not.'

Jonson's double man. And honest about it. I wished that he had lied and exposed himself as mean-spirited.

I looked away out of the window and tried to fix my thoughts on an ivy leaf that quivered on its long stem just beyond the glass.

Voice clichés, I begged him. Be tedious. Be vain. Try to flatter me . . . anything to bring me to my senses!

If he felt as I did, why didn't he step forward and embrace me?

He smiled. 'Does that mean that I've lost a possible patron?'

'What?'

He uncrossed his arms and pointed to my hands. 'Or have I merely gained yet another critic?'

I looked down. Unwittingly, I had twisted one of his *Satires* into a spill for lighting the fire.

Regain control of this interview! muttered my mother's voice. Send him away now!

But his absence would already be a loss beyond bearing.

'You'll know when I burn it.' I began to smooth out the paper.

'The fire waits.' He held out his hand. 'I'll burn them all, if you say they deserve it. If they don't please you, I'll happily consign them to oblivion.'

'Didn't Jonson warn you about me, in turn?' I asked.

'I've had some little experience with dramatic gestures. That's a fine performance, but I'm quite certain that you have other copies.'

That stopped him.

'Your satires are brutal, cocky, and cold,' I said. 'Even that fire won't warm them. They are witty but cruel. I like the world less since reading them.'

He threw back his head and laughed with apparent pleasure at my insult. 'Jonson did say that you're a rare creature – a patron who is also a poet and therefore understands both the craft and the soul of poetry. And the deceptions.'

'He flatters me. A gentlewoman's verses are mere needlework of the mind. An acceptable pass-time if she's lettered.' Though not in my husband's eyes.

'Neither of us believes that.' Donne brushed away my words with his long fingers. 'I will confess all. I've read your work. You alarm me, even cause me twinges of envy. You will drive me past my easy games.'

This is flattery of the highest order, I told myself. This man is even more dangerous than I first thought.

'Write a verse just for me,' I said. 'In a kinder mode.' The next step in the poet – patron courting dance. 'I will consider it then send for you to tell you what I decide.'

I can't handle him, I thought after he had left.

That spring, I had borrowed more money to buy the lease of a house at Twickenham Park. Whenever the Queen could spare me from Denmark House, Whitehall or Greenwich, I could then follow Henry's court, and Elizabeth, to the countryside. This new estate, my very own – not inherited by my husband nor held at the pleasure of the Queen, and where I was free to entertain my poets and friends – lay just across the Thames from

163

Prince Henry at Richmond Palace and a little up-river from the Princess at Kew. While I waited for Donne's poem, I began to lay out my new gardens.

Donne will disappoint, I promised myself as I squinted at a tangled riverside thicket where I imagined an avenue of beech. You'll feel a fool for that passing madness of your first meeting. You've been a fool before. You'll survive.

I felt astonishingly cheerful.

My new loan, our growing debts and constant shortage of cash meant that I would have to wait to install the Greek or Roman statues that I imagined on either side of a broad walk, leading the eye away from the house towards a distant fountain. In the meantime, a double row of clipped yew columns would have to do.

My request for kindness had been a trap. Donne would almost certainly write the commonplace effusions of a lover dying in the service of a chilly goddess. Like all the other court poets, he would call me 'Diana' or 'Queen of the Heavens', or even, like Jonson, 'Morning Star'. Quite properly, because I was their patron. A patron knows that gratitude can heave its breast and strike dramatic postures in verse that can be safely ignored in reality.

While I discussed the layout of paths with the estate manager, half of my mind defied Master Donne to find a fresh adjective for my fair, slightly russet hair, my pale skin, my lively eye, my wit, and my unquestioned virtue. I wanted him to save us both from the disaster I felt waiting for us.

His *Satires* should have warned me. What I read four days later, alone in my Twickenham study, was this:

> *Dull sublunary lovers love*
> *(Whose soul is sense) cannot admit*

*Absence, because it doth remove*
*Those things which elemented it.*

I could hear his smooth voice reading it, seeming to disclaim the senses. He wrote in the rhythms of everyday speech, not in the grand Classical images and cadences of court verse like Jonson. No goddesses. No Diana.

*But we by a love, so much refin'd,*
*That our selves know not what it is . . .*

Indeed, we did not! I half-smiled in recognition.

*Inter-assured of the mind,*
*Care less, eyes, lips, and hands to miss.*

I re-read. Then again. 'Inter-assured of the mind . . .'

By the alchemy of his words, he and I were already lovers, advanced far past the 'dull sublunary' moon-struck, rutting couples who grope and wrestle in hedges or canopied beds. He wrote as if he had already possessed my body and was safely entwined in my soul.

'What arrogance!' murmured my mother's voice.

No doubt, she was right.

I looked again at his final line with renewed alarm. '. . . Care less, eyes, lips, and hands to miss.' You can't miss what you don't value. However much he proclaimed the triumph of the mind, he had lingered in final emphasis on the renounced flesh.

I was not deceived by his tactical withdrawal into the realm of the mind. His lines were still both cocky and brutal. I read no kindness here, just clear intent. He was telling me that he meant to have me, eyes, lips, and hands as well as mind.

I refolded the poem. With alarm, I noted that the light, the floor beneath the soles of my shoes had changed. The air entered and left my lungs with new fluidity.

I would be firm. This time, I would write the script. I understood that, like me, he refused to accept the gap between our desires and the reduced rations that life is willing to give us. But he had met his match in me. He would learn that we were equal in obduracy. If I were firm, it might be possible after all to enjoy a kinship of the mind, without the other.

Against my will, the scene in my head revised itself into flashes of impossibility.

His mouth on my breast. His wife. Looking down at his sleeping face. Edward clutching his arm, divorcing me now that all my money was gone. Dancing with Donne before the King and Queen, our eyes meeting through the slits in our vizors, the heat of his hand on my waist. Jonson grinning at us both.

I sat holding the paper that he had touched.

I would keep these images trapped in my head. He and I would be chaste but inter-assured of mind.

It would not work. To try would be dangerous.

Revise . . .

He was indeed an interesting poet. Even Jonson respected him. My reputation at court would gain lustre from being patron to the poet, if I could control the man. And he needed a patron.

Revise.

In spite of what my husband said, I knew the difference between a good story and the truth.

I sent my letter of refusal to him by my good friend who was also Donne's friend, Sir Henry Goodyear.

That was that.

# 25

## LUCY – TWICKENHAM, 1613

The boy looked at me uncertainly, not convinced that I was the Countess. When I assured him that I was she, he gave me a letter. Opening it clumsily with my muddy hands, I saw that it was a poem. 'Twickenham Garden'. My garden. A second poem from Donne.

'He's waiting outside the gate now,' said the boy.

'Here? Now?' I wore an old woollen skirt and heavy boots to help my small crew of gardeners with the planting.

I had wild thoughts of rushing into the house to wash and change into a finer gown. Then I thought, So be it! I did not need a fine gown to lay down the law to an importuning poet.

I would dismiss him for the final time. My present turmoil made it clear that I should. I had already refused him once. Let some other patron have the reflected glory.

I watched the boy run back towards the main gate. With the poem between my teeth, I brushed my hands on my skirts. Then I sat as elegantly as possible on a stone bench still wrapped in straw from its journey. I tried to read while my hand refused to hold the paper steady. I kept my head down as footsteps crunched towards me over the new-laid gravel. I pretended suddenly to hear him and looked up. 'Master Donne!'

Deceiving neither of us.

My face felt as red as an apple.

'Madam.'

I wanted to scrub the half-smile from his face. 'Poor Master Donne,' I said. 'Do you expect me to be moved by this self-pity?' I read aloud the first line of the poem. '"Blasted with sighs"? And "surrounded with tears"?'

'To protect your reputation, madam, I disguise myself as an ordinary poet.' He wore his black coat again. It occurred to me that he might have no other. 'I beg you to read on.'

> . . . *Hither I come to seek the spring,*
> *And at mine eyes, and at mine ears,*
> *Receive such balms as else cure every thing.*
> *But O! self-traitor, I do bring*
> *The spider Love, which transubstantiates all,*
> *And can convert manna to gall;*
> *And that this place may thoroughly be thought*
> *True paradise, I have the serpent brought.*

I should not have allowed him past the gate into my new unrealised garden where the ground was strung like a fiddle with strings tied taut between pegs, marking out unmade paths. Nothing was itself yet. Everything still needed explanation. And I was unarmoured, dressed in an old blue wool gown and ancient sleeveless jacket, a farmer's wife.

A pair of gardeners digging nearby pretended not to be listening.

I stood and led Donne away past heaps of bricks, curving beds of churned mud, piles of horse manure and straw-wrapped shrubs from the Netherlands.

We arrived at the top of the newly planted beech avenue, for which I had borrowed again from Edward's aunt. I stopped to root myself. My eye saw noble, rounded green crowns overlapped against the sky, echoing the clouds. The infant reality stood fragile and naked, too far apart to comfort each other, tied to posts that would steady them against the winds and frost of their first year. I would never see them as I imagined when I planted them. What I did in the next few moments would shape my immediate future more surely as anything I had ever done.

At the far end of the avenue, beyond the brick wall and the towpath of the Surrey bank of the Thames, above the onion domes and flags of Richmond Palace on the far shore, the rising sun flared suddenly into view over Richmond Hill.

I finished reading his poem. 'It will take more to bewitch me than this frustrated lover bewailing a hard-hearted mistress,' I said with a fury that astounded me.

No more wishful lying to myself.

I had wanted a reason to give way to the unreason that I felt waiting for me in him. He had not given it to me. It would take more than this ingenious wordplay to pay for the danger I felt in him . . . And it was ingenious, I had to admit. 'Spider-love . . .' he had written. I had never read such a love poem before. If that is what it was.

> *The spider Love, which transubstantiates all,*
> *And can convert manna to gall;*
> *And that this place may thoroughly be thought*
> *True paradise, I have the serpent brought.*

But it was not ingenious enough after all to shake me out of my familiar self: the young Countess of Bedford, favourite of the Queen, generous, witty, the lightener of hearts, at the centre of every lively entertainment. Overflowing with ideas. Given to no one entirely, safe in that internal space where I guarded the kernel of myself that had gone elsewhere on my wedding night, and ignored the whispered envy of the Queen's love for me. The kernel that still mourned a dead, newborn son. The solitary kernel that wanted more and, startled into unexpected new life, had felt the twitch of possibility in this man.

'And "Paradise"?' I asked. Donne had played on the Latin word *paradisus*, meaning 'garden'. 'A stale image . . . even if you do play the serpent in this Paradise.' I shook the paper.

'Do I not give the image a fresh turn?'

'Fresh enough, I grant you. But you wrote this verse before you ever saw this place. You write of trees that aren't here and never will be. "Twickenham Garden"? It could be Richmond, or Nonsuch, or Windsor. Or Scotland!' I did not understand my own fury. 'In short, you do not transform reality. You lie. Ingeniously, for all your "lover's tears" and "chrystal phials", which I have often read before in the work of other men. Your garden here has nothing to do with me, only with you. It grows entirely in your imagination. By giving it a true name, you counterfeit reality.'

Jonson would have killed me by now.

'Should I be flattered to count for so little?' I demanded. 'I exist in your verse only to break your heart. You! You! You play games with your heart. You hide from me and from true emotion behind all those clever, glistening words.'

He looked at me wide-eyed, without a hint of the anger I expected. 'Is that true?'

I nodded, breathing as hard as if I had run all the way from Kingston.

He dropped to one knee in front of me. There was theatrical flourish in the action, but a deadly earnestness as well. 'Madam,' he said. 'In you, I have found a mistress more severe than my own conscience. I beg you to do battle with me! And promise me that you will show no mercy.' He stood again and brushed the dark spot of damp on his muddy knee. 'I speak as a writer. We will accommodate the rest, but this is more urgent.'

'You try to trick me. Don't think to flatter me that you woo my wits and not my body.'

'I'm in deadly earnest. Jack Donne, the clever, cruel satirist . . . you told me so yourself when we first met . . . the man of wit with a cold eye for folly, his own and that of other men, is offering . . . begging you to allow him . . . to open the dark conflicts of his heart and mind. Earnest John and Wicked Jack . . . will you be referee between them? I pray to God for His help but He remains curiously and stubbornly silent.'

'My money is limited.'

'Money, like our bodies, will make its own way.'

I noted that he did not disclaim money entirely, however.

'Do you understand what I ask? You are my own better mind in another body.'

This is outrageous, I thought. Flattery of the most ingenious sort. Beware. He is drawing you into that suffering that Jonson mentioned.

'You don't believe me,' he said. 'Come. I've not found the words yet to express what I mean. I must show you.'

'Where do you go?'

171

'We won't leave your Paradise.'

'This must be your final argument,' I said. 'But be warned, I am resolved to refuse you, no matter what you say.'

He did not touch me, but I followed him as if his hand grasped my arm.

With seeking eyes, he walked inland, away from the Thames and the concentric circles of my intended formal garden. We doubled and redoubled like hounds tracking a scent. We entered an old, untouched woodland through which ran the stream that I meant to divert into a series of small waterfalls flowing down to the Thames and the sea. All the time, he searched.

I watched him study a leaf-covered bank above the stream. The sun had heaved itself over my southern wall and tumbled down through the trees. He unfolded his cloak from over his arm and spread it on the ground.

'Lie here,' he said. He waved away my protest. 'No, not that. I keep my promises.' He gave me his hand to help me down onto the cloak. I tried to ignore the brief distraction of his touch. Smoothing my skirts, I saw that straw had stuck to the back of them.

He stretched himself out facing me, full length on the leaves a short distance away. He propped his dark head on one hand.

'Good morning,' he said.

# 26

'I feel foolish. I'm certain we look like a pair of fools.' I spoke from the need to say something rather than real conviction. Then I felt like a clot for saying what I didn't mean.

We lay facing each other two and a half feet apart, a little more than the length of his forearm, which lay flat on the ground, reaching towards me but not touching me. I was half-curled on his cloak, my head propped like his on my right hand, my left hand lying loosely across my belly. He had stretched out full-length on his side with his legs a little bent. He wore white stockings and had fine ankles and well-shaped calves.

The distance between us was a chasm.

The morning sun spilled slowly over the edges of leaves and crept along the arching stems of couch grass, feeling for new earth to invade. Near the base of a pine, which I could see by turning my head a little on its supporting hand, a corm of sows' bread cyclamen dangled a low pink crown. The pointed tongues of its furled oak leaves had begun to poke up between the blooms.

Though he still held tight to the rein, the short distance

between us vibrated with the force he was keeping in check.

'What are we doing here?' My new, terrifying desire suddenly snaked out from my fingertips. The heat in my belly seemed to bend the Lady's Bedstraw between us like a blast from an open oven.

'Testing my belief.' He rolled onto his back, linked his hands behind his head and turned to look at me. He did not touch me, but he looked. His eyes flowed into my veins.

I had never been wooed like this . . . if wooing it was. Perhaps he was mad.

I suffer from a strange new malady, I thought. And will die of it.

His eye-beams were lances. Replacing my bones with cold liquid metal. I had to look away. His breathing sawed minutely at my hearing.

I studied every detail lying between us. Single twisted grass blades. Little blunt hearts of Shepherd's Purse and their hair-like claws that would grab on to my hems. A wood louse, a minute upturned cooking pot, skittering on numberless hair-like legs. Six ants, laboured in a line, tiny boats beneath the sails of leaf fragment clutched in their jaws, struggling through a giant tangled wilderness that suddenly looked as huge and overwhelming to me as it must have seemed to them.

Just below the suspended fingertips of my left hand, I saw with total clarity a piece of half-rolled leaf. Black where it touched the bare soil, drying upward by degrees to bright rust.

The morning passed. Slowly, I grew bored with resisting him. I looked back at him.

I let my eyes rest on his chest. Behind the faint sound of his breathing, I heard a questioning phrase being sung over and over by water passing over a rock. I watched the rise and fall of his ribs, and how the folds of his coat stretched and retracted with each breath. I looked at the barely visible stirring of the cloth over his flat belly. Hurriedly, I raised my gaze. His white linen collar, edged with narrow lace, trembled rhythmically with his pulse, faster than in sleep but much slower than mine.

The skin on his wrists and hands was browned by foreign suns.

I glanced at his face.

He smiled. 'Patience. We will spend today only as friends.'

'I hope you intend nothing more for tomorrow.'

'I can't imagine tomorrow.'

I felt the ground grow hard under my hip. The coldness of the earth began to seep through his cloak, my wool skirt, jacket, linen petticoat and shift. I felt the earth pressing up against me, and myself pressing back down, weighty, planted like a stone.

I tightened when he flung out his arm. But he let his hand lie as if arrested in the act of reaching for me, as relaxed as a sleeper's hand. He closed his eyes.

'Listen,' he murmured. Then the flesh of his face relaxed onto its bones.

He was asleep.

I felt a sudden illicit pleasure, like entering someone else's chamber in their absence and opening their chests and cupboards, seeing their empty stockings stretched by the shape of their toes, or finding half-eaten bags of walnuts. He had surrendered himself to my eyes. I was free to study him openly.

His fingers were stained with dark brown oak-gall ink on the thumb and first two fingers. There was a softer smudge on the side of his hand under his little finger.

A hard hand, busy hand. A hand fit to hold a pen, but also a knife. A hand that would hold firmly.

His belly was flat. His crossed calves in white stockings were lean and strong.

He was snoring gently. Without waking, he turned onto his side to face me. The skin of his face was pulled a little askew by the hand on which it lay. I smiled as I would smile at a sleeping child and found myself drowned in sudden tenderness.

His eyes opened. 'Will I do?'

Yes, said my heart.

I was warm rain. I was the breeze that lifted the lock of his dark hair and stroked his cheeks and the line of the arm that lay extended towards me. I felt him like the sun, gilding my face, throat and breasts with its warmth. The heat of his concentration warmed my ribs, my legs, my feet that lay half-folded under me.

I stretched. I felt safe, as if I too could fall asleep under his gaze and know that all would be well.

'You are beautiful,' he said. 'I must say that at once, because it's true. And you might wonder why I, of all those who praise you, failed to say it.' His extended hand plucked a grass stem. 'You frighten me. I need fear.'

Before my newly born sense of safety could vanish, he added, 'You also comfort me. I want you, but if I can't have you, nothing in this moment will change.'

We looked at each other, eye-to-eye.

He was my world, I already knew. Reason had nothing to say; nothing it could ever say could make me not know what I felt now. Reason could only shout warnings and instruction. Reason could try to dictate my behaviour. By now, I was far out of its reach.

'I knew at our first meeting,' he said.

'So did I.' Drinking a butt of claret could not have

176

shaken that same honesty from my tongue. 'Will you make a poem from this day? When you find the words.'

'Almost certainly.' He watched me stir uneasily. 'But the poem will not be this moment. Nor us. It will be itself, with a different time, a different Lucy, and possibly a different Donne flowing through it.'

'You will hide behind your words again?'

'Unless I find the courage to go naked without metaphor and ingenuity.' He leaned forward intently. 'Lucy, listen to me . . . in plain, naked, trembling words. This moment . . .' His hand flung a spider's web around us, wrapping us together. 'This is what there is. Willy-nilly, we have it.'

Midday had passed. For the rest of the afternoon, we lay by the stream, moving a little from time to time, looking freely into each other's eyes. Greeting, questioning, resting at ease on the other's unknown thoughts. At times, one or the other would look away to think then look back again.

I wanted never to move again. It was enough to lie here with him while the afternoon cooled and the sun withdrew again, inch by inch through the trees, leaving cool patches of shadow like dark footprints. The future would look after itself. I watched the stream darken and grow more opaque. The water threw sharp-edged chips of brightness back at the falling sun before plunging into the black shadows at the base of stones.

At last, the evening chill probed too hard for us to lie still. We shook ourselves and stirred, awaking. He rose and touched me for the second time, helping me to stand. We laughed at our legs, as wobbly as newborn colts. We stood helplessly by the darkening stream, still in our bubble, unwilling to make ourselves break it.

'I want to kiss you,' he said, 'but if I do, I will not be able to leave you.'

I nodded mutely.

But all was agreed between us.

He read me his poem a few weeks later. Warned about the alchemy of transforming life into verse, I did not expect to see my exact self, nor our day in it. I braced myself for a different moment, different time, a different Lucy. Even a different Donne. But one verse brought tears of recognition to my eyes,

> When love with one another so
> Interanimates two souls,
> That abler soul, which thence doth flow,
> Defects of loneliness controls.

I had not known what to call those defects of loneliness before he named them and healed them in me.

# 27

The right moment to make love eluded us. We wanted it just right, both knowing that it would come.

No, we would decide. Too public. No . . . no . . . no . . . too quick. Too sudden.

'You must not throw away your career again for a woman,' I told him. 'I'm not even a wife. We must take care.'

I could not begin to calculate what damage our liaison might do to my own life. I knew that it would not be a casual breeze that blew in through the door and out through the window.

Autumn closed in. The weather was growing colder. Opportunities grew fewer and fewer. People were being driven indoors again, crowded together around the fires. Privacy grew harder to find. The pressure of constant eyes and ears drew in like the nights.

In the end, we were driven to a sudden, almost brutal consummation. Unable to wait, just as we had not wanted. At risk, just as we had laboured so hard to avoid.

In only my shift, naked under the linen shift and in my cloak, but wearing boots against the wet cold grass.

In my new garden, against a tree like a stable groom and maid, we achieved a desperate, uncivil, ruthless sealing of our bond. I was beyond thought. My body, so neglected, so quiet, so meek, awoke with a roar and consumed him.

'My maenad,' he said afterwards. He leaned his head against the tree beside mine. 'Alas, Lucy, I fear there's no escape from this for either of us.'

'I don't want to escape!' I gripped my own wrist behind his back like a wrestler around an opponent.

His head moved against mine. 'Nor I. But God help us!' Then he pressed my head to the tree. I was caught between the trunk of the tree and his mouth.

But all that was in the past, killed by us both. What did he want from me now?

180

# 28

## LUCY – LONDON, 1621

I take Elizabeth's letter to Holles and follow Turnor alone across the Strand towards the Thames. Sir Kit watches me go. To the very last moment, he has tried to persuade me to let him come with me.

Dusk is already wrapping itself around us. The Thames, now thawed, looks as sullen and as opaque as lead. Thin jagged plates of rotten ice linger and bob wherever the sun does not reach. Dogs bark furiously at each across the river, secure again in their forced separation.

Turnor leads me to a private wherry. After wrapping me in the piled furs, he takes a seat behind me. He wears brown wool and leather, an unremarkable man. To the careless eye, he might have been any ordinary serving man. We fly down-river with the outgoing tide.

I see the first lanterns spring into life ahead of us across the river. Bright rectangles of doors flash open and close again. Windows glow. Behind us, in the City, servants and householders are lighting the lanterns required by law to hang over every door. To my surprise, we have angled towards the far side, the Southwark bank.

Though it is early spring, the wind out on the river needles through every gap of the new gown made to armour me in London. I pull my cloak tighter and duck my nose and chin down into the hired furs.

I hear a faint cheer from Southwark, then another. After a few more strokes of the oar, I begin to make out the discordant battle between bands in the different inns, competing for the ears of passers-by. 'Come drink here! Come to me! Come to me!' the fiddles cry, one on top of another.

I had expected the noblemen and knights of the Virginia Company to gather in one of their great houses in the City. Instead, we seem to be headed for Sodom and Gomorrah. Southwark. London's unruly Ward Without, on the wrong side of the Thames. In Surrey. Outside the locked street-bridge that kept the City safe at night. In Southwark, the watch have given up on enforcing curfew and all other order. In Southwark, every thing and every one can be bought.

I had been there several times in the Queen's party, to see a play or play bowls while we pretended that no one recognised us in our half-masks, in spite of our rich clothes and the men-at-arms who cleared our way. But only in daylight and only inside the bubble that always surrounded majesty, even when in disguise.

I follow Turnor up the water stairs at Paris Garden at the top of Bankside. He pushes ahead of me through the crowds and warring shouts and fiddles, down the Bankside, past the Falcon, and the Cross Keys. He moves around obstacles like water and the crowds close at once behind him so that I have to elbow and shove, yanking at my farthingale, in order to keep up with him. I throw off importuning hands, wave away offered mousetraps and tobacco pipes.

He turns into the Bear, an inn wedged between the Little Rose and the Hart's Horn, facing the river. With my hood shadowing my face, I follow him into a thick fog of tobacco and woodsmoke. Inside, the laughter, shouts, and clanking of pots almost drown out the fiddles. The room smells of heated animal bodies like a kennel or stable, and of wet wool, spilt ale and hot boozy breath.

I must look like his doxie, I think. Trailing behind him like this. Just one more of those women who sit on laps at the crowded tables then follow a mark upstairs to a private room. A few eyes assess me as we pass. No one pays attention to the man I follow.

Leaving behind the worst of the racket, we climb a flight of dark narrow wooden stairs that stink of stale ale and piss. Turnor knocks at one of the private rooms. We wait in silence while the lock rattles.

'Lady Bedford!'

In the corner of my eye, someone leaps to his feet. The rest of the men in the room already stand by the fire. The room feels crowded, but there are far too few men present for a full legal meeting of the Virginia Company of New England.

The noise from the inn below bangs at the floor. The fiddles twine thinly through our talk. The number of bodies crowded into the room is making the fire smoke. Their combined force and solidity make Turnor feel insubstantial. His clothes and beard are the colours of the wood-panelled walls and plank floor. He retreats to the far wall. In the firelight, which is the only source of light in the room, he becomes scarcely more than a thickening of textures and lines in the shape of a man.

I know most of these men as old friends. Two of them

have partnered me in masques. I have sat with several of them listening to poets read their work, then drunk wine with them and debated who was the finest writer. I have flirted with them all for the sheer, shared game of it, whether or not, in truth, they prefer boys. The firelight casts an orange light on their faces, leaving the side away from the fire black with shadows.

'Lucy! Gentlemen, our muse returns to us!' Henry Wriothesley kisses me warmly. The Third Earl of Southampton is Treasurer of the Virginia Company and one of the most passionate supporters of its attempts to colonise the New World. A rival patron when I was at court, he is still a dandy, still exquisite in dress and manner, if a little broadened by age. The long, fair, ribbon-tied lover's lock that once fell over his shoulder has given way to the short hair and beard of mature dignity. But he still hums with the fervour that once sent him racing around Italy in the company of the King's Surveyor, Jones, in search of architectural manuscripts and the perfect building.

Over his shoulder, I see Holles bobbing his white beard at me. Beside him stands a younger self, his son Denzil, whom I had last seen as a boy. The son wears puritanical black and is said to have grown into an even fiercer Protestant than his father.

Like me, several of the other men here have been patrons of Master Inigo Jones, the designer of the Queen's masques and now the King's Surveyor, who is at the moment busy replacing the old wooden Banqueting House, recently burned down. Wriothesley has commissioned paintings, songs and poetry. We have all competed, sometimes fiercely, to buy the finest antiquities from Greece and Rome, and the most important works by Continental painters like the German Hans Holbein and the Italian Titian.

All of them had served Henry, the Prince of Wales, at his golden court at St James's Palace. Most of them were part of the fierce group of Protestant warriors who had shared the Prince's passions, both artistic and military, before he died. Most of them suffered my fate, losing their place at court with the death of their royal patron. One or two had survived the breaking-up of the Prince's court and gone on to serve under James. Unlike me, some of them still have family lands and large estates to provide a comfortable income.

After Wriothesley, I kiss Sir Robert Preston, one of my former dancing partners, still lean and looking younger than his years, who had ridden with Henry in his Accession Day Tilt.

Then I greet Sir William Alexander, Gentleman Extraordinary of the Privy Chamber. And then Lord Sheffield. And Robert Ker of Ancrum.

Our greetings are punctuated by bursts of laughter rising through the floor.

I smile with special warmth at Sir Arthur Gorges, a Devonian now in his fifties, who might as easily have been seventy, with a face as wrinkled and seamed as an old shoe. Naval commander, cousin of Raleigh, and himself a poet, he is rough-edged, tainted by two plots against James, and, like Holles, always ready for a scrap. At St James's, I had liked him and found him always amusing, even when he did not necessarily intend it. A conversation with him could leave you flushed and out of breath like a brisk walk in the cold air.

Sir David Murray, Groom of the Stole and Gentleman of the Bedchamber to Prince Henry, is also older than many of the others, having come down from Scotland with the King when he arrived to claim the throne of England.

Murray takes my hand and holds it while he kisses me. He always had a soft spot for me, and I for him. 'I am indeed overjoyed to see you again, madam!' I can still hear Scottish granite in his voice.

'And I, you,' I reply with equal warmth. 'But please don't say how the years become me.'

He pulls back and studies me as if I have posed a serious question. Then he nods. 'Nothing is as it was. Time spares no one. Nevertheless, you remain beautiful.'

'I dare not call you a liar,' I say. 'But having protested, as I must, I assure you that my pleasure in being flattered is utterly unchanged.'

Looking at their smiling faces, I can almost imagine that we are all back in St James's again, or the queen's court at Denmark House. Donne's 'First Good Angel' or Ben Jonson's 'Morning Star' and her attendant suns. They, with a male freedom denied to me, had ventured out into the wider world of maps and seas then returned to venture with me into the realm of the imagination.

The Queen's court and the Prince's court met in these joint ventures. The two courts shared the playwrights Daniels and Jonson, and the artist Jones, along with the musician, John Dowland, and Salomon de Caus whose gardens strove to be Paradise. Brandishing my pen and my purse, playing battle cries on my lute, dancing in my jewelled shoes, I had led our search for the El Dorado of perfect expression and beauty.

They now vie so gallantly for my attention, smiling and mouthing court words that stroke and soothe me, that I might have thought myself once again to be shining brightly. For a moment, I forget Donne's letter and Turnor, and the reason I suspect that I have been invited here.

Their heads turn to the sound of feet pounding up the stairs. Hands go to swords. Then a woman's laugh and a slammed door raise smiles. Any moment, a bed will begin to creak. I feel them suppressing the coarse jests that my presence prevents.

How much do they feel the change in our circumstances? I wonder. This rowdy, tawdry Southwark inn signals more than a need for secrecy. When we had all been younger, ambitious, hopeful fools, we did not doubt that we had the power to change the world of the mind . . . even I, a mere woman . . . even if the material world, in which men killed each other over Baltic oak and the supremacy of the Pope in Rome, would not bend to our wills. Pursuing Perfection, we made our own joy in the face of unkind circumstance.

The raucous noise from below thumps at the soles of my feet through the floor.

The sharp eyes of old Adam Newton, once tutor to Prince Henry, read my mood. '"A Glimmering light of the Golden times appeared . . ."' He quotes from a sermon preached after Prince Henry's death. '". . . all lines of expectation met in this Centre"'. In Henry. The old tutor has aged badly since I last saw him. 'In whom do the lines of expectation meet now?' he asks, to no apparent point but to absolute purpose.

The death of his royal pupil, and of so much hope, has squeezed the juices out of him. He has shrivelled like the body of a mouse in a dry barn.

'I did not know, sir,' I say, 'that you were a venturer in the Virginia Company.'

'I was never able to sail with His Highness to the Americas. Furthering his wishes for a colony there is the next closest that I can get.'

All the time, at the edge of the group, Holles thrums with impatience.

To my knowledge, there isn't one Papist, either known

or resurrected, among them. And not one attendant. I had seen no waiting men among the guests drinking below, neither. They are undoubtedly here, but keeping their heads down.

'I half-expected to meet Arundel here tonight,' I say, testing.

There is a tiny quiver in the air. 'He had hoped to come,' Wriothesley says. 'He is desolated not to see you again.'

Thomas Howard, Earl of Arundel, is a Catholic. He was the only known Papist in the Prince's court.

The fiddles below begin a reel.

Last of all, with a faint disdain that can be read only by those who know him well, Henry Wriothesley introduces two new faces, two knights who are unknown to me.

'And this is my son,' says the elder of the two, Sir William Sennett, who is a thin man made all of tufts. Tufted beard, tufted hair, tufts of hair growing from his nose and ears. 'Young Sir Walter.'

'Madam, your faithful servant always.' Again, the surprisingly deep voice that should belong to a portly ageing knight. The son blushes and bows. The firelight glows through the rims of his ears as he tangles with sword and cape, taking up far more space in the room than his thin frame merits.

I watch the other men step out of his range. He's one of those people, I think, who spill wine on other people's clothes and tread on other people's toes and are given wide berth for safety's sake.

He untangles himself and looks at me expectantly, waiting for me to acknowledge that we have already met. His father seems to have claimed all the family hair. He is the beardless, blushing youth who brought me the news of Elizabeth's whereabouts.

'Sir.' If, by chance, he likes older women, I decide to

give him something to blush about. I smile into his eyes and set off another dangerous bow.

I catch Wriothesley's faint, cool smile and wonder what the ageing lions of Prince Henry's former court make of this awkward, lank-haired youth. Made-up knights, both of them, says his smile. Father and son. Part of the new Stuart order.

In a more private moment, I will ask Wriothesley if the father, Sir William, had paid the King for a double knighthood at a special wholesale price. Bought a job lot. The question would amuse him.

He might or might not have forgotten that my father was part of this new order, a made-up baron.

But all such men have their uses, no doubt. The Company has already used young Sennett as their running-groom to me.

'And Master Turnor, you know, of course.'

Young Sir Walter shifts his gaze onto Turnor like an eager hound, ready to wag his tail if only Turnor's eye would turn onto him.

I let them lead me closer to the fire. In the absence of attendants, the ageing Scot Sir David Murray stoops to the fire, a little awkwardly, to warm me some spiced wine with the poker.

Wriothesley raises his glass. 'To the return of the Heavens of our Morning Star!'

I smile back. 'I am delighted to see you all again, but I'm certain you didn't call me here to relive the past.'

'But you can help us rewrite the future!' Gorges cries. Old scars stand out white against the scarlet of his sudden passion.

'And so we arrive at the matter with a sudden jolt.' Wriothesley arches his eyebrows at Gorges. 'Before the Countess's wine is cool enough to drink.'

189

'The Countess is right, sir.' Gorges is unabashed. 'We stand here like a gang of gelded dandiprats, kissing and smiling and trying to pretend that England hasn't just been made the laughing stock of Europe! And all Englishmen with her!'

Holles nods. 'True! God save us!' His truculence feels muted in the presence of Gorges.

'Gentlemen,' says Wriothesley. 'Order! I beg you.'

Gorges turns on Wriothesley. 'Before the debacle in Bohemia, you volunteered to fight in Germany on the Protestant side! Where's your stomach gone? Where's the honour in a Hapsburg victory? Where's the honour if England's forced at swordpoint to turn Catholic again?'

'Gorges! Guard your tongue!' Wriothesley's voice has lost any hint of languidness.

'For fear of what I might report?' I ask. 'If you don't trust me, why did you invite me here?' I take the cinnamon stick from my wine mug and suck on it indelicately. Behaving like the old familiar Lucy to reassure them all. The cinnamon makes my lips tingle.

I weigh the warmth of the cup in my hand. Weight and heat, sensed by living flesh. The sensation feels suddenly fragile and beyond price.

This meeting is even more real than the letters I have carried under my bodice. We could all find ourselves kneeling at the block. In the moment before I lost my head, such good company would be small consolation.

'Cecil is dead,' I say. 'To whom would I report now? From the moment Master Turnor arrived at my door, I have assumed that whoever employs him also wrote the letter I took to The Hague.'

Several pairs of eyes slide in his direction.

If I leave now, I think. . . . I might be a little tainted, if any royal agent is watching the Bear, but still with room to argue my innocence. For more convincing innocence, I should have torn up their letter on the ship on the way to the Low Countries and scattered the pieces overboard into the North Sea.

'I ask your pardon.' Wriothesley has recaptured his earlier careless tone. 'We've fallen into the habit of discretion. In truth, we whisper an open secret. Many in England . . . many more men than the small number here . . . are even now raising men and money to send to the aid of the Protestant princes and our princess. And may God speed them better than the others we sent!'

'An earlier force of English volunteers has been wiped out by Tilly's Spanish in the Palatine,' Newton explains. 'I fear that we throw cups of water into the sea.'

I do not want more aid sent to the Protestant princes to prolong Elizabeth's will to fight.

'We have nothing else to throw!' Preston, the tilter, speaks for the first time.

'We must fight with wroth and fire!' cries Sennett senior. 'We must be bold traitors.'

'We speak of England's honour, not of treason.' Wriothesley cools the rising heat by taking the high-backed chair-of-grace at the top of the table. Holles holds a chair for me on the Treasurer's right. Wriothesley becomes a dark profile between me and the fire.

'But which is it? Treason against king or against country?' asks the irrepressible Gorges, brightly lit at the far end of the table. 'The best interests of England and the will of the King are opposed.'

'And that assertion is open treason, sir. Please, sit down.'

Turnor does not join us at the table but sits on a bench by the wall.

There are no papers on the dark red tufted table rug, no agenda for a meeting. The only sign of the purported excuse for this meeting is a shadowy curling map of Cape Henry and Jamestown pinned to the wall beside the door, ignored. They do not even pretend.

Wriothesley follows my eyes. 'The Jamestown colony struggles, as you've no doubt heard. Our present hopes lie on the Continent.' He leans back. 'How did you find the Queen of Bohemia when you were in The Hague?'

'Desperate. But grateful for any message of support. The King claims that her complaints make Doncaster look a fool on the royal peacemaking missions.'

'It's the Spanish who make him a laughing stock!' Gorges rises again to the bait. 'They pretend to listen to his proposals for peace and draw out the marriage nego-tiations merely to gain more time . . . to build up their forces against us.' He glares around the table. 'Doncaster tries to tell the King, but is not believed. Does Buckingham not read the intelligence reports he must get from his agents abroad?'

'Can Buckingham read?' Wriothesley murmurs across Gorges's flow.

'Or perhaps, his agents fear to write what they know he doesn't want to hear.' This is from Holles.

'More likely, Buckingham himself doesn't tell the King what the King doesn't want to know,' offers Ker.

Holles shakes his head, entirely shadowed, with his back to the fire. 'The man's a jumped-up fool! The King could afford to ignore governing while Cecil was still alive to do it for him . . .!'

'. . . Whereas now he still hunts all the time and we've no one speaking and thinking for him but that snake of a male prostitute!' Gorges cuts in again.

I step in. 'As well as your letter, I also carried one from the King.'

Wriothesley inclines his dark profile.

He already knew, I think.

'Did you read it?' asks Gorges.

In the side of my eye, I half-see Turnor re-crossing his legs on his bench.

'And break the royal seal?'

Turnor gives an impatient twitch to say that he would not have had my scruples.

Adam Newton frowns down at the table, not seeming to listen. A narrow quarter moon of firelight shows his lips moving silently.

'Did Her Highness tell you what the King wrote to her?' asks Murray, on my right.

'You don't already know?' The silhouette of Holles again. 'Let me think . . . mmm . . . She's to hold her tongue for fear of angering Spain. "Yer intemperate stirring of sedition, madam, displeases me, blah, blah, blah." We know that her pleas for help have already put him in a rage. She can save her breath. No matter how she begs, the King will not go to war to save her . . . which is why we must.'

'She fears that her father has cast her adrift on the Continent. Saved only by the Christian charity of Prince Maurits.' I have broken the cinnamon stick into curved splinters that now litter the table rug.

'It can hardly be credited,' cries Sir William Sennett from beyond Murray. 'That a princess of England is treated so shamefully!' His son nods and leans to look at Turnor for confirmation.

'At least, she's warm and dry in the Wassenaer Hof, which Maurits has given her as a refuge until her fate is settled.' I brush the cinnamon fragments into my empty glass.

'The lines of expectation . . .' murmurs Newton, as if talking to himself, '. . . now meet in the Princess Elizabeth.'

'May I remind you all that to defy the King's stated wishes in matters of state is treason.' Wriothesley again.

'Every Englishman who is mustering men and arms knows the risk,' Murray says after a moment.

'Don't mince words,' says Holles. 'We're traitors already.'

I now understand Arundel's absence very well. After his family had been tainted more than once with treason, he climbed, with difficulty, back into royal favour.

'Is it not a greater treason to betray England by allowing the Catholics to invade other countries as they please?' Denzil Holles takes over from his father. 'We all know that they'll attack England again as soon as they're sure of their strength.'

'We must be armed with wroth and fire,' repeats Sir Walter Sennett.

'We welcomed that bloody foreigner from Scotland as our king . . .' Holles points his beard across the table at that other bloody foreigner from Scotland, Sir David Murray. '. . . because he was a male monarch with two male heirs – and a daughter to barter in political marriage! But with Prince Henry dead and his sister exiled, we're left with only . . .' He pauses scornfully, unwilling to trouble his tongue to shape the name.

'. . . Charles, who will be married to Spain by his father, if the King has his way, and will turn the country Catholic again.' Gorges finishes the sentence for him.

'The people already hate him for not being his brother.' Preston again, a three-quarter moon on my right, next to Gorges.

'Poor boy,' I venture.

Someone on my left snorts.

'Poor boy or not, the runt of the litter will be our next king.' Gorges's glare dares me to protest.

Wriothesley is sitting back, watching the others. 'Madam, you will observe a divided purpose here.'

'We must strive to send soldiers, and money to pay their wages,' says Murray.

'Elizabeth should be queen of England,' Young Sir Walter Sennett pipes up for the first time, crimson under the eyes turned on him. 'If England needed her, surely, she would come!'

Gorges pounces. 'You're right, young sir. Frederick has lost both Bohemia and the Palatine. He would lose nothing more by becoming king consort in England.' His meaning takes a moment to sink in.

'You go too far, sir!' Bones show white in the bridge of Murray's nose. His lips have a pale rim.

I go cold. 'You don't mean to harm the King or the Prince of Wales?' Even to imagine a monarch's death is treason. To speak of it aloud shoves you up the steps of the scaffold.

'No! I mean no such thing!'

'Then what do you mean? If Frederick is king consort of England . . .?'

Wriothesley cuts me off with a raised hand. 'Gorges, allow me . . .' He leans towards me on his elbows. 'Our first purpose has always been to support the Protestant Union. But the Hapsburgs now have a tight grip on Bohemia. We once hoped to restore Frederick and Elizabeth to the throne. Now we begin to fear that the war will last too long . . . that Her Highness may be taken prisoner before it ends, along with the royal children. Until Charles breeds, those children on the Continent are the only future heirs to the English throne.'

'The Hapsburgs have arrested and condemned to death all the leaders in the so-called "rebellion" against them,' says Gorges. 'Including their candidate for king before Frederick.'

'Mere posturing,' Murray counters quietly. 'They'll never risk the rage the executions would cause. In any case, Maurits will protect Her Highness.'

'If Maurits can.' Gorges goes dark in the face again, showing up the pale scar that interrupts his left eyebrow. 'Spain now sits on his borders after taking the Palatine . . . without a squeak of opposition from the other German princes of the Protestant League.' He makes a noise of disgust. 'And those are the allies we struggle to help!'

'Can the Dutch States fight off both the Austrians and the Spanish to defend the English princess?' I ask.

'More to the point – will they?' demands Denzil Holles. 'What ruler would put his own country at risk to defend a foreign refugee?'

'Maurits once offered to marry the Princess,' Murray protests.

'That means naught! And you should know it!' Preston thumps both hands onto the table. 'The Elector of Brandenburg once entertained her as honoured guest at his *fêtes champêtres*. But turned against her at the first Hapsburg sword shake. Denied her refuge – her husband's own cousin! Sir Richard Weston, ambassador to Prague before the invasion, wrote to me . . .'

'Aye!' Gorges cuts in. 'She had to trick Brandenburg in order to give birth to the new prince under a dry roof, not in a snowdrift!' Rage seemed to spark from his hair and beard. 'Forget Bohemia! Let those cowardly Germans fight it out amongst themselves.'

Newton looks up at us all. 'Once, it was Henry,' he announces, having at last remembered the quote he sought. '. . . whose "magnetique virtue drew all the eyes, and hearts, of the Protestant world".'

All eyes turn to him thoughtfully.

'Now those eyes and hearts turn to Elizabeth,' Newton

196

concludes, bringing the meeting neatly to its crux. 'She is now the centre of the Protestant world.' The sharp old eyes look to see that his pupils understand.

'Agreed. I say, bring her home!' says Gorges. 'It would be best for England and for all Protestants.'

'The King himself told me that he doesn't want her home,' I say.

'Then we must teach the King a reason to want it.'

'Wroth and fire, I say!' Sennett slaps the table.

'There is no treachery in bringing her home to safety.' Holles. His son nods.

Tick, tock, tick, tock. Jonson could have written their smooth exchange in one of his plays. I look from one face to another. They have argued this many times before, whether to rescue or to fight.

In the side of my eye, the dark heavy lump of Turnor sits apart on his bench, weighing down one corner of the delicate fabric being spun as I listen.

'But what does Her Highness want?' Wriothesley, too, has been watching and listening. 'She writes to us all with the gallant courage we expect from her. But what do you think, madam, having seen her? As a woman who was an intimate of the royal family?'

I feel the sudden stillness around me and know why I have been brought here. My answer to this question is the pivot on which the future is balanced. Turnor catches the light as he leans forward on his bench.

'How do you judge her true feelings and wishes?' asks Wriothesley. 'Does Her Highness believe that the war on the Continent can be won? What does she wish us to do?'

All I have to do is speak the truth.

'You may read for yourselves.' I give Holles the letter addressed to him. He passes it to Wriothesley.

'In speaking, she was as gallant as I suspect she proves

197

in her writing. But she confessed to me that she fears the war cannot be won. Their allies desert. The Hapsburgs are too powerful and surround the Protestant forces. Frederick is in despair. If she were a different woman, I believe that she would be afraid.'

Wriothesley nods as he reads, holding the paper to catch the firelight.

No more than a small revision.

I do not harm her. She had confessed her fear. I had felt it and acted now to spare her unneeded suffering, perhaps even the loss of Frederick in battle. I improve the ending. I will save her, and her family, whether or not she will admit that she wants saving.

I watch Preston read next. Then Murray puts on a pair of spectacles and reads.

'She will never admit it,' I say. 'We all know her too well. Her letter will be filled with determination and courage.'

'We expect no less from her,' says Alexander. He holds out his hand next for the letter.

'But I believe that our princess secretly wants to come home.'

It is done.

I can offer only my belief, I tell myself. Never certainty. We can only ever surmise the secret mind of others. Even their words cannot be entirely trusted.

'I vowed to help her if I could.'

'There it is!' says Gorges, shaking the paper now in his hand. 'It's plain as the nose on your face what we must do.'

I know that I have won, even before Wriothesley speaks.

'We are already resolved to do as Her Highness asks here,' he says. 'To muster men and raise funds to defray the costs of war. But I think we must also heed what the

198

Countess tells us. Whilst we remain resolved to defeat the forces of Rome and restore the deposed Frederick and Elizabeth to both Bohemia and the Palatine, we must decide whether or not our princess is safe, being so close across the Dutch border to hostile forces.' He watches the letter passing from hand to hand. 'Do you truly believe, madam, that Her Highness wishes to return to England?'

'How can she wish it openly? When her husband still stays to fight? But I know that she fears.' This version of the truth grows easier with repetition.

'Bring her back to England,' says Gorges. 'There's no risk here. If the German princes ever beat back the Hapsburgs, she can return to Bohemia.'

'Though I've disagreed in the past, I'm now of your opinion, Gorges.' Wriothesley looks around the table. 'The Countess has persuaded me. Who else would bring her back?'

Preston shakes his head. 'I won't defy the King so far. Have never agreed, never will.'

'You dive into dangerous waters.' Murray removes his spectacles and folds them with great care. 'You don't know the King as I do. It's risky to presume how he might respond.'

'We note your warning,' says Wriothesley. 'Although I believe that some of us have already tasted his anger under threat, whether imagined or otherwise.' He looks around the table. 'Is anyone else of Murray's opinion? No? Who would bring Her Highness back?'

I watch the nods and raising of hands. Including Turnor on his bench by the wall.

'Then perhaps Sir Arthur would like to tell how we might set about persuading the King.'

Gorges looks startled to find himself suddenly without opposition. He clears his throat. 'The deposed Queen of

199

Bohemia is second in line to the throne of England. If anything should happen to her younger brother . . .' In spite of the clamour in the inn below us, he drops his voice. '. . . King James is reduced from three certain heirs to one. The weakest one. The one least loved by the people. If the King saw a danger to Charles, that single remaining heir, His Majesty might also see the need to protect his daughter.'

I shove my chair back from the table and rise to my feet. 'I vowed to help Elizabeth home, not to murder her brother!'

Chair legs scrape and clothing rustles as they stand with me.

'How can you even think it? It would destroy the Princess to lose two brothers. You are false, dangerous friends! Pray, excuse me!'

'Madam, wait!' Again, as when he had snapped at Gorges, I see the Wriothesley once given to passionate causes and brawling, who had been saved again and again by his friend and patron, Robert Cecil. 'Remember your vow to the Princess. We all want the same end. Please continue, Sir Arthur.'

'I swear that we will not harm the Prince in truth, madam, merely in seeming. A harmless sham, a toothless threat, but real enough in seeming to make the King grasp how fragile the succession has become.'

We stand in an awkward circle, caught between table and chairs. Then Murray steps away from the table. 'I will not listen further. And I pray that this remains talk only.'

We listen to the door close behind him and his feet receding down the stairs.

'Will you at least hear me out, madam?' asks Gorges.

'To be brutal . . .' says Holles, '. . . you need our help to fulfil your vow.'

'But why do you need mine?'

'We need you to grow close to the Prince of Wales,' says Wriothesley.

'But the Prince hates me! I always took his sister's part, was in his brother's court, and the Queen's. I was never part of the King's court nor that of Prince Charles.'

'That was many years ago.' Turnor speaks unexpectedly. He moves away from the wall into the firelight. He is suddenly moulded into a solid shape by highlights and shadows. 'Prince Charles may have adulation now and obsequious flattery, but ever since his mother died and he outgrew his nurse, he has lacked a woman's soft sympathy.'

'Isn't Lord Buckingham woman enough?' Wriothesley pulls at a lace cuff.

'Only for the King,' says Turnor. 'Buckingham is the Prince's rival for the King's love, wants to replace Prince Henry in the hearts of both King and Prince.'

None of the men interrupts or contradicts him. I feel heads nodding around me. I begin to think that I might have misjudged the part Turnor plays in the group.

My opinion of him grows, along with my wariness.

'Buckingham bullies the Prince like an older brother,' Turnor continues. 'Soft sympathy from the Marquess? I think not! Why do you suppose the Prince has so many dogs?'

'I'm to serve as another of his dogs?' I ask. 'As a soft, sympathetic bitch?'

The men around the table look startled.

'Turnor! For shame!' says Wriothesley, quicker than the others.

'Madam, forgive me.' Turnor sounds more amused than penitent. 'I did not mean . . .'

Gorges interrupts, his white beard trembling with emotion.

'We all want the same thing, madam. And we put our faith in your "learned and manly soul", as Master Jonson once put it. You are a fellow soldier, but armed with different weapons.'

'Please sit down again,' says Wriothesley.

I look after the departed Murray.

'He doesn't hate you, madam!' Newton again, Prince Henry's old tutor. 'He fears you and your scorn. You are a court wit . . .'

'Was . . .' I murmur.

'. . . Prince Henry and his sister may have been your friends,' he persists. 'But you were the chief favourite of Prince Charles's mother. You've spent enough time among that family to understand the power this gives you with her son.'

By chance or cunning, amongst all the other flattery, Gorges has hit upon the one piece that secretly pleased me. My 'learned and manly soul'. I hesitate a moment longer, then sit down again.

'What sham do you intend?' With that question, I cross a line. They know it too. I feel their tension ease a notch as they settle back onto their stools and chairs.

In the silence, the sound of rhythmic clapping accompanies the reel beneath our feet.

'A false accident, perhaps during exercise.' Turnor stays on his feet, taking over from Gorges. 'Followed by a heroic rescue. No harm done to the Prince . . . it might even win him popular sympathy.'

'An accident to remind the King that his last son is as mortal as the first proved to be.' Gorges again.

'All of us except Master Turnor are tainted in the Prince's eyes by our love for his brother,' says Wriothesley. 'Whereas you've been away from court since the Queen died. You no longer have clear alliances. You share His

Highness's passion for collecting and can help satisfy his hunger to acquire. You know how to charm. You'll have no difficulty in gaining his trust and access.'

'And once I have gained those?'

'You can tell us where and when he is to be found, what exercise he takes, where he most often walks or hunts. You might even suggest to him . . .'

'How long have you been planning this for me? You might have consulted me sooner about my own script!'

'Most vitally,' says Holles, 'you will become the patron of Master Turnor, in his other guise as playwright and poet.'

I look at Turnor.

'Yes, madam,' Turnor says drily. 'And I have manuscripts to prove it.'

Those 'execrable verses', I think. Real after all.

'After a time . . .' Wriothesley turns onto Holles a look I cannot see. '. . . you will introduce Turnor into the Prince's court. From tonight, for your own safety, you had best cut yourself off from us and speak to us only through him. Helping us shape an accident that will harm no one, including ourselves.'

Holles juts his beard at me. 'I assure you, madam, we're soldiers, not martyrs.'

'You've always been one of us.' Wriothesley looks at the other men for confirmation. 'We have always counted you as an ally.'

I feel a twitch of irritation. He must see that such flattery is no longer needed. He crosses his arms and leans back in his char. 'You must admit that the scheme has an elegant innocence.'

'A seeming accident.' A rescue.

These are men of consequence, used to command. They make the air glow with their confident words of doing and happening.

'An elegant innocence.' How cleverly he chooses his words.

I won't be caught by mere words. There's nothing innocent about what they mean to do. But I would not be conniving to spread war, after all, but helping to preserve the English peace.

A feigned accident . . . a scripted rescue.

I try to imagine the reality.

The venture does not feel so very different from writing or performing in a masque – a masque to act on the King's mind, like Prince Hamlet's play to catch the conscience of the king.

Perhaps.

'It is still an attack on the Prince,' I say. 'I don't see the King appreciating the fine distinction between sham and real.'

'That's why we must take care to find circumstances unlike any other attack,' says Gorges. 'No cut girth. No accidental arrow while hunting. We must find circumstances that are safe but appear dangerous. That's why we need you.'

'Will Murray betray you?'

'I think not . . .' Wriothesley considers the question as he speaks. 'He's with us in wanting to protect the Princess. And left before his conscience could be burdened too far.'

I face Turnor. 'Why did Doctor Donne write you a letter of introduction to me?'

If I had thought he would answer me straight, I would have asked Wriothesley whether Doctor Donne was still a friend, as wild Jack Donne had once been. 'Did you or anyone here ask Donne to write that letter?'

'He wrote because I told him I was in need of a patron in England,' says Turnor.

I do not believe him.

Wriothesley does not answer me.

They must think me a fool after all.

If Donne were not working with them, he was working for the King. It seems very likely to me that Donne, rejected as Company secretary, was building another upward step for himself by working for the King, against us all.

'Doctor Donne is not with you in this?'

'The Dean of Paul's knows nothing of what has been said here today,' says Wriothesley. 'He does not concern us.'

I hear their words. I feel a deeper, colder current flowing underneath, but I want to believe the promise in their words.

If they succeeded, with my help, James would bring Elizabeth home. Elizabeth would be safe. I would be reunited with my friend . . . my almost daughter.

She would form a new court from her loyal friends. We would once again dance and sing and share laughter. I would play midwife to poetry and music, again put on a veil and scarlet feather. Jewelled shoes would turn my steps into a trail of fire.

She would give me the right to grant commissions, licences and favours, and to collect the fees. I would again have power to make money, to pay our debts. Replace my sold jewels. I might even buy back the lease of my house and garden in Twickenham.

I would be needed.

I try to imagine John Donne betraying me. He had broken my heart, but I had willed the end as much as he.

I cannot not see him betraying me.

Even for ambition?

Out of my thoughts! Go! I tell him.

But enemy or friend, he will not be banished. He is still a poet. I had heard the poet still alive in his sermon. At the very least, he would see me again offering bounty and inspiration to court poets. To men who lacked his talent. He would burn with jealousy in his pulpit. He would envy . . .

Ignoble creature! I berate myself, scarcely hearing the farewells of my fellow plotters around me.

Ignoble thoughts! Childish and revengeful when you mean only to do good. But, as I have said, our thoughts and actions are seldom pure.

# PART TWO

# 29

## LUCY – LONDON, 1621

Why wait to do a thing you dislike? Prince Charles is my quarry. The soft bitch will sniff him out.

At this time, the Prince of Wales is in residence at Richmond. Buckingham stays in London with the King.

I do not need to see Villiers again to know what he would say, if he deigned to speak to me at all. I write to the Prince, direct. Buckingham will not like it, but he does not yet rule the Prince as he does the King.

These bloody Stuarts, I think as I wipe the ink from my pen. A dead heir who might or might not have been poisoned, if popular rumour could be believed. A king who acquiesced to the execution of his own mother and fears his own children. What hope can there be for the surviving son?

I can hear Buckingham now: 'The Prince does not want his sister back in England. Are you mad, pleading to him for his greatest rival? Would you make an enemy of our next King?'

But I promised Elizabeth that I would speak to her brother.

Three days later, on a damp grey morning, I take a public wherry up the Thames to Richmond. As we travel upstream, the day suddenly recalls that it is early summer and turns unexpectedly benign. The sun stretches like a late sleeper and beams on us through the large gaps appearing in the clouds.

My humour does not match the change in the day. My body feels tight. I am not so certain of my success as my venturer friends are. I once knew well enough how to play the courtier, but while serving the queen, and attending on Henry and Elizabeth, I grew soft and lazy. My ambition and my heart had agreed. I found at least some amusement in most people and truly disliked very few. I even enjoyed occasional battles of wits with the King when the humour took him. Safe inside the bubble of the Queen's court and protected by her love, I had, for the most part, ignored the under-size, sullen boy who worshipped Henry and plagued his sister, Elizabeth, and whom I now must charm.

You'll pay now for any earlier disregard! I look down into the twisting braids of dark water that flow out from the boat. My fingers touch the package that I hope will be my weapon of last resort.

Our keel slides over the quivering ghosts of other boats making other journeys up the Thames to Richmond Palace, when Prince Henry still lived. We pass my parents' former house at Kew, where they moved from Combe to keep an eye on their royal charge at Whitehall.

In the corner of my eye, I seem to glimpse Elizabeth in my father's garden there.

Go away! Please! Just for now. I need to keep my vision clear and my aim fixed on Charles.

Stubbornly, she leans back on her hands on a stone bench and blows a lock of unruly red Scottish hair out of her eyes. Not yet a distant foreign queen and mother, she is plotting how next to alarm my poor parents who were so weighed down by official care of her.

I am suddenly hollow with missing her.

I watch the bank slide past. Both my father and mother are dead. And she is far away, a refugee sheltering from Hapsburg armies.

I imagine a flash of gown through the trees on the riverbank, Elizabeth walking from Kew to Richmond Palace to see her beloved Henry. The fair, noble warrior and king-to-be. The perfect Protestant knight with his army of trained gentlemen around him.

Brother and sister had ridden into London like a pair of angels. The crowds roared and flung their hats into the air. They threw posies like a blizzard of coloured snow at these miraculous, beautiful, Scottish royal children who now belonged to them.

'Mark those two,' my mother had said to me. 'They will be the making of us. And of England.'

A gull swoops, folds its wings and lands, just-so, on the prow of the boat. Once, that instant of perfection would have made my heart want to burst with the clean pure delight of childhood, when each moment arrived fresh and peeled raw. Smelling, sounding, tasting only of itself. Now, every experience feels clouded with shadows of an earlier time, the future shaded with a new unease.

We round a wide, generous bend. On my right, on the Twickenham bank, I see the wall of the garden I had made and where John had read his poems to me. Twickenham Park. Sacrificed to debt. Through the trees glints my little waterfall, John's 'stone fountain weeping out my year', described by him even before I'd had it built.

If Bacon, who bought the lease from me, should be convicted of corruption, someone else would walk there on the paths I had laid, among my trees. Someone else would lie on our bank above the stream.

The opposite shore is no kinder to my thoughts. A delicate fantasy of onion domes, fluted towers and wavering reflections is doubled by the river. Richmond Palace. Prince Henry's palace.

He rowed against the outgoing tide. With his boat pointed upstream, Henry matched his mortal strength against the pull of the sea. His boat hung stationary in the water, his power matching that of the Thames in a perfect balance between Nature and man. His boatman sat in the stern as he did every day when the Prince took this exercise, even though his presence was unneeded. On the shore, I stood with the Prince's retinue, watching the golden head and smooth-working shoulders of our future king.

A thought nudges. It dives again, disappears like a coot. When I try to look straight at it, it had never been there at all. Then I think I see Henry's sleek fair head among the jagged shards of sunlight bouncing off the water, swimming in the Thames as he often did, both here and at Whitehall.

He had gripped the stone edge of Crane Wharf just below the palace and swung himself up, easily, laughing and shaking off water like a dog. He palmed the water from his eyes and sighed in pure pleasure. And the rest of us sighed at his beauty and the thought of one day being ruled by such a king.

The nudging thought almost pops up again, then vanishes without breaking the surface.

What I do think: if Henry had been king, the Hapsburgs

would not have dared to attack Bohemia where his sister was queen. Had he not died, he would already, though still only Prince of Wales, have gathered his Protestant knights, defied the King and been at war on the Continent, fighting for his sister and the Protestant cause.

I take the boatman's steadying hand and step onto the slippery water stairs. I am no longer a privileged friend, merely a humble petitioner to another Prince of Wales. Poor tongue-tied, bandy-legged Baby Charles, who had once trailed after his older brother and sister like a tiresome puppy. And who later eyed my breasts and turned scarlet when I smiled at him. Now he is heir to the throne of England. If Henry had lived, I would not be here, stalking this younger brother with a treacherous heart.

I look up at the double-tiered onion domes with the wrong colours snapping on their flag poles. I shake my skirts and tweak my lace cuffs back into orderly pleats. I was once the closest companion to England's dead queen, welcomed by her older son, heart-sister to her daughter. Surely I can manage her youngest pup.

The heavy door of the river entrance opens.

My mother would not have flinched. Help me! I beg her severe, implacable little ghost.

See where it lies and ride towards it, her voice murmurs up from the water that slaps delicately against the weed-covered steps behind me.

But my seat has been unsteadied. In spite of every charm I raise against him, my husband, and exile, have diminished me. And I do not like my present purpose.

# 30

The spaces inside the palace are both known and strange at the same time, like the distortions of a dream. Following a waiting gentleman through familiar hallways, I pass unfamiliar paintings of life-like fruits and flowers. I am watched by the marble pinhole eyes of unfamiliar gods and Roman generals. Strange new shepherds and sheep wander across bright new tapestries from Mortlake. We pass through a new pair of gilded Italian doors.

In the short distance from the water gate, I have already decided that rumours Kit brought me about Prince Charles are accurate.

'The Prince,' Kit had reported over an evening pipe, 'is said to care more for art than for politics.' His voice betrayed his disbelief at such a preference in a king-to-be. 'And vies with other collectors to increase the great collection left to him by his older brother.'

Looking about me now as I walk through Richmond Palace, I see that, as a collector if not as a soldier, the new Prince of Wales can hope to match the old one.

A marble nymph offers me marble anemones. A stern bronze Roman bust glares at me across the tiled floor.

My humour lightens. I share the Prince's taste for art. I may find that we share a true bond, like the one I had shared with his mother.

I see us together, the runt grown in stature and dignity, turned king-in-the-making. And I, a kindly, still lovely older woman, with a good eye and bold tongue for a bargain, who could advise him . . . He would never be his brother, but . . . We share wine. Admire his collection. He danced beautifully as a small boy. The near-man had now added other graces . . .

A dog whining outside the further door wags its tail when it sees us coming and paws at the door panelling.

I see the scene on the far side of the door . . . I speak to the Prince openly . . . He agrees to ask the King to bring his sister back to England. And in doing so, he spares both of us having to go through with the sham intended by the venturers.

Revise . . . Even better, I take him into my confidence. The Prince understands the necessity and volunteers to act his part in the mummery, in order to persuade the King to bring his sister home.

I enter the Great Hall. At the far end of the hall, beyond groups of courtiers, a comical manikin sits in Henry's chair.

Reality.

I waver between the opposing dangers of too much respect and not enough. I read the sulky droop of his shoulders and decide on a deep, formal reverence.

'Your Highness.' I rise to meet a pair of hostile, pale, suspicious eyes, alert for any sign of mockery.

Charles Stuart, Prince of Wales, the runt of the royal litter whom no one expected to survive past babyhood, is still undersized at the age of eighteen. Years have not increased his dignity. Raised above me on the dais under a new red velvet canopy, he perches uneasily at the front of the gilded royal chair, his toes stretching down to reach the floor. His face is still thin, his hair sparse and fine. He still looks eight years old in spite of an attempted moustache.

'Why did you ask to see me?' He touches his upper lip as if feeling my gaze on it. The huddled courtiers eye me curiously, but none are close enough to listen. Several dogs lie curled on the dais like random rugs.

'Sir . . .' I feel my way. 'I am lately returned from The Hague . . .'

'I am aware of your journey.' He looks around as if for Buckingham, tightens his mouth and grips the carved lion heads on the ends of the chair arms. His eyes already droop at the outer corner like those of an old man, anticipating life's disappointments before their full weight can descend.

Looking at his clamped mouth, I decide against the brief, comical anecdote I had prepared about the great storm that tossed us about on our voyage back. And how we had feared for our lives almost as much as for our dignity as we leaned, lords and grooms alike, spewing over the gunwales. Elizabeth would have relished it.

'Your sister, the Queen of Bohemia, sends you her faithful love and wishes for Your Grace's good health . . .'

'She is no longer the queen of Bohemia,' he interrupts. 'Nor the Electress Palatine.'

'So she fears . . . if there is no aid from England.'

'There will be no aid from England.' He clutches the chair arms more tightly. His pointed chin jerks up in defiance. Clearly, he thinks I will dislike his news. His eyes move as if searching again for the absent Buckingham.

'Has the King decided so absolutely?'

'Did he not tell you so himself?'

He is old enough to have his own spies, then. In spite

216

of his slightly comical appearance, I must not underestimate him. This is no longer the old Baby Charles.

'I daresay that Your Highness has opinions of his own.'

There is a flicker in the pale eyes. His thumb and forefinger smooth the infant moustache. But if I had hoped to provoke a show of independence, I am to be disappointed.

'The King, my father, will not permit the Princess and her German Protestant husband to ruin my chances of making a marriage with Spain. Buckingham agrees. She must not be allowed to ruin England's chance to gain the Spanish as firm allies, at last.'

'Sir.' I drop my head in seeming agreement. So much for brotherly love. The Virginia Company venturers had been right. It is unanimous – King, Buckingham, and the heir to the throne. If she remains abroad, Elizabeth must survive without England.

'Did she commission you to beg me for help?' he asks.

'She would value your thoughts,' I reply truthfully enough.

He looks gratified.

'Could she not return . . .' I begin.

'. . . to England?' His voice is incredulous. 'You believe that she should return to England?'

I recognise the rising notes of his childhood rage.

'She chose to leave us and become German,' he says. 'The Princess no longer belongs to England.'

Buckingham's words, almost exactly.

'Forgive my presumption, sir,' I venture. 'But does Reason not advise that there might be a risk in leaving the Princess on the Continent?'

'Risk?' he asks coldly.

'As a rallying point for the Protestant cause. A loose cannon.' At my most courtier-like, I have never before dissembled from so deep in my heart. 'Surely, it would be more politic to have her here in England, under your eye. Here, where she could be more easily controlled.' I shrug, dismissing her.

'Controlled by whom?'

'You hit it exactly, sir. Left on the Continent, she remains vulnerable to hostile influences . . . a target for England's enemies. A good prize, the second in line for the English throne . . .'

'I fear that she would be first!'

'She has never seemed so ambitious.'

'Because you're a foolish, ignorant female whose wits are dulled by life in the country. You don't understand. The people are ambitious for her. She'd be even more dangerous here in England than abroad. If she were here, the people might rise up in her favour as some threatened to do with Henry, to put him on the throne instead of our father.'

'A few reckless fools . . .'

'Buckingham says that I must not risk bringing her home, Spanish marriage apart. I would sooner die than bring her back!'

'Sir.' I curtsy again.

There it is. He has made my choice for me. On with the mummery. Without costumes or music but mummery nonetheless.

I cannot imagine that the Prince will enjoy the experience, whatever it proves to be. Praise God, he does not risk death, merely indignity. Meanwhile, my part is to charm when I no longer feel charming. Nor inclined to do so.

I will need my last-resort weapon after all. I suppress a deep sigh of regret.

'Sir,' I say. 'Forgive me if I've angered you with idle questions. They were not my purpose in coming here.'

'I hope your true purpose pleases me better.' He whistles for one of his miniature spaniels. 'Good girl,' he croons when it jumps onto his lap. He begins to scratch its head as if I were not there. Then he turns over one floppy ear and examines it for ticks.

'The . . .' I choose the safer way. '. . . your sister commissioned me to bring you a Holbein drawing.'

He looks up, eyes unguarded for the first time. 'A Holbein?' The great Flemish master, painter of royalty and now dead. 'Where is it?'

'Waiting under guard by the river entrance, still wrapped against the voyage.'

I had hoped to leave it there. If the Prince had shown any sign of weakening towards his sister, or if I believed there was the least chance of bringing her home without the stratagem of the false accident, I would have taken it back to London with me.

I had bought it from an old nobleman in a damp palace in The Hague. Another button gone.

I am yours, it had whispered. You know that I am already yours. To leave me here now is to abandon me. I could not imagine the world without that drawing. I could not afford it, but my heart had to have it.

It gives me joy each time I look at it. Its presence glows in my awareness even when I do not look at it. It gives me delight as little else has done for months. I brought it here with me reluctantly but had seen no other way to carry out my purpose. Elizabeth didn't know that it existed.

'Send for it at once! I will see it here.' He pushes the dog off his lap. 'What is the artist's subject?' He does not ask how his sister had managed to salvage a Holbein drawing while in flight with scarcely more than her children and clothes. And dogs. He calls for wine.

219

Nor does he ask why she might send it to a brother who has disclaimed her.

'It's a study for the betrothal portrait on wood of Anne of Cleves, already in . . .' I almost say *your brother's* but correct myself in time: '. . . in Your Highness's collection. I thought it best to wait until you instructed me where to send it.'

When the wine arrives, Charles takes a lugged Venetian glass goblet and nods graciously to me to take one as well. He hands his glass to his taster. The man sniffs, then takes a careful sip and swills the wine around his mouth. I imagine a distant, fearsome drum roll. He swallows.

In the brief pause that follows, I see him shrieking, clutching his belly . . . his throat . . . dying.

Who knows better than I do that there is good reason to take care? With Henry gone, Charles has become the second most important male in England.

The taster nods, wipes the rim of the glass with a napkin and hands the glass to the Prince.

While we wait for the picture to arrive from where I had left it, I count ten men-at-arms ranged along the wall. It strikes me that an apparent accident will be as hard to arrange as a true one. Why should a mummery be any easier than a real attempt on his life? The Prince is surrounded always by waiting gentlemen, guards and serving men.

Charles catches me counting and eyes me suspiciously from behind his glass. I am still an enemy, though perhaps improving. In spite of the promised drawing, his eyes still hold a sulky wariness.

Suddenly, heir to the throne or not, he looks very young and very vulnerable. Mouthing the words of his elders. Still afraid to challenge the fully grown men around him. He must feel the weight of expectation pressing down on him, as Henry had done, but he lacks entirely his older brother's courage and grace.

I look away, lest my thoughts show in my eyes. He must know how far short of his brother he falls in the popular opinion.

To my surprise, I feel a twist of pity.

The drawing arrives. I unwrap it carefully, grieving already for its loss. The tranquil face of a former queen gazes at me out of the frame, looking at being the price of the trust and goodwill of the next king of England.

I hold her up.

Farewell.

The Prince snatches the drawing from my hands, banishing my earlier compassion. 'Oh, yes,' he breathes. For the first time that I can remember, he looks happy.

I watch him for a moment then gaze under lowered lids at the other paintings and statues in the Great Hall. All of them are as unfamiliar as the ones in the passage-ways. I need not have worried. It does not matter after all that I am a mature woman. This prince would not care that I am still considered beautiful even so. I have guessed what beauty truly moves him.

He props the Holbein drawing against the back of his chair. We stand side by side for a moment, just as I had imagined, studying the delicate grey lines that magically conjure up a dead, German princess. Her finely drawn face floats in a sea of delicate lines that only hint at the details of her coif, jewels and gown.

'It's beautiful,' he says softly. 'Even more beautiful for not being finished. We see the woman, not her gown.'

'Your Highness looks with an understanding eye.'

After a moment, as if diffidently, I throw up my next lure. 'I've seen a fine double portrait of your grandfather with a youthful friend. In a house in Bedfordshire.'

I do not say that this house belongs to my husband's family.

The Prince looks away from the gentle smile of Anne of Cleves. 'By whom?'

'I can soon learn the artist's name.' I tilt my head to study the drawing. 'I must do so quickly, however. I hear rumours that the Earl of Arundel has been sniffing after it.'

Indeed, he might well be. I give a quick prayer of thanks to quicksilver Rumour, so hard to prove or disprove.

Thomas Howard, Earl of Arundel, who had not attended the meeting of the Virginia Company, had been the only Catholic in Prince Henry's inner circle. He had travelled to Italy with Inigo Jones when the painter was still Henry's surveyor. From his tour of Roman temples, galleries and ruins, Howard had returned with a passion for all things Classical, determined to bring both the vision and the objects to England. Before the Prince died, he and Howard had competed to be England's most avid collector of art.

'Arundel must not lay his hands on a portrait of my family,' says Charles. 'The royal collection must have it.'

In spite of Sir Kit's reports over a pipe in my parlour, I had not guessed at the deep hunger to acquire that the Prince's voice now betrays.

I leave him sitting in his chair again, gazing at the drawing as if the rest of the world had disappeared, leaving only the hungry beams of his eyes and the tranquil miracle of lines between his hands.

The smiling marble nymphs, victorious Roman generals and painted kings watch my retreat. I understand the Prince's passion. I share it. But I am not fated to govern a country.

If fate had lusted for a royal sacrifice, Charles should

have died, not Henry, I think with a heavy heart. Better for England, for Elizabeth, for all of us.

I look quickly around me, as if this dangerous, private thought were booming around the high, ornate ceiling and echoing from the gilded panelling. But my escort never falters. Passing minions ignore me. Only one, very young, groom with a bucket of coal sketches a hasty bow.

The waiting gentleman closes the palace door behind me. His lack of ceremony tells me how low I had fallen.

That will change.

I should have felt triumph. Instead, I feel confused. My belly cramps as I ride back down the Thames. I want to wrap my arms around myself and curl up like a grub in the bottom of the boat. Instead, I brace myself upright in my corset and point my eyes ahead, down the midline of the river. I do not look left at my Twickenham garden, though the side of my eye catches the shifting leaves of my growing beech avenue. I do not look at my parents' former house in Kew.

I want to be sick. The gentle surge of the barge with each stroke of the oars becomes the tossing of sea waves. I cannot fix my eye. My life with Edward at Moor Park sucks me back down like the bottom of the sea. I have merely imagined that I might escape.

But you have succeeded, says my mother's voice. In this first step at least. You've stirred the Prince's lust for that painting. He begins to trust you. What ails you?

I've won the dubious privilege, I reply, of becoming a prying, invasive agent for a Prince of Wales I do not respect. To search for beauty that I will discover, love and lose. To abuse a thing that truly matters to me by using it to deceive.

Then don't deceive! Where's your ambition, my girl?

retorts my mother. And your Reason? A prince is even better than a princess. Forget those dangerous Protestant nobles and knights. Stop struggling. Accept the world as it is. Insinuate yourself into his court. Align yourself with him. You could do worse than the next king.

Align with Charles? And Buckingham?

My mouth tastes of tarnished silver.

I look up at the sky. Mother, I am a counterfeit of my former self. I'm no longer the daughter you raised.

I think you're afraid, she says scornfully.

Empty, I say.

I close my eyes. Affection. Love. Once they had been mere words, a little false, a poet's building blocks. 'Affection' and 'love' – a dancing amphibrach and a severe, one-footed full stop. I had secretly curled my lip and believed that poets exaggerated for effect.

I remember the leap of true understanding from one mind to another. The wordless but inarguable truth passed from one skin to another. The solid essence at the centre of my being. My anchor. Without love and affection, I am a floating husk empty of meaning.

How long could I go on living as a husk? Even if it meant that I could be at court again.

True ambition cannot afford a heart. Therefore, I have lost true ambition.

Warm tears begin to run down my face, overflowing from a mysterious, unexpected spring. Startled, uncomprehending, I let them flow, whether the boatmen see or not.

The breeze cools the water on my cheeks. Once I would have smiled brightly and hidden my true feelings. I had wiped away the tears of others and not burdened them with my own tedious sorrows. But I cannot stop these tears.

They continue to flow as we pass the opening of the Brent into the Thames. Then the River Crane, the Efra, the Tyburn. When we reach the outflow of the Wandle in the Surrey bank above Lambeth, my inner poet begins, wryly, to observe the irresistible watery metaphor. Self-awareness and control reassert themselves. The mysterious, overflowing truth retreats like a prodded snail, back into hiding. I feel poised, like the river at the turn of the tide, trembling in stillness between going one way and another.

I write to the venturers in our agreed cipher, reporting on my progress with the Prince. I mention the elusive thought that had nudged at me on my journey to Richmond. It had resurfaced into my awareness on the journey back to London, as the wherry again slid past Crane Wharf. A possible shape for the Prince's sham accident. The Prince emulated his dead brother but was far less able at almost everything.

Kit delivers the letter for me to Turnor at his lodgings among the tenements of the old Savoy.

'A strange choice for a gentleman,' he says when he returns. 'Surrounded by beggars, debtors and rogues. I wouldn't let my wife go there alone.'

'I wouldn't trust her in Turnor's care, neither.' I shut out my own memories of the Savoy and offer him a filled tobacco pipe. 'What do you make of the man now that you've seen him face-to-face?'

We sit by the fire in the little parlour overlooking the dark garden. Kit inhales thoughtfully. 'He was civil enough to someone he thought was a serving man. In a brawl, I'd want him on my side.'

'Why do you say, "brawl"?'

'I don't think he fights by the rules.'

225

I blow out a double smoke ring. Then poke a finger through the second. 'Neither do I.'

Lodgings in the Savoy are as ambiguous as Turnor himself. The old hospital had fallen into ruin, then been partly reclaimed to house paupers, students, pensioners, scholars and poets. Or, in this case, a minor playwright and execrable poet. Rooms there were more than modest. I knew them far better than I should.

At the same time, the lodgings lie close to Bacon's York House and to the big houses on the Thames of the Cecils, the Howards and other powerful men. In the Savoy, Turnor has quick access to the freedom of the river. He is near the Royal Mews, the Jewel House, and Whitehall itself. A short wherry ride will take him across the Thames to the top of Bankside and Southwark. In the Savoy, he has a base suited for quick action in many directions and a warren of single rooms, larger lodgings, and dormitories in which it would be easy to lose himself.

He is also very close to Bedford House. I feel him watching me from across the Strand, even here in the little parlour, where he would have to be hidden behind a ball of clipped box.

'I think he was praying when I arrived,' says Kit.

'I can't imagine him on his knees, even to God.'

'Or perhaps just reading a Bible. I'm certain I saw an open Bible on his table.' He taps the dottle out of his pipe on the sole of his boot. '. . . a fat book, in any case.' He gives me a half-smile to mock his own lack of learning. 'I am absolutely certain, madam, that it was a book.'

'If it was a Roman Missal, we're all in trouble.'

Kit opens his mouth to say something more, but closes it again. I don't press him. He advances at his own pace in our long but still-growing friendship.

Then, falling asleep that night, I suddenly see the

rightness of Kit's piece of information. Whether or not he had been praying, Turnor has the implacability of certain Puritan clerics, a cold fire too chilly to be called fervour.

To complicate my unease, I must give Turnor bad news. I have failed to insert him into the court. Neither the Prince of Wales nor Lord Buckingham had been impressed by his verse. I had, myself, refused to commission enough poor poets to know the bitterness I will cause in him if his fervour is born from poetic ambition rather than policy.

I delay.

# 31

I would like to cross out with dark, wide lines my visit to Woburn Abbey in Bedfordshire, home to Cistercian monks until their abbot was convicted of treason and hanged from a local oak. It was given to my husband's family, the Russells, by Edward VI in 1547, three years before John Russell was created the First Earl of Bedford for diplomatic services to Henry VIII. In late summer, the ignoble, low-born wife of the damaged, disappointing, penniless and heirless Third Earl, humiliates herself by begging from the wall a double portrait identified as Lord Darnley and a friend. I promise Edward's cousin that he would be paid for it. In effect, I steal it.

As I cannot dislike myself any more than I already do, I then ride to our house at Chenies and inform the tenants now living in our former rooms in the Old House that I have come to remove a drawing from the gallery. They watch me closely as if I might also steal their silver plate. I can hear the unspoken words: 'the court cormorant!' An unseemly, greedy bird.

Before riding back to London, I go into the other part of Chenies, built to entertain royalty, which we had never occupied and which now crumbled slowly back into the land for lack of money to maintain it.

Tick, tick. I listen to the beetle in the oak beams. The cracked tile floor of the great hall grits under my shoes. A plaster rabbit lies at my feet in fragments, fallen from a wall frieze, his head looking wistfully back towards a missing leg lying two feet adrift.

The great gilded hall where I walk was built to entertain King Henry. Elizabeth, his daughter, had danced here on the floor patterned with her father's Tudor rose. The chilly air that pokes cold fingers up my skirts and sleeves was once warmed by human breath and the tiny flames of scores of honey-smelling wax candles. Men and women had pumped the heat of their ambitions and lusts into air filled with whispers and laughter. And music.

I have never seen it peopled. By the time Edward married me, Chenies, like the Russells' fortunes, was already in decline, the neglected hall and royal lodgings falling into ruin. But walking through the ruined chambers, I can imagine how it had been, the ornate plaster friezes, the gilt, the glowing coloured glass in the high bay windows and the now-leaning walls of the great range built to receive royalty. In the overgrown hedges and lumpy green leafy pillows in the great terraced gardens, I detect the ghosts of ordered pathway and neat globes of yew.

Patience, I tell the sad, echoing space. I may yet be able to bring you to life again as well as restore Moor Park. My present humiliation is the price of that hope.

A letter from Turnor waits for me at Bedford House. He grows impatient with the difficulty I seem to be finding in introducing him into Charles's court. An outsider may do his best, but . . .

Though his language is veiled, I grasp his meaning. Within a day of my return, he brings me a play.

'Perhaps the Prince will prefer this to my verse,' he says.

'It must please Lord Buckingham first.' I read the first pages to avoid meeting his eye. *Revenge for Honour.*

'A fashionable title,' I say. Revenge had taken over the public stage several years ago. Though they are falling out of fashion, I prefer the court masques with their gods and goddesses, their music and dancing and their hopeful glimpse of finer worlds.

He nods. 'I chose it for that reason.'

'I will read it. But you must understand that I can't tell Buckingham or the Prince that they inconvenience us with their delay in responding.'

I read it after he's gone.

He'll not get far in this court with this, I think. Is he mad? Apart from its fierce attack on Papists and a grotesque, syphilitic character named The Whore of Rome (who lacks a nose), it's a dreadful piece of work. The characters are dead puppets existing only to mouth his words. Nothing is true. Nor, on the other hand, is it wonderful. His world is dark, ugly and false. I will destroy the last shreds of my last reputation as a patron if I pretend to like it.

I will have to think of a lie to put him off. Meanwhile, I must advance my own wooing of the Prince. I dress warmly against the growing chill of autumn and once again take a boat up the Thames to Richmond.

# 32

Prince Charles sits up in bed, wrapped against the damp chill of the river. Ten gentlemen of the bedchamber attend him, along with a chamberer, four grooms, including one who did nothing but tend the fire, and a messenger standing by to carry off any royal request.

'Is Your Highness ill?' My face flames. The venturers have moved fast! I look for a doctor, covered close stool or other sign of illness.

He has been injured. He is being poisoned.

Then I think, if the false mishap has already happened, I am set free from my task. I am free to dislike the Prince, and he, me.

'I'm quite well, madam,' the Prince says. 'Why should I be ill?'

He is merely holding court in bed, as his father is known to do. A greyhound, two spaniels and single pocket beagle lie curled on the gold-crusted coverlet near his feet. He holds a third spaniel. To my relief, I do not see Buckingham.

When they understand my business, the waiting gentlemen settle to a game of cards at a table by the window.

Charles waves me close to the bed. 'What joy, madam?'

I lower my voice, a conspirator. 'The double portrait of your grandfather and uncle was painted by the Fleming Hans Eworth. The owner protested that he would not part with it under any circumstances.' Until I told him otherwise.

'Has Arundel asked to see it?'

'The owner didn't say.' Because I did not ask him.

'Is it very costly?' The Prince looks wistful.

More costly than he can know, I think. My pride still stings.

'Trust me, sir,' I say. 'I will get it for you. In the meantime, I hope this might find favour with you.'

The drawing taken from the wall at Chenies is a detail study for the portrait of an unknown man, a falcon.

The Prince takes it and turns it to the light. Again, I see pure joy brighten the narrow sullen face. Again, against my will, my heart twists with pleasure.

This is my proper part, I think. Giving him joy. I should be delighting with him in the God-like capacity of our fellows to spin true worlds of paint or words, *ex nihilo*, from nothing. Not plotting his downfall.

'Even without colour,' the Prince breathes, 'the feathers look almost real!' He holds the picture close to his face to study how the painter has captured the difference between the soft down of the breast and the slick, sleek pinions of wing and tail. His sallow face is flushed with excitement.

Watching him lay the drawing carefully on the coverlet, I ache to grow fond of him. But I do not dare. He stands between his sister and safety. He refuses to help her. He is the enemy.

'And now, sir . . .' I call the groom waiting outside the door with a large wrapped picture.

He tears away the linen wrapping. 'The double portrait! But I thought you said . . .'

'Did I not say you could trust me?'

The suspicion has left his eyes. Together, we gaze at the painted figure of the young Darnley, the Prince's grandfather, with a companion.

'Are you angry with me, sir, for teasing you?'

He scarcely seems to hear.

'I shall get up. William! George!' he calls. 'Come dress me!' He flings off his burden of cloak and coverlet. The dogs scatter from the bed. 'Pray excuse me, Lady Bedford, until I am dressed. Then you must meet me in the long gallery and we shall decide where to hang these new treasures you have brought me.'

A little later, we stand shoulder-to-shoulder, gazing up at the fish-scale array of paintings on the wall of the gallery, in easy intimacy.

Perhaps I could contrive to have him hit by a falling picture frame.

He points for the benefit of a serving man on a ladder who is hanging the double portrait. 'A little farther to the left.'

Then he turns to me with a small frown on the royal brow. 'Next I must have a finished painting by Holbein. Not merely drawings. I must add my own Holbein to the collection.'

He must have heard my intake of breath. 'Please don't disappoint me, madam.'

I smile. 'I thought that you trusted me.'

We have no Holbeins left at Chenies, finished or unfinished. I can't bear to make a second raid on Woburn. It would ruin me to buy such a thing, and if I ask the Prince for the true market value of what he wants, his sprouting favour would wither.

233

'I know one possible . . .' I say at last. It would test my friendship with Arundel to the limits. 'An allegorical group, far more rare than Holbein's portraits. *The Triumph of Virtue*. A procession of the Virtues . . .'

'It sounds tedious.'

'If you could only see it . . .' I shake my head, dismissing what I was about to say. 'Your Highness will think me a fool, but I fancied . . .'

'Fancied what?'

I wave away my foolish woman's words. 'I imagined that I saw your face on the rider leading the procession. . . . and that another of the mounted figures in the procession wore the face of the King. It can't be, of course,' I say quickly. 'We both know that the painter died before he saw either you or your father, but I feel that he might have foreseen . . .'

The light eyes sharpen with suspicion. He is not his father, but he is no fool, neither.

'Forgive me.' Again I wave away my fancies. 'I would not have spoken if Your Highness had not insisted.'

'He might have foreseen what?'

'In a dream perhaps . . . a divinely inspired vision . . . such things happen.' I shrug and laugh. 'I'm certain now that I merely fancied the resemblance.'

'Your fancy is not beyond Reason,' he says thoughtfully. 'Master Holbein painted my Tudor forebears. A resemblance might have sprung unwittingly from his memory.'

'Perhaps.'

'And it's a rare piece of work?'

'Most rare.'

'Does Arundel know of this painting?'

'I suspect he does, sir.' Arundel owns it.

'Can you get it?'

'I will try.' I recognise the reckless need to acquire.

'Don't tell George,' he says. 'He will scold me for spending without consulting him.'

I imagine Charles throwing off Buckingham's influence. With my encouragement. 'It will be our delicious secret until you can unveil your new possession in triumph. Then my lord Buckingham will see that you are indeed a full-grown man, a future king with a mind and will of your own.'

The royal eyes suddenly look anxious. 'He might be angry at my deceit.'

'Sir, a king is the spy of God. He must know and keep to himself matters that ordinary mortals, who are not royal, cannot share. You must begin to practise. It cannot be treason to imagine that one day . . . far in the future we all pray . . . you will become what you were born to be – the King of England.'

He nods. Then nods again with more conviction.

I feel like a traitor to his sister. What has changed? I am being no more insincere than any person at court would have been.

I may have lost the taste for being a courtier, I think with surprise. Donne infected me with his disease of paradox – a hopeless longing for truth coupled with the fatal ability to argue the truth in all sides.

Forget the *Triumph of Virtue*, I imagine saying. I feel the relief that follows this honesty. It's part of a ruse to bring you down, I would say. I have been abusing the best part of your nature to work against you. And the king-to-be would be grateful for my honesty.

Then I remind myself of the sulky boy who had listened to his sister's misfortune and declared that he would rather die than have her brought back to England. This is the king-to-be who sets alliance with an old enemy of England above the life of his own royal sister, who is also his heir.

I write that evening to the venturers, through Turnor.

*The Prince seems most vulnerable in his love of art and desire for acquisition, My present favour grows entirely from that love and desire . . . He intends to remain at Richmond until November, when he will return to London to be with the King for the annual celebration of the escape from the Gunpowder Treason.*

Letter back:

*Does the Prince take regular exercise?*

My letter back to them:

*When at Richmond, the Prince exercises as his brother did. He retains many of his brother's old teachers . . . tennis, riding, rowing, bowls, running, sword-play . . . who find him filled with resolve whether he fences or, in fine weather, rows against the current of the Thames opposite the palace. He does not enjoy the tilt as his brother did but rides like a Centaur, often in Richmond Forest . . . is a weak swimmer and will not walk a step farther than he must.*

I cross out 'opposite the palace' and write 'between the eyot and the palace' in its place.

# 33

I will never be innocent again, I think. I had been most innocent when the world, and my husband, would have called me sinful, even depraved. When I was with John Donne.

*Mon amour.* My love.

Donne had always liked to ride alone, he told me. Without a destination, letting words find him, turning his horse towards a wood where he half-glimpsed an idea waiting for him. He would set off to the west into the open heart of England. Alone in a space free of walls, of will, of noisy children, and of the fetters of expectation, he found his poems.

He asked me to ride with him.

A married woman and a married man, not wed to each other. He did not concern himself. I was the mirror of his soul. If he did not worry, neither did I.

For our first ride, we met at High Holborn and turned our horses north towards the rising slopes of Hampstead.

I felt awkward with fear. I kept silent lest he see that

he had written me better than I was, and that our bond was counterfeit.

I glanced sideways at his preoccupied face. A rogue's face, I thought. Too handsome by half. Worrying lines of dissatisfaction furrowed the skin between his eyes.

I felt suddenly cold. I had written him better than he was. Our flesh had conspired to madness. My pride could not accept that I had merely fallen into animal rut and must dress it up with talk of souls. I had let myself believe the ordinary flattery of an extraordinary poet.

He leaned over and touched my hand without speaking. His fingers pressed lightly on the back of my hand for a long moment as if he passed some force from his body into mine. I felt his pulse and the rhythm of his horse in his fingertips. Suddenly, all was well again.

We rode on in friendly silence.

He named his fifth child, a daughter, Lucy, and asked me to be godmother.

I collected words of love like a child snatching up perfect pebbles on the beach to put safely in a pocket. *Vita mea*. My life. . . .

*Il mio amore. Agapairma*. My love.

*Mein Hertz*. My heart.

From ambassadors, in other tongues. *Moja lubov*. My love. *Solnyshko moyo*. My sun.

And from foreign retainers of envoys. *Meu amor. Mein liefde*. And from the Queen's own Danish Anna, *Min kaerlighed*.

The word caught the reality.

He gave me himself wrapped neatly in his own words: '. . . meteor-like, of stuff and form perplexed . . .'

He gave me myself, a creature of 'quick soul' and bright

'through-shine front'. I wanted to believe in her. I blossomed into her.

Words created truth.

When I could neither see nor touch him, I read him. By firelight, by candlelight, under my covers, in my gardens, in the slanting light of a window bay.

I wore him in my senses. He rustled under my clothes.

We did rut. We took every chance we could get to strip off our clothing and join flesh to flesh. When he could not enter me, I caressed the skin of his wrist. If all else failed, the touch of his shoulder against mine was enough. But I did not feel sinful. How could it be sin, if I had no other choice? I fed on him with a child's simple, absolute appetite. I felt as pure and free and innocent as an animal in Eden.

I grew kinder to others. I even wrote in a friendly fashion to Edward and shared a civil meal with him when he came briefly to London on a visit from Chenies. He no longer enraged me. His resolve to be miserable made me want to weep instead of shout at him. I pitied him for never knowing joy and for having destroyed all chance of it with me.

I saw the same kindness mirrored in John. I felt no jealousy at his tenderness to his wife Anne and to his brood of children. It merely confirmed that he and I felt the same compassion for those unfortunates who were excluded from what we had.

'What do you hope to find out here?' I asked him on our second ride.

He looked towards the setting sun. 'The face of God.'

I accepted his words the way my body accepted the water I drank.

# 34

**LONDON, 1613**

I had not thought. I was the childless countess. Motherhood did not like me.

I had forgot how his wife had borne him a child a year. I did not think that his loins would be as fertile as his mind.

Cold fingers squeezed the back of my neck. Edward would know that he could not be the father.

I waited to lose it like the others.

It lodged. Grew inside me. My womb was as eager as my heart.

The sky looked brighter, my eyes sharpened. The birds sang more loudly.

Fool! Fool! This is true life, not a piece of verse, I told myself. There will be consequences. But even my morning retching did not lessen my joy.

At night, I glittered even more brightly at court gatherings. I cheered for my poet . . . father of my secret child . . . at his readings and watched with pride while men of power and influence clapped him on the back and begged for copies of his work. I glowed when he recounted how he had entertained the King at his table of wits. The penniless lawyer had begun to rise.

'But beware,' he said, laughing into my eyes. 'My old reputation lives on. Every day, some hopeful poetaster asks my opinion of his imitation of a scurrilous epigram by Wicked Jack Donne.'

The extreme emotions that I had secretly scorned in poetry now quivered with truth. I'd had dust in my eyes. I was fully awake for the first time since my wedding night. I found myself walking carefully, balancing the brimming cup of myself.

Edward, not yet injured, arrived unexpectedly in London from Chenies, making some excuse of business matters. But the cold eye with which he studied me convinced me that he paid someone in the house family to spy on me. My morning retching was hard to miss. I could not think why I hadn't seen the likelihood of a spy before.

But I did not care what Edward thought. If the child were a boy, he might even be willing to pretend it was his. Better a false heir than no heir at all. It would depend on how much it pained him to see the title pass instead to his brother's line. It could be our secret . . . I saw the Fourth Earl in his rocking horse . . . Donne's child grown to manhood, rebuilding the lost wing at Chenies . . .

Revise!

Did I truly believe that Edward would tolerate a cuckoo in the Russell nest?

I did not care. I brimmed with a new sense of purpose. My life had suddenly acquired a reason far more urgent that the happiness of the Queen, who had begun to drink too much and often sank beyond even my reach. I had a purpose that was totally my own. I was growing a child.

I imagined holding it, bending my face to sniff its head.

Feeling its hands pat the skin of my breasts as it explored its new universe. A new person yet part of me. The future grew warm with promise. How could I have imagined that playing midwife to poetry and to other people's joy was enough?

While my belly did not show, I told no one, not even John, who continued to rain poetry on me. We shared joyful conceptions of verse. We stalked ideas. He then caught them with his words, delicately, arrogantly, wildly.

> *Whoever guesses, thinks, or dreams, he knows*
> *Who is my mistress, wither by this curse . . .*

He grinned with mock blood-lust.

'I can't stomach venom today,' I said.

I carry your child. I carry your child, sang my blood.

He studied my face, then sat beside me on the stone bench in the garden behind Bedford House and took my hand.

I felt the pressure of eyes and looked up to see my husband watching us from an upper window. I did not remove my hand nor call him to John's notice.

'I must try to remember . . .' he said. '. . . didn't bring it with me.' While he thought, I studied him for signs of his recent illness.

Thinner, I thought. Nothing more.

He lifted his face to the sky.

> *The sun itself, which makes times, as they pass,*
> *Is elder by a year, now, than it was*
> *When thou and I first one another saw.*
> *All other things to their destruction draw,*
> *Only our love hath no decay;*
> *This no tomorrow hath, nor yesterday.*

A passing gardener muttered, 'madam . . .' and lowered his eyes as he hurried on. I did not care that he might report to my husband. My love at my side had caught it exactly. This moment had no tomorrow, nor yesterday.

Then he laid his hand tenderly on my belly.

'I suppose that if anyone would know . . .' I said.

He nodded amiably. 'I've had practice.' He removed his hand at the sound of the returning gardener. 'Our best work.'

That evening, when John had ridden back to his house in Mitcham, I sang to the babe growing in my womb and felt a listening stillness. I searched the trunks in my closet for a tabor I had kept when we had to let our company of musicians go for lack of money. When I found the little drum, I beat out the quick syncopated rhythm of a galliard and could have sworn that the child danced in my belly.

I scarcely heard Edward at supper that night when he called me 'whore' from behind his napkin.

# 35

When Kit leaves to deliver my last letter to Turnor, I want to call him back and tear up what I have written. I am worse than a whore. I betray the best in myself and in the Prince, to serve my own selfish ends.

The past is gone, I tell myself. Let it go. Turn your eyes to what lies ahead. Make your peace with God if you can't make it with yourself.

Let go of John Donne.

I stand suddenly on the very edge of a precipice, looking down into darkness. The earth loosens beneath my feet. It begins to crumble. It will give way and send me falling down into Nothing.

Revise . . .

Nothing. Without the past, I have nothing. If I cannot recreate the past as my future, I will become nothing.

Nothing. The word creates the reality. A cold fog spreads through me, blurring my thoughts. I feel myself growing indistinct, like distant hills when a rainstorm moves in. Soon I will disappear.

I had retreated with my swelling belly to my little kingdom in Twickenham. My poets, Jonson and Donne followed me. Doncaster, Goodyear, and Arundel attended my little court in the country. Master Jones visited when he came to Richmond Palace to speak with Prince Henry. The designer of gardens, de Caus. The architect, Smythsson. Sir Arthur Gorges, a sea-faring Devonian poet who was a cousin of Raleigh. Arundel.

Then the news came from the Russell estate at Woburn that Edward's horse had thrown him against a tree. Duty called me there.

I left Twickenham.

I found my husband with a crippled arm and askew from his fall in ways that were not just of the body. He seemed almost triumphant when he related his accident, as if he had succeeded at last in a thing he had been striving to achieve.

He looked at me across his freshly bandaged arm. 'Not only am I now a broken man, our debts still grow. I must lease out parts of Chenies. And you must sell the lease of Twickenham Park.'

'Where will we live?'

'I have bought an old estate at Moor Park, near Rickmansworth.'

If he could afford to buy it, I knew that it must be in even worse condition than Chenies.

I returned to Twickenham for the last time to arrange its sale to Lord Bacon, who, whatever his shortcomings as merry company, had always admired the gardens.

Then I rode to Moor Park to examine my new home,

lying in a valley near Rickmansworth, between Chenies and London.

A straw and clay bird's nest had fallen down the chimney into the dank fireplace of the entrance hall. Unlike Chenies, where the old wing still stood, Moor Park offered no refuge. All of it was in disrepair. The air felt hollow and cold, with a lingering smell of dog and ancient piss.

The derelict manor house of modest size was filled only with the sound of mice, drips, and birds in the chimneys. Somewhere a door banged gently in its frame.

I kicked at a shattered piece of coloured glass fallen from a broken window. A seedling tree had dug its toes into a crack in the high stone sill. The walls leaned. The rooflines sagged. Rain gnawed at the ornate twisting brick chimneys and dug at the stone window frames. I ran my fingers over the ghost of a carved 'W' on a worn stone boss.

My husband, at least, should be content here. He loved his misery above all else. Failed as a courtier, failed as a soldier, he chose to excel at suffering. Moor Park would suit him perfectly.

After half an hour of desolate wandering, I squinted my eyes and imagined.

Torches had once burned in the rusting holders on the panelled walls. The hall fireplace, which was large enough to stable a horse, had once roared with flames. Cardinal Wolsey had once dined before those flames.

The hall could be friendly again, I decided. If we cleaned the chimneys and I hung my favourite Mortlake tapestry from Chenies on the end wall – unless Edward insisted that I must sell the hanging too.

I imagined fire and candles, and a procession of dancers advancing hand-in-hand from the far end of the hall, but the silence around me stifled all memories of music.

246

Here I am again, I had thought. Back in another ruin. Escaped from Chenies by way of Berwick, only to end up at Moor Park.

I don't call Turnor back with my letter to the venturers. I now see possible escape from Moor Park even if I dislike the price. If only my queen still lived. If only Prince Henry, the hope of England, had not died. If my princess had not married and gone to be a foreign queen. If her younger brother were not a spoiled, uncertain, self-willed weakling set on a Catholic bride.

I put away my pen and ink in my writing chest then go out into the gardens at Bedford House, hoping that the touch and smell and sight of growing things might lift my spirits.

Shears spread, a gardener pauses to greet me.

I walk through the arched gate. The late summer abundance of the kitchen garden, beans, turnips, salads, cannot hold back the chilly fog spreading from the river. I scarcely notice the three weeding women who stand to curtsy as I pass.

In the solitude of the orchard, I reach up for the smooth solidity of a half-ripe apple. My bodice stays cut into me. The first pain had gripped my belly as I was reaching up like this, but then it had been for a pear.

Suddenly, I'm weeping.

I drop my arm. My body clenches with remembered pain.

My hard milk-swollen breasts had leaked wetness into my shift. It had been pain without purpose. The mouth that should have suckled had closed forever.

I hug myself and rock on my feet.

She had never wanted to eat. Two short days. Scarcely counted as a life, but she was as entire to me as if she had lived to bury me.

247

My daughter, with John's dark hair and long fingers. And his eyes. She was too quiet from the start, but her stillness did not keep her from looking at me with startled recognition when I first held her. Her eyes were clear and filled with awareness that I did not expect in a newborn babe. As if she were complete, her soul already full-grown. Her tiny body was too small to hold it.

'There you are!' said her eyes. 'We have found each other at last.'

I stared back in joyful recognition. My daughter. I was no longer 'I' but 'we'.

She was our best creation, John's and mine, more perfect and absolute in beauty and meaning than any poem. I felt huge with the future. Flesh, blood and bone, I was all ruthless purpose, to protect this child whom I had grown inside me. A seed that had chosen to grow while I stood by with expectant heart. Now a fragile, beautiful flower, as fragile as the dust on a butterfly. A May fly. I was almost afraid to hold her lest I damage her.

We gazed into each other's eyes.

Then her lids fluttered and dropped. In the sleep that followed, she became a mere babe again, blind, terrifyingly new, not yet lodged in the world. I held her. Rocked her. Felt her heartbeat, fast as a frightened mouse. Pinched her to try to make her cry so that I could put my nipple into her mouth.

'Use a wet nurse, madam,' the midwife had said. 'A woman with experience of babes.'

'But not with mine!'

She lived for two days.

I shrank into a small hard clod of earth. I did not weep.

I stoop now and pull up a thistle. Then throw it away. This is not even my own garden. It is a Russell garden. My garden was in Twickenham and in the words that had grown there along with the flowers. My gardens were at Chenies and now at Moor Park, where I defy my Russell husband by cramming it with cuttings and seedlings I have nursed. Trees I have planted. Everything in the vegetable world burgeons and thrives for me, from oak trees to delicate Blue-eyes-in-the-grass. Why could my babes not live?

'Motherhood does not like me,' I had said to John when he arrived back from France, too late to see her. There were whispers, of course, among my household. Edward does not have dark hair and long slim fingers.

She had been born too soon, the midwife said. Before she was ready. If I let myself think about feeling the tree root that had caught my foot . . . just like a tree root . . . a sly tree root, even though we were just rising from dinner in the hall . . . which had sent me flailing forward, against the edge of the table, onto the stone floor . . .

Even now, I do not let myself think about it or I would cut my husband's throat while he slept.

# 36

After my daughter died, I never felt entirely well. Sharp pains twisted my belly. Sometimes I felt a sensation of falling under my breastbone. I slept too long. I put food into my mouth, chewed and swallowed, but without appetite.

Prince Henry died, and Elizabeth married, both within five months. My knuckles began to ache so that I could neither write nor play the lute.

I read a poem John sent to me while I was visiting Edward, being a dutiful wife to an injured husband in the country.

*Thou shalt be a Mary Magdalen, and I, A something else thereby . . .*

Magdalen. Magdalen Herbert. One of his first patrons. A patron of Wicked Jack. An older widow. Cultured, still wealthy. Recently remarried, but then, I too was married. They were still friends.

I could not be jealous of a friend.

Why did her name occur to him, even as a figure of speech?

The serpent stirred in Paradise. I coaxed it back to sleep. It would swallow me whole if I let it wake.

I tried to read.

*A bracelet of bright hair about the bone . . .*

Perhaps my bright hair, perhaps not. I could see the felicity of his image. I could not find joy in it. My eyes went again to 'Magdalen'.

The alchemy of poetry, I reminded myself. Not the same moment, not the same woman. He has made a thing complete and distinct in itself.

Don't be a jealous fool.

Serpent, go back to sleep!

I returned to London and my lodgings near the Queen at Denmark House. Suddenly, I saw how the gilt fringes on the bed-hangings and cushions had tarnished. I ran my fingers over the chipped inlays of ivory and ebony.

Her Majesty now danced less and drank too much. She no longer sang at all. It was forbidden to mention Prince Henry in her presence.

'Even by royal measure, Bedford . . . it's so bad!' She meant her marriage. She held out her glass for me to fill again as we sat drinking together. 'Here's to Buck-buck-buck-bucky!' She raised her glass. 'May all his teeth fall out and bite him on the arse!'

'We can always hope that one of the Prince's dogs might do just that,' I said, to steer her away from the threat of sudden tears.

'Hope?' she asked. 'I see no hope in this world. But I still have hopes for the next one.'

'And I hope that you're in no hurry to find out!' I set the jug back down with a thump. I did not refill my own glass.

'I'm too weary to hasten anywhere.'

I watched her stare out of the window as she had done in Berwick.

'God is bad,' she said. 'He's very, very bad! Don't you think so, Bedford? Doesn't listen. Reminds me of the King . . .'

'Would you like me to sing you to sleep tonight?' I must not let her dark humour infect me. My knuckles might ache too much to play the lute, but I could still sing. 'I know a Spanish lullaby you've not heard.'

I made myself sing it to her. I had learned it while I carried my daughter, to sing to her. It remained like the tip end of a thorn that breaks off in your thumb and will fester and swell up with pus if you can't remove it. It felt hot and red, the way my eyes often felt.

'*Duerme no llores* . . .' Sleep without tears.

While the old chamberer, who had come with the Queen from Denmark, rubbed Her Majesty's swollen feet and ankles, I sang it again and again until the queen slept and I had sung it out of myself.

I grew reckless in search of joy and visited the two small rooms that John had rented in the Savoy. We made love and read his work. I read him some of mine. I was loved with heat and sweat and rumpled sheets, as I had thought I would never be loved.

But I felt a distraction in him. The other half of the double man was somewhere else.

'What is it?' I asked once. 'Where have you gone?'

'Here! I'm here with you.'

'You try too hard to reassure me,' I said.

'You shouldn't need to be reassured. We're together,

no matter where you or I may go. I've said it. Written it. Your heart in me, and mine in you. You see with my eyes and I see with yours.'

That's a poem, I thought. Not speaking to me. But I kept my mouth shut. He had laid his face against my right palm, with his eyes closed. His other hand held tightly on to mine. My love for him replaced my flesh inside my skin. The truth of him there, with me, touching me, filled me with heat and light. I pressed myself back against the door I held closed against a first whiff of loss.

I conceived another babe and lost it so early that I held it in my hand like a strange small fruit. I buried my little misshaped cherry under a tree at Moor Park and told no one, not even John, whose wife was carrying their seventh child, which survived.

My skin grew hot. I sprouted spots on one arm, shoulder and half of my face, so that I looked like an Italian *commedia* mask, one half myself, the other monstrous. The court doctors suggested that I might have a rare form of the small pox. Then my spots vanished as suddenly as they had come, but left behind a smear of pain and four small scars on my face.

The Queen became impatient with me. Her own ill health worsened. She complained of gout and grew irritable with drink.

'For God's sake, go elsewhere to recover!' she said.

'If the light and laughter ever fail,' I had told her all those years ago in Berwick, 'you may banish me!'

She went to her palace in Greenwich and left me in London.

Then Edward decided that we could not waste money

running Bedford House when I had other lodgings in London with the Queen. He ordered the city house shut up and returned to Chenies to begin our move to Moor Park.

# 37

## LONDON, 1621

The venturers don't tell me when it will happen, but I know that they must. I will have my own part to play and must be ready. I'm uneasy. I've tried to tell them through Turnor that a false accident will be as hard to arrange as an assassination. Through Turnor, they thank me for my opinion and tell me nothing.

I can still hear the edge of dissent in the voices at that first meeting. I had felt a crack in their purpose, admitted by Wriothesley. I can't see exactly where the crack runs, nor how deep.

Murray stands on one side, I'm certain. Most likely with Wriothesley, though it's hard to say exactly where the dry-voiced Earl stands on anything. They will try to raise men. They will fight abroad. They do not want to challenge the King in England. They are loyal subjects of James, who happen to believe that their monarch is misled by his single-minded determination on peace.

Murray will not agree to the false accident, but I don't think he will betray his friends, neither. I watched him at the end of that first meeting, ruffled and flushed, still brimming with unspoken words that he knew would fall on deaf ears.

Gorges is most certainly on the other side, with the angry men, with Holles and his Puritan son, and Sir William Sennett, who wants to fight with wroth and fire. His son, Sir Walter, will follow his soldier hero, Turnor, who is the angriest man of all. He hides in seeming ordinary because, if he unveiled himself, he would burn like a tar barrel set on fire and rolled flaming through dry hay.

I know that it's safer for me not to meet them again. But I feel set to one side, ignorant of what they mean to do. Ignorance frightens me, as indeed it should. Any attack on the Prince will be treated as treason, sham or not. The penalty will be the same. Then I grow angry that they are willing for me to serve our shared purpose in dangerous ignorance.

Not one of you would agree to such terms, I think.


Turnor brings me another play. *The Devil Loose in London.* I read it closely. It's another show of violence and deceit in a world without the faintest gleam of light. His characters are creatures from nightmare. The play might almost make me laugh. A murderer and rapist is disguised as a nun. A son kills his own mother from ambition and is then accidentally disembowelled.

In truth, the play terrifies me. Jonson had been imprisoned for less. Turnor unveils himself in his plays. Every word exposes the writer's deep rage.

Surely, Turnor can't despise the King enough to believe him blind to the parallels in this play? James acquiesced to the death of his own mother, Mary Queen of Scots. He then acceded to the throne of the woman who had signed the execution warrant. Suspicious, fearful, sharp-witted

James would not miss the echo of a traitor's death on the scaffold in the accidental disembowelling.

I re-read the final scene in which the matricide's house falls and crushes him, and is then set on fire by a lightning bolt from a cleansing God. The bodies of the wicked burn. As the Gunpowder Plotters had meant them to burn in the ashes of a blasted Parliament.

Does Turnor imagine that metaphor and costume can disguise his true meaning? Does he not understand that these things create a new, more vivid truth that men often remember more clearly than the facts themselves?

It does not matter that, as a patron, I would never put forward this dismal piece of work. For my own safety as well as Turnor's, I must not show the thing to anyone, least of all Buckingham.

I think a little more. I have a copy made of the play. Then I send Kit with the copy to Wriothesley. A mere courtesy, if he already knows the true nature of his lieutenant. A warning, if he does not.

I try to think of another delaying lie to tell Turnor. Once our mummery has been performed, he may no longer care what anyone thinks of his writing.


Turnor comes to Bedford House to tell me. He interrupts me while I am packing warm clothes and books to take to Richmond where the Prince has offered me a bedchamber and parlour. I don't want to go, but Reason says that I must accept this honour with a semblance of gratitude. I do not tell Turnor that I am going.

They have chosen the river, he says. Using information I have given them about the Prince.

After Turnor leaves, I finish packing for Richmond. Though my part in it is done, I want to be there when it happens.

257

Rumour will seize any story in its jaws and run away with it. Something could so easily go wrong. I will see for myself what happens. I trust only my own eyes.

I pray that Murray was wrong and that the King will react as the other men judge that he will.

We are using the best that lies in the Prince of Wales to work against him.

Elizabeth feels very far away.

# 38

## RICHMOND PALACE, LATE AUTUMN 1621

The Prince's skiff points upstream against the tide that runs down to the sea. Small and awkward, wearing only his shirt, trunk hose and a loose doublet, he rows grimly against the current, imitating his dead brother, trying to build his strength. One oar jumps out of the water, splashing both the royal rower and his boatman.

I wear the inconspicuous clothes of a farmer's wife, the colours of the earth and sheep. Watching from the flat sloping Twickenham bank across the river from the palace, in the shadows of my old garden wall, I can hear the Prince's grunts of effort as he labours against the pull of the water.

Remembering his brother's effortless rhythm, I feel another stab of unwelcome pity. I know, because I had written the fact to the venturers, that the boatman, who would row back if the Prince let the tide carry the boat too far downstream, had also been Prince Henry's rowing master. Charles had taken him over from Henry's household, along with Henry's Master of Horse, after his brother died.

The Prince strains backwards against the oars. Uneasily,

I eye his padded trunk hose. The wool bombast stuffing around his hips would soak up water like a sponge.

Across the river, the Prince's retinue wait on the palace water stairs. A red-liveried groom, slumped shoulders signalling 'boredom', stands holding a pile of pale linen towels. Another groom squats to tend the charcoal brazier that will warm both the Prince on his return to land and the poker for heating the wine in the silver jug held by a third groom. A fourth groom holds a clean, folded shirt. A fifth hugs the Prince's heavy jewelled doublet in both arms as if it might try to escape or thieves might try to snatch it. And because the Prince sometimes missed the step while getting out of the boat and plunged ankle-deep into the water, a sixth groom waits with dry stockings draped over one arm and a pair of shoes dangling from his other hand. Four waiting gentlemen trade desultory gossip on the stone terrace at the top of the steps, their voices and laughter carrying clearly across the water. Eight men-at-arms block the gate to the gardens. Two more stand on either side of the entrance to the palace.

At last, I see the man I'm looking for. Though Charles can swim, he lacks strength. Below the main retinue, a little down-river to allow for the fast-flowing current, Henry's old swimming master stands at the front of the quay just above Crane Wharf. He watches the Prince intently, standing by to save the royal life, should the need ever arise.

I look closely at the passing horse riders, farmers and market women on my side of the river. The wide flat shelving Twickenham riverside is a main thoroughfare from Twickenham to Brentford and Syon. Any of these passers-by could have been an intelligencer working for Lord Bacon, for the King, for the Company, or for any of the many powerful men who hired their own agents to gather the information that underpinned their power.

But most people pause only briefly to watch the Prince before walking on. Had he been Henry, they would very likely have set up permanent camp.

No one can know what is intended, I reassure myself. But guilt makes my drab partridge feathers feel as conspicuous as a shimmering peacock display. Guilty intent swirls over the surface of the river like a cloud of gnats.

I watch three boys who wade in shallow water parallel to the shore, looking for dropped pins, shoe buckles and coins. Boys, curiosity, and sharp eyes go together. I do not let myself look back up the river to where two fishermen steady their boat in the current opposite the Ham water meadows. One holds a rod. The other sculls gently to hold their skiff in position. Though they are just too far for me to see their faces clearly, I am certain that the fisherman is Denzil Holles.

The three boys are now searching the shore directly opposite the fishermen. My heart tries to break my ribs from the inside. I want to shout a warning. But Turnor swore that witnesses on shore would notice nothing.

I lack his confidence. My eyes follow a well-dressed rider who has paused for what felt a little too long to watch the Prince. I'm certain I know the set of his shoulders. I watch him until he disappears around the bend towards Twickenham before I turn back at the labouring Prince.

The tide is running fast. Leaves, feathers, bubbles, and carefree ducks race by me, riding the outgoing current. A broken branch spins past. An old shoe bobs, nosing above the surface like a swimming water rat. Then clots of waterweed and dead grass. A larger raft of tangled rubbish seems to overtake the two fishermen on its way downstream.

The sun glows pink through a pair of ears at the corner of my eye. I turn. See no one. I had imagined the presence of young Sir Walter Sennett.

The three boys stoop to dig something out of the mud. The raft of rubbish passes them. As it draws closer to me, rising and falling with the water, I see a gleam of bright gold winking at the centre of the nest of broken branches and weed.

The Prince sees it too, close by on his right, shouts in excitement, and digs in his left oar to try to turn his boat. 'Over there!' he shouts again. He tries to point then hauls at the oar again.

The boat jerks, then swings too far. When he tries to correct his course, the right oar splashes and slips from his hand. The boatman stands, moving forward from his seat in the stern, reaching for the oars.

'Get it!' Prince Charles shouts to the boatman. 'Now! Or I'll lose it!'

The raft of rubbish is bobbing past his skiff. The Prince leans out over the water, stretching to reach the golden cargo, his back turned to the palace.

Because I am watching for it and am on the Twickenham side, I see what happens next. Too fast for anyone on the other shore to see or say.

Changing direction to dive into the water as the Prince had ordered, the boatman steps hard onto the gunwale. In a confusion of splashing, the skiff overturns, dumping Prince and boatman into the river.

Through the splashes and the shouts of alarm from the palace stairs, I hear a dull thump. I forget that I am hiding and run down to the edge of the water. Apart from the half-submerged belly of the overturned skiff, the river surface is empty. The skiff already moves away downstream in the current. Then I see the boatman's head break surface.

One head.

Where's the Prince's head?

I think again about his trunk hose that would soak up water and weigh him down. The overlooked detail that could spell disaster.

The boatman gasps for air and dives again.

The swimming master is already in the water, headed for the overturned skiff. Boats are pulling away from the palace stairs. The boatman surfaces, farther downstream. Again without the Prince.

'. . . think he hit his head!' he shouts into the sudden pandemonium. Then he knifes back down under the water.

We've killed him! The river suddenly looks vast. It has swallowed him. I find myself in the water. The current tugs at the hem of my skirts. I wade farther out, straining to see through the dark choppy surface, praying to see a pale submerged shape.

'What happened?' The three boys pant from their sprint back down the bank.

The boatman surfaces again, far down the river.

I strain my eyes. A single dark shape. Then it resolves into two heads.

'I have him!' he shouts. Both go under. The swimming master reaches the spot and dives after them.

My bones jangle. The overturned skiff has already passed Crane Wharf, headed for the Kew bend. The boats that had put out from the palace stairs pause uncertainly. The boatmen bend to peer into the water.

Dark heads bob to the surface, much farther down-river than I had been looking.

How many?

I stare until my eyes felt like steel.

. . . two men, swimming awkwardly, hauling something

between them. One of the palace boats reaches them. The two men in the boat haul a limp shape out of the water, throw it face-down over the seat and pound it on the back. I wade back out of the water and run along the shore, shoes squelching, wet skirts hobbling my ankles.

Two men on the Twickenham side have now dived in and are swimming out to the rescue, or for a closer look.

How much did they see?

'What happened? Did you see?' asks a man trotting at my shoulder.

'Was it the Prince who fell in?' A woman flushed with excitement tugs at my sleeve. 'It was the Prince rowing! I think he fell in!'

'I think he's dead,' announces another male voice. 'He looked dead to me.'

Across the water, I hear the Prince cough. Then he begins to retch. His spasms rasp the air.

Alive.

Farther down the river, the bouncing whale belly of the skiff spins gently out of sight around the Kew bend. The tangled nest with its golden cargo has already disappeared, or else is lost amongst the other rubbish on the surface of the Thames. Someone in the hire of the venturers would fish it out, I was certain. It would not have mattered if anyone else were to find the mysterious golden flotsam had it not been for the almost invisible strand of spider's web that would serve as a hangman's cord – the long length of fishing line on which the little ark had been guided into the Prince's path.

I watch until I'm quite certain that the floating nest must have rounded the Kew bend. Then I turn to look up-river. The two fishermen have disappeared.

Everything is changed.

# 39

That night, I find a parcel waiting in my lodgings at Richmond. There is a note with it, misspelled and barely literate.

*Wun a my cowes fownd it at Brent Forde. I pray god ther mite be a reward for the finding.* It is signed *G. Hickson, drover* but I recognise Turnor's writing. On the outside of the letter is written *for his hines the Prince*.

I open the little parcel then sit thinking about unanswered questions and my own ignorance. It seems clear enough what I am meant to do. I even see that the venturers might mean to protect me further from the royal alarm that must follow the Prince's mishap. But the little gilded casket on my table feels as dangerous as an unexploded rocket shell.

Though the afternoon sun nudges through hazy cloud outside, it is night in the Prince's bedchamber where he holds court the next day. When I am announced, the shutters are closed. Constellations of beeswax candles scent the air with honey and mingle with the sharper smoke of fortifying herbs that burn in a fireplace large enough to stable three horses.

Prince Charles sits up in bed wrapped in a cloak and coverlet, with a posset mug steaming on a ledge of the ornately carved bed-head. A large poultice seems to grow from the top of his narrow head. The outer corners of his eyes droop more than ever, intensifying his resemblance to a bloodhound pup.

I curtsy as gracefully as I can while hugging my bundle. As I rise, I note the three hovering doctors. Ten gentlemen. To my relief, Buckingham is absent. But six new men-at-arms stand outside the door who had not been there before, and two more inside the room itself.

'I am filled with joy to see Your Highness alive and . . .' How would he wish to be seen? '. . . so resolute in the face of pain.'

'I thank you, madam. I am alive but still clouded in my memory.' His eyes go to my bundle. His lust to acquire seems undiminished by near-drowning. 'Have you brought something for me?'

'A most wonderful surprise, sir, which I hope might help ease your suffering.'

Prince Charles seems to forget his recent ordeal. He leans forward eagerly like a child at Twelfth Night wanting the gift in a visitor's pocket. 'What is it?'

I lay my bundle on the silk coverlet.

'Open the shutters to give us light,' he orders. A groom leaps to obey.

He hauls at the strings. I could have cut them for him, had I been allowed to carry my knife into his presence.

'Allow me, sir.' I ease the bindings and pull back the wrappings from the gilded wooden casket carved in the Roman style, a tiny temple with a hinged roof, egg-and-dart moulding around top and bottom edges, and miniature columns at each corner. I recognise its origin in one of Jones's Italian drawings.

The Prince frowns at it, his face pinched with thought. 'I think I was trying . . .' He looks up at me, puzzled, worrying at a memory. Then his face clears. 'I saw this very thing yesterday. I remember it now! It was the cause of my accident.'

'Forgive me, sir! I did not mean to upset you. Let me take it away at once!'

'No!' He slaps both hands on the little golden casket. 'It doesn't upset me! Where did you find it?'

'I'm told that a drover fished it out of the river at Brent Ford.' A dangerous moment for me. 'My taste for collecting is still known hereabouts, it seems, from my days at Twickenham Park. The drover brought it to me, hoping for a reward. As, indeed, I gave him. He noticed it only because one of his cows was sniffing at it.'

Enough! No more embroidery. Now shut your mouth! I warn myself.

He slides open the clasp and lifts the lid. 'Oh!' he gasps.

Inside, on the red silk velvet lining, lies a tiny golden king mounted on horseback. He is as tall as my little finger, wears classical robes and carries a spear. He is made of solid gold. I know because I had held him.

'Do you know who he is?' He strokes the golden figure with his fingertips.

I pretend to study the figure for the first time.

'I believe it must be the Greek Alexander,' he says. 'Both a general and a king.'

'I believe so too, Your Highness.' I still cannot believe that the venturers risked losing such a rare and costly object in the river, even to lure the Prince.

Charles lifts the little king from its cushion of silk, climbs from his bed and goes to the sunlight falling from the now-unshuttered window. 'Was he truly found in the river? Could he have sailed past my palace?'

I nod, unwilling to voice what I was almost certain was a lie. This golden figure is no mummer's prop.

'I'm certain it must be the same that I saw.' He turns the gleaming figure in the light. It shines like a small warm sun in his hands. 'It's a sign! Do you think it might be a sign?' A child begging for reassurance.

I cannot help myself. I give him what would make him happy. 'Yes, Your Highness. It's a double sign: of God's mercy in sparing you yesterday and of a glorious future like Alexander's.'

He smiles but then sucks in his lips to hide his pleasure in my reply. Which makes him look like a toothless old man. 'Is it . . . was it . . .?'

I read his unease. 'It's a gift, Your Highness, which my gratitude for your safety is happy to procure. It's a gift from God, who set the little king afloat like a modern Moses.'

'In which case, madam, you must be one of His angels, knowing at once when the drover brought it that such a thing belonged to me.'

'Sir, you're too kind. I aspire no higher than the Pharaoh's daughter.'

The touch of arrogance in his last words eases my guilt, if only a little.

I know that I should now report back to Turnor, who will tell the Company that, thanks to their foresight, I am reconfirmed in the Prince's favour.

I eye the poultice on his head.

These great ventures seldom go exactly as planned, I reassure myself.

But watching Charles caress the golden figure, I think again of my long, stricken wait for the boatman to re-surface with the Prince.

I am quite certain I had seen both the Prince's head

and that of the boatman at least once. But then they had disappeared again. There had been so much splashing and shouting and putting out of boats that I can't trust my memory.

The blow to the Prince's head could only have been an accident. No one can be certain of making an overturning boat hit a man on the head.

Again, I was searching the surface of the water, praying to see two heads. Seeing only the leaves racing down on the tide, clots of weed, the disappearing belly of the skiff.

Men often drown in the attempt to save someone else.

But the boatman is a strong swimmer. He often raced against Prince Henry. The two of them had swum against the outgoing tide in the same way that Charles had tried to row. I had watched them compete, along with the swimming master, to see who could swim farthest under water without coming up for air. Only when the swimming master dived for them did boatman and Prince return to the surface.

I shake my head. It was meant only to be an accident. This is not a play or piece of tragic verse. I am making things up, just as Edward says I do. But I can't help it. In my head I see the boatman holding the Prince down like a submerged tree branch snagging his clothes.

# 40

'How dare you come here?'

Turnor has followed me to Richmond Palace but has not been allowed to enter. An usher takes me to him where he waits by the river entrance under the eyes of four men-at-arms. Security in the palace has been doubled since the Prince's mishap. I don't want him inside and, rather than vouch for him, I lead him back onto the riverside terrace.

'Your guilt overrides your good sense,' he says. 'My presence here is entirely innocent. I have a perfect excuse to seek you out. Though you appear to have forgotten it, you are my patron.'

This is the moment to give him the bad news about his literary offerings. I cannot. To be honest, I am afraid.

'I have given both your plays to Lord Buckingham,' I say.

'And?'

I shrug.

'Fortunately, I have now finished a new play.' He takes a neat sheaf of papers from his leather pouch. 'Our failure on the river makes it even more urgent for you to introduce me into the Prince's court circles.'

I do not take the offered manuscript. '"Failure on the river"? I saw success.'

'But the King has not taken our message. Instead, he has increased the guard on the Prince.' He jerks his head back at the heavily guarded river gate, then at the two men stationed on Crane Wharf. 'We will not so easily be given another chance to try again outside the palace.'

I do not like sharing that 'our' and 'we' with him. 'Try again? You're mad even to think it!' But I now understand their purpose in lodging me even more securely in the Prince's favour and inside the palace. 'I'll have nothing more to do with it.'

'Read the dedication.'

Reluctantly, I take the play and lift the title page. The early dusk of the shortening days leaves just enough light to see.

'That was sent to us from Prague.' When I recoil from what I see, he smiles. 'Don't fear, madam. There's no guilt in having it. Those bills are being distributed all over Bohemia, Silesia and the German states. The Hapsburgs want to make their intentions plain beyond all argument.'

Beneath the title page lies a crude wood engraving on the cheap paper used for public handbills. Even if you could not read German, the engraving makes the meaning clear.

'Twenty-seven men dead in a single day of victorious butchery!' The tight rage in his voice sits oddly on the surface of the crisp air.

'They did it after all.' I stare at the severed heads spiked on the towers of the Charles Bridge in Prague, bleeding from the mouth where their tongues had been cut out. In another part of the picture, the quartered bodies of the men are stacked like butchered carcasses in an abattoir.

271

A pool of black ink floods the stone paving of the town square.

Feeling hollow and cold, I read the list of names. Lords, knights, military commanders. Men of the highest rank. Former leaders of Bohemia. The Protestant patriots who had fathered Frederick's short-lived rule. The rector of Prague University. And ordinary burghers of the city. All the most prominent men who had dared to oppose the Hapsburgs and their empire.

'Did anyone in England know this was to take place?' The pale face of a passing boatman turns to the sound of my raised voice. Elizabeth knew. I hear her saying, 'Some of my train fear for members of their family.'

'Seven squadrons of horsemen were needed to keep order in the town square. The last report we heard, the German princes had sent envoys to negotiate to have the sentences lifted.'

'All the Bohemian leaders.' I look at the handbill again in the failing light. 'There's no one left to fight for them in Bohemia.'

'And no one left on the Continent who would dare.'

I lead him up the narrow stone staircase to a riverside walkway on the top of a wall. A gust of wind nearly carries off Turnor's manuscript and the handbill with it, but here on the broad stone walkway, we can see everyone who approaches and speak without fear of listening ears.

'Will the Hapsburgs stop before they've captured Frederick?' I ask.

'I think not. And then what will they do with him? Butchering twenty-seven honoured men in a single day is not the act of a power than means to settle for peaceful compromise!'

'Has the King voiced an opinion?'

He swallows what he clearly wants to say. 'England

had sent an official envoy to barter for the lives of these men . . . Lord Hay, again made a laughing stock. This is another slap on the King's face! Do you think the Hapsburgs wouldn't relish delivering the greater slap of capturing his son-in-law? And executing him? Perhaps even the Princess. Everyone in England must fear for her now. And for the little Crown Prince.'

'Surely, the King must now bring her home, with her children,' I say. 'He must know his daughter's danger. The Dutch were welcoming, but they are also frank. They can offer refuge but dare not undertake military support.'

'Nowhere is safe for her but England,' Turnor agrees. 'Alas, our King does not share the same fear as his subjects.'

'Then he's a blind fool!' I say hotly. I point to the engraved handbill, which I still hold. 'They executed Slik, who was nobility, and the candidate for king before Frederick. Why not the King himself?'

He lowers his voice even further. 'These executions increase our urgency to make a blind man see.'

I stare across the river at a herd of cows drinking on the Twickenham bank. Behind them rise the trees of my former garden, my lost *paradisus*.

I do not want to expose any weak point to Turnor, but I must know. 'Who in the Privy Council wants the Princess home? What does ambassador Wootten think? Or the King's own envoy to God, Doctor Donne?' I turn my face away, as if watching the sea coal barge that is tying up at Crane Wharf.

The shouts of the boatmen and porters cut across our words, carried on the wind.

'That counterfeit divine, Donne, can't speak for God to anyone,' says Turnor.

'Easy!' yells a boatman. 'You trying to kill us all?'

'He was busy in Germany with Doncaster as his chaplain,' says Turnor, 'praying for the peace negotiations. I thought perhaps that you might have seen him when he visited The Hague.'

I do not want to hear what Turnor has just said. I watch while the shape of a youth throws itself onto the counter-weight of the crane. Two excited dogs bark around his legs. The white arm of the crane rises and begins to swing.

'I knew you for one of us after that first meeting,' says Turnor. 'I read your ambition in your eyes. You're in this with us all the way. We must try again.'

The wind snatches at the papers in my hands. They rise and scatter like startled gulls. Flip and spin. A few head for Syon.

I lean and try to catch a page as it drops past me. I watch it skim out over the dark river and settle on the surface among the floating leaves.

'Try again,' he had said.

Turnor stoops to pick up pages that have fallen onto the walkway terrace.

'You would not have liked the play in any case,' says Turnor. He mimes to the men on Crane Wharf to crumple up and throw away the pages that have landed there or on the barge.

# 41

That night when I try to sleep, the scenes from the handbill take on colour and move against my closed eyelids. I hear the guttural roars of pain from men whose tongues have just been cut out. I see Frederick on the scaffold, Elizabeth trying to climb the steps after him. Men-at-arms rush to hold her back.

I blink up at the dark canopy of my bed. I turn my head.

The windows are latched closed. Church bells, barking dogs, a distant rumble of inconclusive thunder, all would usually have lulled me, being other people's business which I could ignore. Nothing needed from me.

Bark, bark, bark . . . a small dog, challenging. Bark! Bark! Bark! A much larger dog unable to reach its impudent, pipsqueak challenger.

'Oars here! . . .' Faint but insistent at the edge of my hearing.

I turn onto my side with a pillow over my ears and find myself talking to my dead mother.

A woman must put up her hair before she is beheaded, she says. And be sure to wear a clean shift.

I'm not going to be beheaded.

I'm glad to hear it, she says tartly. I taught you something at least! At times, given your behaviour, I did wonder.

Against my will, through an unguarded crack in my thoughts, John steps into the debate.

'Why are you here?' I demand wildly.

'Lucy, don't be so slow-witted.' He crosses his arms across his chest and waits for me to catch up.

I look at his hands, remembering. But not what I feel he wants me to remember. 'Stay right where you are! I order. Not a step closer!'

He smiles and moves aside. 'Look whom I've brought to see you.'

I had not noticed the little girl standing close behind him, leaning against his leg. She has his hair and dark observing eyes.

'Lucy?' My voice croaks. His daughter, my god-daughter. But I already know better.

'Are you blind?' he asks. 'It's not Lucy.'

Joy floods me. With a cry, I fling myself from my bed. 'Where did you find her?' She has grown out of recognition, a miniature beauty.

'We found her together. Don't you remember?'

I wake in tears, with the old sick feeling in my stomach.

I've cut you out of my soul. How can you be so cruel? Go away!

I can't, says the echo of his voice. And you can't cut me out. In any case, I'm already back.

I wake fully. The dream clings on to me in wisps. The darkness in my room stirs.

Without looking at the shadows, I climb from my bed and stoop to light a taper from the banked fire. I light a candle. The light blooms. But my uneasy sense of near-madness does not melt away.

I sit up in my bed with the covers pulled to my chin.

He is already back. In my effort to avoid thinking about him at all, I had kept pushing away an important piece of information.

First came his letter.

Then came Turnor.

Then the Company of Venturers and its war-like cause.

'Write the rest of the verse yourself, Lucy,' says John. 'I've begun it. You finish . . .'

'John?' His presence feels so real that I speak aloud. Waiting for his reply, I begin to feel foolish. I am fully awake now. No excuse.

My dream of beheading had led straight to him.

I will not think about my daughter . . . our daughter.

I know now what I had not known when his letter reached me. Doctor Donne had been on the Continent during the disaster in Bohemia. He had been to Heidelberg and Berlin. He had visited The Hague. He had been in the suite of the King's envoy, Doncaster. Elizabeth's beloved Camel Face, who was busy arguing against her, putting the King's case for peace to enemies who pretended to listen and continued to prepare for war.

Once, John had been my champion and secret other soul. Ambitious John Donne now seemed the creature of the King and Buckingham. Now, though born a poor Catholic and with time in the Fleet prison against him, he has risen to become the Anglican Doctor John Donne, Dean of St Paul's.

I lie awake, thinking about his letter. He would be brutal in his honesty, so don't you shirk, Lucy. I need to ask him my most urgent question. Was his letter to me written by a friend or an enemy?

I thought you needed a miracle, says a voice that is not quite mine nor his but both together. Surely, that's your most urgent question. What miracle might knock the scales

277

from the eyes of the blind, stubborn, opinionated Scot on the English throne?

Is that question itself a trap?

A miracle to make a blind king see.

I give up on sleep, wrap a coverlet around my shoulders. With my bare feet on one of its corners, I watch a reluctant dawn edge the night away to the north. I cannot avoid the truth that insists on thrusting itself at me. Whether or not he is himself a traitor, John Donne has set me on the path to treason.

If you need me gone from this world so urgently, I tell him, you might have found a kinder way to end my life than the scaffold.

I see Donne whispering to the King that he has drawn me out of cover with a false introduction.

'Well done, laddie!' says the King. 'I always suspected the woman.'

The Countess is a secret traitor, says Donne. It runs in families. Her husband had once been traitor to the previous ruler, Elizabeth I.

'Weel,' says the King. 'I hope you dinna want me t'crown ye Pope!'

'To serve you, Majesty, is reward enough,' murmurs Doctor Donne. He knows that his reward will follow soon enough.

The scene might almost have been written by Turnor. Revise!

I refuse to believe that the ending of our love had contained the seeds of such terrible anger. We had felt like enemies, but I cannot accept that I had known him so little when I thought I knew him so well. My John could not be so changed that he would harbour a cold, scheming, patient rage that could wait for three years or more before it destroyed.

# 42

**LONDON, 1615**

Like an amputation.

The beginning of the end was my fault.

'You write the word "love" twenty-one times!' I brandished 'To the Countess of Huntingdon'. All my jealousy, buried after reading his poem to Magdalen Herbert, has leapt red-eyed and snarling from its kennel.

'She's stepdaughter to my employer. She, and he, expect to be flattered. How else should I write?'

I shook with sudden, unconstrained rage.

Elizabeth Stanley, Countess of Huntingdon. Countess Nose-in-the-air. Younger than I was by seven years, still in fresh bloom. Daughter of the Earl of Derby, wife of Henry Hastings, the Fifth Earl of Huntingdon. Also styled Lady Hastings of Hungerford and Lady Botreaux by her marriage. Third in line to the English throne by her descent from the younger sister of Henry VIII, Mary Tudor, but passed over on the Old Queen's death in favour of Scottish James, who was descended from the King's older sister, Margaret. She was a true noblewoman by both birth and marriage. Not the daughter of a made-up lord.

This Elizabeth was beautiful, with a high noble forehead and hair a little lighter than mine. Like me, she was a writer and patron. She danced in the *Masque of Queens* to wide acclaim. Nicholas Hilliard, who captured all the great in miniature, had painted her portrait. He had not painted mine.

I loathed her.

I had slipped into the Savoy hospital, where Donne kept a room for escape from his noisy brood, now moved from Mitcham to live with Sir Robert Drury in his London town house.

'. . . "love's cold ague"?' I demanded, quoting his poem to her. 'She puts you in a fever?'

'You will note that I end by praising her virtue and innocence.'

'As you once praised mine? I seem to remember that you did it only to put rumour off the scent.' I read another line from his poem: '"I may be raised by love, but not thrown down"?' I shook the paper at him. 'I know how love raises you! She's not so virtuous if you can write to her that love "raises" you!'

'Can you not see the poverty of my inspiration in those twenty-one repeated '"loves"? I did better by you than that!'

'But what of those "Violent profane heats"?' I demanded.

I was a coward. I did not tell him which line upset me the most.

*. . . his wandering rage of passion, love . . .*

I would not make it easy for him to tell me that his wandering rage of passion had wandered to another woman.

280

'Lucy, my love does not wander.' He sounded weary. 'But my children must eat. Come over here to me. I need to share violent, profane heats.'

By the miracle of our shared hearts, I was already there. And he had understood my secret fear at once. I had already forgiven. We were still one.

But later that night, back in my bedchamber in Denmark House, I could not sleep. Listening to the gentle snores of my maid on her pallet on the floor, I stared up into the pleated silk canopy of my bed. Stripped of daylight reason, I lay awake in the dark turn of the night, helpless in the grip of cold, nightmare certainty. I was a gullible fool. He shared his heart just as he shared his poems. As clearly as if I stood in the doorway, I saw his other female patrons lying naked against him amongst the crumpled sheets in that little room in the Savoy.

I sat up. Reached out for the harsh reality of the twisted golden fringe on the bed-hangings. In the darkness, the petals of the embroidered lilies on the coverlet looked as sharp as trident blades. I swung my legs to the floor, hoping that that shock of cold on the soles of my feet would jolt me fully awake.

But the gullible fool still looked from the doorway of his room at the other woman in his bed.

You imagine, I told myself. Don't imagine before you know.

# 43

**LONDON, 1615**

I had to learn from someone else that John meant to turn clergyman.

Lord Hay, Viscount Doncaster, wandered one day into Scotland Yard, where I was standing with Master Jones inspecting a painted backdrop. In spite of the Queen's growing ill health, and continued drinking, she planned a masque for the coming Twelfth Night celebrations. Among others, the cast would include the Countess of Huntingdon.

I watched Doncaster amble closer and closer to me, seeming fascinated by all he saw, a tall, slope-shouldered, long-nosed man, with a weakness for pretty lace and wide boot tops.

'Very fine, very fine,' boomed Doncaster when he arrived behind me.

Before Jones could prostrate himself with gratitude for this noble compliment, I led Doncaster away. 'What's the gossip?' I asked.

This amiable former soldier – Elizabeth's 'dear Camel Face' – had the keenest ear for rumour that I had ever known. His unerring discretion about what to say to whom, and precisely how much, made him equally valuable for learning news and for starting it. The King trusted him for both purposes. So did I.

Doncaster placed one hand on the nearest wall and examined a patch of sawdust stuck to the sole of his kidskin boot. 'I fear that Taunton has lost its Member of Parliament.'

'Master Donne?' I didn't know whether Doncaster had guessed my true relationship with my favourite poet.

'I may beg the King for a new chaplain for my next peace-broking *ambassade* to the Continent,' he said.

'How so?' I did not see how Donne as Member of Parliament and Doncaster's need for a chaplain might fit together, but I trusted Doncaster to have a reason.

'The King sent for Donne yesterday.' Doncaster, who had been present, performed the conversation to me almost *verbatim*, imitating the King's thick Scots accent and mimicking Donne's obsequious bows.

'I re-read that work of yours, *Pseudo-Martyre*, Master Donne.' (Being a Scot himself, Doncaster caught the King's voice exactly.) 'A keen attack on the Papacy. You've the mind for theological argument! I'm of a mind to see ye ordained.' Doncaster leaned back as if sprawling in a chair, with the air of a royal godparent giving a long-wanted gift.

'Majesty . . .' (Donne's voice) '. . . I'm deeply flattered by your good opinion . . .' (Doncaster bowed twice in imitation) '. . . but I am unworthy to be a churchman.'

The King had snorted. 'Y'mean you're a conniving, ambitious arse-licking bastard? Nay, laddie! You're perfect for the Church.' He leaned forward, elbows on knees, and studied his victim. 'The Church needs men like you, with a subtle, contentious wit. We drown in religious debate. Need a thoughtful man who can talk the balls off a monkey. I'll see to your ordination.'

'You should have seen poor Donne's face,' said Doncaster. 'He's been pressing hard for a diplomatic role abroad. Like mine, or even Wootten's in Venice. Envoy . . . ambassador . . . some diplomatic post – and the knighthood to go with it. Secular preferment, in any case. But I'm afraid that he's hoist by his own petard . . . should never have written so well on religious matters. Drew the straw marked "God". You don't refuse a king!'

'Donne's to be ordained?' I asked in disbelief.

'So Majesty decrees.' Doncaster nodded with glee.

'But Donne writes well on all subjects. No one has asked him to turn glass-maker or astronomer.'

Doncaster gave me a sharp look.

'Poor Master Donne.' I tried to imitate Doncaster's glee. 'Will this mean that he must give up writing love poems and write only holy sonnets and sermons?' The ground seemed to tilt like the deck of a sinking ship. John would have told me when we last met, I assured myself, if I had not distracted us both with my jealousy.

But I had been right to fear.

Doncaster's long homely face crumpled as he suddenly thought what Donne's ordination might mean for me. Though he gave the impression of lacking subtlety, it was a cultivated impression. Behind the lugubrious camel face lay a quick, shrewd mind. And nothing could be kept entirely secret at Whitehall. He was also kind.

'Even holy sonnets need a patron. The Lord's rewards tend to be reserved for the Afterlife.' He did not quite meet my eye.

My thoughts balked. Surely, Doncaster was teasing me.

The King was jesting. It would never happen. Donne turned churchman? I could not imagine him weighed down by church vestments, constrained by the public expectation of morality.

'The whole truth is less amusing than my anecdote,' Doncaster said. 'There's been talk for some time of having him join the Church . . .'

If I had still been at the centre of court, among the highest circles, I would have heard this talk too. Not learned it as amusing gossip in a yard filled with woodpiles and half-built theatrical props.

'. . . The Archbishop is also in favour. And Buckingham,' Doncaster went on.

'In spite of Master Donne's scandalous epigrams and immoral sonnets?'

'Even churchmen are allowed to be young, so long as they outgrow it.'

'He has always shown a taste for wearing black.' I knew that I was not deceiving Doncaster for one moment. 'Perhaps the King read his secret desires.'

There are scandalous churchmen, I tried to tell myself. John might become one of them. Add the 'Wicked Doctor Donne' to Jack and John. But while a wife was allowed to a clergyman, a married mistress might be questioned.

Ever since his loss of a son and two daughters within two years, I had been waiting like a rabbit under the shadow of a hawk. Edward had been right. I did lie to myself.

'. . . talk for some time,' Doncaster had said.

John could have told me about this move to ordination himself long before our last dreadful meeting. We had shared one mind. Why had he left me to learn from someone else? I would not think about what his silence might mean.

'. . . make a fine chaplain, given his languages and experience abroad,' Doncaster was saying, 'when His Majesty sends me to Germany as peace-broker.'

My rival was not Elizabeth Stanley nor Magdalen Herbert. Not another woman, after all.

He is going to abandon me for God and his conscience, I thought. And only a wicked, sinful woman like me could object to his choice.

. . . And for his career, I reminded myself. If he leaves you, it will be for God, his conscience, and his career.

He should have told me before anyone else.

I had to see him again. Talk to him. I would know at once if he had left me.

# 44

Leaving all my attendants playing cards, gossiping or napping in Denmark House, I startled Donne in his rooms in the Savoy. Future Doctor of Divinity or not, he set aside his pen happily enough.

I was a coward and went into his arms without speaking.

We lay silent later, wrapped in a cocoon of sheets and odours. 'Why didn't you tell me that you are to be ordained?' I asked.

I listened to his shallow breathing. At last, he sighed.

'I lacked the courage.'

'Even with me?'

'It will make no difference to us,' he said. 'Perhaps a little more discretion . . .'

'You can't continue with a wife and a mistress.'

'You know that I'm a fraud in any case. Always have been. The King knew my history when he pushed me towards the Church.'

'The word "doctor" will change who you are.'

'It's only another word. It won't change me with you. Without you, my verse dries as hard as summer mud.' He blew gently into my hair. 'Like the turds of an old billy-goat.'

In the next weeks, watching him pace when we were alone together in his room, I began to feel helpless with him, as I had at our first meeting. He retreated from me, out of reach in his own thoughts. I could do nothing. He was no longer satisfied. Not by his own words. Nor by what money I could still afford to give him.

When I had to leave him to attend the Queen, fears attacked me. He would be thrown from his horse and killed. He was, at that very moment, laughing about me to Magdalen Herbert.

His work began to frighten me.

'You speak to God as passionately as to a woman,' I said once, after reading a new sonnet. 'It's strange, but moving. I like . . .'

'Give it back to me.' He snatched the paper and threw it into the fire burning in my parlour at Denmark House.

I wondered how often his wife had seen this restless anger before he fled from their home.

'Flawed, heavy with intention, plodding with purpose . . .'

I chose to think that he spoke to the burning page and the words on it: our ugly, unacceptable children.

We watched his words turn to a fragile grey veil over the coals between the brass fire dogs. 'I'm certain that God is a forgiving patron,' I said.

'No, Lucy. He judges men's deeds, not words. I'm damned.'

'Then I am too.'

He scarcely heard me. I wished I did not know him so well. I wished I could be blind and not understand.

His real anger was with himself. He wanted . . . He

288

hungered . . . He knew that It lay just beyond his sight, waiting for him, if only he could . . .

He could blind himself to me, if he wished, but he could not make me stop seeing the truth of him.

Both Wicked Jack and Doctor Donne agreed. John Donne was growing weary with debate. He was worn out. He wanted resolution.

Helpless, I watched him pace and suffer.

Jonson had warned me that Donne was a double man, when he first introduced him.

I had lost my grip on my part in his life. Edward, buried at Moor Park, did not need to play the jealous husband against John. My husband's debts curbed me better than a beating. Smirking Poverty rubbed the lustre off my angel wings. I could no longer buy the freedom for John to empty the stones of financial need from his pockets. I had played midwife to verses that he now threw in the fire. Even our bodies had turned enemy. I could not buy off his tormented conscience.

I fled from London to Moor Park before we could do more damage to each other.

# 45

The Queen's health continued to decline. Eaten by Melancholy, she was now drinking as heavily as the King. Her pleasure in dancing and masques withered while her feet and legs swelled. Company and conversation, including even mine, wearied her. When she decided to move yet again from Denmark House to her palace of Placentia in Greenwich, she scarcely noticed when I asked permission to stay behind.

At Moor Park, I found Edward shut away in his own chambers, all day it seemed, dining there alone with whatever gentlemen chose to join him, tended by his old nurse and served by the house family as if his increasing isolation were an everyday condition.

When I first entered, the stale air of his large parlour reeked of wintergreen, damp and dogs.

'You.' He hugged the bundle of his bandaged arm.

'Why don't you open the shutters?'

'You've decided to come back and tell us all how to live, have you?'

'I'm happy to find you so well, sir.'

'I don't imagine that you care one way or the other.'

After a few civil questions from me, which he answered with terse words and sour looks, I left him alone, just as he wished.

I ate in the hall with Agnes and Kit, who had come with me to prospect for a possible house for himself and his wife, who was at last, miraculously, with child.

I tried to stay busy. The late summer garden at Moor Park needed my attention. I had to decide how many hogs to slaughter for bacon . . . how many supplies should be sent to London for the winter . . .

Goodyear wrote that the Queen's health worsened. As I read his letter, it occurred to me that I might not still be needed in Denmark House or at Greenwich when winter came. I had not let myself think what I would do if the queen died.

One grey afternoon, I went to inspect the derelict cottage Kit had found.

'It's yours, if you can manage the repairs,' I said. I nodded at his eager drawings and even sketched a few possible details of cornice and chimney. I made an inventory of the work that needed to be done on Moor Park itself, until my list grew so long that I put it away in despair.

Kit began to teach the stable grooms (and our startled riding hacks) how to fight on horseback.

One morning, I tried to lose myself in the unwrapping and planting of six precious grafted cherry saplings, newly delivered by barge from the Low Countries. Slowly, with my hands careful on tender young saw-toothed leaves and shiny peeling bark, the smell of damp earth tinged with horse manure anchored me. My thoughts grew settled, calmed by the vision of an almost-certain future of white blossom, bees, and sweet, dark fruit.

Donne arrived without warning.

The day quivered, then reformed, slightly askew.

From the look of him, he had been riding all night. He had caught me in my oldest clothes, as if I had been working in the fields.

Balanced as carefully as an over-filled glass, I led him into the house.

Absently, he accepted wine and a chair in my little parlour at the back of the house. He pulled several folded papers from the breast of his jacket and slapped them onto the table between us.

'I'm a fraud,' he said.

'I've heard that before.' I kept my voice light. 'Have you come here to have me contradict you yet again?' I brushed the remaining dirt from my hands and tugged at the waist of my plain old woollen jacket.

He did not smile. '. . . a poetaster of the meanest sort.'

I picked up my own glass with care. 'You're in danger of insulting my literary judgement.'

'I lick arses with my words,' he said. 'My titles creep along the ground, whining and begging like beaten dogs. "To My Lord Big Pocket". "To the Countess of Bed and Board" –'

'Do you mean me?' I stiffened.

I waited for the quick look, the half-smile that would tell me he had set a trap, was testing me.

He continued to glare down at the papers on the table as if I were not there.

I set my glass down again lest the stem snap in my hand. '"The Countess of Bed . . ."?' A sudden white rage blossomed in my chest. 'You once asked for plain-speaking, John! So tell me, plainly – is that all you've been doing with me in your room? Licking my arse? In order to beg?'

Rage pushed me to my feet. 'Forgive me if I imagined that we were making love. And that my opinion and suggestions counted for something with you. Should I let "kind pity choke my spleen"?' I threw words from one of his poems back at him. 'How long do you think you can insult me and expect me still to continue as your patron?'

'You know that I insult no one but myself.'

'Do I?' If we shared a single soul, his soul must know how he had just hurt mine.

'Whom else do I insult?' he demanded.

His new blindness shocked me out of caution. 'Your other patrons, perhaps? Those women you keep assuring me are so virtuous, like the Countess of Huntingdon. And Mrs Herbert.'

He threw crumpled pages into the fire. 'To hell with you,' he said.

'Me? Or those papers? Or your other madams?'

'For God's sake, Lucy! I told you I must have more money.'

'Why am I then the fortunate patron who must watch you have a tantrum every time you decide that your latest work is merely ordinary?'

I looked at the fire, where his papers had turned to shimmering opaque ash. 'As it happens, I agree that the last two poems I read were not your best work.'

'So how do we disagree?'

'Writing's too easy for you. You expect constant perfection. You've been spoilt with ease, John. Not like the rest of us.'

'Don't instruct me how to write!' He turned eyes as hot as the fire from the burning papers to my face. 'I don't settle for "ordinary". I don't trot out verses as a pretty game for bored ladies and gentlemen with nothing better to do.'

The words that sprang into my mouth were hooks to haul out his guts. But even I had the sense to keep silent.

He looked startled by what he had just done. And a little defiant.

'I mistook you again,' I said at last. 'I thought that you valued my poet's eye and understanding . . . even my occasional gifts of words. Did you not once convince me that my work filled you with awe? I understand perfectly now that the opinion of a "bored lady with nothing better to do" does not matter to you. Only her purse matters. And mine's no longer generous enough.'

I was disappointing him in every way. He had lost his trust in my judgement. His ingratitude made me breathless.

I understood his ruthlessness as a poet, even now, when I wanted to tear his head from his shoulders.

'I believe you've come here to be rid of me,' I said. 'If you want to hate me, you clearly don't need me to help you find a reason. Or do I speak too plainly for even your taste?'

I left the room and went out into my gardens, cold with a finality I had not intended.

He might recover his good humour, I told myself. Might forget his hurtful words and bring me a new poem that he found worthy to survive the fire. I would try to forgive.

I stooped in a pool of skirts and pulled up a seedling hawkweed from the gravel path. I stood with it in my hand. A light breeze blew a cool curtain of mist from the fountain across my hot face along with a dreadful thought.

Could his anger really be the fear that he had forgotten how to write?

Such things happened. His young wife was pregnant yet again, with another child still in clouts. He lacked money – I knew that aching tooth of distraction far too well. He was taking Holy Orders in the Anglican Church when he had been born a Catholic. He was ambitious but saw the folly of ambition.

So much weight on his spirit could paralyse a man.

I loved the poet. But did I also love the man alone, with the poet ripped from his heart? I feared that he was already falling out of love with the patron as her pockets emptied, turning her into just another of his adoring women. And it was now clear that he despised the would-be poet in me.

I found myself wandering between the tall hornbeam hedges of the Wilderness in the flowing space I had designed to calm the spirit.

Calm eluded me. The space was empty and lifeless. I knew every turning. My bones knew exactly how many steps I could take before a hidden wall barred the way. My green creation was turned as barren as his pages.

'Lucy?'

His voice. The hornbeam rustled.

I stood still, heart thudding.

Don't answer, I told myself. You can see the end coming. Make a clean cut now with the knife in your hand, not his.

I knew that he was standing as still as I was, his ears just as keenly tuned to the rustling of the hornbeam. His dark eyes would be flicking from leaf to leaf as he listened with his entire body for my reply.

I knew that the poet in him was ruthless. How ruthless was I?

I was foolish. I wanted just a little more.

I moved towards the Grotto with careless, noisy foot-steps. I didn't know if he followed. Scarcely looking at one another, we collided in urgency in the shadows of a false underworld. I had raised my skirts even before he finished untying the front of his breeches. I felt the dampness of the wall soaking into my back and tasted blood on my upper lip where his teeth had cut me. Then I felt him lick the wound as tenderly and purposefully as a mother cat.

As he was leaving Moor Park, he leaned down from his horse, our heads close. 'All will be well,' he said.

I nodded, unable to speak. Our coupling in the Grotto had felt like a farewell.

I can scarcely remember the time that followed. The Queen sent for me again. I returned to London and Greenwich to try to raise her spirits. John vanished into his new life of study, ordination, becoming a deacon and priest. Henry Goodyear, a close friend of many, including John, kept me abreast of his progress though I pretended not to care.

I saw him sometimes in company. We would nod then look quickly away.

I joined the gossip. 'How earnest he has become . . .' 'Who'd have believed it?' '. . . Still scandalous as a writer of religious verse . . .'

# 46

I intended to sneak to St Paul's alone and in disguise, with only Sir Kit to guard my person and reputation, to lurk unseen where no one I knew could see my face or try to guess my thoughts. I had not seen him in private since Moor Park. His new duties as Royal Chaplain, vicar at both Keynston and Sevenoaks, and as Reader in Divinity at Lincoln's Inn kept him too busy.

But the excitement in London and Richmond was too widespread for me to escape. Expeditions were planned. The sharing of carriages arranged. Tongues clacked.

Imagine! Wicked Jack Donne, writer of immoral verse and savage satires! John Donne, the courtly seducer. The King's own Doctor Donne. Become God's John Donne! Was it possible? Doctor Donne, the former libertine poet, was to preach in St Paul's Churchyard.

They all wanted to hear him: the cynics who could not believe his elevation, the envious who begrudged it and hinted darkly at how he might have earned it, his former patrons. The many whom he had charmed and would

297

praise any word he uttered. And me, who pretended that she needed to judge what manner of man he had become.

I agreed at last to ride to Paul's with the cheerful Henry Goodyear, my faithful letter-writer; not the most noble company on offer, but the most bearable.

I had to see John again, even from a distance, to feel his eyes pass over me, whether he knew it or not. Merely to be in the same space. To imagine that even one atomie of the air I breathed might have entered his body, been warmed by it and left it again.

I needed to hear what words he sent out into the universe now. And learn to whom he sent them.

I was a pitiful spectacle, even to myself! He had done worse than give me the pox. He had infected me with his images. If his heart was mine and mine was his, but he had taken his back again, what did I have left? If we had shared a single soul, what poor shredded scrap occupied me now? There had been more body than soul in that last frantic rut amongst the hornbeam.

Nobles and shop-keepers crowded into the churchyard. They murmured and hummed. They sneezed, coughed and sent up belches of laughter.

John Donne appeared suddenly under the pulpit roof, having climbed the steps at the back.

The crowd made a sound like a wave breaking on shale. There he is! There he is!

A surge of bodies carried me forward. I pressed even closer, until I could see him clearly.

He still wore black, but now it was the black of a priest's vestments, no longer the moth-eaten coat of a poet.

He raised his hands. Silence fell.

How he must relish such power, I thought. I looked at his fingers. I remembered his naked body pressing down on mine.

Then he began to speak. His voice carried easily to the crowd.

And I knew beyond all doubt that we were finished forever.

He was magnificent. Himself, but grown greater in stature. Though he was easy to hear, he seemed at times merely to muse to himself in the hearing of close friends. He gifted us all with his private thoughts.

The poet still flew, but he flew towards God. He spoke to God as if He were a woman, with the same passion. The same spirit that had once driven his flesh now spurred on his soul:

> . . . by withdrawing himself from his calling, from the labours of mutual society in this life, that man kills himself, and God calls him not.

The King's sharp eye had seen the truth.

Donne was born to be God's man, after all, I thought. He has found his calling and left me behind in the profane mire.

He saw me. His eye flicked away, then back. A flicker. Then he looked back and smiled. But all I could see was the easy, ambitious charm that dared risk offending no one. Not even me. I looked at a stranger.

I turned and shouldered my way back through the crowd.

Then, in August, he sent an invitation for me to ride with him again. We had not ridden together since he entered the seminary. I remembered his black moods, our last coupling, and his final words, 'All will be well.'

Hope surged, unreasoning and violent.

# 47

'There was a cleric and his lass,' I sang defiantly as we rode along Hog Lane through Finsbury in the late summer heat. The dogs barked in the Lord Mayor's Kennels we had just passed. The heavy rains of the north had not yet reached us.

'And his lass, and his lass, and another lass. Tralala la la . . .' I trilled.

My mare flattened her ears at the edge on my voice.

He kicked his horse and galloped ahead.

'If I'm truly part of you, running away won't help!' I shouted. '*Doctor* Donne!'

After a moment, he reined in his horse. I trotted slowly to catch up with him. He would not look at me.

Don't do this to me! I wanted to shout. What do you want from me?

With every thud of my heart, I found it harder to speak plainly, as I knew I must. Ignored, my horse dropped her head. I heard the hollow chomp of her teeth on the yellowing grass. I heard the creak of my own bodice. The vanes of a windmill turned slowly on top of a hill to our left, the machinery clanking and groaning. I heard John take a jerky breath. Silence. Then another sharp inhale.

My anger turned to terror. He was weeping.

'My wife Anne has died.'

'My love,' I cried. 'I am so sorry!' I was. Though he reached out and took my offered hand, and clung to it, coldness washed through me. Knowledge from beyond the realm of Reason told me that her death had finally killed me too.

'. . . Giving birth to our child.'

'All is not well,' I said. 'And never can be.'

He did not contradict me.

I had not been jealous of Anne Donne in life, but I could not bear to read the epitaph he later wrote for her. She had died one week after giving birth to their twelfth child. She and I had shared the duties of bearing his fruit, serving the two halves of his urgent need. But seven children of his flesh still survived, while he had rejected all the poetry in whose birth I had played a part. I was not midwife to that epitaph. And in his words, his public face he turned to the world, she had been everything.

Watching him weep on his horse, I accepted at last that I had lost him, not to Anne, nor Magdalen Herbert, nor the Countess of Huntingdon, but to a rival more powerful than any mortal woman.

I should have let Jonson warn me when he had said that Donne suffered. Instead I had tried to ignore John's underlying terror of death and of the punishment to follow for a sinner.

'Oh, my black soul,' he had written, when he still showed me his work. 'What if this present were the world's last night?' The eve before Judgement Day. The dreadful moment before Eternity.

I had tried to pretend that his 'profane mistresses' did not include me.

> Take me to you, imprison me, for I
> Except you enthral me, never shall be free,
> Nor ever chaste, except you ravish me.

He wrote those lines to God, not to a woman. John ached for spiritual absolution. He hoped like a child for a smile from his Father. I stood in his way. I could not rival God.

Sitting on my horse that day, with the windmill clanking on the nearby hill, I thought I did not care if I died.

Until that day, part of me had believed I could still make magic. That I might again, somehow, become a patron, a woman who mattered. And then John and I would also start again. We would find a way to be at ease again, as if he were still the blood that flowed in my veins and the mirror of my thoughts. As if he still lived in my senses and rustled under my clothes.

Thinking I might not have heard the news, Doncaster wrote to me at Moor Park to say that Donne's wife had died in childbirth while delivering their twelfth child, which was stillborn, leaving seven alive. He himself was preparing an embassy to Germany for the King to try to broker peace between the warring Catholics and Protestants. He would take Donne with him as his chaplain to take the man away from England and his sorrows.

> . . . he, no doubt, will find good use for his fluency in so many different tongues . . .

I fell asleep wondering whether or not Doncaster had intended a double meaning.

Then John was gone from England. The poet Jonson went to visit Scotland. Meanwhile, the Queen grew more and more sluggish and easily out of breath. The royal doctor set her to sawing wood to increase her circulation, but she threw down the saw after a few strokes and swore she could not breathe. Doctors said that she died of dropsy, a fatal swelling of her limbs and vital parts. I feared that she had willed herself to die.

While her court was dissolved and my world fell away around me, I sustained myself by writing to Elizabeth and lived for her letters in return.

Then I heard that Doncaster was back and Donne with him. Soon after his return, John was made Dean of Paul's. At the time, I had wondered how he had managed to rise so far so fast. Now I feared the reason.

# 48

## LUCY – RICHMOND PALACE, 1621

'Have you ever been a spy?'

Ben Jonson's head jerks up at my question. I look down at the dark inkblot left on his paper by the stutter of his pen. We sit at a table in one corner of a large receiving chamber in Richmond Palace. He is revising the script of his new masque, *The Gypsies Metamorphosed*.

At the other end of the room, members of the Prince's court are trying red and gold costumes of silk cut to look like rags. I should be among them, a minor performer.

I look to see that no one is standing close enough to hear. 'You're the King's Poet. What price did you pay?'

I see a flare of the rage that had once killed a man and put my hand on his solid arm. 'You know me too well to fear me. And know that I take no pleasure in prodding at old sores. But I need to know whether it's possible.'

He looks down and dips his pen again. Then he sets it back on the table and crumples the page of his masque with ferocity. 'Spoilt!'

'I'm sorry. But I need to know!'

He glares. 'Is what possible?'

'Please . . .' Suddenly, I can't continue.

'It's not like you, madam, to be at loss for words.' He stands and stalks out of the door.

After a moment, I follow him. 'Wardrobe,' I murmur to the tailor kneeling nearest to me, pinning up a curtain. He nods abstractedly, his mouth full of pins.

I walk slowly, shaking out the costume that I had snatched up as a flimsy excuse to leave. In the passageway, Jonson's paw grabs my arm and guides me up some narrow stone stairs onto the open walkway above the river.

'What the devil did you mean?' he demands.

'I believe you've already answered my question.' I fold the spangled veil over my arm.

'Which was . . .?'

'Is it possible for a poet, who was born a Catholic and has served a time in prison . . . who has come close to being a convicted traitor . . . can such a poet be promoted, for his verse alone, to the highest of honours granted by a fearful, Protestant king?' I draw breath. 'A king with the wits to penetrate this poet's metaphors and to read the subversion often hidden behind the words?'

Jonson leans on the chest-high parapet and pretends to look out at the Thames. 'Do you speak of me or of Doctor Donne?'

'Both similar cases, are you not? Both of you, swift-risers.' Jonson is a bricklayer's stepson. Donne, an ironmonger's. Both are well-schooled. Both have soared. 'Which one would you like?'

In truth, Donne has risen the higher with less formal learning. Jonson is still a mere poet and playwright, a step above players but not much of one, even if he is the King's Poet.

He gnaws his thumbnail for a moment. 'Why do you care if Donne has been a spy?'

'Perhaps I've turned intelligencer myself and sniff after you.'

'Bull's bollocks!'

'Please!'

He must have heard my desperation. He swivels his head and examines me thoughtfully. 'What are you up to, madam? I thought all that business finished when our Jack donned black vestments and climbed the steps of the pulpit of St Paul's.'

'It did.' I no longer care what I admit. 'You have only to read his sermons to know.'

'I have read them, and I still see the old sinner's words. Even if he claims to address them to God instead of a worldly mistress. And the change hasn't seemed to help him – he still suffers.'

'Did poetry alone push him up those pulpit steps?'

'He's always been an elegant arse-licker.' He shoots me a sideways glance. 'You know that as well as I do.'

His brutal coarseness jolts me back to a clear head. 'You still avoid my original question.'

'"Spy" is a harsh word.' He sighs hugely, in proportion to his size. 'Nothing now is as it was in the days of Walsingham and then Cecil . . . men with foresight and organisation . . . who knew better than to waste men with a gift for both languages and charm.' He can't keep a faint ping of satisfaction out of his voice. 'They sent men abroad, not as spies, but simply to report. To gather gossip at the Spanish court, or, perhaps, pillow talk in Italy. Indiscretions snatched while drinking late in France or Flanders.' Eyes slanted sideways at me, he shifts uneasily now.

Cecil and Walsingham – men who had feared the wealth

306

and power of the Catholic Church more than anything else. And who knew better than to waste any tame Catholics eager to prove their loyalty. Two Catholics, like Jonson and Donne, eager to shed the handicap of their religion and to advance, who also had foreign languages and charm.

'Cecil's death didn't end the need for intelligence,' says Jonson.

I feel a flicker of dislike for both him and Donne.

'Whatever Jack has done,' says Jonson, 'he punishes himself even more than I daresay the Almighty will ever do. "Doctor" was forced upon him. Did you know?'

'I had heard.'

'King and Archbishop both. Left to his own wishes, our man would have chosen cheerful roguery as a special envoy or ambassador. Then his conscience would have been clear. Everyone knows that ambassadors, like poets, always lie.'

I could not have asked for a clearer confession. I had been certain before, but Jonson has just confirmed it. What I still do not know is whether John . . . Doctor Donne . . . was serving the King when he wrote to me introducing William Turnor. And, if so, what did he intend?

'Jack was too clever for his own good. He misjudged with *Pseudo-Martyre*,' says Jonson.

I nod absently.

Did John, like Buckingham, still smart from some slight that I had neither noticed nor intended?

I shake my head. Not my John. He would have thrown words at me sharp enough to strip off my skin and shred my soul. I would have been twisted and turned inside out, tied into a knot in metaphor, cut off in a short line. When he had been angry, by God, I had known it! Our thoughts had been too closely joined for deception. His hot, energetic soul had always spilled over and burned me. He would never punish me coldly, three years later, by setting me up to be a traitor.

I forget the bulk of Jonson at my side. I gaze out but see nothing. My thoughts scramble for footing but slip and fall. I have another even more urgent question but dare not ask it.

Jonson stares across the river towards my former garden, lost in his own uncomfortable thoughts. Thank God, he seems to believe that my interest in Donne's past springs only from my heart. Learning this much has been risky enough. The question I dare not ask is this:

How likely is it that a former Catholic who has climbed by royal favour from prison to Anglican Dean of Paul's would risk everything in a plot against the same crown that has lifted him up so high?

# 49

## LUCY – RICHMOND PALACE, 1621

Turnor brings yet another play script as his excuse for coming here to see me. Today, it is raining too hard to walk on the terrace by the river, so I wait while he gives his sword and dagger to the men guarding the river entrance. He opens his coat to show that he does not carry a pistol. He permits a search of his boots. He smiles and answers civilly to every question, but I see his eyes, sharp and searching, assessing, thinking. I know that he is judging the strength of the guard and their care in searching for weapons.

He takes his leave of the guard, friendly, not too craven. He is one of them, a military man. A brother-in-arms but making little of it.

'We need to talk.' He counts the passing pairs of ears. 'Somewhere private.'

He is different today. Now that he has finished his performance with the guard, the rage bubbles closer to the surface. He looks at me with a new intensity. The reek of high emotion comes off him, the stink of men who have been fighting or just ridden in a race.

309

'Everyone is within, trying to stay warm and dry,' I say. 'We can talk here.'

We stand under a loggia of arches that runs the width of the internal courtyard.

All my dislike of the man comes together in a rush of loathing and fear. My hands make folded fists on the ledge of my farthingale. The hair rises on my neck. Like a good watchdog, I sense danger. My lips pull back from my teeth. A growl stirs in my throat.

'Madam?' He offers the manuscript.

I do not move to take it.

'No? Perhaps you're right.' He replaces the script in his pouch. 'We must speak of more important matters.'

'I have nothing more to say to you. I wish to speak to Wriothesley again.'

'But I have much to say to you . . . can we sit?' He walks towards a stone bench set against the back wall of the loggia.

'No. We're done.' I nod to a pair of the Prince's men carrying tennis rackets, who pass us in the loggia.

He inclines his head in mock resignation. 'Briefly then, before some other buffoons can come upon us. We have an unfinished task. The next attempt must succeed. Another botch will see him so closely guarded that his dogs will be searched before he is allowed to scratch their ears.' He reached into his pouch again for the manuscript. 'If you will only tell me where the plot falls short . . .'

I see Buckingham enter the far end of the loggia. Turnor doesn't know that he could have saved himself his literary subterfuge. Buckingham turns away so that he does not have to walk past me. But he sees us.

'Or perhaps your ambition has spied better opportunity?' says Turnor, looking after Buckingham. 'A change of loyalty would explain your failure to introduce me here.'

'Your work explains it!'

'Listen to me,' he says low and fiercely. He would like to grab me by the arm, but does not dare do it here where he might be seen. 'All those still loyal to the Prince's brother have been moved to other positions, away from his person, or banished from his palaces altogether. You saw what I endured merely to be allowed past the door. Strangers, Protestants, disappointed petitioners . . . me, for instance . . . are not to be allowed even in the same room. And, alas, the creatures closest to the Prince are too stupid and doggishly loyal to serve us.'

I stare at him.

'His hounds, madam,' he says as if I were too slow to follow him. 'Therefore, you must carry out the cleansing.'

'Get out!'

'Calm yourself, madam, or I shall shout out your intentions. Send for men-at-arms.'

'*My* intentions? You confuse me with a character from one of your own appalling plays.'

'Madam Revenge? Mistress Blood?' He smiles again.

I like his smiles even less than his cold stares.

'Don't imagine that you can insult me,' he says. 'I'm not one of your tame poetasters who pretended to hang on your words while they pocketed your money. It's you, madam, who confuses reality with a two-hour traffic of the stage. Do you imagine that you can turn back now and cast off the character you have chosen to play?'

I go numb. My brain will not work.

He shakes his head and digs into his pouch again. He offers me a letter. My own hand. 'Don't snatch!' He jerks it out of my reach. 'I'm afraid that you have already written yourself into our script.' He replaces my letter in his pouch.

'Who else is with you in this?'

311

'It doesn't matter,' he says. 'You're the only one of consequence. You alone are left in place to drive the threat of the Whore of Rome from England. This time we will use a woman's weapon. Poison – the weapon of the weak. You will kill the Prince.'

When he is gone, I plead a headache to Agnes and go to my sleeping chamber. I haul my little writing chest from under my bed. There are bright new scratches around the keyhole. I try twice before I manage to slide in my key.

Thank God, I did not keep any of the letters I received from the venturers.

My silky blank Italian paper is still there. And my silver-mounted quill and inkpot. I riffle through the piles of letters. From Goodyear. From Chamberlain. From Doncaster. I find two from my friend Cecilia Bulstrode, now dead and no doubt trying to flirt with the angels. It takes a moment to see what is not there.

Elizabeth's letters are gone.

But I had burned the ones I thought treasonous and kept the harmless gossip from The Hague that makes me feel close to her.

John's letters are gone, including his letter introducing Turnor. And all of his poems. I know that grief will ambush me later.

I look through the chest again. There's something more, if only I can think . . . I feel under the blank papers. My fingertips find only the smooth polished wood of the bottom of the chest. Forcing myself to calm, I lift out pen, inkpot, letters and blank paper until the writing chest is empty.

The King's seal is gone.

I can't breathe. My hands grow cold and clumsy. My fingers turn to stones.

What is the worst that Turnor can do with it?

My thoughts scatter. Fool, fool, fool, fool, fool! Foolish, gullible, self-deceiving . . . I had talked myself into believing what would best serve me and my pitiful ambition.

I had heard the true intent in Gorges's words at that first meeting. I had even challenged him. I had let myself be persuaded that I heard wrongly and sat down again at their table.

Not all of them want him dead, I thought. Remember the crack. The undercurrents of discord at the meeting, and Wriothesley trying to guide them away from the unspoken.

Most likely not Wriothesley now, I tell myself again. Not Murray. Not Newton . . . most likely not Newton. Though he had loved Henry and mourns him still.

Gorges. Angry, a cousin of the executed Raleigh, who had been sacrificed by James to win Spanish goodwill. A cousin executed to placate the Catholics. Gorges, for certain.

The Sennetts? Newcomers. Hard to judge what their words truly meant. 'Fire and wroth' might mean nothing when it came to an act as extreme as Turnor intended.

Who else? The boatman, who had caused the accident, just as I had tried not to believe. Prince Henry's other old retainers, now moved away from the new Prince of Wales.

And the implacable Turnor with his cold Protestant fire and talk of cleansing. One of Death's serving men. I had seen it in his eyes. Even without a cause, he ached to kill.

Had I written myself into my part beyond escaping?

I had taken great care in all my letters, both those in cipher and those in plain English.

Suddenly uncertain, I try to remember if I had ever written any words that would prove my guilt. Court gossip to acquaintances . . . invitations to harmless-sounding dinners and gatherings.

But there were cracks where a knife blade could enter. I had always known the risks. I had indeed given the Prince Turnor's poem, in spite of my distaste for the man's writing.

The accident . . . My imagined image of the boatman holding the Prince under the water.

Not imagined after all.

And Turnor means for me to replace the boatman.

Kill the Prince.

There is no decision to make.

I'm sorry, I tell my mother. I will fail you here. I can't do it. I won't do it. I will not even think it.

There is a way, if I can only devise it.

Surely, I can outwit a mercenary soldier who does not know how to write the plot of a tolerable play.

# 50

I think. I revise. I rewrite. For two days, I lack the courage to go forward.

I attend the Prince. I advise him on frames, and on the best positions for new paintings. I help him unwrap an equestrian statue in bronze. I assure him that I am in pursuit of *The Triumph of Virtue*. I try to keep my guilty thoughts out of my voice and face.

I try to think like a soldier, and a man. The battle has changed. I am fighting for my life.

To postpone all action for another day, I swallow my pride and set off to Sussex, to Arundel's estate. I return to Richmond. Two days later, I know I can delay no longer.

*If you wish me to do it, you must bring me the means,* I write in cipher. *You must bring it to Bedford House where I will meet you. I am too much watched here in Richmond, which is only a village. And you will understand that I cannot send a lady or maid to make such a purchase, even in London.*

I send this letter down the river to Turnor and any of the venturers who share his intention. I ask Kit to wait for the reply and bring it to me at once.

I am distracted at supper. After supper, I cannot make myself pay proper attention to the final masque script that Jonson has brought me.

'What ails you, madam?' He glares. 'Is it so dull? Should I have saved myself that damned uncomfortable journey here!'

'I'm sorry. I'm unwell.' I make a vague gesture at my belly. 'May I read it in the morning?'

As expected, the impropriety of my admission placates him.

Alone in my sleeping chamber except for Agnes, I write a letter to Sir Edward Coke, who had been Lord Chief Justice and is now a member of the King's Privy Chamber. Poor Kit would have another journey to make to London.

He arrives back after supper but while the cards are still out on the tables. I excuse myself and take him to my own lodgings in the palace.

'He took his time in replying,' Kit says. 'Three hours waiting by the gate of the Savoy and not a whisper of food or drink.'

I send a palace groom to bring him bread, cold meats from supper, and wine. I sit with him while he eats at a table in my receiving chamber.

Turnor's note is terse: *After supper on the evening four days hence. Bedford House.*

Kit pretends not to watch me as he folds a slice of cold venison and tucks it into his mouth.

I have four days.

I give Kit the letter for Coke. I will tell Kit everything. I imagine unburdening myself and asking what he thinks I should do.

I can't tell him. He is already in danger for being my messenger to Turnor. He's too open to burden with the need to lie.

For a flash, I see Kit being tortured to make him betray me.

'If you love me,' I tell Kit, 'you must now go straight back to Bedford House. See that Sir Edward gets my letter at first light tomorrow. Then find at least two stout armed men of good reputation, whom you trust and whose word will be believed in court. Bring them with you to Bedford House just before suppertime four days hence. Wear your sword and be ready for a possible fight.'

He stops chewing his bread. His face suddenly reminds me of the ashen boy who had bent over me after my fall on the way to Berwick. 'Turnor?'

'Yes. He must be taken. I will tell you when. I don't like his present play,' I say in an attempt at lightness.

He looks at me and swallows with effort. 'I'll haul him from the stage by the scruff of his neck.'

'That's what I hope. But above all, you must not be hurt. Trust your dislike of him. Choose your men accordingly.'

I see him off back to London on the last night boat.

# 51

The night is pleasantly cool. I wait to watch the wherry disappear and listen to the quiet muttering of ducks settled on the lowest water steps. I want to walk away, down the towpath towards Kew and the remembered safety of my parents' house. As I return to the river entrance of the palace, a man steps out of the shadows of the wall.

Turnor.

He should not be here. Kit has just left. Coke has not had my letter.

'What are you doing here?'

'Do you think I'd give you four days to devise trouble for me?' He smiles. 'Nothing succeeds like an unexpected night raid.'

I look at the men-at-arms guarding the door.

Call to them.

And say what?

'Shall we go within?' He lowers his voice. 'Not a word, madam. I can read you. I promise you, my story will persuade better than yours. And I advise you to hear it.'

I will not take him to my chambers. Agnes and my maid are there. I won't have his presence taint my rooms.

Nor be alone with him in the gardens at night.

Private, but not alone with him . . . I lead him to the long gallery. Men-at-arms guard the staircase. Men-at-arms guard the door to the Prince's apartments. All within hearing of a shout for help.

Pairs of torches flank the doors at either end to light the way of anyone passing through. No one is in the long, wood-floored tunnel, eighty paces from end to end. The windows at either end are shuttered. No fire burns here tonight. Drinking and gaming take place in smaller, more private rooms. Lines of chairs stand with their backs to the wall. Five small tables mark out the long axis. It's a place to walk in bad weather or to admire the Prince's collection of portraits that hang as close as fish scales on the panelled walls. A place where balls are sometimes hurled at ninepins and drunken races are run on rainy days. In a palace where you are always attended or attending, it is a place where you can hope to be alone. At least one babe is rumoured to have been conceived here.

'No more accidents.'

I look at the flattened glass vial in Turnor's hand. It's too dark to tell its true colour, but torchlight glints from the glass ridges. The Angel of Death lies coiled inside, waiting to unfold its wings.

He cocks his head. In the shadowed holes of his eyes, I see his knife slipping under my ribs on a dark evening. My horse's girth breaks where it has been cut; I slide helplessly, face-first towards the ground. I see Kit surprised alone in a narrow street or as he slips his key into his door. Two assassins, perhaps three. He stands no chance.

'I told you to come to Bedford House.' My voice seems to echo down the gallery. Kit is at Bedford House. His reinforcements will be at Bedford House. Here, we are dangerously close to the Prince.

'But, as you can see, I've come here instead.'

'I'm not ready.' I'm whispering now.

'You will never feel ready.' He too speaks in a near-whisper, but I feel ears listening from every chair along the wall. The portraits hanging above us listen. Their painted eyes watch us.

'We can never serve the Princess by murdering her brother!' My words escape through a tight jaw. 'She has lost one brother already. Do you imagine that she'll thank us for killing the second?'

He stands too close to me, so that I can hear. I smell him: wool, leather, and sweat. 'Her feelings do not matter! We serve England, whose next king will hand the country back to Rome! The King and Prince will sell us to the Papists in exchange for a royal Spanish whore, with Buckingham as their bawd.' He raises his eyes to the wall above us. 'You won't be the last Papist to lose your head, madam!' He is not speaking to me.

The shadowed image of Mary, Queen of Scots, mother of the present King, and a Catholic, stares over our heads.

'I would do it, but I must not be tempted to self-sacrifice,' he says. 'I shall be of far more value fighting in Germany than dead in England. Whereas, you're of no use to anyone, not even yourself . . . a female player tainted by her stage. A burnt-out court whore who displayed herself in lewd costume until her beauty faded. You should thank me for forcing you to achieve one moral act!'

I had not realised until now how much he hates me.

He continues to hold out the vial of poison to me. I feel the pressure of his will.

I must not take it. I must not touch it, nor have to lie when I swear that I had not touched it. I put my hands behind me.

'Whilst you consider, I would be grateful for a few rations,'

320

says Turnor. 'I mean to stay here in Richmond until it's done. Which must be soon. Tonight, by preference, before I sail for the Continent.'

I have to walk away. I can't think so long as he's in my sight. I hear his feet following me on the wooden floor. I can't bear to have him behind me, unseen. I turn to face him again. His eyes catch the torchlight. I see the reflected sparks and the tiny dark pinpoints of his pupils.

'If you're afraid,' he says, 'consider this: kill the Prince and you may escape detection. Even if suspected, you would have time to flee. The poison is subtle. It will take several hours to stop his heart. No one will be certain when it was given.'

'I will not poison the Prince,' I say in a low steady voice. 'You may threaten me, but you cannot force me.'

He shakes his head at me in a way that reminded me of Edward, silently reproving one of my stupidities. 'Your chances of staying alive are far better if you act as your duty demands. I've made certain of that. When I sail from England tomorrow, I will leave behind me in my lodgings my witnessed confession. I will tell how you brought me – a hired mercenary – into a plot against the Prince. How you have introduced me into the palace, though not as I had hoped. How you helped to devise the so-called accident. I will tell how I suborned the boatman on your orders – for, who knew better than you, who had once been an intimate of Prince Henry, which of his retainers was still loyal to the dead Prince?'

'You turn the truth inside out!'

He goes on as if I'd not spoken. 'The boatman will be arrested . . . an honourable man who still grieves for his dead prince and for the England that has been lost. Under question, he will almost certainly confess the truth . . . that he meant to drown the Papist weakling, Prince Charles,

321

when he overturned the boat. But, alas, the quick response of the Prince's men prevented him from assassinating the Prince. So . . .'

He holds up the poison again and continues his twisting of the truth:

'Your famously quick wits at once devised a new stratagem. You brought the Prince what he believed to be the cause of his near-fatal "accident". You profited from the failure by twining yourself more deeply into his confidence and favour, preparing to try again. This time with poison.'

'Who will believe the confession of a turn-tail mercenary against the word of a countess?'

'A frightened King and his timid whelp. But I will also leave confirming evidence for them to find. Letters, for instance.'

'There's nothing in those letters that will convict me!'

'Not in the ones I took from your writing chest.'

It takes me a moment to understand.

'The venturers never saw my letters to them?'

He nods ruefully. 'I fear that I kept them all. Including that in which you gave details of when and where the Prince took exercise. And, of course, your letter instructing me to bring you the means for your intended murder.'

He bows in mock leave-taking. 'To save His Majesty's men the trouble of pursuing and arresting him, the mercenary soldier William Turnor will vanish in battle. And you will either hang for attempted murder of the next king or be beheaded for treason.'

'Sir Christopher Hawkins knows the truth,' I say. 'The man who has carried you my letters. Do you think he has no eyes . . . can't think for himself? He will be witness to the truth. He's well known as an honest man.'

'And I have eyes. He's well known as your creature . . . another of your paramours, by chance? A bindweed

322

knight who has never served England as I have. But he won't be able to speak for you, because he'll be dead. Like the Prince. Do you think I'm fool enough to leave such a patently honest witness alive? My confession will also tell how you had him killed to prevent him from betraying you.' He shakes his head again. 'Madam, I fear that you should have studied more military strategy and less verse.'

If I let him leave Richmond, Kit is dead. One way or the other.

I walk in a tight turn. The floor creaks under my feet. The painted faces of five royal Henrys spin past me. I take two steps, as if it were possible to run. I look towards the doors nearest this end of the gallery. See a narrow dark line where they meet. Tightly closed. The other end of the gallery is too far away for eavesdropping. I stop and face Turnor.

'Put that thing away!' I say quietly. 'I will do it, but not from fear. And not with poison.'

'How then?' He sounds truly interested in my reply.

'When the Princess lost her older brother, many people believed he was poisoned. I will not rob her of a second brother in the same way.' I don't know what to tell him I will do instead. 'You must give me time!'

'I believe that poison offends you in reality as much as it did on paper!'

'It's a feeble woman's weapon, the weapon of witches and beaten wives. It will point to me at once.'

He makes a rueful face and, to my surprise, hides the poison in his trousers again. 'You'd rather masquerade as a man?'

He unbuttons his leather jerkin. 'Would your "manly soul" prefer to use a man's weapon? Like this one?'

Turnor reaches for the small of his back under his jerkin

and produces a short Italian stiletto, the needle-like blade six inches long, sharp-edged for only the first two. 'If only a man's blade will satisfy you, I pray, use mine!' Dull, sharp steel with a simple basket guard. Made for killing, not for ornament, small and easy to conceal.

I grip my skirts in my fists and step back. 'How did you get that blade into the palace?'

'The guard know me by now. Your creature. And I know where they search . . . You are afraid of it, I'll be sworn!' He teases me with a turn of his wrist. Torchlight touches the moving steel.

I fear; not the dagger, but my own sudden newborn thought.

'Forgive me. Your behaviour sometimes makes me forget that you're a gentlewoman.'

He steps closer, teasing me with his blade. I retreat again. Anyone who thinks him ordinary has not looked closely enough at his eyes.

Order and clarity arrive in my head. I see where I must ride.

'Alas, poor Madam Morning Star, you're too nice in your breeding. Your gentle education has taught you to wield a pen but not a blade. You learn to use needle but not a sword.'

I hear his scorn. I listen for any sign of weakness.

'Privilege can't come to your aid when you must help a man across the boundary between life and death. Any beggar can murder as easily as a king. And kings die as surely as beggars. Don't mistake your fragile power as a countess for true power.' He raises the knife between us. 'This is true power.'

I fix my eyes on the blade. I write it into my hand.

He nodded. 'Is it beyond you? True death, I mean, not that brief carnal spasm that poets presume to call "death".

Or perhaps you don't wish to become a martyr any more than I do? But it's a risk you must take. Unlike me, you've no choice, as I trust I've made clear.'

We are a pair of shadows, murmuring in a silent, echoing space. I hear now that he is in love with his own performance. A little giddy with having a helpless audience.

'I will not use poison,' I say again.

'If you attack with a knife, most of all with a short one like this, they'll cut you down in an instant,' he warns. 'With luck, you might be able to kill a guard or two before they kill you . . . if you know what you're doing.'

I shake my head. I don't know what sound my voice will make if I try to speak.

I feel strangely absent from myself, as if I merely watch. A mouse being tossed by a cat must feel like this. Helpless to escape. Allowed to run until the inexorable paw stops it again, its life shrinking with every heartbeat. Time shrinking. But that mouse knows exactly where it stands.

I am in John's 'dreadful moment that will determine all eternity'.

Turnor feels something of my thoughts. I see him smile. He seems to broaden. He is no longer ordinary.

'It's harder to kill a man than to kill his reputation,' he says. 'And harder still to kill him with a short blade like this one. So long as you do not make the common error of stabbing at the heart through ribs and clothes. To strike a man most surely to the heart, you must strike with words. But you already know how to do that.'

I turn my head aside as if I can't bear to look at the knife any longer. My trembling grows from a rising fury. I let it fill me.

Turnor holds the stiletto point upwards and assumes a schoolmaster's tone that does not hide the tight winding of his springs. 'I must put right the defects of your

325

schooling.' He points at the stiletto with his left hand as if at a book. 'Pay attention. In battle, an armoured man is vulnerable in only two places – armpit or groin.' He mimes the blows. 'Armpit . . . groin. But, in this case, you must merely dispatch the runt of the litter. Like a butcher in a shambles, bleeding a pig. With a short blade . . .' He touches the point of the blade to the side of his throat. '. . . you must cut here.'

I can no longer hear his words through the thunder in my ears.

His lips ask, 'Do you wish to try?' He offers me the dagger, handle first.

He is close enough for me to smell his excitement through the wool and leather. He is aroused by goading me. I take the knife gingerly, as if I have never held such a thing. As if I have never pruned nor sliced through a tree root, nor punched holes in leather harness.

He steps back a little, hands on hips, arrogantly confident, smiling. The torchlight turns him into a man of sharp angles, deep shadows and bright corners of bone. 'There will be blood, of course. It will ruin your gown. Be advised by me: poison is the safer choice for your wardrobe.'

The metal hilt is still warm from his hand.

'Go on, then. Try to strike me.' He pulls aside his soft linen collar and tilts his head back to expose his throat. 'Do you fear to learn how hard it is?' His left hand sits casually by his side, ready to knock away my hand. 'So?'

Not the throat. One chance. Ride towards it. Do it!

I move before he can see the thought in my eyes.

I see only the small, shadowed, slope-sided bowl of bone. Only the centre. As his left hand comes up, too low, aiming to protect his throat, I drive the blade into his right eye.

He roars when I strike, a garbled shout of surprise and rage. He reaches for me.

I leave the knife in his eye, stumble backwards, almost blind and deaf from the blood pounding in my head.

But I have not killed him. He does not fall. Panting, he keeps walking. One hand pulls at the hilt of the knife, the other gropes for me. He keeps coming, still pulling at the knife.

I run to a table, put it between us.

'Help!' I scream.

There is almost no blood.

Turnor takes another step towards me. He will not fall. Stays on his feet, still comes after me. With him close behind me, I run to a farther table, closer to the door. He moves around the table towards me, still reaching for me. He will not die.

'Guards – here!'

He is between me and the door. The dark shape of his mouth moves.

'Lucy . . .' He wavers. I think he will fall at last.

He keeps coming.

I grab a chair from the wall and throw it at him. Strike his legs. He stops and looks down at it as if confused. Still, he does not fall. The knife moves with his head when he turns it back to me. An obscene beak.

'Guards, here!' I scream again.

He steps clear of the chair, unsteady as a drunk. Only the devil can be animating him now.

I turn to bolt in blind panic for the far end of the gallery.

I must not. I must know that he is dead.

A spasm shakes him. He staggers into a table, falls forwards. The dagger hilt hits the tabletop and skews sideways. The end lodges against the base of a marble bust.

I begin to retch. I am leaning over a chair seat, braced on my hands, voiding my stomach when the first of the Prince's guards bursts through the door.

'Assassin!' I gasp. I retch again. 'Assassin.'

The men-at-arms lift up the still jerking body. 'It's Master Turnor, the playwright.'

I hear his feet still scrabbling at the floor.

Two more guards pound towards us down the length of the gallery.

'Madam, did he hurt you?' Hands touch my hair, my stomach, my back.

I brace myself upright on the chair back. My body begins to quiver, turned to jelly and water bones. 'He . . .' I try to draw breath. 'He . . .' I can't find words. 'I . . . he told me . . .'

'What happened, madam?'

I now have no choice of script. 'He meant to kill the Prince of Wales.'

# 52

## LONDON, 1621

I disappear from sight, transported down the Thames under guard into a locked chamber in Whitehall. The lively luminous quality of the light that leaks through the single tiny shuttered window tells me that the room overlooks the Thames. A man-at-arms guards the door. I am allowed to talk to no one except my poor Agnes, locked in with me.

I read the tiniest signs to try to guess my likely fate. The silk coverlet on my four-poster bed is a good sign, though the bed itself lacks a canopy. My custodian is a fair sign, if I wish to believe it so. He's an upper servant wearing the King's livery, who treats me with respect, gives me candles and a fire, feeds me well, but tells me nothing. I am allowed to wash my face and hands in a basin, but no more. I am not in the Tower.

The candles are made of tallow, not beeswax, and smell of sheep. This is not a good sign. Nor is the tiny fire that neither warms the room nor dispels the damp. Nor is being forbidden to send to Bedford House for clean clothes or admit any of my people. This room does not feel like lodgings for a woman who has just saved the life of the heir to the throne.

I don't know what to make of my seclusion. I ache to question my gaoler but won't lower myself to exposing my ignorance. I must seem steady in the knowledge of my own innocence.

For the first day, I fix my mind on my release. All will be well. My story will be accepted. I have saved the life of the Prince of Wales . . .

Please God, let Kit not have been surprised by Turnor or one of his men! . . . I will return to Whitehall and Richmond a heroine. Be fêted and rewarded.

This is no lie. I did save the Prince. It's the truth, if only a part of it. The part that must become the entire reality. I must wipe the rest of the tale from my mind like a poet or playwright crossing out bad lines.

I must not fear, because I am innocent. More or less.

Cross out the 'less'! I tell myself.

I am innocent enough.

But Turnor stands biding his time in the shadows of the dark, shuttered room. He will not fall, even with the knife in his eye. He is a nightmare unicorn. He toys with me. Pretends to catch me, then lets me run again. I understand his garbled speech.

You conspired in an assassination attempt, he says. You're as guilty as I am.

I break my nails on the shutter to try to let in more light.

Agnes sits in a corner on a stool with her hands over her face. She knows only that I killed a man. I don't like her lack of questions. I fear that she fears me. She has known me for twenty-seven years.

'All will be well,' I tell her, as if telling will make it so.

I dare not voice what I fear to be the true reason we are here.

The first afternoon, soldiers come for her, to take her to be questioned. When she turns back frightened eyes as she is taken out, I hold up a reassuring hand. 'Tell the truth,' I call after her. 'Don't fear. There's nothing to fear.' My words are meant for her escort as well as for her.

My first official visitor comes on the second day of my imprisonment. Sir Edward Coke. Killer Coke, who had destroyed the cream of the Catholic gentry after the Gunpowder Treason and, before that, had prosecuted Essex for the Old Queen, and thereby helped to ruin my husband.

Coke, to whom I have written.

Heart galloping, I rise to greet him, as uncertain as a would-be lover.

Like me, Coke had been born into minor gentry. He became a Norfolk barrister who has bounced in and out of favour with the King. Six years earlier, he had been dismissed from the office of Lord Chief Justice, with the help of Lord Bacon. Now re-installed as a member of the Privy Council and having savaged Raleigh on behalf of the King, he has his old enemy Bacon in his sights, charged with corruption. Bacon will pay.

In his sixties, with fine white hair framing a high, intelligent forehead and a long, soft, unshaped beard, Coke has the air of a scholar rather than of what he now is – one of the King's hunting dogs, no longer whipped out of the pack. He can also use his teeth on his own behalf, as Lord Bacon is learning.

The civil gravity of his greeting, the set of his thin mouth with its slight jut of the lower lip, his searching look into my eyes, all of these tell me nothing. I do not like his black lawyer's robes.

He bends his thin lips in a smile.

That means nothing.

But he arrives alone, without guards or secretary, like a friend come to visit.

'Sir Edward, am I under arrest?' I keep my voice light. Asking an absurd question, almost a jest. 'I wrote to you. You know what I intended.'

'Indeed, madam, you are under arrest. And will be brought before a hearing.' He might be discussing the merits of a hawk or horse. But then, this is a man rumoured to have beaten his daughter to force her to marry Buckingham's brain-sick brother. 'And I know only what you wrote me of your intentions. Only a fool accepts without question every word he hears or reads.'

'And only a fool discounts every word before testing it.'

He nods. 'A fair point.'

He may be known as Killer Coke, but he is also famed as a judge and jurist who holds fast to the logic of the law.

'What need is there for a hearing?' I ask. 'Beyond doubt, Turnor is dead. There's no question that I killed him. I have freely confessed it. I did it to prevent him from killing the Prince. I would expect thanks, not a trial.'

He peers at my face like a doctor seeking for morbid signs. 'You also face a possible charge of treason and the attempted murder of the Prince of Wales.'

I feel Death visit me then, testing the size of my limbs for fit. It stops my heart, dries up my juices. 'Possible?' I echo at last. I remember that I must be surprised. 'Treason?'

'There is strong evidence against you, contradicting your letter to me on every point.'

'What is this evidence?'

He ignores my question. 'Tell me what happened.'

Listening closely, he makes me repeat my story. Then

332

he summons a secretary, who has been waiting outside my room, and has me repeat my story yet again, slowly enough to be written down.

'Who knows that I am here?' I ask.

He shakes his head.

'Not even my husband?'

'Not even the Earl. Not yet.'

After he has left, I sit on the bed, arms wrapped around my ribs, anatomising every twitch of his face and nuance in his voice. I rock a little on the edge of the bed. I repeat my story to myself. I go over my interview with Coke. The 'strong evidence' against me.

'Possible charge of treason.' Not a certain charge. My salvation lies in that word 'possible'. There is some doubt about my guilt. In spite of that 'strong evidence'.

The secrecy around my arrest would prevent embarrassment when I was released, as I must be. Turnor had never returned to London to carry out his threat. That 'strong evidence' is a threat to frighten me into confession.

On the other hand, if the King's Council are certain of my guilt, they might also want secrecy. If certain that I represent a wider popular threat to the Prince – as indeed I do, like it or not – they may want secrecy in order to avoid inflaming the threat.

I remember what Gorges said . . . how the Commons had petitioned the King to send armies to the Continent. And what Wriothesley had said about the popular love for Elizabeth and the fear of Charles. It is possible that I am being kept *incommunicado* to avoid any chance of rescue. Rumour of the case could trigger a popular uprising. If publicly tried, I might become a martyr.

Perhaps.

I am not dead yet.

I pace the little room, rehearsing the revised truth in

which I must now believe as if it springs from the bottom of my soul.

I pause in mid-step.

My stolen letters.

Coke did not mention my letters.

Expecting to return to London, Turnor might have left them hidden too well to be found.

Or he might have laid them out ready to send.

There is nothing fatal in the letters Turnor found in my writing chest, I tell myself.

I begin to pace again.

Agnes does not return.

My hearing is to be held *in camera* in a modest room I have never entered, in the King's Side of Whitehall Palace. Not in a regular session, not under the dreaded starry ceiling that has seen so many men and women condemned to death. I will have no counsel to speak for me. I do not expect to have one. Those accused of treason must speak for themselves. They do not see the evidence against them in advance. Their chances of acquittal are slight.

I have not seen the evidence against me. I must speak for myself. But I have not yet been accused of treason. I can't judge my chances.

My guards and I pass Agnes in a hallway on the way to my hearing. Her eyes press an unreadable message into mine. She clasps trembling hands as if praying. I smile and give her a little nod of encouragement. Thank God, she seems unharmed.

Buckingham is already there in the room, when I am brought in, seated beside the King's chair in the centre of a temporary dais. He watches me being led to my chair as coolly as if I were a baiting bear being brought into the ring and set at the post.

On either side of Buckingham and the King's empty chair, four members of the Privy Council wait. Coke is one. Sir Henry Montagu is another. White-haired but younger than Coke, he is a close political ally of Bacon and much in the King's favour, and in Buckingham's. Until recently he sat on the King's Bench and served as Lord Treasurer. With the help of Bacon, he had displaced Coke as Lord Chief Justice. He has now resigned that post at Buckingham's request and the world waits to learn what Buckingham intends for him instead.

He and Coke ignore each other.

Coke and I incline our heads.

I don't know what to expect from him. He has a fearsome reputation for tenacity and blood. But even now he is said to clash with the King over the right of the monarch to make legal judgements in his own person. There have been rumours in Richmond that he thinks of running for Parliament.

The King is carried in. His legs are now too weak to support him. It takes several moments to settle him in his chair. He is growing old.

'What've ye done, Lucy?' he demands, still tugging his coat straight, his Scots accent thicker than I remember. 'You'll need a quick saucy tongue now to save yer neck.'

'You'll hear soon enough, Majesty,' I say. 'But I still promise not to dance.'

I can tell by the blank look in his eyes that he has forgotten our last brief duel of wits.

'Go on, Steenie,' the King says. 'Let's have it over with!' He gazes about him. 'Where's the intended victim of treason? Didn't I make him Lord President of the Council?'

'His Highness is still too disturbed by the attempt on his life to feel able to attend.' Buckingham does not need

335

to add that he will report to the Prince whatever he feels the Prince needs to know.

I remember wondering if this former friend would ever be willing to name me a traitor.

'Let's get on, then!' The King waves an impatient hand. Montagu steps forward. It seems that he is to serve as prosecuting attorney.

This is not a good sign. Montagu is a man of the highest consequence and power. He has a lively intelligence and a reputation for being both fair and informed in his judgements. On the other hand, he is the King's man and close to Buckingham and must have expectations of further advancement. He and Coke are enemies.

He puts a pile of letters on the table in front of the judges.

He stares at me silently for a long while, frowning a little. He has a gentle, good-humoured oval face, with a forehead perpetually crimped by faint concern. Then he strokes his sparse white moustache and shakes his head, as if trying to make himself believe the dreadful facts of my case.

'The Countess of Bedford,' he begins, 'has been as a star, at which the whole world gazed. But stars may fall.' He does not point at me, the fallen star, but his head inclines in my direction.

'Having fallen, she has been determined to avenge herself on the sphere that she once troubled until it thrust her out into darkness. Having once stood as the poet's "Morning Star" that shed its light on all Whitehall, she is now bent on destroying the brightest lights that remain shining high above her. From envy and bitterness, she would have put out the Sun!' He smiles at the King and judges to signal the double meaning in his metaphor.

We are all lettered men, says his smile. We have all

read and judged her extravagant praises for ourselves. We all know how empty such praises can be.

Buckingham nods encouragement. I see their quick exchange of glances.

I see it. Buckingham has asked for Montagu in this hearing.

Buckingham wants me to be charged with the treasonous intent to murder the heir to the throne, driven by nothing more than simple envy and bitterness. Steering men's thoughts away from the dangerous subject of Spain.

'You conspired with a pack of wolves,' says Montagu. 'Men who shared your treasonous malice, other treacherous malcontents.'

Malice endangers no one but me. It does not threaten to stir up a popular revolt. Malice reduces. I must lead them away from malice.

'How am I said to have conspired?' I demand.

'Wait your turn, madam.'

'Let her speak, Montagu,' says the King. 'She'll be at least as entertaining as you are. Go on, Lucy. Here's a chance to flap yer tongue.'

'Thank you, Majesty.'

My heart thuds. I believe that I have the measure of a part of my audience. But in this case, a bad performance might cost me my life.

Ben Jonson whispers in my ear, 'Whilst you play a goddess, you *are* a goddess. You must believe it for the short time you are onstage.' A rivulet of chill runs down my neck as if his breath had indeed stirred my hair.

I remain seated, head raised. My hands lie folded calmly on my lap. I ignore the stink of my body, still in the clothes I wore when I killed Turnor.

I must gamble on where the power lies here in this room.

337

'I would like to swear.' I nod at James. 'On the new King's Bible.'

Majesty grunts. Neither satisfaction nor dismissal. Acknowledgement only.

I lay my hand on the jewel-embossed leather cover. I swear to tell the truth.

'And now, madam . . .' The King leans back.

'Under oath, I swear that I have acted ever only for the happiness and safety of the First Daughter of England.' I hear my voice begin to climb and grow thin from lack of breath. I inhale and lower my voice.

Sing in your chest voice. Remember to breathe.

'I confess to wishing to give Her Highness comfort when she seemed in danger from her enemies. Is this a treason?' I look at the judges in turn but avoid Buckingham. 'Beyond doubt, she has enemies. That is fact. No one can dispute that she and her husband have lost both Bohemia and the Palatinate, to the Hapsburgs. Again, that is fact. They are without a country to call home, under Ban of the Empire. Her plight is not a matter of opinion nor religious sympathy. No one can dispute it.'

Coke breaks my gaze and looks down at his hands.

Yes, my lords, I think. The issue is politics, not a woman's petty personal malice and bitterness.

But don't rub their noses in the fact.

'It is surely possible for one woman to wish to comfort another. It is our nature to wish to comfort.'

'You'd best ask the Earl of Bedford whether his wife's nature is truly so generous!' Buckingham says.

The sally wins him a smirk from his master.

I try not to see him. He sits at the edge of my vision, disbelieving, wanting to think the worst of me, sucking at my attempts to order my thoughts. I know now that he wants me exiled or dead. Leaving him without competition for the favour of the malleable Charles.

He and I are competing today also, but not for Charles.

Coke has fixed his eyes on the tabletop.

'Please tell me if I do not understand,' I say. 'Having admitted to the death of Master Turnor, I believe that I can be accused only of visiting the King's daughter in The Hague. But I was permitted to go only because I acted as a messenger from the King himself.'

Buckingham pounces, not as clever as he thinks himself. 'Was this so-called visit of mercy not part of your scheme? Did you not offer yourself for this *ambassade*?'

'My lord, you know that I did. Indeed, you arranged it. But I see no treason in such an offer, only loyal service. Any more than there was treason in your arranging.'

I see suppressed smiles behind the dais. The King, however, frowns and pulls at his lower lip.

I also catch a flash of irritation in Montagu's eyes.

'But did you not also deliver a letter to the Princess written by the King's enemies?' he continues.

'I delivered the letters I was given, my lords. One from the King. The other from a friend, and a good loyal subject, so far as the world knows.' Loyal to whom, I do not say. My voice heats with indignation. 'I did not think that I needed permission to act as a running groom.'

'We will come shortly to that other letter you carried.' Montagu looks at the King. 'But first, if I may return, Majesty, to the case I was making before the Countess interrupted . . .?'

The King waves an impatient hand.

Montagu is not reading him, I think.

'As I was saying . . . From envy and bitterness, she would have put out the Sun.'

'You're all mad!' I exclaim.

The King sits up, as alert as if watching a cockfight.

'I've been accused of most sins, but never envy. Nor bitterness. Is that not true, Majesty?'

I have lost Montagu now. But then, if he is Buckingham's man, I never had him.

'Generous to a fault, Lucy,' agrees the King.

I see Coke place his closed fingertips on his mouth.

'What do you imagine that I hope to gain by "putting out the Sun"? Though I would prefer to call him the earthly son of the flesh, who is still only the Sun-to-be.'

'And she knows how to talk,' Majesty murmurs.

Montagu chooses to ignore my final diversion. He consults his notes. 'You don't hope to gain; you plot from malice and to prevent loss. Your family profited from pillaging of monasteries. You schemed against an English alliance with Spain because you fear possible reparations and restitution of property stolen from the Catholic Church . . .'

Stolen? I think. Reparations and restitutions! Our Protestant Peacemaker King listens without a flicker or flinch. If Montagu feels safe to say such things, the temper of the times is truly changed. The Protestant venturers of the Virginia Company are right to fear.

'. . . If the Prince of Wales marries the Infanta of Spain, you and your family risk losing everything.'

'Faithful service to the crown is never so badly rewarded,' I say. If Montagu has any sense, he will abandon this line of attack. The King's own daughter had been raised in the 'stolen' abbey given to my father. If this is the worst accusation he can make, I am tempted to feel a cautious hope. But the pile of letters still lies waiting on the table.

'Majesty . . . my lords,' says Montagu. 'It's time to stop playing the Countess's games.' He nods to his clerk, who hands folded sheets of paper to the judges, Buckingham and the King.

'You have been given a copy certified by magistrate, of the confession of Master William Turnor, stabbed to death by the Countess, a murder to which she has already confessed and which I don't think even she would now dare to deny . . .'

'I don't deny it!' I cry. 'You are wicked to suggest that I might try! I have never denied it. I made my guilt in his death clear from the moment the first man-at-arms entered the room. But I swear, again, that I killed him to save the life of the Prince!'

'That is not what Master Turnor says in his confession.'

My hands clench on my lap. Now I understand Coke's evasiveness, and Montagu's hostility. I've been a gullible fool again.

'Where did you find this document?' asks Coke, looking up from his reading.

'In the victim's lodgings, properly witnessed.'

There is a moment of silence. A rustle of turning pages.

He has outwitted me after all.

Turnor had written his false confession before he came to Richmond. He did not know that he would not return to carry out his threat. He had never intended to wait. He had already damned me when he pretended to give me a choice.

Kit . . .! I think. Had Turnor already killed him too?

'You will see,' says Montagu, 'that he confesses on pain of eternal damnation how he was drawn into a plot to assassinate the Prince of Wales. He tells how the Countess recruited him for this purpose. He describes the first attempt on the river on His Highness's life. And how it failed . . . praise be to God! He tells how he then felt remorse, and tried to withdraw, but the Countess threatened to denounce him to the King if he did not finish the treacherous task. And how she offered him money to do so. Hence, his decision to flee from England, and from her. Alas, as we know, she prevented him.'

He turns to me for a long moment as if reading my soul. 'I say that the Countess of Bedford conspired with her unfortunate creature, William Turnor, to murder the Prince.'

Turnor had always meant to denounce me.

This is no longer a performance. My hands turn clammy. I cannot breathe.

'I summon one of her own people to testify against her,' says Montagu. If it is Kit, I will at least know that he is alive.

It is not Kit.

My steward, John Mudd begins as a fervent witness in my defence. 'The Countess is the best, most generous mistress a man could ask. Devout, industrious . . .'

'Thank you, Master Mudd,' Montagu interrupts drily. 'Your loyal support for your mistress is noted.'

These are hard, sharp-witted men who are not impressed by eulogy. But I feel tears start to my eyes. Though I know it is not the reason he has been called, his trembling sincerity is beyond doubt.

'Did you ever see the Countess in conversation with Master Turnor?' asks Montagu.

Don't be too grateful, I try to warn Mudd silently. These men are too sharp. Speak the truth.

The steward gives me a look of anguish. 'Yes, sir. But only when he came to Bedford House as a petitioner for her patronage. With his plays and verses. The Countess always had her lady or some other woman there with her. No one ever heard them speak of anything but his work.'

'Did she praise him as a writer?'

Mudd pauses to consider. 'No, sir. She spoke her mind after he was gone. She didn't reckon him as a poet. I had half a mind to run him off to save her from being troubled any further.'

Montagu raises his eyebrows. 'She did not think him a good writer?'

'I just said as much.' He does not see, as I do, where this is going.

'Perhaps she also met him elsewhere?'

Mudd gives him a long, level look. 'I wouldn't know, sir. If you're hoping I'll lie either to save the Countess or to damn her, you read me wrong. I'll say no more than I know, but what I know, I'll say.' This even-handedness is more impressive than his earlier praise. He is no fool and is learning fast.

'May I speak my mind?' he asks.

'If ye'll swear that ye have one to speak,' says the King. The effect is not comic. King James can jest while watching a man hanged, disembowelled, beheaded and butchered.

My steward gives me an apologetic nod. 'Lady Bedford is a generous-hearted woman, but she can't always curb her tongue. She may like to misbehave for effect, but I'd swear on a Bible that she'd never plot anything wicked in cold blood.'

'Then you know that she plotted?'

Mudd repeats his cool look. 'I'm not so solid between the ears that I can't draw conclusions from the fact that she's here, and I'm here, and you're asking me such questions . . . sir.'

Montagu flushes slightly. 'Is it possible that the Countess may have been hiding a flirtation, or more, with Master Turnor? Such deepening of the bond between poet and patron is not unknown . . .' His voice insinuates.

343

'She had no bond with him!'

'I'm done with him,' says Montagu. 'Bring in the next witness.'

The ears. I had seen young Sir Walter Sennett on the Twickenham shore after all. And he had seen me.

'I came forward after I heard what happened . . . that the Prince almost drowned. I saw Lady Bedford on the riverbank at Twickenham just before . . .' He looks at me with hatred. '. . . just before it happened. After the Prince capsized, I saw her run into the water. Now that I know she killed Master Turnor, I feel certain that she meant to hold His Highness under water if she could and . . .'

'Your certainty does not concern us.' Coke interrupts from the judges' table. 'Only your testimony that she was there.'

Montagu's left hand makes a fist in his black sleeve.

'Why were *you* there?' I demand of Sennett. 'My lords, ask him why he was there! Ask him how well he knew Master Turnor!'

'Do you instruct us in how to proceed, Lady Bedford?' asks Montagu.

I sit back in my chair. Reason tries to reassure me that they have no absolute proof of anything more than an accident. Only Turnor's lies.

Coke clears his throat.

'Go on,' Montagu instructs Sennett.

'With the sly, seeming-innocence of Eve, she murdered a noble soldier to protect herself!' Sennett stares at me as if at the Antichrist.

'We already know she killed him,' says the King. 'Give us news we don't know!'

Coke makes a note.

Sennett is a clown. They can't take him seriously.

Montagu dismisses him.

The next witness is very different.

The Prince's boatman. Two guards have to hold him upright. His hands are swollen. His wrists bleed where they have been strapped.

'Yes, I tipped the Prince's boat.' His voice creaks with dryness. His eyes defy. 'I held him under. A Papist pup that deserves to be drowned.'

He's a dead man, I think. Has nothing more to lose.

'Did you act of your own free will?'

'With a willing heart and I would do it again.'

'Did you act alone?'

'No. Not alone.' He looks at me.

'On whose authority did you act?'

'On that of the true friends of Prince Henry and his sister, the Queen of Bohemia, who should be Queen of England!'

'Who gave you the order?'

The room is so silent that I can hear water slapping the wall under the window.

He smiles at me with swollen lips. His sister in the cause. 'She did.'

'The Countess ordered you directly?' Coke interjects over the exclamations of his fellow judges.

'This is false!' I cry. 'Someone has forced him to lie!' I turn on Buckingham.

The boatman stares at me with sudden scorn but speaks before I can attack Buckingham. His quick anger saves me from a terrible blunder. 'I do not lie, my lords! Master Turnor told me that the orders came from her. I believed him when he said that she shared our purpose – to free England from the claws of Rome.'

'Turnor told you to kill the Prince!' I say. 'I did not! You had only his word for it that I gave the orders.'

He shakes his head. 'Now I know better, madam. You

345

are a traitor!' His eyes brand me a despicable coward, renouncing the cause to save her own neck. I watch him being taken away, almost certainly to die for what he believed.

They do not call Kit.

Because a dead man can't be called, I think.

Truth and lies tangle in my head. I forget my story.

'And now the Countess will condemn herself by her own words.' Montagu picks up the pile of letters at last. 'My lords, these letters were left by Master Turnor in his lodgings.'

I am certain that I burned Elizabeth's most incriminating letters, those asking for help, written in the first heat of her flight. I should have burned them all.

But the first letter is not one of those stolen from my chest. It is one that I wrote and sent to the venturers of the Company, which Turnor had intercepted and kept.

'*The Prince seems most vulnerable . . .*' Montagu reads. '"Vulnerable"?' he asks. 'You are schooled in Latin, madam, and know exactly what your words mean. '*Vulnus*. A wound. *Vulnerabilis*. That which may be wounded. Does that word not suggest a search for weakness, for "vulnerability", in order to attack most effectively?' He points the little wisp of his beard at me, a teardrop of white hair under his lower lip, daring me to reply.

Turnor had not passed on my letter to Wriothesley and the venturers. He had kept it. He had always meant to use my letter against me, even while he used the information I had written. I wonder suddenly if Wriothesley, Preston and Newton had even had foreknowledge of the false accident on the river.

'Please read the rest of my sentence.' I speak my own words from memory. '". . . most vulnerable in his love

346

of art and desire for acquisition." When you hear all my meaning, my use of the word "vulnerable" becomes clear at once. It's a metaphor. The Prince is vulnerable in his passions only.'

'Then why, in this following letter, do you list all the Prince's physical exercise, implying the circumstances in which he might also be "vulnerable"? Fencing in the tiltyard, riding in Richmond Forest, for example.'

I try to remember exactly what I had written. I can remember only a dangerous lack of respect.

'Majesty . . . my lords, Rumour is greedy,' I say. 'For better or worse, often to my own discredit, I have always fed the beast. Shameful, perhaps, but not treasonous.'

I am beginning to talk too much.

Speak less. To more effect.

'Why did you cross out "opposite the palace" and write instead "between the eyot and the palace"? Is that not to make more clear exactly where the Prince could be found and . . .' Montagu pauses for effect. '. . . *vulnerated*?'

I know something is wrong even before he smiles and offers me my letter.

'Will you read aloud what you then went on to write?'

Below my signature, a *post scriptum* is written in the bottom margin of the page. I work out the simple cipher, the same that I had used in all my exchanges with the venturers.

'We have made a copy,' he warns, seeing my hands tighten on the paper.

'I did not write this! I will not soil my tongue with it!' Speaking the words will stick them fast to me, even if they are not mine.

'My lords, I expected this refusal,' he says. 'The Countess is far too clever to condemn herself with her own words. I will do it for her. Here is the translation of her cipher.' Montagu reads. '"In my opinion, the Prince is best attacked on the water, away from his retainers and where his own weakness in swimming will make him easy prey."'

You must put your hair up, said my mother. But I think you a weak fool. You're going to die for the wrong reasons.

'Give it to me again!'

He holds it up for me to see but not to snatch and destroy. His belief in my guilt chills his eyes.

I point at the letter. 'Does any man here think me fool enough to write such open treason in such simple disguise? It's an insult . . . and an attempt to terrify me out of my wits. I admit to the rest of the letter. That last line, the *post scriptum* is a forgery!'

'I'm not surprised that you deny writing it.'

'Because I did not.' I had forgot another lesson from the Old Queen: cross out every inch of clear space around anything you write.

He waves away my denial.

'Lastly, why did you have in your possession an impression of the King's seal? For what purpose did you mean to use it? Another forgery? Is it not treason to impersonate the King, in writing as in all else?'

I had forgot the seal.

'You strain to make a case against me with insinuation and surmise!' I draw a deep breath. I will not be a weak fool but a bold one. The truth about the seal, or the near-truth, is thin ice, but it just might hold.

'Her Highness took the seal from the King's letter I had delivered to her and gave it to me to keep safe. She could not bring herself to destroy that symbol of her lost England, that track of his royal hand. But she feared to keep it in The Hague where enemies might find and use it.'

The King raises his brows. For a dreadful moment, I fear that he will begin mocking applause. Then he frowns and pulls at his lip again, vanishing into private thought.

'How did you come to know William Turnor?' Montagu demands, suddenly shifting his direction of attack.

I look at him.

John.

I can't make my mouth shape his name.

Coke leans forward, intent on my answer.

John Donne, the new Dean of St Paul's. Enemy or friend? No use to me either way. If he's Turnor's ally, no one will believe me. If he's not, I must not pull him down with me, whether he's friend to me or not.

'How did you know William Turnor?' repeats Montagu.

'He asked me to be his patron.' Safe enough.

Buckingham gives a bark of derision.

'And were you?'

There had been witnesses to our meetings . . .

'I allowed him to petition me for a time. He proved to be a mediocre poet. I won't argue otherwise. But he was the only poet who wished to serve me. I was flattered into giving him more attention than he deserved.'

Too much talk again. Don't let fear loosen your tongue.

'I suggest that your patronage of a writer you "didn't reckon" – if I may quote your own steward – served as a disguise for your shared involvement in the treasonous plotting. Not knowing of Turnor's confession, you thought to hide your own guilt by killing the chief witness against you.'

I had underestimated Turnor as a writer. He had been far better than I at rewriting the truth. Had failed only in writing his own ending.

One small lie to the boatman had been enough to turn the truth inside out.

'Majesty, my lords,' says Buckingham, 'corroboration of her fantastical lies is scarcely needed. But I would offer one last confirmation. The Countess had already aroused my suspicions. On the evening after the Prince's ordeal, when the Grace of God preserved his life, she came to Richmond, claiming to have found the lure that almost killed His Highness.' He bent out of sight and lifted a covered object onto the table. 'I have it here.' He lifted the cloth from the gilded casket. 'Do you recognise this, madam?'

The doctors, the taster, the waiting gentlemen had all witnessed . . .

'Yes, of course. I took it to the Prince as soon as it was brought to me.'

'Why was it brought to you, if you were not part of the plot?'

'I'm known both for my taste for antiquities and for the generous prices I have paid.'

Now Coke clears his throat. 'Madam, you seem to have an excuse to answer every point raised against you. Yet your own letters point clearly to your guilt. How do you explain them away?' His voice is gentler than his words. He does not mention my letter to him.

The mouse has one last chance to escape the inexorable paws.

Now I stand. I move into the middle of the speaking space, forcing Montagu to step aside. I do not rush. I breathe in. I take command of the audience, with the King, as always, the central point of focus.

The King and Coke.

I ride straight at my innocence. I must ignore the paralysing thought of death. Blind myself to ambiguities and half-truths. Nothing must distract me nor make me break stride. I must not fall.

350

Jonson whispers in my ear again. When you play an innocent, you are innocent.

'Majesty, my lords, you have heard the evidence produced against me. Now I ask you to revise . . . *revisere*. To look again. To re-examine. To look again with the aim of correcting or improving.'

'By God, the woman's turned Latin tutor now!' The King looks left and right at his councillors, inviting mirth.

Montagu steps forward to take command again.

'I hope, Majesty, that you will allow us to enjoy this uncommon tutorial,' says Coke, before Montagu can speak.

'We sit before you as ignorant scholars,' says the King. 'Set to, Lucy.'

Montagu steps back to Buckingham's end of the judges' table.

'I ask you to see my letters,' I say, 'my dealings with Master Turnor, as an attempt to confirm my own suspicions. For that was all I had – suspicions.'

'Ha!' The King leans forward, elbows spread on the table. I can't read his tone.

I glance at Coke. I argue just as I had written to him.

'I had strong suspicions, but nothing to take to the law. A woman's feelings that something was amiss. I hoped to lure Master Turnor and his colleagues into the open. To acquire evidence to show your lordships.'

Buckingham laughs loudly.

'Every accusation can be turned to its exact opposite – proof of my loyalty.'

'Ingenious,' says the King. 'Wasn't expecting that.' I imagine approval in his voice. But he is not a simple man. To be entertaining is not to be innocent.

'Ingenious, indeed!' Montagu steps back in and refastens his grip on the proceedings. 'And what of Master Turnor's confession? The confession of the boatman?'

'The boatman had only Turnor's word that I gave the orders.'

'Therefore you killed Turnor to prevent his denying it.'

'I killed him to save the Prince.'

'We argue in circles,' murmurs Coke. 'Please advance the debate.'

'Aye, get on with it.' The King sighs and scratches his jaw. He re-crosses his legs impatiently.

Montagu looks at Buckingham.

'It does no harm to nail down the truth,' says Buckingham. 'It seems clear that Lady Bedford killed Turnor to prevent him from exposing her treasonous intent, not knowing that she acted too late. Unless that is true, why did he trouble to condemn her when he had already confessed his own guilt?'

'I can't explain why he was so eager to condemn me,' I say. 'But I'm certain that as judges you've known cases where petitioners, like some dismissed lovers, respond to rejection with unreasoning rage . . .'

'Let me interrupt to summarise.' Montagu overflows with disbelief. 'You say that we are mistaken in our understanding of the evidence, and that, in part and in effect, Master Turnor forced you to kill him because he would not accept your low opinion of his verse? Madam, I believe that I might wish to revise . . . *revisere* . . . your testimony right back to where we started – with the truth of your guilt.'

The King smiles a little, dangerously entertained now by the enemy.

'Why should we take her word . . . the word of a frivolous woman, a fallen court favourite whose false nobility is borrowed from her husband . . . against the word of a tested soldier?' demands Montagu.

Coke purses his lips and wrinkles the high forehead

above his long, strong nose. 'In my judgement, Reason can still tilt the argument either way. I would like to examine one last witness.'

'You should have given notice,' says Montagu coldly. His little fluff of a beard juts again. His perpetual frown deepens.

'We need no more proof of her fantastical inventions!' says Buckingham. 'For which inventions, I might add, she was once famed in Whitehall.'

Coke quickly turns to the King before he can agree with his favourite. 'We have not sought the opinion of God, Majesty. Surely, we should seek His opinion in a judgement that may lead to a capital charge. Whether or not He chooses to advise us is another matter. A man of God may be able to help us.'

'Ye never know,' says Majesty. 'Anything's possible.'

An usher brings in Coke's witness.

'Doctor Donne!' the King exclaims. 'It's been too long since we last debated.' He beams. 'Welcome! Now we'll see the Countess pummelled with heavy-footed metres and scourged with long lines.'

All arguments flee from my grasp. I stand gaping at him. His presence snatches all weapons from my hand.

The Reverend John Donne, newly made Dean of St Paul's, wears a prelate's black silk robes in place of his coat. A little grey at the temples now, his beard neater and shot with grey. Still slim with wide shoulders but the beginning of a stoop. The almost-smile still lurks in ambush at the corner of his mouth. After a first quick glance, he does not look at me. A faint scent of incense reaches me from the folds of his robes.

'How do you know the Countess?' asks Montagu. If he has heard past rumours, he hides it.

'I'm sure that you all know she was my chiefest patron,

my lords, while I still wrote poetry for the court instead of sermons for Paul's.' He aims his words at the King, clearly no more willing than I to let Montagu lead the proceedings. 'Because you will all have heard them sung far too often, I won't repeat her infinite praises.'

'Thank God,' says the King, *sotto voce*. More loudly, he asks, 'But how d'ye rate her as a servant of the crown?'

'As a faithful servant, Majesty. A devout woman, but neither Puritan or militant Protestant.' Now Donne flicks a glance at me. 'In that respect, I would call her a worldly saint.'

'Nay, John!' The King sits forward. 'From what I've heard, no one knows better than you that the woman's no saint!'

I hear suppressed gasps. Veiled eyes watch to see how Donne will deal with this blow, to both his testimony and his new high position.

'Aye, Majesty.' Donne looks unperturbed. 'You know me. I never use a simple phrase like "good, loyal woman" when I can spout poetic hyperbole like "worldly saint".'

He moves closer to the King and lowers his voice in confidence, but it carries through the room as clearly as his preaching voice had carried through Paul's Churchyard. 'You didn't hold my former appetites against me, Majesty, when you put me forward for ordination. Is the Countess not allowed a chance to reform as well? What value is virtue to any of us if it's too easily won?'

The King laughs.

Then Donne shifts into magnificence. He holds up his hands to command silence from his congregation. 'The Countess of Bedford has won virtue in the most painful way possible,' he says. 'She violated her soft nature as a woman, like a lioness aroused to defend her cubs, in order to kill an enemy who would have killed the Prince. This is virtue hard won. Causing her the spiritual torments of a martyr. And for that suffering, I call her a "worldly saint".'

'But how does she come to plot with a man as vile as Turnor? How does she even know such a man?' Montagu half-turns to the judges, triumphant in this demand.

'Because, Majesty . . . my lords, I gave her his name.'

'You!'

'I gave him a letter of introduction to her. As a playwright and poet.'

'Is this true, Lady Bedford?'

I nod wordlessly, made breathless by his performance.

Donne gives me a small bow. 'And I beg you a thousand times to forgive me, madam, for sending you such a paltry talent . . . and in a man who proved so dangerous. But I had my reasons, my lords, which were the same as hers. My letter may even be amongst those on this table.' Donne points.

Looks are exchanged. Heads are shaken. In his letter to me, Donne had never used Turnor's name. Nor mine, nor his own. Turnor had not thought the letter worth leaving to be found.

'A pity,' says Donne. 'It would prove what I say, beyond argument.'

'Are you saying that you conspired with her?' asks Buckingham.

'My lord, I prefer to avoid the word "conspire". It makes a man sound guilty even when you accuse him of nothing worse than conspiring to show Christian charity. I trusted her to make good use of what I gave her.'

'And that use was . . .?'

'To try to draw him out. I had heard rumours about him and his activities on the Continent while I was there acting as chaplain to Doncaster. When I heard that he had come to England, I decided to test the rumours.'

'Why did you choose a frail woman for such a purpose?'

The half-smile pounces. 'In spite of his dangerously puritanical politics, Master Turnor aspired to be a poet and playwright. Anyone who approached him as a soldier, he would suspect. But to a possible patron, he would crawl, suspecting nothing while hoping for everything.'

He looks at me again, more directly this time. The faintest lift of his brows asks, is it good?

I drop my head minutely. Yes.

'I regret that I did not realise just how poor a writer the man was, nor how dangerous. Furthermore . . .' He cuts off a threatened interruption from Buckingham. '. . . I could think of no better "conspirator" of either sex.' He treats Buckingham to the flash of smile, still playing with 'conspire'. 'The Countess of Bedford strikes awe and admiration into stronger hearts than mine. She is famous for her quick wits, broad understanding, fierce loyalty, courage and infinite generosity.'

'D'ye truly think her innocent?' asks the King.

'I know her to be innocent of treasonous intent. And I believe that her plea of defending the Prince should be accepted. God urges my conscience to speak. As Dean of Paul's, I cannot say otherwise.'

Through the Dean of St Paul's, God Himself has cast His vote.

The King nods. 'That'll do for me.'

The two other judges nod. Buckingham looks stony.

'And for me,' says Coke. He and Montagu stare eye-to-eye. Then Coke adjusts the set of his ruff with the faintest hint of satisfaction.

*    *    *

356

I am judged to have killed William Turnor in self-defence and to protect the life of the Prince. There will be no charge of treason. The Prince will be reassured that I am, after all, a loyal subject, though I hope that it won't be Buckingham reassuring him.

I murmur my thanks to Coke.

Donne is carried off by the King before we can speak together.

I am innocent, but Elizabeth remains abroad. Buckingham will not welcome me at court. I will keep my head but have risked my neck and achieved nothing. I must not stop yet . . . more to do.

Buckingham is overseeing the carrying out of the King. As he prepares to follow, I catch his coat. 'By all that the two of us ever achieved together, I beg a word.'

He hesitates. I see 'no' forming on his lips.

'Hear what she has to say, Steenie,' the King calls back over his shoulder. 'It's the least . . . Ow, you clumsy clot . . . Take care how ye go!'

Buckingham keeps the table between us. He wrinkles his lovely nose as if the reek of my filthy clothes offends him as much as it does me. 'I don't trust either you or Donne. You may have been freed without charge, but I want you out of Whitehall and Richmond. Stay away from the Prince of Wales.'

'One last favour, then, before I return to Hertfordshire with my tail between my legs.'

'You have the impudence to ask?'

'I would speak with the Prince one last time.'

Two court clerks still work at their table near the judges' dais. Buckingham turns away from them and lowers his voice. 'Do you dare imagine that he wishes to see you? He didn't feel that he could tolerate today's proceedings.'

'How will I upset him? He is to be told that I fought to save him!'

'Did you?'

'If I am innocent, then that must be the truth.'

'I think you and Donne made fools of them all.'

'Including the King? A fool?'

His eyes waver.

'You will no doubt be present when I see him. If you feel that His Highness grows distressed or you see danger of any kind, send me away at once.' I look him in the eye. 'I will hazard my life that I will not distress or harm the Prince. And, at this moment, I assure you that nothing is more precious to me than my life.'

He sucks in the exquisite lower lip and shifts the fine shoulders uneasily. 'You've caused me only trouble.'

Whereas, I helped put you where you are, I think.

'Tell me now what you mean to say to him,' he says.

'I beg you to excuse me. It's not fitting if news meant for him were to reach your ears first.'

We both know that most news for the Prince reaches Buckingham first. He, too, knows how to lift a seal and bribe informants. Though I swear that my cause pleases God better.

'I mean to raise his spirits, not cast them down. Will you deny him a message of cheer?'

The last clerk is still gathering together his papers and making final notes. He pretends not to hear and tilts his head as if to judge what he has just written.

'I wish only for His Highness's happiness.' Buckingham leans closer. 'And then we shall be rid of you for good?'

I have no doubt that he will do his best to renew my exile.

'If His Highness wishes it.'

He looks satisfied with that answer. What Buckingham wants, Charles now wants. Buckingham asks, Charles grants. Just as the ageing King humours his favourite's every wish.

'It may take time to arrange,' he says.

Which suits me perfectly. I have made a promise I'm not certain I can fulfil.

Not for the first time, neither. And I have made this promise to the Prince.

My arrival at Bedford House with Agnes is muted. Mudd has gone to Smithfield so I must wait to thank him. Clearly, he has said nothing. I have been absent for only five days and most of the house family assume that I was at Richmond.

I don't see Kit.

A messenger arrives on our heels. The porter brings me a letter with the Prince's seal. To my dismay, and, no doubt, that of Buckingham, Charles has summoned me to come to Richmond the next day.

'But I'm not ready!'

'You must bathe before you go, madam!' Still ferocious with relief, Agnes mistakes my meaning. 'And put on a clean gown! You've time before tomorrow.'

We are both a little unsteady as we climb the stairs.

I wear my cloak up to my bedchamber, where Agnes helps me peel off my layers of filthy undergarments and gown. Though my chamberer brings ale, bread and cheese, our stomachs are still too tight to eat.

Agnes dismisses my maid, calls for hot water and fills a large basin in front of the fire. I stand naked up to my shins in the wonderful, steaming heat that sends delicious thrills through my legs and arms and let her help me wash away the smell of fear. I lift my hair so she can wash the back of my neck. I feel the cloth falter just as I remember my mother's instruction in the dream.

'It didn't happen,' I say. A rivulet of warm water runs

down my chest from the motionless cloth. 'But I thank you for your prayers. I'm sure they prodded God into sending me His spokesman.'

Silently, she finishes washing my back and wrings out the cloth into the basin.

Then she calls for more hot water and washes herself more modestly, still wearing her smock, while I dry by the fire and try to think what to tell the Prince.

When I go back downstairs, Sir Kit is waiting at the bottom. Like Agnes, he is angry with relief. 'There you are, madam. Thank God! Next time, please tell me when you mean to . . .'

'You're alive!' I cry. I want to embrace him. I beam at him instead.

'Yes,' he says, looking puzzled. 'What did you fear had happened to me?'

He doesn't know, I remind myself.

'More to the point, where have you been?' he asks. 'You weren't at Richmond and no one knew where you had gone. I feared . . .'

'You haven't heard?' I can't bear to weigh him down with too much knowing . . . that I had killed a man in part to save him.

'Heard what?' He looks at me closely. 'Master Turnor is dead. I wondered if you knew.'

I nod, unable to speak.

His eyes sharpen. He looks down at my hands clenched in front of me. 'Is the rumour true, then?'

'What's being said?' Again, I see Turnor, reaching for me, refusing to die.

Suddenly I feel hollow, as if my head might topple. I grip Kit's arm as I had done after being thrown from my dying horse. I see the same terror and sense of responsibility in his eyes that I had seen then.

'Never mind, madam. Come sit.'

I let him lead me to a bench.

'I must go to Richmond,' I say.

'Don't think of it just now. I'll arrange it. Take you there myself. Just sit for now.'

'Don't be angry,' I say.

'Angry?' He looks astonished. 'I'm glad to see you safely back, madam.'

'I need a pen and paper.'

Without leaving my side, he calls for a groom.

Still giddy, I pen a letter to Arundel.

I give it to Kit. 'Do you forgive me enough to ride with this through the night to Arundel in Sussex? And to bring back my lord's reply with the same haste?'

'As urgent as that first ride?' he asks. A glint of relish sparks in his concern.

'Not urgent enough to break your neck.'

But he's already taking his leave, in haste to be gone.

Now I must wait.

Now I can stop.

Sudden exhaustion weakens my knees. Somehow I achieve my bedchamber and my bed. After a week of sleepless nights, I've barely time to think that I've wagered again on friendship before I sink into a wonderful oblivion.

# 53

The next night, the Prince is once again in his bedchamber, still dressed but in his shirtsleeves, drinking and playing cards with his gentlemen. Remains of supper sit on another table.

When I enter, Charles stands and applauds as if I have just executed a difficult dance step or sung a high C in an aria. The others jump to their feet and join in the applause. Buckingham applauds but skewers me with his eyebeams.

Rumour has rushed up the Thames ahead of us.

I look back at Kit, returned from Sussex and now waiting by the door.

'I hear that you killed a man for me, madam!' Prince Charles turns back to his companions. 'How many of you have done as much? Not even you, Steenie!' And back to me. 'I shall ask Ben Jonson to write a masque about the fierce Amazon queen Penthesilea just for you. And I will dance as your partner. You deserve as much!' He lifts a rope of pearls over his head and drops it over mine.

I make a grateful curtsy. As I rise, I meet Buckingham's cold eye.

This fit of gratitude will soon pass, it says.

'Have you eaten, madam? I shall serve you with my own hands.' Flushed with excitement, Charles pours me a goblet of wine. 'To my spiritual mother . . . I shall call you my spiritual mother because you have given me my second life.'

'It was not so close as that,' I protest. 'And it was a service any loyal subject would have performed.' I lift my glass. 'May Your Highness have a long, healthy and happy life!' Everyone snatches up his glass. We drink. Then I say more quietly, 'And you will have *The Triumph of Virtue*. Holbein's visionary dream.' I nod to Kit to come forward with his linen-wrapped package.

'How long must I wait?'

'You may have it now, Your Highness.'

The Prince already looks past me to Kit in joyful disbelief.

I pull the wrappings from *The Triumph of Virtue* and put the finished painting by Holbein into the royal hands.

The Prince's gentlemen crowd around us to see.

'You are my good angel, madam!' cries the Prince. 'My agent of a good fortune! To give me two such gifts at once – my life and my soul's desire.'

'Look closely at the picture first, sir, to judge whether I imagined.'

Charles bends close to the painted surface to peer. 'I, too, see the resemblance.' He turns to his gentlemen and shows the picture. 'Whose face do you see here?'

There are exclamations of astonishment and murmurs of accord. It is the Prince's face, beyond doubt! And could that possibly be the King, riding behind him?

'It's a sign, a good omen for the future,' says Charles. 'I thank you.' He gives me the smile of a happy child.

Happy for the moment, at least.

Tomorrow, I will send Kit back to Arundel with some of the royal pearls to pay for the picture. The lord will not expect such prompt payment, if any at all. Another true friend.

'You must dine with me tomorrow,' says the Prince. 'And tell me all about your battle to save me. And the next day, we shall speak of other paintings you have seen and one or two that I have spied myself and covet.'

Buckingham is staring at me. I shake my head gently. I do not want war. This is not the court I want. But I will not refuse its bounty neither while it is being offered to me. I should feel happier than I do.

Two days later, I ride to Moor Park, taking Mudd and his wife with me.

'Have a good look around and consider every possibility for increasing the income from this place,' I tell him.

Edward does not come out to greet me. Nor does he wait in the hall.

I know for certain that he's not out riding or hunting.

After watching my eyes search, our chamberlain clears his throat. 'Madam, my lord, the Earl . . .' he begins, flushed with unease.

'Is he worse?' I hand my cloak to the house groom.

'Please come see for yourself, madam.'

I follow the chamberlain to the little parlour at the back of the house.

Edward sits staring down at a polished black wooden ball of *lignum vitae* the size of a baby's head, on the floor in front of him.

'He sits there in the same chair every day,' whispers the chamberlain. 'All day. Ever since his old nurse died.'

'I used to be able to hurl that ball straight,' Edward says when I come in. 'Can't even pick it up now.'

364

'I'm giving instructions to pull down the derelict east wing. We can begin to rebuild.'

'Do as you wish,' he says, without looking up. 'You always have. Go away! You make my head ache.'

I wait a moment for him to speak again. He clamps his mouth shut. He sits, staring at the heavy black wooden ball. I might not have been there. In the silence, thoughts churn round and round behind his eyes. I back away, out of the room. I had not expected so much decline.

'I've tried . . .' the chamberlain says, when we have left the parlour again. He looks at me, fearing my anger.

'I'm sure he could not be looked after any better.'

'He won't go out . . . says that his chair is his only safe place.' Eagerly now, with a trembling voice, the man unloads the weight of responsibility. 'He sleeps in that chair . . . I always make certain he's wrapped in a fur rug.'

'He won't sleep in his bed?'

'It's the ghosts in the hangings, madam. And the last time he ventured out of the house into the gardens, he said a tentacle reached up from the fishpond and wrapped round his ankle, made him fall.'

In the great hall, the little tree rooted high above my head on the window ledge has grown at least a foot taller. A few of its brown fallen leaves skitter across the floor in the draught stirred up by my skirts. I study the great hall, turning slowly, hands on my waist.

The end wall must be braced. A huge task that will eat money.

But I will have a little money again, made by the Prince's favour. And I will be alive to see the work done. I have time. I am alive when I had feared I might die.

I do not need to stable my horse in the vast crumbling fireplace.

I suddenly see it. My thoughts scramble into sudden urgent life. The joy of renewed purpose floods me. I want to sing. I will sing in a moment and Edward and his megrims can go hang. But now I am thinking too hard.

It is possible. Not mere repairs.

Charles's favour will last for as long as I can help him find new paintings and antiquities for his collection. I will make the most of his gratitude. I will not push myself forward at court nor ask too much. I will not challenge Buckingham past his endurance. I will be modest and stay out of sight. I will be ingenious but not greedy. Mudd will devise new schemes for making money from the estate. I will have enough to do it.

I will leave Chenies as it is and tear this house down. Rebuild Moor Park entirely. No larger, nor grand, but raised on the gentle swell of the nearby hill, above the frost that pools in the bottom of the valley. A pale house of stone with large windows to let in the light.

I run into the parlour and throw open a narrow, diamond-paned window to look up at my new house, which I already see glowing in the sun.

There it will stand. Noble. Square-cornered. Symmetrical and finely proportioned in the new Italian style. I will ask Jones to design it for me. He has grown very grand since he first designed masques for the Queen, having also built her a house and designed a new banqueting house for the King. But he will do it for me, for old times' sake. I will persuade him. If Jonson behaves himself, and he and Jones don't kill each other, I might even commission Jonson to write me a masque that Jones will design.

The last thought sobers me. There will be no queen to dance in my masque. No Anne. No Elizabeth.

I have failed in what I set out to do. And almost lost my life in the trying.

You wanted it, not she, says my mother briskly. She still wants to stay and fight. Who are you to tell her that she should not?

I will write to Elizabeth straight away, tell her that I wait to love and serve her whenever she is able and ready to return. I will not write that I had thought I knew better than she did. Even I do not push royal friends that far.

I close the window. I head for the dairy to inspect it. I change my mind in mid-stride and turn back. I go up to my chamber and tell Agnes and my maid not to unpack.

# 54

This time, I cannot see what shape my goal might take. Back in London, I ride from the Strand into Fleet Street, alone. No Sir Kit, in spite of his protests, not even a maid. I cross over the stench of floating rubbish at Fleet Bridge and clop into Ludgate Hill. I had lied to my horse on that snowy ridge between Moor Park and Chenies when I promised not to drive us together off the cliff. I am taking him with me now over the edge.

I must expect nothing more, I think. The gift of acquittal should be enough.

But here I am.

I rein in and look up at the Cathedral of St Paul. Solid and real under its stumpy tower where the tall steeple destroyed by lightning has never been replaced. It is a contradictory place of pulpits and market stalls. In the Cathedral aisles and the churchyard just outside, the worlds of man and of God intermingle. Prayers with hope-filled business handshakes. Priests walking among apprentices who are selling themselves. Bibles being sold along with obscene books. John has not escaped from contradictions after all.

There is a block in the Deanery Yard. I dismount and hand the reins to a Cathedral groom. I have not warned Donne I was coming. I half-hope to find him away.

He is there. A servant leads me to him.

He stands up from his table, comes from behind it. He watches me enter, without speaking.

The servant leaves. We face each other in silence.

I gaze around his study in the Deanery of St Paul's Cathedral. The room is all black and brown. A single branched brass candleholder stands on a sideboard heavy with books and scrolls. On his table, he has a seamstress's candle-stand with a lens to focus the light. A pair of spectacles lies on an open Bible almost as large as the tabletop.

'How sober you have become, Doctor John,' I say at last.

'With effort.' The new Dean of St Paul's seems as much lost for words as I am. 'Sobriety sits uneasily on me.' He looks down at his black gown, then reaches down to his table and moves a goose quill pen an inch to the left.

The first crack has opened in the solid block of our silence.

'You always dressed in sober clerical colours,' I say. 'I sometimes thought it was an affectation to set you apart from the court dandies who imitated you.'

'But now the colours fit, uneasy or not. Lucy, I've found my way to peace.'

'You? At peace?' I ask sharply. But my ears catch the unneeded use of my name. 'You did a service for Doncaster, or the King, which brought you a rich, if sobering, reward!'

'I won't deny it. But the position as Dean exerts its own power on the mind. It forces self-examination. You're right. I'm not yet at peace, but I've found the path. I search for it through my sermons . . . I write sermons now.'

'I know. I came to hear you preach once . . .'

'Yes. I saw you.'

We run out of words again. No doubt he is remembering, as I am, the moment our eyes had met over the crowded congregation. I hope he did not see my panic-stricken flight. I want to ask, but dare not hear the answer, whether his sudden plunge down the steps of the pulpit had been to come after me or to escape.

'I heard the poet still speaking that day.'

I hear him exhale.

'A muzzled poet,' he says. 'A true poet is free to observe and to play, without moral responsibility. As a cleric, I must try to help others resolve their struggles.' He pauses. 'The passion behind the words is no less now.'

'I heard that too.'

We fall silent again.

'How do we get out of this terrible unease?' he asks.

'By plain speaking?'

'If we still can.'

Having come this far, I jump from the edge. 'That was a handsome apology you made at my trial. And I accept it.'

His head jerks back. 'Not too florid?'

'Amazingly straightforward.'

'I grow simple with age.'

'I think not. Those were not simple lies you told.'

'What lies?' Now the half-smile flashes.

'Did you truly suspect Turnor and hope that I would draw him out?'

'I introduced him to you, did I not? He had importuned me. I thought him at least a rogue, possibly worse. I thought you could handle him and might even find him amusing while you learned more about him. I was a fool.'

'As I was.' I blow out a puff of breath. 'Do you truly think me innocent?'

'I would not have testified, else.' He moves the pen

back to its original position. Picks it up again. 'It's your opinion of my guilt that concerns me.'

'I came to thank you for saving my life. How did you know that I was "innocent of treasonous intent"?'

'I knew. You don't answer my question.'

'About your guilt?' I watch him closely. 'For most of the last year, I was unsure whether you meant to help me or to kill me.'

'What do you believe now? From their reaction to my performance, it was clear that you'd not given the councillors my name. And Coke later confirmed it.'

'The new Dean of Paul's was safe at last. I could not risk destroying that safety.' I see his face contract but can't read it. 'He had no need to risk it by tainting himself with attempted murder and treason.'

'But he did risk it. Just as you protected him.'

'But how did you know how I meant to defend myself? I had scarcely decided myself how to argue my case. I don't understand how you knew, nor what your knowing meant. I've tormented myself ever since.'

'I didn't know.' He laughs. 'Does it truly surprise you that we invented the same lies?'

'Once, it would not have done.'

Then I let myself hear the enormity of what he has just said.

Our silence now is delicate and filled with questions but also warm with possibility.

'We managed that exchange quite well, did we not?' he asks cheerfully. 'Onwards?'

I hug myself with crossed arms.

'And what do you conclude from the risk the Dean of Paul's decided to take?' He looks down. 'Lucy . . .'

Again, my name. A little spangle of light released into the air.

371

'. . . I owe you several apologies, not just one. For my paroxysms of doubt. For insulting you and belittling what you had given me.'

I feel my face go warm. My head bobs to acknowledge his apology.

He takes my hand then looks at me for permission.

I nod. My heart should have been thundering, but, in truth, I feel an incoming tide of deep calm.

He looks down and studies my hand as if it were a thing he had lost and he wanted to be certain he had found the same one. For a few moments, we both think about this touch and what it might mean. 'Your poet is just as confused as he always was. Just older, not much wiser.'

If he lets go of my hand now, my skin will bleed from the tearing.

'I won't let go.' He has read my thoughts.

We sit down at his table, hands joined, our arms outstretched towards each other.

'I don't know where we . . .' we say at the same time. We stop and laugh.

'There!' he says. 'Proof!'

I take refuge in metaphor while I try to catch up with where we seem to have arrived. 'If my poet is still confused,' I say awkwardly, 'your "First Good Angel" is worse. Trying to smooth her tattered pinions.'

His cocked head urges me on.

'Flying lop-sided, like an ageing goose . . . paddling furiously as she struggles to get airborne . . .'

'Into the overwhelming weight of the sky,' he concludes.

We both smile a little at this exchange. Once familiar ground.

Angel and poet look at each other across a table littered with papers, pen and ink, with years, and battles, quarrels, kisses, caresses, with lust, and guilt, and ruthless hunger. With imperatives and gentleness, betrayals, clumsy groping for goodness. Two mirrored souls who invent the same lies.

'I'm sure that God laughs,' he says. 'Watching us struggle to be good. And some of us give Him more amusement than most.'

'Still as arrogant as ever, I see.'

'Merely willing to consider the most humiliating possibility.'

We smile at each other openly this time. Suddenly I feel safe again.

Safe enough.

'I failed,' I say. 'But I can do no more.'

We look down. Our intertwined hands make a single complex map of tendons and veins.

'A continent of shared history,' he says.

Time that has passed leaves dark pitted caves in the hillsides and valleys carved by streams. It uncurls the nut into a tree.

The richness, I think. Oh, the richness.

'You see me straight and still don't flinch,' he says. 'A woman of courage.'

I quiver like the turning tide, afraid even to smile. I feel for the shape of the moment.

It holds his company, his friendship and his respect . . . Memories of a shared wildness that touched a holy darkness in my soul. It holds the feel of his hand, then and now. And believing that we could open any door whatsoever and pass through together.

'I still don't fit, but please don't tell anyone,' he says. 'Never did. Too wicked to be a cleric. Too devout to be a poet. Too ambitious to be a man of God. Too fearful and filled with self-doubt . . . and mockery . . . to be a courtier.

I could lick arses with the best of them, but I thank God daily that, against my will at the time, I was spared the fraudulent life of an ambassador. I was altogether too self-flagellating and hungry for spiritual grace to have carried off the part.'

And yet he would have been forgiven, as he has always been forgiven but refuses to see.

'Yet I've been rewarded.' He looks at his books, his study. 'My work now is to speak of my spiritual struggles aloud, to a full congregation. I don't deserve such a luxury.'

'Your congregation are fortunate to have a fellow sinner leading them, not a judge.'

'You never fitted, neither. Too womanly to be a man. Too male in spirit to be a docile woman.'

'I like my woman's body,' I say.

'So do I.'

There is another pause.

'How does your husband?'

'You've never asked after him before.'

'But now I'm curious about the rest of my life.'

'Please don't . . .'

'Why not? It's true.'

Our glances collide and hold.

'I shall build him a safe place in the new Moor Park,' I say. 'With strong walls, filled with sunlight. No corners for shadows, no closets with closed doors. Where he can be as miserable as he likes for the rest of his life.'

'And you?'

'I mean to rebuild Moor Park. And I will ask Master Jones . . .' I do not mind that he begins to laugh. I hear his pleasure at recognising the old Lucy.

We still heal the defects of loneliness in each other.

We are still mirrors of being, I think. A miracle. We still reflect the truth to each other. Face-to-face. I think we will remain so now until death clouds the glass. There is no other joy on earth like this shared, flawed, salty, cobbled-together trotting past of time. Reason enough to be alive.

'May I read you a poem?' he asks. He looks a little shy as he riffles through a pile of papers and pulls one out.

> *No spring, nor summer beauty hath such grace,*
> *As I have seen in one autumnal face . . .*

I listen. I watch his mouth. Hear his fervour. His words float up to join the wider air of the heavens. I don't care if he wrote it for me. He offers it to me now and cares that I think it good.

This moment, where I have arrived . . . where we have arrived. This moment is what there is. We will pass through it into what we cannot know or see. But this moment also shapes the future.

He rests his head on his hand. 'Good morning.'

We smile at each other across the table.

# Epilogue

## ELIZABETH STUART – THE HAGUE, THE NETHERLANDS, 1661

*'God will not always prosper ill actions, as you see by the King's restoring and his rebels' pulling down.'*
— Elizabeth, Electress Palatine

On the flat shore, all mud and rough grass, their rich dresses look as out of place as jewels on a goat. Elizabeth lifts her skirts to keep the hems from fouling, but she does not mind the mud. She is growing old, a widow now, but today nothing can lower her spirits. She smiles at a pair of raucous, evil-eyed gulls fidgeting on the pilings of the wooden quay. She smiles at the tiny sucking pop of a vanishing mud crab. She smiles even at the mud. Far out on the water, round-bellied Dutch ships wait to take her home.

She squints across the choppy grey water. The wind whips loose strands of hair into her face, blowing from behind, in the right direction, towards England. Even the weather blesses her return.

The fair white face that England offers to the Continent is too far away to make out through the low cloud. She last saw those chalk cliffs as a fifteen-year-old bride, watching them blur into mist as she sailed into her future in Heidelberg. In her absence, England had torn itself apart with war and murdered its king, her younger brother Charles. She herself had become an embarrassment, the deposed Queen of Bohemia from the overthrown royal line of England, surviving on the charity of the Dutch.

Her child-self feels a moment of terror. What if nothing lies beyond that blurred line of cloud that might or might not be the horizon?

When she had first heard the news from England – that the Beast, Cromwell, was dead – she feared to let herself believe it. The Beast who had fought, defeated and beheaded her brother no longer ruled England. His soldiers no longer stabled their horses in Rochester Cathedral. His agents no longer smashed statues, slashed paintings and arrested men for writing the wrong words. She had not dared to believe that Parliament had voted to restore the monarchy, and the Stuarts, her family, to the throne of England.

But then she had heard English sailors cheering her nephew Charles onto his ship, taking him home to England to be crowned.

'We have him, we have him!' the sailors shouted as they took him on board. 'God bless King Charles!' Charles the Second.

Then she had seen the name of her nephew's ship. Once called *The Naseby* . . . Her tongue still refused to shape it . . . Naseby, that place . . . that battle between Englishman and Englishman where the Beast had won and royal hopes had died. *The Naseby* has been renamed *The Royal Charles*. Order has returned to a world that was upside down.

My turn now, she thinks. My dearest Bedford, how I wish you were still alive to welcome me! I need you here to tell me that all will be well . . . that a soft landing waits for me, if only I will jump.

She listens to the grey sky but hears only the wind.

To you alone, I will confess how I fear the changes I know I will find. The old England is a stubborn ghost in my head, walking spectre-like, a chilly mist across the new reality. You are dead and I am almost past dancing . . . Bedford . . .? Are you there?

Conversation with the souls of the dead can be a little one-sided, she thinks.

Then she imagines that she hears a tart familiar voice.

'Best talk only to yourself, madam,' murmurs Lucy. 'You might at least get a reply . . . and never say that I would be past dancing.'

The barge is ready to take her out to the ship.

Unexpected tears ambush her as she kisses those she will leave behind. 'Visit me in England,' she begs. She lifts her head to the sound of a horse on the road.

Other heads turn. A courier has galloped after them from The Hague.

'Your Grace! A letter from the new king of England.'

She sees uneasy glances exchanged around her. She smiles, but the fingers that break the royal seal are cold.

She reads. Stops breathing.

The King is not yet ready to receive her, it says. Her presence in England at the moment might cause political embarrassment. She must wait in The Hague until he chooses to invite her.

She hears the silence around her. Eyes watch her. No one moves. The only sounds are the gulls and the slap of waves.

She refolds the letter and smiles at them all. 'His

Majesty, my nephew Charles, is so eager to welcome me that he can't contain himself until we can embrace at Gravesend. He sends his words flying ahead to bring me home.'

She tucks the letter into her bodice. 'And here they shall lie above my heart until I set foot in England.' She turns to the barge that will carry them out to the ships. 'Come! We must not miss this following wind!'

Later, at the rail as if looking back for a final view of her old home, she tears the paper into scraps and lets them fall over the side of the ship onto the water.

We've done it at last, dear Bedford, though it has taken a little longer than we wished. I'm on my way home. Nothing will stop me now.

## THE PEOPLE IN *THE NOBLE ASSASSIN*

### HISTORICAL
LUCY RUSSELL, COUNTESS OF BEDFORD (1581–1627)
– Daughter of Lord Harington of Exton (guardian of Princess
Elizabeth Stuart). From 1603 to 1619, one of the most
influential women in England as queen bee at the court of
Anne of Denmark, wife of King James I. Beautiful and
gifted, Lucy was given a boy's education, like Elizabeth I.
The playwright Ben Jonson (as an intended compliment)
wrote that she had a 'manly soul'. She wrote verse, entered
male debates and was said by the composer Dowland to
know so much about music that she could 'mend my tunes'.

Though one of the most important figures in the social
culture of Jacobean England, she has been unfairly
neglected by history. The Countess was a gifted, intellectual seventeenth-century female in a hierarchical, male
society – which Elizabeth I ('the Virgin Queen') had ruled
as a quasi-man, refusing to marry and be reduced to a
wife. In contrast, Lucy was married at thirteen to Edward
Russell (as his guardian's third choice for bride) and

suffered the handicap of being wed to an unremarkable man. She became his chattel. Her money was his. His mediocre reputation dragged her down. The better-known literary women, like Mary Herbert and Dorothy Sidney, had the good fortune (in addition to their natural gifts) to be wives or siblings of respected literary noblemen.

Lucy turned her ferocious energies to the role open to her – acting as patron to poets, artists and writers, including Ben Jonson, Michael Drayton, Inigo Jones and John Donne. Contemporary anecdote reports that she had more poems dedicated to her than Elizabeth I. Believed by some, both then and now, to have been the lover of John Donne.

EDWARD RUSSELL, THIRD EARL OF BEDFORD (1572–1627) – Husband of Lucy. Briefly imprisoned, fined ten thousand pounds and exiled from court for his involvement in 1601 in the Essex rebellion against Elizabeth I. However, unlike Essex, he kept his head on his shoulders and was restored to favour by King James, along with, and perhaps because of, his gifted young wife. Among the great Russell houses were Woburn Abbey, Chenies Manor and The More (also known as Moore Park). After several years of marriage, he was thrown against a tree in a riding accident and seems, thereafter, to have retreated into relative seclusion at Moor Park. When he died without children, the title passed to a cousin, Francis Russell.

JAMES I OF ENGLAND AND VI OF SCOTLAND (1566–1625) – King of England after the death of Elizabeth I. One of the most intellectual kings the country has had, he was also impatient, bored by governing, erratic, louche, unattractive, and fond of pretty young men. Having been used at the age of two to depose his own mother, Mary Queen of Scots, from the Scottish throne, he was understandably afraid of the widespread popularity in England of his two older children. He may have suffered damage during his difficult, twenty-four-hour birth, which might help explain his uneven walk and short attention span. However, the widely accepted image of him as a shambling, dribbling, cod-piece fiddler arises from a description written by a disappointed suitor and should be treated with caution.

ELIZABETH STUART (1596–1662) – Only surviving daughter of King James and Anne of Denmark. Like her older brother, Henry, she was far more popular with the English than either her father or younger brother, Prince Charles (later Charles I). She made a love-match with Frederick, the Elector Palatine, in 1613. (To learn more, see my novel, *The King's Daughter*.) Her husband's short and disastrous reign, 1619–20, as the elected King of Bohemia gave her the name by which she is best known: 'The Winter Queen'.

CHARLES STUART (1600–49) – Only surviving son of James and heir to the English throne. A sickly child, who was not expected to survive, he became Prince of Wales after the premature death in 1612 of his older brother, Henry. In a later period, not covered in this book, he married Henrietta Maria of France and ruled England, as Charles I, after the death of his father James in 1625. He led England into the Civil War, lost to Oliver Cromwell's armies, and was beheaded publicly in 1649, outside Inigo Jones's Banqueting House in Whitehall, London.

FREDERICK, ELECTOR PALATINE (1596–1632) – German prince and deposed King of Bohemia. Husband of Elizabeth Stuart and father of Prince Rupert, who later led English royalist forces in the Civil War. His daughter, Princess Sophia, was to marry the first Hanoverian and bring together the two royal houses of Stuart and Hanover.

GEORGE VILLIERS, MARQUESS OF BUCKINGHAM (1592–1628) – Later Duke of Buckingham. Powerful favourite of James, taking the place of Robert Carr. Given the affectionate nickname 'Steenie' by the King, he further extended his influence through a close friendship with Prince Charles, assuming more and more powers until he was assassinated in 1627. His assassin, John Felton, became a popular hero.

JOHN DONNE (1572–1631) – Best-known of the English 'Metaphysical poets'. Born a Catholic. Trained as a lawyer but became a much-imitated court poet, famous for his scandalous satire and eroticism. He was almost certainly a government agent. Finally, after Anglican conversion, he was appointed Dean of St Paul's Cathedral, London, celebrated for his religious sonnets and sermons. (See Author's Note pages 391–2.)

JAMES HAY, VISCOUNT DONCASTER (c. 1590–1636) – Scottish aristocrat who came with James from Scotland. A gentleman of the King's bedchamber, created Earl of Carlisle in September 1622. Staunch Protestant. Family motto: 'Spare naught'. Was later to broker the marriage between Prince Charles and Henrietta Maria of France.

BEN JONSON (1572–1637) – Poet and a leading English playwright born at Westminster. A Classics scholar and stepson of a bricklayer with whom he worked before turning soldier in Flanders. Then joined Henslowe's company of players, where he killed a fellow player in a duel. He became the writer of Jacobean court masques and the King's Poet.

INIGO JONES (1573–1652) – Son of a Smithfield wool merchant. 'A picture maker', according to contemporary accounts. Widely travelled architect and theatre designer who rose by ambition and genius to become the arbiter of Classical taste at court. Most famous for the Whitehall Banqueting House and the Queen's House in Greenwich, he also surveyed Stonehenge. Collaborated, and often fought ferociously, with Ben Jonson, his literary opposite number in the creating of court masques. He was Prince Henry's surveyor, later the King's.

SIR EDWARD COKE (1552–1634) – Known as 'Killer Coke' (pronounced 'Cook'). Jurist, judge and member of the Privy Council. A major legal thinker and writer on English law.

SIR HENRY MONTAGU (1537?–1642) – Member of Privy Council, former chief justice of the King's bench, and lord high treasurer (resigned at Buckingham's insistence). Ordered the execution of Raleigh. Later became trusted advisor of King Charles I.

SIR HENRY GOODYEAR (1571–1627) – Gentleman and poet. A good friend to Lucy and patron and close friend of John Donne.

SIR EDWARD CONWAY and SIR RICHARD WESTON – King James's ambassadors to Bohemia, sent to parlay for peace between Catholics and Protestants.

CAPTAIN RALPH HOPTON (1598–1652) – Young officer who accompanied Elizabeth Stuart's flight from Bohemia. Thought to have served in the army of her husband, Frederick, Elector Palatine. Later made First Baron Hopton.

## THE CHIEF VENTURERS

Protestant nobles and knights, former friends of Prince Henry, and/or former members of his household:

HENRY WRIOTHESLEY (1573–1624) – Third Earl of Southampton, Wriothesley (pronounced 'Risley') was a famous literary patron, thought by many scholars to be the 'gentle youth' of Shakespeare's sonnets. He angered Elizabeth I by his involvement in the Essex plot, but was restored to favour by King James. Interested in the colonisation of the Americas, he was an officer of the Virginia Company.

JOHN HOLLES (1564–1637) – Later First Earl of Clare.

DENZIL HOLLES (1599–1680) – Second son of the above. Entered Parliament 1624. Pro-presbyterian.

SIR ARTHUR GORGES (c. 1569–1625) – Former Gentleman of the Privy Chamber to Prince Henry. In 1597, he had commanded the *War-Sprite* in which his cousin Raleigh also sailed.

SIR DAVID MURRAY – Part of a large and influential clan serving the crown. First Lord Scone and captain of the guard to James in Scotland. Former Groom of the Stole to Prince Henry (*q.v.*).

ADAM NEWTON (d.1630) – Scottish, former tutor to Prince Henry from c. 1600. Greek and Latin scholar.

Translator of Classical texts and an art collector. Like Lucy, interested in the works of Hans Holbein.

THOMAS HOWARD (1586–1646) – The Second Earl of Arundel shared the late Prince Henry's passion for collecting art. The only member of the Catholic Howard family tolerated by Prince Henry, he made the first-known sale of a picture to Henry, for two pounds.

## REMEMBERED

HENRY STUART (1594–1612) – Prince of Wales and heir to the British crown until his tragic death at age eighteen. A fierce Protestant champion. Had he lived to become Henry IX, England would almost certainly have avoided the Civil War and there might still be Stuarts, rather than Hanoverians, on the British throne. He was the first royal to buy art as a passionate collector and acquired much of the basis of the present Queen's Collection, or as much of it as survived the Commonwealth. I write in more detail about how he may have died in my novel, *The King's Daughter*.

ANNE OF DENMARK (1574–1619) – Queen of James, mother of three surviving children: Elizabeth, Henry and Charles. Close friend of Lucy.

FREDERICK, LORD RUSSELL (1602) – First of Lucy's two lost babies, who lived for only two months. Lucy also had an unnamed daughter who survived for two hours (1610).

SIR JOHN HARINGTON (1572–1614) – Lucy's older brother, later Second Baron Harington of Exton (not to be confused with his adventurer cousin, Sir John Harington, who was godson of Elizabeth I and inventor of the flush toilet).

## AND IN A CATEGORY OF HIS OWN

WILLIAM TOURNEUR/TOURNOR/TURNOR – Soldier-of-fortune, date of birth unknown. Possibly aka CYRIL TOURNEUR/TOURNOR/TURNOR. Cyril was an adventurer and Jacobean playwright. He is now denied the chief work once attributed to him (*The Revenger's Tragedy*, credited to Thomas Middleton) leaving him with only a single play, the less well known *The Atheist's Tragedy*.

Intriguing evidence suggests that William and Cyril might have been the same man. William turns up mysteriously on one of Cyril's title pages. In any case, whenever Cyril appeared in London, William vanished, and *vice versa*.

## FICTIONAL CHARACTERS

CHRISTOPHER HAWKINS – Groom and later Master of Horse to Lucy.

LADY AGNES HOOPER – Widow of a Buckinghamshire knight and lady-in-waiting to Lucy.

SIR WILLIAM SENNETT – One of James's 'made-up knights'.

SIR WALTER SENNETT – Son of Sir William. Title likewise purchased.

PETER MUDD – Steward at Bedford House, London.

Also the many who would have existed in reality, largely invisible to historical record but appearing in household rolls, identified as often by function as by name. Like the Prince's boatman, the swimming master, doctors, grooms, maids and all the other people who kept life going.

# Author's Notes

## CHARACTERS

The central characters in *The Noble Assassin* are real. People often ask if historical characters are easier to write about than fictional ones, because more is known about them. The opposite is true. Historical records, even when they exist in any detail, almost never tell you what a person was thinking or feeling at any particular time – which is the heart of fiction, as opposed to straight historical account. Even letters can deceive – being often formulaic or politic – except in the very rare cases when they were written to close and trusted friends. Where they exist, the recorded facts, most inconveniently, often put people in the wrong place at the wrong time for the story you want to tell. Most helpful are the small details of daily life found in household records and rolls, which help you to build up your imagined world. You can learn far more easily what a mason was paid, for example, than how he felt about his work, or his wife.

I will not change the facts so far as they are known and I can learn them. But history is always a slippery beast, as historians will tell you. The challenge is to learn as much as you can, to make use of what you learn, and then to imagine a plausible, coherent story into the dark cracks between the known facts. Most historians will say that they do very much the same. I am not the first to suggest that Lucy Russell was John Donne's mistress, though I have had to imagine the details of their affair.

## JOHN DONNE
Donne was a special challenge, worth at least three books of his own. However, I had set out to write Lucy's story, not his. I had to show him through her eyes and in her memory. Her point of view shapes what we learn and dictated what, with regret, I've had to leave out.

## THE SPECIAL CASE OF TURNOR
I've taken advantage of the fog of mystery surrounding the real Cyril Tourneur/William Tournor/William Turnor (see character list). Though I imagined the details of Turnor's role in *The Noble Assassin*, you have only to look at the number and fervour of religiously inspired plots against James and the Stuarts to know that men like him did exist. The Gunpowder Treason of 1605 grew out of Catholic grievances and fears of persecution. And though less well-publicised, the ferocity on the other side was just as vehement. Many Anglicans and Protestants were convinced that Prince (later King) Charles was dangerously pro-Catholic (perhaps even a secret Papist) who would sell the country back to Rome. He did indeed go on to marry a French Catholic, Henrietta Maria. In 1620, England had not yet finished paying in either psychological or military coin for Henry VIII's rupture with the Catholic Church of Rome. The English Civil War, though still unimaginable, was already brewing. That bloody convulsion had many complex causes, but religion was one, embodied here in Turnor.

## LANGUAGE

My ear was somewhat tuned by four years working as resident choreographer and assistant director with the Royal Shakespeare Company, hearing seventeenth-century English spoken day and night, every day. Outside rehearsal, we played at speaking like characters from Shakespeare, Marlowe or Jonson. Actors ordered tea and bacon butties in iambic pentameter. This experience made me comfortable with the language of the period and gave me confidence I would otherwise have lacked. At the same time, I loathe pastiche and work on the principle that people in the seventeenth century sounded as normal to each other as we do to ourselves – a tricky balance but fun to attempt.

The prosecutor's speech in Lucy's hearing is adapted from the judgement against Raleigh in 1603. On occasion, I also use the rhythms and syntax of a particular speech of Shakespeare as a template for my own different vocabulary and purpose.

## THE POEMS

Most of Donne's poetry was not published until after his death. The exact dates of writing, the categorical groupings and the female objects of most of his poems still provoke speculation. Only a few of them are addressed to a named person or can be linked to a particular historical event or place. Interpretation of internal clues and evidence in the poems varies widely, leaving scope for imagined alternatives. In *The Noble Assassin*, Donne also admits to quoting himself when appropriate, regardless of when he might have written the poem in question. As the postman said in the film to the poet, Pablo Neruda, 'Poetry is for the person who needs it.' And when he needs it.

Because Donne is so often the subject of attempts to detect biography in works of creative imagination, I have given him an opinion on the shimmering boundary between the autobiographical and the imagined, which most writers know well and many scholars curse. However, his part in the still ongoing debate has nothing to do here with schools of literary scholarship but grows out of his need for emotional clarity between himself and a subtle, intelligent and passionate woman.

I have quoted from the following poems by Donne: 'Twickenham Gardens', 'To the Countess of Bedford', 'Elegy 9, "The Autumnal"', Holy Sonnets XIII and XIV, and 'The Ecstasy'.

And I invite lovers of Donne's poetry to find the scene for which I took great pleasure in using 'The Ecstasy' as a plot template.

## THE PLACES

Combe Abbey is now a hotel. Nothing remains of the old house at Moor Park, which is thought to have stood more or less on the ninth tee of the present golf course. The fine house now at Moor Park was not built in Lucy's lifetime. Part of Chenies Manor stands, is occupied, and can be visited by the public, although the existence of the missing great wing that I describe, though real, has only recently been discovered.

The site of Lucy's garden on the Thames at Twickenham can be seen on the Surrey riverside, if you look down from Twickenham Bridge at the area known as St Margaret's.

Of Richmond Palace, only a stretch of Tudor brick wall and a gateway remain. Crane Wharf can be seen on old maps. Several old paintings show both the palace and the opposite riverside, where cattle drink and Lucy witnesses the attack on Charles. This flat, sloping shore is now the retained bank along Duck Walk. Though the egot I mention is still there, Richmond Bridge had not yet been built and crossing was by ferry. (After London Bridge, there was no bridge until Kingston.) And because Charles had not yet built his controversial enclosing wall, Richmond Park was still a mix of open hunting forest and farms. For those who know it, the view from Richmond Hill was just as beautiful and just as famous as it is today, if without the distant tower blocks and airplanes in and out of Heathrow.

# Some Helpful Books

**ORIGINAL SOURCE MATERIAL**
Chamberlain, John, *The Letters of John Chamberlain*, ed. Norman McClure, American Philosophical Society, 1939.

Donne, John, *Selected Poems*, Penguin, Ashton, Robert (ed.), *James I by His Contemporaries*, Hutchinson, 1969.

Jonson, Ben, *Bartholomew Fair*, Nick Hern Books, 1997.

Jonson, Ben, *The Complete Poems*, ed. G. Parfitt, Penguin, 1975.

Middleton, Thomas, A *Mad World, My Masters and Other Plays*, Oxford University Press, 1995.

Scholfield, John (ed.), *The London Surveys of Ralph Treswell*, London Topographical Society, 1987.

**OTHER BOOKS**
Akrigg, G.P.V., *Jacobean Pageant*, Hamish Hamilton, 1962.

Bergeron, David M., *King James & Letters of Homoerotic Desire*, University of Iowa Press, 1999.

Blakiston, Georgia, *Woburn and the Russells*, Constable, 1980.

Crystal, David and Crystal, Ben, *Shakespeare's Words*, Penguin Books, 2002.

Haynes, Alan, *Sex in Elizabethan London*, Sutton Publishing, 1977.

Oman, Carola, *The Winter Queen*, Phoenix Press, 1938.

Pedrick, Martyn, *Moor Park: The Grosvenor Legacy*, Riverside Books, 1989.

Prockter, Adrian and Taylor, Robert, *A to Z of Elizabethan London*, London Topographical Society, Publ. No. 122, 1979.

Ross, Josephine, *The Winter Queen*, Weidenfeld and Nicolson, 1979.

Stewart, Alan, *The Cradle King: The Life of James VI & I*, Pimlico Books, Random House, 2003.

Stubbs, John, *Donne, The Reformed Soul*, Penguin, 2007.

Thurley, Simon, *The Lost Palace of Whitehall*, Royal Institute of British Architects, Drawings Collection, 1998.

Weinreb, Ben and Hibbert, Christopher, *The London Encyclopaedia*, Macmillan, 2010.

# The Noble Assassin –
# TIME LINE

1572    John Donne born.
        Edward Russell born.

1581    Lucy born, daughter of Sir John Harington.

1585    Edward Russell succeeds to title, 3rd Earl of Bedford.

1588    Donne probably leaves Oxford.

1592    Donne at Lincoln's Inn.

1593    Donne's younger brother Henry dies in prison for association with a Catholic priest.

1594    Lucy, thirteen, marries Edward Russell, 3rd Earl of Bedford (then twenty-two). She is third choice of his guardian, Countess of Warwick.

1596    Donne sails on Cadiz expedition with Essex.

1597    Donne on Islands Expedition.

1601    Edward Russell involved in Essex Rebellion. Fined
        £10,000.
        Donne elected MP for Brockley.
        Donne secretly marries Anne More.

1602    Russell son born Jan. 19. Lives one month. Buried
        at Chenies, Feb. 1602.

1603    Lucy rides to Berwick to meet Queen Anne. Made
        a Lady of the Bedchamber. Begins period of great
        influence at court. Patron of arts/poets.

1608    Lucy buys lease of Twickenham Park. Lives at
        Twickenham until 1617.

1609    Smythsson makes drawing of gardens and new
        house. It's uncertain whether these are a survey
        of existing house or a new design.

1610    Lucy's daughter born, lives two hours.

1611    Lucy has a miscarriage.
        Donne visits the Continent with Sir Robert Drury.

1612    Death of Prince Henry. And of Lucy's patron and
        protector, Robert Cecil.

1613    Elizabeth marries Frederick, Elector Palatine.
        Leaves England.
        By autumn, Frederick ill (breakdown?).

1614   Lucy's brother dies of smallpox. She inherits his art collection and begins avid interest in art.

1615   Donne ordained.

1616   Lucy, with Duke of Lennox, gains her father's patent for coining farthing tokens. Charles made Prince of Wales.

1617   Frederick proclaimed King of Bohemia.
Lord Russell buys Moor Park, Herts. Lucy moves there.

1618   May – Defenestration of Prague.
July – Austrian troops enter Bohemia.  Defeated by bad weather.

1619   March – Hapsburg (Holy Roman) emperor, Matthias dies.
Anne of Denmark dies.
Oct. – Frederick and Elizabeth move to Prague.

1620   Nov. – Hapsburgs attack Prague. Battle of White Mountain. Protestant Bohemians routed by Catholic armies of Hapsburg Empire. Frederick and Elizabeth flee from Prague.
Dec. – Elizabeth gives birth at Custrin Castle in Germany.

1621   Donne made Dean of St Paul's.

1623   Frederick dies.

1627   Edward Russell dies.  Lucy dies shortly after.

1631   John Donne dies.

1661   Elizabeth Stuart returns to England. Her daughter
       is mother of the first Hanoverian King of England,
       thereby uniting the Stuarts with the present Royal
       Family.

# Q&A

## WITH

# CHRISTIE DICKASON

**Tell us about a typical day in the life of Christie Dickason.**

It depends on which day you pick – which is one of the good things about being a writer if, like me, you fret at inflexible routine. When I'm deep in a book, I like to surface slowly in the morning, day dreaming about the people and story. If it's early enough, the birds sound, for about an hour, as if they think they own the world. Then always, COFFEE in bed. And talking to my husband. Sometimes, I rise around 6am, to get daytime chores out of the way, not from virtue, just restlessness and wanting to outwit the temptations of the washing-up later in the day. (Yes, the washing-up can be a very seductive form of procrastination. Like the spice shelf that needs immediate sorting, now! When struggling with his work, a writer friend sorts and re-folds all his towels.)

When I'm drafting, I try to keep office hours, though it is often much longer, sometimes up to twelve-hour days. When my fingers are moving freely, I get pushed into that other place and forget time. However, a typical writing day is more often made up of carrots and sticks. Carrots: more coffee, time-out in my garden. Eating chocolate. Calling a friend. Going for a quick walk to clear my head. Even a trip to the supermarket is a treat! And the garden centre is a super reward for a good session. Sticks: more words ON THE PAPER. Now! No excuses! Do it!

I do let myself define 'office' rather loosely. My goal is one to five thousand words a day – it doesn't matter where I write them. For months at a time, until the book is finished, I tend to go down into a well and stay there until I'm done. (Family and friends are very forgiving.)

Research days can mean anything: from accosting a falconer flying his bird in the park and asking nosy questions to looking at original documents at the Kew Archives. Or visiting a National Trust property to see what my characters might have seen when they stood at their gate.

Every once in a while, I have to take a day just to catch up with the rest of life and do something about the refuse tip my poor neglected house has become. I think writers must always feel guilty that they're not doing the 'other thing'.

**Where do you normally write?**

I've written everywhere. In the middle of my living room, racing an absolute deadline, with a toddler screaming and pressing his nose to the window. On busses. I love cafes, where no one can find me. On walks and beside the River Thames, near where I live.

Now I do most of my serious drafting in an electrified shed at the bottom of my garden – no phone or internet, just me and my computer and reference books. And my coffee mug.

In early stages of a book, I sometimes find that the computer inhibits creative thought, so, when I'm not quite ready to formalize the story onto a typed page, I take a notebook to my local Italian coffee shop. Or Kew Gardens. Or Richmond Park. Or the Thames towpath, or anywhere else that I can stop and scribble. (I suspect that I've been spotted as a potential burglar taking notes outside houses.) Then, when the mulling suddenly takes shape, I'll belt for home and my PC to get it all down.

**What inspired you to become a writer?**

Indignation. I've always written, since before I could spell, from about the age of five, but I never thought of it as a possible career. Writing was a private vice, too much fun to be work. So I went to university, then into theatre, and worked in a real job as a director and choreographer.

I didn't start writing seriously until illness forced me to give up theatre and do a job that let me eat and sleep. While bed-ridden, I read one particularly dire book (among the hundreds of others) and I thought if I couldn't do better than that I should throw myself into the Thames. So I wrote my first novel. It was pretty dreadful, but an editor thought that it showed that I could write, and she commissioned my official 'first novel'. I gave in to the inevitable and found that I had come home at last.

**Do you think your past career, as a theatre director and choreographer, influenced your writing? How so?**

I can't imagine writing novels if I hadn't worked in theatre. After years of having to visualize printed plays as moving, breathing, 3-D events and helping the actors bring them to life in real time, I still see the action of the story unfolding in my head like a play or film, which I then describe for the reader. I need to see the 'set' and 'costumes'. I need to hear the voices of the characters in my head. Theatre left me with a vivid sense of physical reality. Even when actors and audience all know that a performance, like a book, is a joint conspiracy to pretend, they still can't escape being real people in a certain place at a certain time, surrounded by smells and sounds and colours and pheromones. If a cup of tea was needed, the playwright Alan Ayckbourn always wrote in enough time for the actor to make a cup of tea. I think readers, like play-goers, feel this kind of physical plausibility even if they're not aware of it, in the same way that falsehoods and impossibilities make them uneasy without knowing why. Therefore, I hope, they also trust that I'm being truthful about the bigger realities that are the heart of fiction.

Last but not least, theatre taught me the importance of (and some techniques for) making the audience leave their drinks in the bar after the interval because they're eager to go back into the dark to learn how the play ends.

### How do you create such vivid worlds?

Thank you for finding them vivid. I think I'm a sensualist. I love to cook and eat. I like the feeling of exhausting myself with dance or mountain climbing. I like to dig earth and smell horses. To stroke dogs and cats. And I try to communicate these sensations. I try to avoid generalizing or using ready-made images. Truth lies in the detail.

### When you are starting a new novel how much planning and research do you do before you begin to write?

Two different questions there. You need to research the broad sweeps before you can even start imagining a historical novel. Is there a possible story alive there among all those historical facts? Do you want to write it? And to live with these people and their story for the next year or so? These days, publishers ask for a fairly full synopsis of the plot before they'll commission a book. This means researching a subject (and falling a little bit in love with it) before you're certain that you're going to write the book. Then, if it goes ahead, you can start to research the specifics – the shapes of dwellings, the food (and the cutlery used to eat it), clothing across the social spectrum, horses' saddles, the name and colours of currency, how people brushed their teeth and cured illness, and all the other details of daily life.

I plan much more fluidly. I decide who my people are, where I'd like to end up and roughly how I might get there. Then I loosen the reins and let the characters and story find their way step-by-step. (Which is not the same as letting them take over. You're in charge and can always nudge them back into line – or adjust the destination.) Those researched details make up the terrain of their journey and help to define the internal logic of your world.

**Which period in history most inspires you as a writer?**

The Jacobean, in the early 17th century, fascinates me. It's a black hole in English history, just after the Tudors and before the Civil War. The people had the vigour of the Tudors, but the world was growing more and more complex in ways I think we would recognise today. King James (who took the throne after Elizabeth I) was one of the most interesting and complex monarchs (if not, perhaps, the most lovable) that Britain has ever had. It was a time of cultural diversity, religious struggles, strong women forced into constraining clothes and roles…I think I'd better stop before I go on and on!

When you write historical novels, you hope to illuminate the past but also to see our own time through the filter of the past. This period for me has just the right balance of fascinating strangeness and familiarity.